Canticum Tenebris

Wrath of the Old Gods Book II

John Triptych

1. The Conclave

Vatican City

For the fourth time that evening, Cardinal Giancarlo Buffoni knelt down in front of the small altar at the side of his office and prayed as hard as he could for the Lord to return. As he gripped the crucifix with both hands and continued his silent chanting for over an hour, he had a feeling of pending disappointment because his god was just not listening to him. Giancarlo had begun to get a gnawing sense of realization that his forty years of selfless service in the name of God had all been for nothing, as the other gods were all out there but not his own. The cardinal had a gnawing sense of realization that he had been wrong all these years. He had turned sixty-one a few months ago, and his knees were beginning to go numb as he continued to kneel on the hard wooden kneeling bench. Looking up at the crucifix that was the centerpiece of his personal altar, Giancarlo had finally had enough as he gripped the edges of the small desk on top of the kneeling bench, then pushed himself up to a stooping position before his backhanded slap sent the two-foot long wooden crucifix with the ivory figure of Christ toppling over and onto the marble floor.

As he wiped the tears of frustration from his eyes with the forearm of his cassock, Giancarlo limped over to the tall window facing his oak desk and looked outside as circulation slowly returned to his tired legs. His office was dimly illuminated by candles ever since electrical power across the entire city had gone out weeks ago. The night was strangely quiet as the riots that had gripped Rome seemed to have taken a night off. From his office window in the Apostolic Palace, he could still see the smoldering remains of the bonfires that littered the Piazza San Pietro, the oval-shaped square that fronted the Vatican. Just last night, the rioters made one final push to get through the contingent of Swiss Guards and volunteer police units who manned the barricades. They tried for the cardinals and most of all the Pope, as they demanded to know where their god Jesus Christ was, and when he would save them from the demons, monsters, and pagan gods that were now rampaging not just in Europe, but across the entire world. The Pope himself was locked away in his inner apartments within the palace. He refused to comment at all about the growing sense of despair among the entire church and the faithful as to what was happening to the Earth. His Holiness refused to see anyone except the two nuns who faithfully brought him food and water. Meanwhile, the cardinals and priests tried their best to allay the public as to why the Pope wasn't revealing himself and taking the lead as hell had finally come down to them all.

Giancarlo was thankful that the Vatican compound was completely surrounded by ancient stone walls that enabled them to withstand the almost daily riots that began a week after reports of the pagan gods returning. There were still sporadic radio signals from the Italian government and private stations but the stream of information from newspapers, TV, and the internet had by now ground to a halt. When news reports had begun to filter in about demons coming into homes and slaughtering whole families, Giancarlo and the other cardinals began to express gnawing fear that the entire city would soon be a slaughterhouse. They feverishly prayed for salvation while telling the faithful to stay calm and continue to believe that Jesus Christ would return, but as the weeks went by and the killings and disappearances continued, the people began to lose faith in the Church and all of its teachings. There were hushed rumors that parts of the city had even begun to worship these pagan devils since it was obvious to them that Christ wasn't real after all; not as real as compared to the unholy monsters they had seen with their own eyes.

A series of knocks at the doors of his office instantly brought him back to reality. Giancarlo made his way to the large wooden door and unlocked it before pulling it open. Outside stood his secretary, Father Salvatore Rossi, a young priest from Florence who had been serving him faithfully for six years now. Giancarlo could see that the younger man's vestments were partially torn up. There was a bruise on his left cheek and he nursed a split lip.

"Come inside quickly," Giancarlo said as he stood aside while his secretary shuffled in before closing the door and locking it again. "What happened to you?"

Salvatore's forehead was bathed in sweat as he caught his breath. "I'm sorry, your Eminence, but I just came from the entrance to the Papal Apartments nearby. I wanted to ask a question to Cardinal Martini when I heard a scream."

Giancarlo's eyes squinted in confusion. "A scream? Coming from where?"

"From within the Papal Apartments, your Eminence. It sounded like a woman screaming so I started knocking on the door to the outer chambers of His Holiness, but I didn't see the man standing nearby because he was hidden in the shadows until he came out and attacked me."

"Was it someone from the outside? Are the rioters here? Then we must alert the Swiss Guards."

"No, your Eminence, it was one of the Swiss Guards that attacked me, I think his name was Franz because I had met him before. He punched me and I fell to the ground and then he put his hands on my neck and tried to strangle me!"

Giancarlo's eyes were as wide as saucers now. The entire city was in the grip of this madness. "Go on."

"The pain was too much and I started to pass out, but I was able to grab hold of something that had fallen to the floor, I think it was a metal box or something, but took it and hit him in the face with it. Then he just fell over. I'm not sure if I killed him, but I got up and ran all the way here."

"If the Holy Father is in danger, then we must go to him, come on."

Both men walked out of the office and into a darkened corridor. Giancarlo had taken a flashlight from his desk and pointed the thin beam of light straight ahead as they started moving towards the stairway. The old cardinal sensed something was lurking in the shadows around them but he dared not point the flashlight around for a closer look, Giancarlo had a deathly fear that whatever kind of horrid things were with them might just come true if he expected hard enough for them to be present. The younger man seemed too concerned about the Pope's predicament than sensing the things lurking around them, Giancarlo thought.

As they ascended up the massive stone stairs and into the floor above them, they both sensed an eerie quietness, as if whatever being had initiated the brutal violence that Salvatore described had decided to take a break and prepare for an even worse orgy of terror. This feeling of dread made them silent as they both got to the opened outer doors of the Papal Apartments.

Salvatore stepped through the open double doors first. The first room that they entered was actually a small chapel where the Pope would sometimes conduct a private mass. Giancarlo could see that several of the pews were overturned and the altar near the entrance had fallen on its side. The crucifix of Christ had somehow been turned upside down. As the cardinal pointed the flashlight at the upturned figure of Jesus, he noticed that there was real, dripping blood on the statue, and its mouth and eyes had somehow been chiseled off.

"Cardinal Buffoni, over here," Salvatore said as he crouched down by one of the overturned pews.

Giancarlo made his way to where the younger man was and aimed the flashlight at what Salvatore pointed to. He noticed bloodstains that nearly blended in with the bright red carpet, some pieces of broken teeth but nothing else.

"I swear, this is where that Swiss Guard attacked me," Salvatore said.

At that moment as Giancarlo swung the flashlight around in a wide arc to get a better view of the chapel, both men noticed that a door along the side of the hall was ajar. Having been to the Papal Apartments a number of times, the cardinal knew that the open door led to an inner corridor with several other doors further inside which in turn, further led to a meeting room, a small dining room, a private study, and finally the modest bedroom where

4

the Pope rested at along with a second bedroom that the personal attendants of the Holy Father slept in. Without any further words, both men walked over to the door and opened it further before peering inside.

That was when they noticed that the once cream-colored walls were now stained with blood. Salvatore gasped as he could see bloody handprints as well as hoof prints that seemed to have been layered onto the sides like some diabolical wallpaper. The bloody prints that looked like they were made by both man and beast extended all the way up to the high vaulted ceiling, as if someone or something had dipped their extremities in blood and just walked up and down the walls in haphazard fashion. The younger man looked around and quickly saw a used antique candelabrum sitting on top of a high table along the side of the corridor. He grabbed a hold of it by the stem and took it with him just in case he needed a weapon of some sort.

The first door they saw led to the small meeting room. Salvatore stood to the side as Giancarlo opened the door and pushed it inwards before shining the flashlight to illuminate whatever was in there. As the flashlight's beam illuminated the center of the room, both men shrieked in horror.

Lying on top of the table was one of the nuns. Sister Maria Parisi, a kindly old lady who had served as a personal attendant to two previous popes, lay eagle-spread on the table, her nun's habit had been torn loose and was on the floor in little pieces. Her mouth was wide open, frozen in a silent scream that signaled the intense agony that she went through before finally dying. But the most horrific part was that her breasts had clearly been chewed off by some unholy beast that also eviscerated her stomach. Her intestines were splayed out like an open can of giant red worms while all sorts of tools and implements had been thrust through her orifices. Giancarlo could see flies buzzing around the room as they eagerly feasted on the blood and entrails of this poor woman. The sharp, metallic smell of blood was combined with the earthy, pungent stench of excrement that hung in the air like a miasma of death and disease.

Salvatore turned to the side of the door as he had dropped the candelabrum on the ground and began to vomit. Giancarlo remembered the atrocities he had witnessed when he was a priest in Africa during the events of the Rwandan Civil War, but nothing could prepare him for this horrific sight as he too began to gag, but he was quickly able to control himself as he stood back and turned away from the room.

As the younger man started to get up from his knees after his near violent retching had subsided, he noticed that the blood on the floor had a definite trail that seemed to lead further down the corridor. "Your Eminence, look," Salvatore said as he wiped the off the remaining spittle from the sides of this mouth using his wrist.

"Come on," Giancarlo said as he helped the younger man on his feet and both began to follow the crimson trail. As they looked in the other rooms, there seemed to be nobody else around. The path of blood appeared to have ended at the Pope's bedroom, right at the foot of his hand-carved wooden bed.

Salvatore carefully peeled back the bloodstained sheets on the bed. "Lots of blood, but no bodies, only Sister Maria in the meeting room."

As Giancarlo used his flashlight along the wall beside the bed, he noticed a slight indentation that ran along the base of the bed, there seemed to be a space between the wall and the headboard of the Pope's bed. "Look at this," he said.

Salvatore placed his hand over the crack. "I can feel a draft coming from behind the bed."

"Help me," Giancarlo said as he began to push the headboard backwards. "There must be a hidden alcove behind this bed."

Both men tried to push the bed backwards, but it seemed too heavy to move. Giancarlo caught his breath as he kept the light shined at the bed. Salvatore could see that the carved symbol on the top of the bed's headboard seemed to be tilted partially to the right. The younger man immediately put his hand on the carving and tried twisting it. Just as Salvatore twisted it counter-clockwise, the bed began to move by itself. Both men were startled and instantly backed away as the bed slid forward into the room. Behind it was a hidden passageway.

Without further adieu, both men stooped their shoulders and entered the barely six-foot high passageway that seemed to have been carved out from the stone blocks that buttressed the building. Giancarlo led with his flashlight as

Salvatore followed close behind. As they moved further inwards, the passageway began to get larger with each step and soon both men could walk fully upright beside one another. They realized that there was a downward slope while noticing that the blood trail had once again become visible on the smooth stone floor of the tunnel.

After walking nearly half an hour in the pitch black tunnel, they soon noticed that it had began to slope upwards once more as they could see carved steps leading up. Giancarlo's flashlight had begun to dim due to its constant use. "I hope we find the exit soon or we shall be fumbling around in the dark," he said softly as they kept on moving.

Beads of sweat once again began to form on Salvatore's forehead despite the chilly gusts of wind in the passageway. He sensed that they were heading towards their doom. "We seemed to have gone in a westerly direction," he whispered.

Both men soon noticed a faint light up ahead. As they moved closer, they could see the opening of what looked like a stone block that had shifted to reveal an elaborately painted corridor. There seemed to be a rising noise nearby, as if there was some sort of orgiastic revelry going on.

"Oh my god," Salvatore shuddered said as he realized just where they were. "This is the corridor that leads to…"

Cardinal Giancarlo finished his sentence. "The Sistine Chapel."

As Salvatore stepped out of the hidden tunnel and into the corridor, he noticed that the trail of blood continued on towards where the world famous chapel was. Although the Sistine Chapel itself was no more than one hundred and thirty feet across its entire length, its ceilings and walls were hand-painted by the great Renaissance artist Michelangelo and featured his masterpiece on the altar wall, The Last Judgment, with its complex visions of heaven, hell, and the people in the afterlife. The chapel itself was also used by the cardinals as the site of their conclave when electing a new pope. Since the entire Vatican compound had been closed off to tourists and the public since the Glooming began, both men were wondering what was causing all the noise that was emanating from the open double doors as they got closer to it. They noticed a flickering illumination similar to firelight coming from the chapel entrance as they got closer.

Marshaling their courage, both men ran up the ramp leading to the chapel before turning to look inside. They were not prepared for what they saw. Giancarlo screamed out in horror as he dropped his flashlight and fell to his knees. Salvatore could not believe what he was seeing either, thrusting out his right forearm to cover his eyes and he began to wail.

Almost all of the other hundred cardinals were there, along with the Pope himself. None of them had any clothes on, and they were in the midst of unspeakable debauchery. A creature with a star-shaped body, each point ending with a hoofed hind leg like that of a goat, was rolling around the hall like a man-sized pinwheel, its human-like head at the center of its grotesque body and speaking in strange tongues. Another creature with three gigantic heads on top of its mushroom-shaped body was crawling along. It had nine spider-like legs that enabled it to move up onto the walls and to the top if the high ceiling where it began to piss on the priceless frescoes. The Pope was kneeling on top of the altar at the far end of the chapel, as a demon with a snake-like lower torso was trying to stick itself down his throat. The Holy Father seemingly encouraged it further by trying to open his mouth as wide as he could. The cardinals were rolling naked on the bloody floor, fornicating with themselves, the creatures, and on the mutilated corpses of the other nuns.

Giancarlo had had enough as he turned around and ran along the corridor, but not before stopping in front of two burning torches ensconced near the exit. They were apparently placed there earlier that evening to provide illumination. Grabbing one of the torches from its holder, the cardinal steeled himself as he turned and started walking back towards the entrance to the chapel.

Salvatore saw the cardinal walking back to him with a flaming torch in his hand. "What are you doing?" the young priest said to him as he tried to grab the torch away.

"Let go of me," Giancarlo said as he tried to push himself away from Salvatore who held him tightly and wouldn't let go. "We must destroy this whole place to rid ourselves of all those devils!"

"No, your Eminence!" Salvatore said as he held him fast. "Michelangelo's masterpieces are in that chapel along with the other cardinals, it will be murder!"

Giancarlo had both frustration and fury in his thoughts. "Let me be hanged as a murderer then, but I must do my duty in combating the forces of the devil!"

Another voice called out behind them. "Buonasera, Cardinal Buffoni and Father Rossi, how nice of you to finally meet with us."

Both men turned around. Standing in the corridor was an old man wearing a dark suit. Giancarlo had just walked along the same pathway less than a minute before and it seemed that the stranger just appeared from nowhere. The man in the suit was gaunt and had long white hair tied back in a pony tail, his wrinkled visage belied years of experience as he rubbed at a large brass right on his right hand.

Giancarlo faced him with the torch in his hand ready to strike. "Who are you?"

"Please allow me to introduce myself," the man in the suit said in fluent Italian. "I'm a man of power and refinement. Seth Solomon is my name and I'm afraid I cannot allow either of you to interfere with my invocations. You see, our Pope is being possessed by about three of my geotic demons and the ritual is almost finished. So naturally, until that is done, I'm afraid I cannot allow any interruptions."

"I've never heard of you," Giancarlo said. "What kind of man are you to help with these unholy defilements? Are you even a Christian?"

Solomon smiled. "I'm afraid I'm more than human now. And I was never a Christian."

"If you are responsible for this, then I will stop you in the name of God!" Giancarlo said as he ran towards him, swinging the burning torch. But just as he got to within striking range, a ghost-like being materialized in front of the terrified cardinal, stopping him in his tracks. All Giancarlo could see was a hazy outline of some sort of manlike creature as if it was made of very light mist. Within seconds, the hazy creature grabbed at his throat with invisible hands as the cardinal was lifted off the ground and began to choke as if being strangled.

Salvatore started moving towards the two as he hoped he could help his mentor, but the three-headed demon from the chapel quickly crawled out from the entryway and pounced on him from behind. As the terrified young priest fell onto the floor of the corridor, one of the demon's frog-like heads bit Salvatore's head off his body, letting his corpse tumble to the ground. Giancarlo struggled to breathe but the spirit's grip was too strong as he finally blacked out and suffocated just as his trachea collapsed.

Solomon walked past the two dead bodies in the corridor while he prepared for the final phase of the possession ritual as the two demons followed him into the chapel. Just before going back in, he turned to look at the barely visible spirit that moved beside him. "All this time and you still haven't told me your name."

"I am called Dantalion," the spirit said.

Solomon smiled. "Ah yes, Dantalion. Great Duke of Hell with thirty-six legions under your command. You are the seventy-first spirit of my namesake. It seems the grimiore is quite accurate after all."

"I live to serve the wielder of the seal," Dantalion said.

"That you do," Solomon said as he walked into the Sistine Chapel.

"For now, anyway," the demon said under its breath so no one heard it.

2. Prey

Kenya

Hendrik Visser watched as the small plane landed on the far side of the runway strip and began to taxi towards him. The afternoon was overcast and it gave some relief from the relentless sun that had been shining over the veldt. He opened the door, got out of the driver's seat, and stood on the dirt airstrip as the Cessna 208 got to within thirty feet of him and began to turn off its single engine. The moment the propeller blades stopped, the side door of the plane had opened and one man who wore khakis came out. Hendrik walked over to him as he pulled out his duffel bags from the plane's fuselage and placed them on the ground next to him.

Hendrik stood beside the man as he put out his hand. "Mr. Winchell? I'm Hendrik Visser, your professional hunting guide. We spoke on the phone a few days ago."

The man turned around and shook his hand. He was pale, balding and wore steel-rimmed glasses. There was a Twins baseball cap on his head. "Call me Langdon, please. I'm so happy that you decided to honor your commitment to me because I had planned this trip for months in advance."

Hendrik grinned sheepishly. "The truth of the matter is I had already spent the money you sent over. So there wasn't any way I could refund you. Let me help you with your bags."

"And I appreciate that." Langdon grinned as he handed over two large

11

duffel bags he had placed on the ground but slung a third over his shoulder. "But I've also wanted to make an additional arrangement with you now that we are here face to face."

Hendrik shook his head in confusion. "An additional arrangement? What do you mean?"

Langdon smiled back at him. "Let's talk in your car shall we?"

Both men brought the bags over to Hendrik's dark green Toyota Land Cruiser and placed them in the back, but Langdon continued to carry the third duffel bag over his shoulder and then placed it on his lap as he slid into the front seat. The plane started its engines again and began to taxi to the back of the runway. Hendrik sat down on the driver's seat and looked out into the vast Savannah beyond.

"This current booking I made with you, I know it's awkward with all these things that are happening in the world right now. I'm sure your business must be suffering just like everyone else's," Langdon said as he smiled and looked out of the windshield. "But I would like to make an additional booking, if you don't mind."

Hendrik turned and looked at him. "An additional booking? What do you mean? Do you want to stay at the lodge for a few more days or weeks to hunt more lions?"

"Not just lions," Langdon said as his smile turned into a wide grin while looking down at the bag on his lap. "I would like to hunt at least one male elephant. Maybe two."

Hendrik looked down. "Mr. Winchell, that would be very hard to do because we will need to apply for a new permit and as you well know with this world crisis and the riots in Nairobi, I don't think we will be able to get the licenses at all. It took me months to get the authorization to hunt one lion for this trip and it must be done within the designated zones. As far as I know, most of the government workers here in Kenya have all abandoned their posts so how could I possibly get you those permits now?"

"You've answered your own question, Hendrik," Langdon said. "Kenya, as well as the rest of Africa, and the world for that matter, is slowly shutting down. I had to pay an enormous amount of money to get a private jet to fly me over here. This means that without any kind of government supervision, we can do anything we want here. Do you get that?"

Hendrik sighed. "But the risks, Mr. Winchell, what about the risks?"

Langdon giggled. "What risks? You yourself said that the Wildlife Service has been pretty much gutted weeks ago. The world is slowly destroying itself and this means there are no more park rangers to enforce these stupid hunting laws anyway. I'm pretty sure you and many others are engaging in hunting to feed yourselves now that world trade has stopped, am I right?"

Hendrik looked away in shame. Just two days ago, he had to kill a zebra just to provide meat for his family. "This is true that people here now have barely enough to survive. We are only one step away from starvation now that all my clients except you are gone. I think I may have to close my business after this trip."

"I can solve all those problems for you," Langdon said as he unzipped the duffel bag and held it out to him.

Hendrik took a look at the inside of the bag and gasped. There were bound stacks of hundred dollar bills and a small plastic packet with raw, uncut diamonds on top of the heap. "W-Where did you get all of this?"

"I'm a partner in a pharmaceutical firm back in Minnesota," Langdon said. "I've got all the money in the world, and I've been hunting big game for years. This so-called Glooming that's affecting the Earth is not going to stop me from engaging in my favorite hobby. What I want from you is to just guide me to wherever I want to go in this country and hunt whatever kind of animal I want. Give me two weeks because that is the arrangement I set up with that flight crew that's going to pick me up at this airstrip and I'll give you everything in this bag. You're looking at twenty million dollars plus in both bills and gemstones."

Hendrik bit his lip. "You know of course that there isn't much use for money in these parts nowadays? Everyone is bartering for basic necessities now."

"I'm sure you can find someone who will take this. After all, once this crisis is over and everything comes back to normal again, you can finally retire as a rich man with all this cash and gold, right?"

Hendrik thought about it for a bit. His client was right. The world had now gone completely uncertain because of the unbelievable events that were happening. Just days before, one of Hendrik's neighbors had disappeared, the entire family living in their winery estate when he had gone over there to try to barter for some supplies. The house and grounds were ransacked as if some giant beast had smashed down the walls. Hendrik had two grown sons along with his wife who managed the hunting lodge located near the Tsavo East National Park. Most of their workers had already left to go back to their villages because of the stories about evil spirits and strange gods that had returned to dispense both justice and terror across the entire continent. Just the night before, the entire family had to arm themselves as a small crowd of natives from a nearby village attempted to take over the compound but were driven away by warning shots. Hendrik knew that if his family was to survive somehow they would need to move away to someplace safe, even if he did not know where that would be. And if they needed to go, then money and jewels would be invaluable.

"Very well," Hendrik said to him. "Two weeks. Then I get everything in that bag of yours."

Langdon shook his outstretched hand. "Congratulations, you've made the wise choice!"

That night Langdon had dinner at the dining room of the hunting lodge. Since power was out weeks ago, everything was by lamplight and he spent most of the evening sitting by fireplace just watching the embers glow in yellow and amber hues while sipping on a bottle of scotch. Hendrik's wife cooked and served dinner herself since all the servants had already gone. Langdon tried to make some friendly conversation with her but she mostly just ignored him. Hendrik's two grown sons weren't any friendlier as they mostly stayed at the porch of the lodge and stared into the night with rifles on the ready. As he was preparing for a bath using well water that Hendrik's sons had placed in a free-standing steel tub, Langdon overheard Hendrik and his wife in a furious argument, but since they were speaking in Afrikaans, he really couldn't get what they were saying, though it was clear what the argument was about. By morning, Langdon's breakfast was already waiting for him on the dining room table when he came downstairs and he never saw the wife again. Hendrik stayed silent as he waited for him by the car.

At midday, they had made it to the entrance of the Tsavo National Park. Langdon noticed two very tall and thin African men who were waiting by a signpost just up ahead of them. They seemed to be wearing red cloaks along with just loincloths and sandals. Both carried spears. Langdon was suspicious at first, and became even more dismayed when Hendrik stopped the Land Cruiser and both men got into the back seat, right after they exchanged a few words in their local language. As the car started to move again, Langdon had begun to rub his nose. The two men in the back smelled of piss, sweat, and something else; an additional stench that was somewhat pungent and metallic, but he just couldn't identify it.

Hendrik noticed Langdon's discomfort at the odor as he kept on driving. "These two men are Maasai," he said. "We need them to help navigate this area. They are excellent trackers."

Langdon lowered the window beside his seat to allow more air into the car. "It would have been nice if they took a bath before they met up with us."

Hendrik smiled as he kept his eyes on the trail ahead. "They smell that way because they rub blood on their bodies. It's part of their culture and the lions of the area avoid them because of their scent. They can tell the difference between the Maasai and everybody else."

"That's nice, but how can I hunt lions if they scare them away?"

"They will not be with us when we hunt, they will bring the prey to us."

"Oh, okay then," Langdon said softly. He figured it would make things easier.

As the afternoon sun wore on, the two Maasai warriors conferred with Hendrik before setting off while Langdon sat down on a folding chair in the hunter's blind and ate his packed lunch. When Hendrik joined him in the shade of the camouflaged tent, the two Maasai had already gone. Langdon had brought two bows with him, one serving as a backup in case his primary weapon had a malfunction. Both compound bows had 80-pound pull draw weights and looked nothing like the bows of old. These new modern bows had diagonal inner-cables, dual cams, stabilizers, built-in sights, and levered strings. Langdon had been working out in his personal gym for months before this trip so he was physically prepared for the rigors of bow hunting. He considered it more sporting to hunt large game with a bow rather than with a gun. Hendrik didn't care either way. For him, it was a job and if his clients needed help, he always carried his Weatherby Mark V bolt-action rifle.

A number of hours had passed while both men waited patiently in the blind. Sure enough, the Maasai were as good as their word as a male lion, its mane a deep brown with streaks of tan, began to wander in close to the blind. A tap on Langdon's shoulder by Hendrik and both men were instantly alert as they waited for a precise shot. Once the large beast was in range, it was just a matter of shooting the arrow in the rib cage behind its right foreleg- right where the heart was in order to bring it down. Langdon carefully placed an arrow on the shelf of his bow and waited. For a number of minutes, the animal kept wandering around but Langdon could just not get the proper angle for the shot. So when the animal turned its back on them, Langdon could no longer contain his enthusiasm and shot an arrow into its buttocks. The lion roared and began to limp away as Langdon readied another arrow. He sprinted out of the blind and started running parallel to the fleeing animal, he loved this part of the hunt. Hendrik made a silent curse to himself as he started running after his client. Langdon fired another arrow that embedded itself on the lion's neck. The beast was seriously hurt but not fatally so. It began to charge at Langdon. The pharmaceutical executive from Minnesota was instantly shocked that such an animal had the guts to attack him. The lion made one last roar and made it to less than ten feet away from him before the large caliber bullet from Hendrik's rifle blew the top of its head off.

Sweat poured from Langdon's forehead as he pushed up his baseball cap slightly and wiped the salty sweat using his wrist as he noticed Hendrik walking up behind him. "Thanks," he said. "I thought it was gonna maul me."

Hendrik's tanned face was a mask of stone. "Why did you take that shot while we were in the blind? It was a bad shot."

Langdon smiled and shrugged his shoulders. "Sorry, I got a bit carried away there. We've been sitting around here all afternoon and I wanted to get this over with."

"Get it over with? Are you in a hurry for something?"

"Yeah, I want to bag as many animals as I can before my days are up. This could be my last hunt, and I want it to be the most unforgettable," Langdon said as he adjusted the body cam on his vest. He wanted to make sure that the camcorder he was carrying had videotaped all of it.

Hendrik snorted and shook his head. The man was insufferable. If it were not for the huge amount of money he was paying him, he would have canceled this stupid American's hunting trip and refunded him his money minus expenses. The man was a poor hunter and it seemed he liked to inflict pain.

Half an hour later, the two Maasai went back to where the hunting blind was. Hendrik talked to them for a bit before Langdon noticed that the once mellow conversation in their language had all of a sudden become animated. It looked like they were now arguing about something. As the minutes passed, it seemed that Hendrik was about to hit one of the men with the butt of his rifle, but at the last minute, the old guide shouted at them as he pulled out a wad of dollar bills and gave it to the two Maasai before they turned around and started walking away in silence. Hendrik shook his head as he started walking towards the Land Cruiser parked nearby.

Langdon jogged until he got close to the other man. "What was that about?"

"They are reneging on their agreement to guide us to the elephants," Hendrik said. "They saw you hunting the lion and say you have angered the gods with your blood lust. They no longer wish to guide for us so I paid them only for the lion kill and let them go."

"Those goddamn bastards," Langdon said. "Just like the damned black thugs in the states. After all I money I paid for this trip- now this. You should have never hired those untrustworthy pygmies in the first place."

"I have seen a herd of elephants not far from here a few days back," Hendrik said. "I will take you to them on the promise that you only kill the old bulls in the herd and nothing else."

Langdon nodded. "Okay, it's a deal."

Hendrik looked at him in the eye. He was tired of this, but he had made a commitment and his word was good. "I want you to promise me that you will not take a bad shot. If you do not shoot at its heart, the animal will be only wounded and suffer. Then we will have to chase it to finish it off."

Langdon saw that he was serious and nodded once more. "I promise."

By the time they got to within walking distance of the elephant herd, the sun was starting to set. Although Langdon was getting impatient once again, Hendrik figured that if they could make a quick kill then the rest of the day's trip would be worth it. Both men put on their bush camouflage jackets and left the car behind. Just as they started to make their way to within visual sight of the herd, the wind began to pick up. Hendrik took this as a good sign since elephants normally had bad eyesight compared to humans but their sense of smell was better. The breeze would hide their scent from these beasts and would allow them to get within range of Langdon's bow.

Another hour had passed. Both men maneuvered their way around the thick bushes until they were less than forty yards away from one of the elephant bulls that was making its way to the perimeter of the herd. They were carefully stalking the old male after they picked it out as the one who had wandered farthest from the others. Langdon began to sweat again as his adrenaline kicked up a notch. A few minutes later, they were only less than thirty feet away as the old bull elephant began to rub its sides against a nearby tree.

After placing an arrow on the shelf of his compound bow, Langdon took a deep breath, then drew the bow string back and began to aim at the elephant's rib cage just behind its foreleg. His arm was shaking because he had never shot at an elephant before. If he made this, he could bring down the animal with just one arrow. But at the split second he released, the old bull sensed something dangerous was nearby, and it pivoted in their direction. The elephant instantly trumpeted with pain as Langdon's arrow struck the animal in the upper part of its right shoulder and it quickly ran off, deeper into the bush.

Hendrik cursed once more. Of all the things that had to happen, this was no doubt the worst. He checked his rifle and began to move to where he had last seen the elephant.

Langdon ran alongside of him. "Where are we going?"

Hendrik didn't pay attention to him as he walked over to where the elephant had just bolted from and checked the reddish sand. He saw that there was a blood trail leading north to the base of a nearby mountain. Depending on how fast that bull could go, it might take at least an hour to catch up with it. He wasn't sure about the severity of the wound, but it was clear from the tracks on the ground that the animal was limping.

A tap on his shoulder made him turn around. It was Langdon. "I asked you where we're going," the American said.

"We need to catch up with that bull and finish it off," Hendrik said brusquely.

Langdon frowned. "But it's evening now. Can't this wait till tomorrow? We can come back then."

Hendrik shook his head. "In all the years that I have done this, I have learned it is best that we catch up with this bull and put him out of his misery right away. Your arrow shot wounded his foreleg. That poor elephant must be in terrible pain."

Langdon sighed. "Look, with all the money I'm paying you, you ought to do what I tell you. And I'm telling you, I want to go back to the lodge now and rest."

Hendrik turned around and started to walk deeper into the bush. "Then go back by yourself, Mr. Winchell."

Langdon just stood there for a minute as rage briefly overtook him. With all the money he was paying this idiot, he had to put up with this? He felt like just telling the transplanted South African to go to hell and give him back his money, but then he realized that the man could easily leave him here to die since he carried the car keys and knew the way out of here. It was clear that he had no choice. After clearing his mind, Langdon started to trot after him.

The sun had finally set but the cloudless night was clear. Both men could see the outlines of the tall pale grass and the dark trees in clumps around them so there was no need to use their flashlights. Hendrik could see where parts of the bush was trampled over by the wounded elephant as he sensed the beast was not that far from them as he kept on moving. Within minutes, he saw the bloodstains on the grass. The night sky made the blood trail look like dark ink spots as he finally saw what looked like the elephant's back just a mere forty yards ahead. He then took out the lens cap from the scope of his rifle and began to sight it. Hendrik moved a little bit to the right of where the animal seemed to be lying so he could see if he had a clear shot at the animal's rib cage. Langdon finally caught up to him and started walking alongside.

As Hendrik finally got to the elephant's flank, he knelt down on one knee and began to take aim using the scope. That was when he saw that there was a smaller, man-sized form that seemed to be right beside the animal. As he tried to get a clearer look using his optical sight, Hendrik made a sharp gasp as if to catch his breath before abruptly getting back up to his feet, and then started to sprint back to where the vehicle was. Langdon narrowed his eyes in complete surprise as the other man ran past him, but he too turned and followed as fast as he could.

Just as Langdon caught up to him once more, he could see that Hendrik was obviously stressed and seemed to be out of breath as the experienced guide's face was deathly pale- it was as if he had seen a ghost or something.

"Hendrik, what's going on?" Langdon said as he ran alongside of him.

The other man kept looking behind them as he kept up the relentless sprint. "We must get out of here," Hendrik half-whispered between heaving breaths of air.

Langdon was in generally better shape since he was ten years younger but the relentless effort was also starting to tire him. "What's going on? What did you see? Why didn't you take the shot for chrissakes?"

Hendrik didn't answer as he kept on moving as fast as he could. When he finally couldn't run anymore, he switched to a brisk walk although still glancing occasionally over his shoulder. Fifteen minutes later, both men could see the black boxy shape of the Land Cruiser that Hendrik had parked underneath a tall acacia tree earlier that afternoon.

As the details of the vehicle were finally clear enough to be noticed when they got closer, Hendrik's heart sank in despair. He pulled out the flashlight from his jacket pocket and shined it over the car as Langdon gasped in surprise. The Land Cruiser was wrecked. The front hood had been ripped off and the windows had been smashed inwards. The tires had been slashed through and the engine block was gutted; the fan belt had been torn out along with the radiator- both were in pieces on the ground beside them. Langdon pulled out his own flashlight, and as he shined the beam along the side of the vehicle, he saw what looked like claw marks that torn right through the metal bodywork like it was made of paper.

"What in the hell?" Langdon said as he began to sweat heavily, despite the chilly air of night. "What kind of an animal could do this?"

Hendrik was hyperventilating. "The Maasai. They warned me."

"What do you mean the Maasai? Did they do this?"

Hendrik looked at him with half-lidded eyes. *The American was so stupid and now he had just signed their death warrant.* "The Maasai told me that the gods were angered at what you had done to that lion. They told me that the ngojama would be hunting us tonight and like a fool, I refused to believe them. Now we are mostly likely going to die out here tonight."

Langdon had a blank look on his face. "What a-are you t-talking about?"

Hendrik noticed some dried pieces of wood lying near the tree and he frantically began to gather them. "Get as much of that wood that's lying around and hurry! We must make a bonfire, perhaps it will scare that demon who is coming for us."

Langdon looked around him and started to pick up some of the fallen branches. "What do you mean? What demon?"

"It was standing near the dying elephant when I saw it with my rifle scope," Hendrik said as he frantically began to place the dried wood into a small mound in front of the gutted vehicle. "And it looked back at me with blazing eyes- it was like staring at the eyes of death."

"What did you see? Why didn't you shoot it then?"

Hendrik took out his lighter and began to spread flame over the pile of dead wood. "I doubt the rifle would be of any use on a demon. Legends state that they cannot be killed by men. The one thing we can hope for is that this fire keeps it away."

The dried wood rapidly caught fire as both of them kept grabbing nearby pieces and fed it. Within a few minutes the flames had become as tall as them. That was when Langdon noticed something that was headed in their direction.

Langdon pointed towards a copse of trees less than forty yards away. "Look, look over there!"

As it got closer, they could finally see its full features as the flickering firelight illuminated the creature. It was clearly man-like as it walked on two legs and had similar ape like arms but that was where any semblance with humanity ended. It was covered in a coat of black fur with taloned hands but the most horrid aspect was its face; it looked human enough with a proper nose and high cheekbones but the eyes were as red as crimson and had no pupils. Its gaping mouth was full of fangs that seemed to drool sticky strands of saliva and blood.

Langdon screamed as Hendrik readied his rifle. The old South African knew that creatures of legend could not be killed with ordinary weapons and that the most he could do was bargain and for his life. Langdon quickly remembered that he still had his bow so he took an arrow from the side quiver strapped to his hip and placed it on the bow's ledge before pulling back on the string. As the creature moved in closer, Langdon aimed for its heart and let loose, but the demon caught the arrow in midair with its clawed hand before snapping it in two.

"Shoot it! Shoot it!" Langdon screamed before he turned and realized that Hendrik was aiming his hunting rifle at him instead. "What in the hell are you doing?"

"I'm sorry, Mr. Winchell," Hendrik mumbled as he pulled the trigger.

3. Yokai

Tokyo

His full name was Yoshiro Kamiki, but he preferred to be called Hiro for short since he felt it was a play on the English word hero. Although he had flunked the entrance test for university three years ago, Hiro liked to consider himself as an educated salary man even though he was working as a dishwasher at a small yakitori restaurant in the Shimbashi district. After he left school, he moved into a small apartment with the Nishimura brothers, his best friends since elementary school. The three of them shared a love for manga comic books and video games. Whatever free time they had was spent either reading their massive manga collection or hanging out in the arcades and picking up the latest mobile games for their smart phones. Hiro and his friends could have easily led mundane lives just like the millions of other young men in the world if it wasn't for the Glooming, but in the last few weeks their lives had suddenly taken a different turn.

When news reports about the return of the ancient gods began to filter all over the internet and the world media, the Japanese government made official announcements that citizens needed to stay calm and remain in their homes while it assessed the situation. Within days of their announcements, the internet began to slowly die out as world trade had virtually stopped. Then a large number of airplanes had mysteriously crashed all over the world forcing the authorities to ground all flights while countless ships had also disappeared

23

in every ocean, the few survivors telling stories about being attacked by sea monsters. Within less than a week, practically every city on the planet had begun to experience blackouts as lack of fossil fuels due to the trade disruption was beginning to be felt. To make matters even worse, citizens of Tokyo had begun to report encounters with strange and varied creatures from legend called yokai. These supernatural monsters soon began to rampage and terrorize people across every city in Japan. Although the police and military were deployed in an attempt to deal with these creatures, their weapons seemed to be of little or no use against these mysterious apparitions.

With the police and military spread thin, a number of residents in Tokyo began to form mutual defense groups and started to fortify their residential enclaves. Both the government and private merchants would regularly attempt to bring in convoys to the most stricken parts of the city in order to deliver much needed food and fuel to the trapped residents. In the daytime, most of the people of Tokyo would spend all their efforts to gather food and other supplies and then lock themselves behind bolted doors when the evening came as the yokai came out of their hiding places and preyed on those foolish enough to venture out at night.

By the beginning of the second month after the Glooming began, Hiro and his friends were lying around on the tatami mat floor of their tiny apartment in the Sangenjaya district. Every other night, they reread some of their old manga comic books. Of the two Nishimura brothers, Shinji was the older one, and he was the expert when it came to cataloging as well as answering trivia questions about their manga collection. He was the one most disappointed when the crisis began because no new manga comics were being printed. Hiro and Shinji's brother Shogo were more into video games, but with the electrical grid being inoperative for weeks now, all they could do was just read the same comics by candlelight, night after night.

The evening air was warm and humid so they had left the balcony doors open in order to let some wind in. Shinji was thinner than the other two and he adjusted his glasses in order to squint less as he took out a comic book from the pile that was beside him and flipped through the back pages first- because in Japan books were printed backwards and were meant to be read starting from the rear.

Hiro was lying on the floor and stared at the low ceiling. The flickering candlelight made strange shadows that danced across the painted white walls. "I'm bored. So sick of reading now," he said to no one in particular.

"Shut up, I'm reading," Shogo said as he sat cross-legged on the tatami mat while thumbing through another manga book. He had broad shoulders and his short hair was in a crew cut. Shogo was short and squat; he was also the fattest and the other two called him Sumo whenever they felt like teasing him.

"You haven't read Cobra Sukiyaki Be-Bop yet," Shinji said to Hiro. "It's on the top shelf."

Hiro frowned as he propped up his head on one elbow. "I need to do something, it's been almost a month and we're trapped here!"

Shogo looked up at them. He was clearly annoyed. "Will you two stop talking? I'm trying to finish this!"

Shinji slowly shook his head. "What do you want to do, Hiro? The building watch told us it's too dangerous to go out at night."

"Anything beats staying cooped up here all night," Hiro said as he sat up. His once purple hair was now fading back to black because he couldn't dye his bed-head styled hair anymore. "We should help people to fight against the yokai."

Shogo put down his comic book and started to chuckle. "Look at this guy! He is so sick of reading manga, now he wants to be in an actual one!"

Shinji looked at Hiro closely. "Do you want to die or something? Not even the military can fight the yokai. All we can do is to lock ourselves in at night and hope they don't come through that door."

"Maybe the military isn't able to kill those monsters because they use modern weapons," Hiro said as he moved quickly to a nearby chest and began to rummage through its contents. "But if we fight them like the old samurai, I bet we can kill a few yokai and we will be hailed as heroes."

Shinji saw what he was doing and quickly got up and stooped over beside him. "What are you doing? That's my chest!"

"Hang on a minute," Hiro said, looking for something in the old wooden box before finally grasping it as he brought it out with both hands. "Here, I found it."

Shinji frowned as he saw that Hiro had pulled out his katana from the old wooden chest. The Japanese-style sword was an antique, given to him by his grandfather. Weapons of any kind were strictly prohibited in the country and so Shinji had to get a permit from the government just to keep it. "Put that sword back, Hiro." he said.

Hiro stood up as he continued to clutch at the wooden scabbard that was holding the blade. "We can fight the yokai with this, Shinji. Let's go out tonight and find those monsters."

Shinji grabbed the sword away from him and hissed. "You are crazy! Even if this sword could hurt those demons, I don't have any experience in fighting with this."

"You did practice iaido a few years ago, Shinji," Shogo said. "Hiro took some kendo classes too."

Shinji turned beet red and glanced at his brother. "You think taking a few classes is enough? You're both crazy and you're both going to get us all killed!"

Hiro walked over to one of the shelves along the wall and brought out his shinai, a wooden bamboo sword that he used when he was taking classes in kendo, gripping it with both hands as he swung it playfully around. "With your katana and my wooden sword, we can live our own manga comic book!"

Not wanting to be left out, Shogo quickly got up and dashed towards the small kitchen area as he took out a stainless steel cleaver from the knife block beside the unused hot plate on the counter. "I'm part of the manga team too! Let's kill some yokai!"

Shinji looked down at the tatami mats on the floor. He couldn't believe this. "Is this what you both want? To die?"

"Well, I would like some more food too. One meal a day isn't enough," Shogo said as he tried to spin the cleaver with his hand but it fell down on the floor. "Maybe we could find some extra food out there."

"Shogo is right," Hiro said. "We are slowly dying as we're trapped in this building. I'm sure you could see all the scared people in their apartments, praying for help that will never come and all they can do every day is just wait for their daily ration of food that will probably run out soon. I'd rather die fighting than starving to death like some caged dog who's scared of its own shadow."

Shinji rubbed his chin. "Well, if you're going to do this, then let's do it right. I've got an old cuirass in one of my boxes, it's part of an old set of samurai armor that grandfather gave me."

"I remember that suit of armor," Shogo said. "Where's the rest of it?"

Shinji shrugged sheepishly. "I sold the rest of the set."

By the time they had started down the stairs, all three youths had equipped themselves as best as they could. Shinji wore an old cuirass on his chest made up of rusted iron and leather while his katana was strapped to his side. Hiro had his bamboo sword and a small knife along with his kendo equipment that consisted of a face mask, shoulder pads, a chest protector made of molded plastic, and thick, padded gloves. Since there wasn't much else, Shogo wore a white kimono as well as a rising sun headband over his forehead while carrying every knife from the kitchen after placing them in a plastic apron that he wore underneath.

The ground floor of the building consisted of a small foyer with stairs leading up to the apartments. Since there was no longer any electricity, the elevators were permanently offline. At night there was a makeshift barricade that blocked the front doors and was manned by at least two people at all times. All three of them had served separately as part of the night watch in the past few weeks since the most able-bodied men in the building were all required to put their time in for guard duty. The women would scrounge in the daytime for food and cook a community meal for everyone just before sunset.

As the three of them got down to the ground floor, they were immediately noticed by the two guards near the barricade who turned to look at them with a mixture of surprise and incredulity. Hiro recognized the two men staring at the. The first was a middle-aged truck driver named Takashi while the second was Goro who worked as a postman for the government postal service. Both of them were armed with long bamboo poles with knives that were bound with tape to form a makeshift spear. Takashi also had a red whistle which he wore on a necklace that he could blow into in case of an attack or for any other emergency. Luckily, the building itself had not been attacked so far.

Shinji, Shogo, and Hiro walked over until they were beside the two guards. Shinji smiled at the two men. "How is everything this evening?"

Goro squinted his eyes as he looked at the three young men slowly from head to toe. "Why are you three dressed like that?"

"We're going to go out there and kill some yokai," Shogo said with obvious pride.

Both guards started laughing. Takashi clutched at his potbelly as if it was going to burst while convulsing with amusement. Goro just shook his head and chuckled while trying not to fall down from laughing as he leaned on his makeshift spear for support.

Hiro placed his hands on his hips in obvious displeasure. "What are you two laughing at? Can't you see that we need to do something out there? We can't stay holed up there forever."

A voice from behind them called out. It was a heavy baritone that commanded respect. "What is going on here?"

All five men turned around as a tall, muscular man with a short haircut had walked out of the small office underneath the stairwell and began to address them. Genjuro had always been the tough guy of the neighborhood, and he had become the leader of the building guards pretty much by default because nobody dared to challenge him. No one ever knew what kind of job he had had, but a few of their neighbors who had seen him with his shirt off remarked he must be an enforcer of the yakuza on account of the many tattoos all over his body. The tenants felt safe with him around.

The two guards instantly bowed as Genjuro walked over to them. Shogo was also in the process of bowing until he saw both Hiro and his older brother just standing there defiantly so he quickly pushed his chin and shoulders back up and stood beside them.

Genjuro looked at the three young men. He had a hunting knife in a belt sheath on his hip. "Are you all planning to leave?"

Shinji straightened his shoulders as he wanted to look tough. "We've decided to make an expedition outside of the building to see what we can do to help and maybe to find a way to defeat the yokai out there."

Genjuro nodded as if he understood. "Very courageous. Since all three of you are adults, that is your choice. But if you leave tonight, do not come back until sunrise."

"What? What if we get into trouble out there? You have to let us back in if that happens," Shinji said.

Genjuro shook his head slightly. "I am responsible for the defense of this whole building and everyone in it. I have seen the yokai attack apartment towers such as these when they pursued their victims from the outside and they ran into the buildings for protection. I will not allow the three of you to lead the yokai back to us here."

"But that's not fair!" Shogo protested. "You said you were sworn to protect us and we are tenants in this building too, you know."

"If you stay in the building then my duty to protect you stands," Genjuro said. "But if you leave, you will not be allowed to risk the lives of others. So think about what you want to do very carefully."

Shinji turned to look at Hiro and Shogo. "Let's just go back upstairs, maybe this was a stupid idea after all."

Takashi nodded in agreement. "Yeah, a very stupid idea. Better to go back to your apartment and stay safe. I heard that Mrs. Katsumi will be making curry for us tomorrow."

Shogo's eyes lit up. "Curry? Wow, I can't wait till tomorrow! I haven't eaten curry for months now and I miss it so bad!"

"No!" Hiro screamed. "All this talk about what we're going to eat tomorrow is nonsense! We have to do something or else we will die anyway! I would rather die fighting!"

At that moment all six of them heard a wailing noise outside. As they all stopped talking and began to listen intently the shrieks continued. Hiro guessed that the sound was probably coming from the elevated highway near the train station, less than a block away.

Goro's voice began to tremble. "Now you've done it, all this arguing has attracted the yokai. They'll be coming here," he whispered.

"Wait," Shinji said. "That screaming didn't sound like a demon, it was more like a woman's scream."

The wailing outside continued. Shinji was trying to place the voice in his memory because it sounded very familiar, like the voice of someone he knew. Takashi had crouched down underneath the barricade as his body began to shake with fright. Genjuro merely crossed his arms as he too continued to listen while Shogo had a blank look on his face because all he could think about was the curry he would be eating the next day.

Hiro was already in a fighting stance. "It sounded like a woman who needs help."

Shinji snapped his fingers. "I know who it is! That's Naomi from the neighboring apartment building down the street."

Hiro remembered her. She was a young widow who recently lost her husband and she also just had a baby two months ago. The last time he had seen her was the day after the funeral when the three of them decided to pay her a courtesy visit. He had remembered growing up with her all throughout elementary and high school. Naomi was a beautiful woman, with a pale, oval face that was almost doll-like and had deep black hair that fell past her shoulders. She had been the crush of half the boys in school and many of them were disappointed when she married a cop right after graduation.

Shogo quickly snapped back to reality when he heard her name. "She must be in trouble! Should we go help her?"

"Wait," Genjuro said forcefully. "My directive stands. If any of you go out there, do not come back until sunrise."

"But she's in trouble out there," Hiro said. "How can you make up a rule like that and expect us to help her?"

Shinji grimaced as he looked at Genjuro. "Don't you get it, Hiro? He doesn't want us to help her. He wants us to stay here like cowards."

Genjuro glared at the young man. He looked like he was going to hit him. "You ever call me a coward again. I will rip out your tongue. I have a duty to protect all the families in this building. I know Naomi is a good woman but I cannot jeopardize the safety of everyone to help her."

"Fine then," Hiro said as he held the bamboo sword in his arms. "If you don't want to go, that's up to you. As for me, I will go help her and if I die, at least I died trying to do something good," he said before turning to look at the Nishimura brothers. "Are you with me?"

Shinji thought about it for a few seconds before biting his lip. "I'm with you, let's go. I'm sure we can find somewhere else that's safe after we help Naomi."

Shogo was torn because he wanted to just sleep until it was time for the communal meal tomorrow. But then he realized that even if they did serve the curry, it would most likely be in such a small portion that it would just leave him hungry again. "I'm with you guys," he said finally. "Let's go rescue the lovely Naomi!"

Genjuro said nothing and merely observed as the three young men moved around the barricade and quickly sprinted out into the darkened streets of the city. Takashi and Goro had just stood there, feeling half guilty for not wanting to help out, yet they were partly relieved that someone else would do that foolhardy task for them.

The black and grey shadowed streets were illuminated by flickering yellowish lights coming from the fires on top of nearby skyscrapers, like gigantic torches in the night. As the three men started making their way upwards on a ramp that connected to the elevated highway, they could still hear Naomi's constant shrieks that penetrated through almost quiet evening. All three still had their flashlights and were using them to light the path ahead. They passed by a number of abandoned cars along the road but didn't linger as Shogo could see the outlines of twisted, decaying corpses still inside them.

When they finally saw her, it was apparent she was standing on the edge of the street, ready to throw herself down into the alleyway below. All three immediately broke into a sprint to try to get to her before she could make the leap.

"Naomi!" Shinji shouted as they kept on running towards her. "It's us, we're here to help you!"

Hiro was the fastest runner among the three of them and just as he got close to her, Naomi turned around, away from the ledge and knelt down on the ground as she covered her face and continued to wail. He carefully crouched down on one knee beside her. "Naomi, what is it, what happened?"

Naomi crawled on her knees to him and hugged him tightly. She was wearing a tattered blouse and miniskirt. "My baby! A demon took my baby!"

Just as the two brothers finally ran over beside them, Hiro pushed her shoulders back slightly so he could see her face. "Your baby was taken? How did you get out here?"

"I was in my apartment on the second floor when I placed her on a chair at the balcony," she sobbed. "The sun was setting so I felt it was still safe as I began to prepare her baby formula but as soon as I turned around and looked at her, there was a woman in a kimono standing over the balcony railings. She just took her in her arms and jumped down!"

The two brothers looked at each other in astonishment as they thought about what she said. Naomi started crying harder as Hiro allowed her to rest her head on his shoulders.

Shinji's eyes were wide open in shock. "B-But I thought the yokai could not venture out in daylight. I thought they only came out at night."

"Maybe it was because night was about to fall," Hiro said to him. "Perhaps the yokai who took Naomi's baby had just woken up?"

"I ran out of my apartment building to try to find her," Naomi said. "But nobody was willing to help because they all said that it would be dark in a few minutes so I kept searching. I thought I saw them but they were gone again!"

Hiro was scared but he did his best to comfort her. "Where did you last see her?"

"I-It was getting dark but that yokai wore a red kimono, and I think I saw a glimpse of her near the university," Naomi said.

Shogo nodded. "The Showa University? That's not too far from here, maybe just three or four blocks away. Let's go take a look."

"Hold on," Shinji said. "It may be close by but it would take us far from our apartment building. If we have to run back, it will be a long sprint if we need help."

Hiro looked up at him. "Forget our building! You heard what that fool Genjuro said. We won't be allowed back inside until sunrise so it's better we find the baby and then go find a safe place where we can hole up until the next day."

"Sounds like a good plan," Shogo said as he pulled out the cleaver from his plastic apron. "Let's go find her baby and bring them back the next day. We will be hailed as heroes and shame the others who didn't help. Perhaps we may even get a bigger share of that curry meal tomorrow!"

Hiro looked at Naomi. She seemed a little bit better now since their arrival gave her some much needed hope. "Do you want to stay here and wait for us while we find your baby?"

Naomi made a slight smile as she shook her head. "No, I think I'll just go with you three. I feel safer when we're together."

The Showa Women's University was a large compound that also had a school for every level up to high school. It had largely been abandoned at the start of the Glooming and now its shadowy entrance loomed before the four of them. The campus had consisted of several rectangular buildings that surrounded a large athletic field in the center of the compound. There was an eerie quietness to the whole place as they walked past the unattended gate and into a small, tree lined street before turning left to the main building entrance.

Shinji stopped in the middle of the small street and looked about. There were other buildings that housed different halls and dormitories all around them. "Do you know which block that yokai went into?"

Naomi shook her head slightly. "All I saw was a glimpse of her red kimono as she took my child and went past the gate where we just came from."

Shogo frowned. "We could be here all night if we search all these buildings one by one and I'm already hungry."

Hiro looked at him with a slight annoyance on his face. "Stop thinking about food and look around for clues."

At that moment, all four of them heard a loud cackling coming from the inside of the Hitomi Memorial Hall. Shinji instantly drew his katana while Hiro pushed Naomi behind him as he readied his bamboo sword. Shogo started to make chopping motions in the air with his cleaver.

"Shogo, stop that," Shinji hissed.

"Oh sorry," Shogo said sheepishly as he stopped playing with the blade. "I thought that yokai was near us."

Hiro pointed at the hall. "The sound came from that big building in front of us."

Shinji squinted as he adjusted his glasses. "The sign on the building says Hitomi Memorial Hall, must be an amphitheater or something."

Naomi was shaking. "M-My husband took me there once to see an orchestra playing, it's like a concert hall."

"Oh, I've never been in a concert hall before," Shogo said. "Then again, I've never been in a university like this either. I didn't even take the exams because I knew I would flunk them."

Shinji glared at his brother. "Will you shut up about where you've been already? Nobody cares!"

As Shogo began to make faces at Shinji, Hiro placed his hands on Naomi's shoulders. "I'm going to go in there, wait for me out here," he said to her.

"No, no!" Naomi cried. "If my baby's in there, I'm going with you!"

"Let's all go in there," Shinji said. "The more of us against that one yokai, the better our chances of beating it."

All four nodded. Since he was the best armed among the group, Shinji led the way, followed closely by Hiro and Naomi as Shogo brought up the rear. The building's entrance had glass walls that were shattered and its pieces were all over the foyer as the four of them entered. Naomi kept close to Hiro since he had given her his flashlight so that he could grip his bamboo sword with both hands. Other than the wreckage at the front, the rest of the outer areas seemed intact as they made their way to the double doors leading into the concert hall itself. The doors were slightly ajar and they all noticed that there was some sort of illumination seeping out. Silently positioning themselves by the sides of the doors, Shogo and Hiro immediately pushed the doors forward as Shinji stood by in a fighting stance, ready to draw his katana.

As the doors gave way, all four of them gasped. The concert hall had a high ceiling and they could see an elevated stage towards the far end. Strange balls of floating fire seemed to be magically suspended in mid air above them, bathing the entire area in a flickering yellowish light. Both the acoustically enhanced side walls and the floor were painted in cream colored white. The audience area had multiple rows of empty blue and black padded seats so they made their way along the aisles.

Shinji let out an exasperated sigh as they got closer. "Look at those things on the stage!"

Naomi shrieked as she stared at what was on the theater. Hiro and Shogo just stood by in silent shock. When all four of them first glanced at the stage when they opened the doors, they all thought it contained several sets of brightly colored kimonos that were displayed. They quickly realized that these traditional Japanese robes contained bodies, but without any heads. Each headless body seemed to be sitting in a carefully arranged row so they all faced a potential audience across the hall. As the four of them got onto the stage and began to examine the headless robed bodies, the entire place seemed strangely silent.

Shinji kept his hand on his katana that was still in the scabbard as he stood on the edge of the stage. "Don't get too close to those things."

Hiro and Naomi had walked over to the other end of the stage. "Just stay close to me," he said to her and she nodded. He realized there was no blood on the stage and began to wonder why didn't those corpses bleed when they had their heads chopped off.

Shogo snorted as he took three steps closer to the bodies but sensing that they were inert, he decided to take a closer look as he moved beside one of the headless figures and used two fingers to tug at the folds of its kimono while keeping the cleaver ready with his other hand.

Shinji frowned at the foolhardiness of his younger brother. "Be careful!"

Shogo had a smug look on his face as he peeled back part of the robe. "Looks like it was a woman, I can see her nice, little breasts," he chuckled.

Shinji just shook his head. *My brother is such a fool,* he thought.

Seconds later, all four heard some sort of rustling noise behind them, where the backstage was, hidden away by the long, dark blue curtains.

Shinji ran over to Hiro as Naomi started screaming beside them. Shogo quickly backed away from the corpse he was examining and ran over to them as well. Hiro had his wooden sword ready as he tried to look at where the sounds were coming from.

"There," Shinji said as he pointed to the high curtains at the back of the stage. "Over there!"

At the top of the curtains, all four of them could see parts of it shaking as if there were things moving behind it. A few seconds later, small lumps that seemed to be the size of soccer balls began to appear beneath the curtains right above them. It was at that moment that the curtains fell onto the stage floor right beside them. The four of them began screaming in unison as the flying

35

heads of the corpses began to attack them. Hiro realized that these were demons called nukekubi, creatures that could detach their heads. He had remembered reading about them in a manga comic book.

Shinji drew his katana as one of the flying heads with a visage of a grotesque woman with a mouthful of fangs floated down on him but his swing was too slow and the nukekubi quickly dodged it. Hiro's attack was slightly better as he swung with both hands and connected with another flying head that had tried to latch on to Naomi's throat. When his bamboo sword smacked the nukekubi on its side, the demon flew back out into the audience area. It was like hitting a softball. Shogo also tried to take a swing, but his cleaver didn't have much reach as two more of the flying heads came in from behind him and started biting his back.

"Shogo!" Shinji cried as he tried to fight off the floating heads that had latched onto his screaming brother, but he too was overwhelmed as a half dozen more nukekubi came down on him like a swarm of bees as they tore out chunks of his flesh with their fanged mouths.

Hiro kept on swinging at the demons as he tried to keep the nukekubi from getting any closer, but as he glanced at Naomi for a brief second to make sure she was all right, he abruptly shuddered and drew back. The woman he had a childhood crush on was grinning wildly at him with fanged teeth and her neck began to stretch until it extended ten feet high above the stage. That was when Naomi let out an ear-splitting laugh. Hiro realized she was a demon who had set them all up.

For a brief second, time seemed to stop for Hiro as he just stood there in complete surprise while the bamboo sword slipped from his terrified hands and clattered onto the stage floor.

But just as the creature was about to sink her teeth into him, a katana blade flashed from behind her and severed Naomi's long neck at the base of her shoulders. The demon screamed as she tried to drag her head on the stage floor, her long neck wriggling like a snake.

Hiro just stood there, rooted to the floor, as a young woman ran up to him. She was wearing a short skirt and a white blouse, the kind of uniform that was issued for girls in high school. A shiny katana was in her hands as she used her shoulders to push away the headless body that was wildly flapping its arms around.

The girl with the sword looked at him quizzically. "Well what are you waiting for? If you want to live, you need to run!"

Hiro's voice was like a short croak. "But m-my friends..."

"They're dead! And you will be too if you don't follow me now!"

Hiro followed her off the stage and through the back exit. He never ran faster than he did that night.

4. Seclusion

Greater Boston

Brookline was a small town located south of the Charles River in Eastern Massachusetts. Considered a suburb of Boston, it was home to a number of prominent people from both the old Boston aristocracy as well as highly-paid professionals that kept the town's median income at such a level only the richest people could afford to live there. It was reported in the official census as the city having the most doctorate degrees in the entire country. The town's prime residential areas were widely spaced along winding roads with plenty of trees in between the large colonial-styled homes south of Boylston Street. The northern part of the city had more of a village feel to it, with sidewalks and easily obtainable public transportation. A few months had passed since the god crisis began and now the city was blanketed in a layer of snow, all of its trees had been stripped bare by the relentless chill as if a vengeful winter god had cursed the northern regions of the Earth and held sway over it.

It was early afternoon when a white-painted Ford SUV, with the blue markings of the New York Police Department, slowly made its way along one of the winding streets near the municipal golf course, its snow tires allowing it to traverse the slippery, ice-coated asphalt until it stopped in front of a modest sized, two-story house surrounded by white skeletal trees.

Detective Valerie "Val" Mendoza stared at the red brick walls of the colonial-style house from her side window as she turned off the car's ignition.

"Wow, now that's one hell of a house you got there, Professor. How many rooms did you say it has?"

"Four bedrooms," Dr. Paul Dane said softly as he unbuckled his front seat belt. "And you need to stop calling me professor, Val. Paul would be fine."

Valerie smiled at him. "Sorry, after that speech you gave to the Secretary of Defense, I now have a whole lot more respect for you. When that happens, I start to address you in a formal manner as a matter of habit."

"You really think it was a speech? It was more of a complaining rant."

Valerie chuckled a bit. The past few months had been stressful so she needed to find as much of an amusement in anything she could. "Not many people I know could tell those generals and senators to screw off like you did, especially since the country is under martial law. That took a lot of guts."

"Thanks, I only wish the president was there so I could have told him what I really felt to his face."

"And they accepted your resignation just like that too."

Paul shrugged. "I figured that unless they wanted to put me in jail, there was no way they could stop me from quitting."

"You really think that was the right thing to do? Resign your position as head of Task Force Omega at a time like this? I've always thought that unit was the one thing that could save the country."

Paul had a momentary flash of anger before his shoulders slumped in resignation. "I was no more than a figurehead for that task force, Val. They brought a nuclear bomb into that museum without even telling me. That's when I realized it was a purely military operation through and through. Seems the only thing those jarheads knows is how to kill things- their only way of solving problems that comes along."

"Well, nukes are one weapon we haven't tried against these pagan gods."

Paul shook his head. "Whatever kind of weapon we have just won't work, Val. I kept trying to tell them this but they just wouldn't listen. You were there in the museum and you saw yourself that the giant worm had somehow been transformed into something else by what means we don't even know. If that bomb had detonated, god knows just how bad it would have been. Most of Manhattan would have been toast."

Valerie nodded. "You're right. I was at ground zero and could have been killed too. We lost so many good people in that mission."

"That's what I mean," Paul said. "And their stupid cover up about your testimony on the soldiers and their actions against the cops. It's insane. They screwed up and now they're just protecting each other's asses. I've had enough of it."

"But without you advising them on the task force, isn't it possible they could screw things up even more?"

"Maybe. But either way, I can't bear the responsibility for all those deaths on my conscience. So many people died because of me. I just can't take it anymore, Val."

Valerie placed a reassuring hand on his elbow. "You can't blame yourself for what happened. General Benteen never told you about the nuke so you're not to blame for the deaths in that museum."

Paul sighed. "It's not just the museum, Val. Ever since this crisis started, everyone around me, everyone I know, is dead. I never told you about what happened in England when it started. I had an assistant named Megan and she never got out. The embassy got me out but a few more people died in helping me in that one too. I keep seeing their faces every time I close my eyes."

"I lost my old partner when this thing started too," Valerie said softly. "He was my mentor and everything I learned about being a cop was from him. Maybe you just need a few days to rest and get a new perspective on things."

Paul took off his eyeglasses and rubbed his tired eyes. "Maybe, but either way, I just can't face any more of this. I feel like I'm about to have a mental breakdown or something."

"New York seems quiet at the moment," Valerie said. "We could fix you up in one of the vacant apartments in Brooklyn. Granted, it's not as posh as this mansion of yours that we're looking at right now, but at least you won't be alone. Joe and Commissioner Donovan are grateful for your help and figure we owe you."

Paul made a faint smile. "Thanks for the offer but I think I would just like some time alone for now."

Valerie winked at him as she opened the driver's side door. "Okay, don't say I didn't make an offer for you to stay with us. I guess we can get started with bringing your stuff to the house."

As Paul unlocked the keys to the front door, Valerie immediately went inside as she pulled out her Glock pistol and did a quick search of the place. The house was deserted. Paul hadn't stepped foot into his old home for months, not since the Glooming had started while he was on a lecture tour in Europe. As he flipped the light switches, Paul concluded that there was no electricity either. He would have to live with candles and the few batteries he had for the two flashlights he had brought along. Paul walked back out into the driveway, opened the rear door of the SUV and carried a box of MREs to the house.

Valerie walked back down the stairs as she holstered her gun. "Looks like it's all clear. The good news is that it hasn't been burglarized while you were gone."

Paul placed the box of military rations on the kitchen counter. "I guess I could be thankful for that even though there really isn't much value in the stuff I have in this house anyway."

"I'm impressed," Valerie said. "You got an antique four-poster bed in the master room, one room just stuffed full of books, like a library, and another room for your computer. The fourth has got displays of historic artifacts from all over the world, and you've got two bathrooms upstairs and one down here. You fit the stereotype of the old professor to a T. I'm surprised you stay at a huge house like this all by yourself."

"I stayed because of Elizabeth. She made me promise never to sell the house."

Valerie looked down on the dusty linoleum floor. She had forgotten that he was a widower. "I'm sorry I brought that up, Paul."

Paul smiled as he walked over and squeezed her arm. "No harm done. It was an honest question."

"Professor Dane? Is that you?" A voice that was coming from the open front door made them turn around quickly. It was a heavyset old man wearing a wool cap and a winter coat, standing outside the entrance.

Paul quickly moved over to him and held his hand out. "Clint, nice to see you again," he said as he turned to look at Valerie. "This here's Dr. Clinton Taylor, my neighbor and unofficial head of the neighborhood watch for this block."

Valerie walked over and shook the old man's hand after he had shaken Paul's. "I'm Detective Valerie Mendoza, NYPD."

Clint took off his wool cap. "It's nice to see you two. I thought you were dead or something, Paul."

Paul smiled. "Came close to dying a few times, but I'm still here. Why don't you come inside? I'm going to gather some wood later so I can start up the fireplace."

Clint shrugged. "It's okay, Paul. I can't stay for too long. Donna starts getting antsy when I'm away from her for more than an hour. I decided to take a peek when I saw the cop car pull up and I'm sure glad you're still around." Dr. Taylor was a renowned neurologist who had been living in the area for decades and was an associate at the nearby Harvard Medical School. He had been loyal neighbors with Paul and was one of the pallbearers at Elizabeth's funeral. When he wasn't teaching at the hospital, Clint and his wife were ardent baseball fans and Paul remembered spending many pleasant afternoons and evenings with them watching the games at Fenway Park.

Paul nodded. "How's the neighborhood going?"

"Well, I'm sure you know by now there's no power. Everyone gets by using candles at night," Clint said. "The reservoirs are frozen so most of us melt snow for water and stay in. There's a food pantry that's been set up in front of the Medical Center, but we have to ration the handouts we're giving out now because sometimes the government food convoys get delayed. Oh, and the medical school has been turned into a full-time hospital. Nobody's starving yet so we're getting by."

"That's good to hear," Valerie said. "There weren't any riots around here?"

"There were some riots in Dorchester and Mattapan when this thing started a few months ago but the cold pretty much sapped everyone's strength," Clint said. "Now everybody just seems to be in a gloom as they huddle in their houses for warmth. The mayor and the cops are stretched to the limit so we have armed neighborhood watches that police the area."

"That's good, better than New York," Valerie said.

Clint looked at her with wide eyes. "There've been rumors about New York. They said something about people being skinned alive or something like that. With the constant snow coming down on us up here and the Canadian refugees moving south, we don't get too much news nowadays."

Valerie rolled her eyes. "Oh, you have no idea. Even with your problems up here, I think Bostonians have it easy compared to the rest of the country."

Clint turned to look outside when he heard a woman shouting his name before looking back at them. "Well, that's Donna calling. I gotta go. Are you staying over with the professor, Detective?"

"I'm afraid not," Valerie said. "I have to get back to New York pretty soon."

Clint shook their hands once more before walking back out into the driveway. "Well, I hope you bring more food and medical supplies next time you stop by, Detective. Talk to you later, Paul. If you have any problems, I'm just across the street!"

Paul smiled as he closed the door after Clint left. "Well, I guess it's not so bad up here."

Valerie looked at the fireplace as she rubbed the scar along her face. There were times when it got so cold she could feel the split skin that ran from in between her brow all the way down to the side of her chin. "You've got enough wood to last for a few days here."

Paul walked over and stood beside her. "You know, you could bring your mother up here and join me. God knows this house is big enough for the three of us."

Valerie turned and patted him on the cheek. "Thanks for the offer, but my mama would never want to live anywhere else but Brooklyn. Are you sure you're gonna be okay here by yourself?"

Paul clasped her hand. "I'll be okay. I just need some time to take it all in for now."

"What if the government comes knocking again? You know how nervous they are when it comes to the southern border." Valerie said. "Let's not even mention that we're now practically connected to Northern Europe because everything north of us has been iced over so anybody or anything from that continent can just walk over here."

"The southern border seems to have stabilized even though the country has lost half of Texas to the Aztec gods," Paul said. "As for anybody coming over from Europe, they're going to have to do quite a bit of walking over snow and ice and not to mention the constant blizzards they'll be facing."

"You really don't want to be part of DOD or NORTHCOM, right?"

"Val, they just haven't learned a damn thing. US Army North is now deployed along our southern border. They've got nukes and they're itching to use them even though I've been telling them it's useless. I would be a pariah just sitting around in their command post if I stayed with them and I just don't want that."

"Why do you think the Aztec gods stopped all of a sudden? They could have swept through most of the south by now."

"I don't know. Maybe they're consolidating before making the final push or maybe it's something else, maybe another god is stopping them from advancing north towards us. This is all just speculation right now."

"But you're sure the military won't stop them if they do start to advance again though?"

Paul shook his head. "Val, I was in the battle of London. The Fomorians took some damage from the British military, but I don't even know if those things stayed dead because they came in an endless wave. Even with nukes, how is the military going to deploy them? You can't hit a god with a missile and the Air Force is pretty much gone. All that they can do is maybe detonate a nuke when their positions get overrun but in the end they'll just be bombing themselves."

"I see," Valerie said as she looked away. "I guess I better be going then. My mama always wants me back to her place for dinner every night."

"Thanks for driving me up here, Val. Can I ask one more favor?"

"Sure. What is it?"

"My car's in the garage and I may need a jump because I would bet its battery is probably drained by now."

"Is that it? No problem, let's go outside- I'll drive the SUV up to the garage and you get the jumper cables."

"You got it."

She kissed him lightly on the cheek and placed something in his hand. "This is a fully charged cell phone with my number on it. I know getting a phone signal is touch and go, but if you're in any kind of trouble don't hesitate to call me. NYPD is in your debt. We'll come charging up here if you call."

"Okay, I appreciate the thought."

"One more thing."

"What?"

"Stay alive. I have a feeling we're gonna need each other again."

Paul screamed as he opened his eyes. Within a few seconds, he realized that he was back home and lying in his old bed. The whole house was bathed in darkness since it was still early morning but the Aurora Borealis was illuminating the night sky and he could see the outlines of the bedroom because of the near twilight. As he sat up, Paul grabbed his robe that was lying on an easy chair and put it on over his thermal underwear, before putting on a pair of moccasins on his feet. Paul stood up and walked over by the window and stared out at the snow covered hills around his house. He just didn't feel like sleeping anymore because of the nightmares. Every time he closed his eyes he could see the faces of the dead staring back at him. How he wished that he could just go into a deep sleep and not dream at all but the furies that tormented him were relentless.

It was then that he sensed some sort of movement upstairs, in the attic. Paul felt like there was someone walking around up there. Grabbing the flashlight that was sitting on the night table, Paul moved over to the bedroom door before briefly pausing in order to listen for more tell-tale signs of intrusion. The house seemed quiet once more, but he needed to know so he clasped the door knob, twisted it, and opened the door slightly before peering out into the second story corridor. All he could see was the faint illumination coming from the bottom of the stairwell so he turned on his flashlight and began to wave it around the passage. Still nothing. Paul made his way into the corridor as he pulled at the door panel in the ceiling and unfolded the wooden stairs leading up to the attic.

Paul made his way up into the attic as he used the flashlight to guide him. The single arched window cast a faint bridge of light into the surrounding darkness. It was then he heard a creaking noise. Paul twisted sideways as he brought the flashlight to bear at the source of the sound.

It was an old rocking chair. Paul remembered it once belong to Elizabeth's mother who in turn gave it to her as a keepsake. It was rocking back and forth even though Paul didn't feel a draft in the room. As he stared at it for a minute, his flashlight began to flicker and then died out. Once more all he could see were the faint outlines of the attic as he shook the flashlight, hoping it with turn back on again.

That was when he saw her. Just from looking at the long auburn hair with streaks of grey that fell down to her shoulders, Paul knew almost immediately it was his dead wife. He could see the outline of her delicate chin and the pupils of her rounded eyes reflected back the pale moonlight that seeped in from the window. She was wearing a white embroidered dress, very similar to the clothes she usually wore when just puttering around the house.

Paul's hands shook and he almost dropped the flashlight. "Elizabeth? N-No, how can this be?"

Elizabeth said nothing as she just stared at him and frowned, blood dripping down her chin.

It was all too much. Paul slumped over and fell on his knees as tears began to flow down his cheeks. "Oh God, I've missed you so much. I need you so much. I'm all alone now."

She held out her hands, palms forward in a strange gesture that belied either peace or reception. Paul noticed there were two identical symbols on each palm that seemed to be written in blood. It was that of two circles, the smaller one within the larger ring and both were connected by forked lines emanating from the innermost circle, like stylized streaks of lightning. Paul recognized the form as some sort of ancient symbol, but he couldn't remember what it was exactly.

He quickly turned sideways as several other people from his past came forward and formed a circle around him. He immediately recognized their faces. All the people he had known and who died when the Glooming began. Megan Abramson, Sir Wilfred Pyles, Constable Steve, Getz and Gover, Captain Laura Niven and the many others stared at him with blank, listless eyes as the crimson drops of blood dribbled from their down turned mouths. Paul was now terrified, but he was somehow unable to close his eyes and just continued to stare back at all of them. He couldn't move and so stayed rooted to his spot in the middle of the attic room. Then all of them raised their hands and once more showed the same symbol on their palms just as Elizabeth had done.

Paul shook his head. He didn't understand what it all meant and tried to speak, but no words came out of his mouth. It was then that they converged on him and began to place their bloody hands on his body. As he felt their cold, icy touch, he began to scream in agony as they crowded in and began to smother him before the all encompassing darkness finally overtook them all.

It was mid morning when Paul opened his eyes as he sat up with a nervous jolt. Looking around, he noticed that he was still lying in the middle of the bare attic room as the sun's rays shined through the lone window. *Was it all a dream?* he thought as he sat up and picked up the flashlight that was lying on the floor. As he flipped the switch, the light beam shined faintly. The old rocking chair was still there, along with some boxes.

Paul walked back down to the second story corridor before folding up the stairs to the attic and pushed the top panel back into place. Then he went over to his library and began to pour through his numerous books on ancient runic symbols. It would have been faster using his computer, but since the internet had gone down, doing research meant going back to the old stalwarts of printed books. After about an hour of searching and scanning through hundreds of pages, he flipped into a page of Germanic runes and saw the exact symbol he had encountered last night.

It was called the Black Sun or the Sun Wheel. The first evidence as to the existence of the symbol came from ancient brooches found among artifacts left behind from Frankish and Germanic tribes in Western Europe. There was a prevailing but unsubstantiated theory that the symbol may have been an ancient stylized Roman swastika, but this was nothing more than pure speculation and not generally accepted among his peers. The Black Sun was then appropriated by the Neo-Paganism movement in the early Twentieth Century in Germany before being adopted by the Nazis when they came to power. As Paul continued to read the entries about the rune, he started to wonder why all the ghosts he had seen last night would show him that symbol as it seemingly had nothing to do with the Native American demons plaguing humanity in this part of the world.

A knock on the front door downstairs brought him back to his senses. Paul put the books down on the table and made his way to the front door before unlocking it and pulling back the knob.

Two children stood outside the door, a boy and a girl. They looked to be around eleven or twelve years of age and both were bundled up in winter clothing. The girl seemed to be slightly older. She was a shade taller than the boy as their similar looking faces made them out to be related.

Paul scratched his salt and pepper beard. "Hello."

"I saw your police car in the street yesterday," the girl said. The boy said nothing as he just stared at him with bright blue eyes while he swayed back and forth.

Paul nodded. "Well, it wasn't mine, it belonged to a friend. What can I do for you?"

The young girl bit her lip. "Oh. Okay. I thought you were maybe a cop or something."

"No," Paul said. "I'm a university professor. My name is Paul. What's yours?"

"Kimberly Desmond, but my friends call me Kim," the girl said as she pointed to the smaller boy. "This is my brother Troy."

Paul held out his hand and they both shook it. "Nice to meet you both, do you need police assistance or something?"

Kim frowned and looked down at the snowy ground. "Sort of. Our parents went missing a few days ago and we haven't eaten anything since yesterday."

Paul smiled as he stood back from the door. "Well, why don't you come inside? I'm going to start a fire and cook some breakfast. You both can join me if you'd like. Then after you've eaten, I can help you look for your parents if you want."

Kim hesitated for bit since she was always told never to speak to strangers but she was starving and her own house was cold and it didn't have a fireplace. She turned around and looked at Troy who just nodded his head. "Okay," she said as she took her brother's hand and walked into the house with him.

5. Fission

Colorado Springs

For the four hundredth time that morning, Oliver Reece silently recited the Lord's Prayer as he knelt by the side of the bed. He had been waiting for the knock on his bedroom door since early dawn. But rather than just sit around and do nothing, he felt his time would be better served by silent prayers in order to fulfill his sacred task on this very special day. Several times before, the other team members had opened the door slightly and asked if he would like something to eat but Oliver always said no. He preferred to fast as a form of penance because he would be taking lives today and he felt somewhat guilty about it, even though he knew it was for a sacred cause.

He wasn't always this way. Oliver had gotten married and had a daughter with a woman he met named Trisha when he dropped out of college and tried to be a stockbroker. But things fell through when the bank he was working for folded up and his clients lost millions under his investment advice. They tried to sue him to recover the lost funds, but since he didn't have any money, they finally gave up after a few years. A four-year stint in the Air Force gave him some stability after that, but it all came crashing down when his two-year old daughter was diagnosed with acute childhood leukemia. When his little girl died nine months later, Trisha left him. After that, he wandered about aimlessly, drifting from job to job, without a purpose. That was when a co-worker at the garage asked him to tag along to a local prayer meeting. It was at that rally which was sponsored by the Rock of God Church that Oliver Reece finally saw the Lord's calling to him and he was saved. He then quit his job and packed everything he had in a small bag and headed off to Kansas to live as a volunteer at the church compound in McPherson County. For the next three years, he had helped build the massive stadium as well as the nearby water treatment plant, steadily rising up the ranks of the church hierarchy. By the time of the Glooming, he was part of Pastor Erik Burnley's inner circle.

When they approached him for the mission, he knew it would require his sacrifice but he was more than willing to do it. Oliver realized that everything that Pastor Erik said had come true. The Lord was indeed testing them and the demons that had been unleashed upon the world was the final mark that signaled the end times were here. The Rock of God Church swiftly organized an armed wing to defend themselves, and they all agreed that it should be named the Soldiers of the Lord. Everyone felt that the United States Government had by now fallen into the hands of Satan and could no longer be counted upon to defend the country. So they had to take drastic measures to ensure the survival of the church as they awaited the return of their Lord Jesus Christ who would smite the unholy and bring his faithful warriors with him to heaven. Pastor Erik had decreed he did not know the exact day when the Lord would return, but they all had to be prepared and vigilant. All able-bodied men must be willing to sacrifice themselves to protect the women and children of the church. To that end, the pastor decreed they would send a statement to the Federal Government that the church must be left alone. Since Pastor Erik knew that the only way the government would ever leave them be was through the threat of force, a political declaration must be made with such severe consequences, the government would have no choice about it afterwards.

And so to that end, the church's inner circle conceived of a bold plan to strike at the heart of the Federal Government. It needed to be powerful to ensure that no further retaliation could be conceived against them. It was a complex operation that involved at least three separate teams, and each group needed to pull it off in order for the entire plan to succeed. There were a number of sympathizers in the military and in the US intelligence community to their cause since the days when Pastor Erik's predictions were proven right. Now they had the exact knowledge and the means on how to pull it off, all they needed were the right men who were dedicated and skillful enough to make it all happen. Just yesterday, the first team had already infiltrated Peterson Air Force Base and was ready to activate their weapon. All that was needed now was for the second team to infiltrate Cheyenne Mountain and insert their device and all would be fulfilled.

Oliver opened his eyes as he heard the three knocks on his door. He stood up as the door opened and another man appeared behind it who was dressed in nondescript clothing. "They spotted the convoy, Reece," he said.

"Okay, start up the truck. I'll be out in a few minutes," Oliver said as the man left but kept the door open. He made sure the small wooden cross was around his neck before he stowed it underneath the collar of his military fatigues before putting on his boots. Oliver had made his daughter wear the very same cross on her neck just before she died. He wanted it with him now because he knew he would see her again very soon. The last thing he took from the bedroom was the military ID sitting on the night table.

As he walked out into the living room of the small house he saw two other men standing there. The third man who came into his room was at the warehouse next door and he heard the truck's engines starting. The other two men just nodded at him and all three made the sign of the cross before they started to shake each other's hands.

The first man bit his lip as he grabbed Oliver's shoulder with a gentle squeeze. "May God be with you, Reece."

"And you," Oliver said.

The second man was a bit more heavy set and his eyes were wrinkled from monitoring the portable radio all night. "We placed a Thermos full of coffee in the passenger seat and a couple of sandwiches in case you get hungry, Reece. You should've eaten something last night."

Oliver smiled faintly. "Thanks, but fasting is good for the soul."

Both men nodded as if there wasn't anything more to say.

It didn't take long for Oliver to catch up with the rest of the convoy of M1078 LMTV light utility trucks as they rolled along State Highway-94. As the dozen trucks turned left onto US Route 24, the third LMTV in the convoy slowed down as Oliver accelerated past the others and took its spot. The unit's commanding officer had briefed the first three LMTV drivers that another light utility truck, that was a last minute addition, would be joining them the moment they got to the outskirts of Colorado Springs so there was no surprise as Oliver effortlessly became part of the line. Although the delivery convoy was supposed to be an active military one, the shortage of personnel forced the top brass to make a last-minute change and employ a National Guard transportation unit to handle this month's food shipment to the Cheyenne Mountain Complex. Even though the original transport manifest said thirteen delivery trucks would be making the journey from Virginia to Colorado Springs, the vehicles only numbered twelve until just a few minutes ago, but now they were at full strength due to the fact that a military checkpoint was nearby. The timing was absolutely critical to make sure the watchers would be fooled.

Oliver's throat was dry as he slowed down with the rest of the convoy when they got near the exit ramp leading to Peterson Air Force Base. Even though he had promised himself that he would be fasting, Oliver gave into temptation as he poured a small cup of steaming black coffee from the Thermos. His lips drew back at the bitter taste when he took the first sip. The others forgot to put any sort of creamer or sugar in it but he was so thirsty that he drank the rest of the cup using short sips anyway. The Air Force base was adjacent to the Municipal Airport and both places shared the airfield. As he began to accelerate the truck again while being waived through the military checkpoint, he noticed the four Marine One helicopters parked out in the distance where the nearby parking lot was located. Since there was nothing but static on the walkie-talkie lying in the nearby passenger seat, he surmised that everything was on schedule so he looked to the front and concentrated on his driving. A few minutes passed and the convoy finally got through the checkpoint, then began to accelerate southwards along the highway again.

The food convoy soon turned westwards as they passed by just south of the city of Colorado Springs. Oliver was specifically chosen for this mission because he had been here before when he was a non-commissioned officer in the Air Force. But most of all, Pastor Erik knew he could be trusted and was motivated to pull it off. Since the military didn't allow any sort of civilian traffic along this highway, it was a relatively smooth drive as the convoy turned southwards along State Highway-115 before going west again along the twisting turns of Norad Road.

Half an hour later, Oliver stopped his vehicle just behind the second delivery truck as the whole convoy was now going through the third and final military checkpoint. As he looked out of the truck's window, he could see the gigantic igloo-like entrance leading into the Cheyenne Mountain Complex. It had been almost a decade since he had last set foot in this area so Oliver was momentarily distracted as he reminisced about old times until he heard some faint rapid panting just below him. Looking down at the road beside his truck, Oliver had a momentary fright as he saw a fully-armed MP soldier leading a military working dog around the idle trucks. As he wiped away a single bead of sweat from his forehead, he realized his fear was misplaced since these bomb-sniffing dogs were trained to detect common explosive materials like dynamite, TNT, C-4 plastic explosives, chlorates, and smokeless powders while the explosives he was carrying were polymer-bonded. Nevertheless, Oliver carefully took out a Glock that had been taped from underneath the truck's dashboard and checked it to make sure there was a round in chamber before tucking it into a concealable holster at the base of his spine. The one thing that worried him about this final checkpoint was if the guards decided to use handheld Geiger counters. Even though the technicians he talked to prior to the mission assured him that they took precautions to shield the device that was in the back of his truck against that kind of detection, he wasn't so sure so he had decided right then and there to ram the truck through the North Portal and detonate it in the access tunnel the moment they detected what he was carrying.

A loud thump on the side of the vehicle door made him jump and his head almost hit the cabin ceiling. As he turned and looked down his window, the solider with dog was signaling to him so Oliver lowered the window as he reached for the Glock behind his back.

The soldier with the dog was pointing ahead of him. "You can go in now."

Oliver turned to look at the front. He realized that the two LMTV trucks ahead of him had already gone ahead and he was holding up the rest. "Sorry, I zoned out for a minute there," Oliver said to the MP as he restarted the truck and drove it into the access tunnel.

The Cheyenne Mountain Complex was an incredible feat of military engineering. Just a few years ago, it had served as the headquarters for the United States Space Command as well as for NORAD, but it had recently been deactivated as priorities prompted a shift in assets and air defense was shifted to Peterson Air Force base, just a few miles away. But just a few months ago, the complex became fully operational once more as the Glooming began and it served as a heavily-guarded home to both the president and the Secretary of Defense while the rest of the United States government were dispersed in similar bases in the Virginia countryside. Built under 2,000 feet of granite into the heart of Cheyenne Mountain, the complex itself was designed to withstand a nuclear attack from the outside since the underground city within was shielded by tons of rocks. The foundation of the buildings even had gigantic springs to prevent the structures from shifting a single inch in the event of a direct attack against it.

Oliver smiled to himself as he carefully parked the LMTV truck along the sides of the central access tunnel just behind the other trucks of the convoy. While the complex itself was designed to protect itself against an outside nuclear attack, it would not fare very well against an attack from the inside. As he got out of the driver's seat and made a short jump onto the pavement, Oliver walked over to the back of his vehicle and started unlatching the sides of the truck bed. The back of the vehicle contained boxes of peppers as well as hot pepper sauces; this cargo was carefully chosen by their head of operations because it would partly throw the scent of the military guard dogs as an added precaution. But what he really wanted was the vending machine sitting in the middle of the truck bed, so he looked around until he saw another soldier manning a forklift and was slowly driving it towards the lead truck.

Oliver ran over to her. The soldier looked like she was working at the commissary department as she got out of the forklift and started to unlatch the back of the lead truck.

"Hey," Oliver said to her. "Could I borrow your forklift for a minute?"

The soldier was a young black woman who wore US Navy fatigues. She turned and looked at him blankly. "I'm sorry but I've got to get the boxes off of this truck right away and bring it over to the kitchens, the crew will be starting lunch very soon and there's a shortage of fresh vegetables. The Defense Secretary is on a restricted vegetarian diet because of his heart trouble so he wants to be served first."

Oliver grinned sheepishly. "I hear you. I have the same problem- only this time they told me I have to get that vending machine over to the executive dining hall ASAP. I'd like to move it myself, but the damned thing's too heavy and all I've got is a dolly. You don't suppose I could just borrow it for a minute and then bring it right back to you?"

She shook her head. "I'm sorry, I can't right now."

Oliver bit his lip before smiling again. "I'll tell you what, I'll haul a couple of boxes of veggies for you using the forklift- I'll just stack it on top of the vending machine and I'll make the trip to the dining area first then to the kitchens and be back as soon as I can, okay?"

The soldier hesitated. Oliver knew he almost had her. "Look, I don't wanna get into no trouble, Sergeant."

Oliver winked at her. "You won't. The third box at the back of my truck has got nothing but chocolate bars on it and it's not on the inventory manifest. I was gonna give it to a friend of mine who is assigned here, but I'm gonna give it to you instead as a favor. You can do what you want with it."

She looked around to see if anyone was listening, but nobody was since everyone else was in the process of bringing their own supplies to their designated locations. "Okay, but show me the box first."

Oliver trotted along with her as she drove the forklift until it was behind his truck. He grabbed the designated box from the back of the vehicle and handed it to her. Taking out a small box cutter from her uniform pocket, she sliced a small part of the top of the box and peered within. She could see the plastic wrapped chocolate bars as well as the other assorted candies inside.

She turned to look at him. "Lemme see the manifest list."

Oliver took out a clipboard from the truck's cabin and handed it to her.

"Check the serial number on the box," he said.

She did. After a minute, she pulled out her own copy of the manifest from her pocket and checked to see if it was there. It wasn't. "Okay, you got a deal," she said before she pointed to the forklift. "The boxes that need to go to the kitchen are on the lift right there. Take them to Corporal Miller at kitchen five. I'm giving you twenty minutes before I alert the MPs in case you don't come back."

Oliver grinned. "Yes, ma'am."

As she walked away with the box of candies, Oliver brought up the forklift ramp until it was parallel to the height of the truck's rear bed. Using the manual dolly, he was able to get the vending machine onto the forklift. The boxes of vegetables would probably fall off if he started driving the machine with any kind of speed so he placed them on his lap instead. Oliver then drove the forklift through the opened blast doors and into a subterranean cluster of buildings. As he was moving along the narrow underground streets between the three-story structures, he noticed the Secretary of Defense along with his staff walking slowly towards Command Center. The day was extremely fortuitous because the president was over at nearby Peterson Air Force Base and would not be affected by this phase of the operation. Oliver made a silent prayer to the Lord, thanking him for all the lucky breaks so far.

The commissary area was a small grocery and clothing store located close to the side tunnels that housed the underground reservoir. With its own water and air filtration system, the people in the complex were prepared for any eventuality. *Well, almost everything*, Oliver thought as he opened the side doors of the store with his key.

A soldier assigned to the commissary walked over to him and Oliver handed him the orders that was on his clipboard. This particular soldier seemed bored and merely glanced at it, telling Oliver to carry on with a wave of his hand. Oliver carefully maneuvered the vending machine until it faced the empty wall where it was assigned to and he lowered the lift until it was now on the same level as the floor. He got out of the forklift and then crouched down while plugging the vending machine into the wall socket. Oliver quickly realized his mission was now done. Pastor Erik had told him that if there were no problems he could even get away by slipping past the convoy and perhaps hitching a ride with someone else but Oliver said no, he would be there when the device was activated. His task on this Earth was now finished and he was ready to join his daughter in blissful eternity. Taking the box of fresh vegetables with him, Oliver headed over to kitchen five to fulfill his last promise.

The moment the vending machine was plugged into the wall socket, a coded transmission was relayed through the underground cables of the complex and a tiny FM burst over the airwaves was noticed by a team sitting in a nondescript house just a few miles east of the city, past Schriever Air Force Base.

A radio technician looked up. "The device is active."

General Chuck Teller of the SOL Army stood over the radio operator and crossed his arms. "What's the status on the Peterson team?"

"They're good to go as well, sir."

"Very well, initiate detonation of Weapon One and put Weapon Two on standby."

"Yes, sir."

The vending machine contained a modified W87 warhead. Once created to be used on the MX Peacekeeper ICBM, all the remaining W87s were to be retrofitted into the Minuteman III missiles since the termination of the MX missile program. A few months ago, the Soldiers of the Lord were able to capture over three dozen of these thermonuclear warheads in an ambush conceived by General Teller. They had spent months carefully placing one of the warheads into a vending machine. The bomb was two stage radiation implosion weapon that consisted of two spheres, the larger of the two was a layered ball of polymer-bonded chemical explosive that surrounded an inner layer of beryllium and plutonium-239. The balls were themselves encasing a central core of deuterium-tritium gas. As the vending machine's internal timer wound down to zero, this explosive ball immediately imploded in on itself, causing a fission explosion that in turn compressed the second sphere that contained a thick layer of uranium-238 surrounding a smaller core of lithium deuteride. With the first sphere detonating, this caused the second sphere to immediately chain react into an even larger fusion reaction.

Within a split-second, the entire subterranean complex underneath Cheyenne Mountain was completely obliterated as a force with the equivalent of 475 kilotons of TNT vaporized everything in its path. The whole mountain shuddered as the entire cave complex collapsed in on itself and an initial radioactive pressure wave blew past the North and South Portals of the caves before collapsing them as it entombed only the shadows of all the people who were once inside of it. The focused shockwaves that reverberated from the tunnels and out into the open smashed through cars that were on the roads like dust motes in the wind. The men, women, and children who were instantly killed by the blast were the lucky ones while those that were somehow still alive were horrifically burned as their clothes, skin and hair melted away almost instantly from the onslaught of kinetic energy, searing heat, and intensely lethal gamma radiation.

6. Clues

Greater Boston

Dr. Paul Dane couldn't help but be amazed as he watched the boy eat. Troy was around eleven and short for his age, but he wolfed down five whole pancakes with lots of maple syrup and was already working on his sixth. *The poor kid must have been starving for days*, he thought. Troy's older sister Kim had only eaten two of them before she got up from the dining table and took her plate to the sink.

Paul placed two pancakes on his own plate while standing in the kitchen counter before looking over at the young boy again. He was thankful for the suggestion Valerie's mom made about attaching a couple of propane fuel tanks to the gas stove, now he had a few months of stove top usage until he had to resort to the Dutch oven in the fireplace. "You want some more, Troy?"

Troy said nothing but he shook his head before downing a glass of melted ice water.

Kim stood beside the anthropology professor as she used a damp sponge to clean her plate in the sink. She was thirteen and maturing rapidly. "He stopped talking when our parents didn't come back. They're never coming back are they?"

Paul looked at her. He needed to reassure the child. "Sure they will, maybe you just need to give them more time."

"It's been over six days now since they left," Kim said as she dried off the plate with a cloth towel. "I hope they died quickly."

"You shouldn't say things like that."

"I know they're dead. Otherwise, they would have come back already. It's as simple as that."

"Let's not jump to conclusions as of yet," Paul said. "Did they take the car when they left?"

"Yes."

"What kind of car was it?"

"A maroon colored Beamer."

"You remember the license plate?"

"No, but I think the paperwork for it is probably in our house somewhere."

Paul started eating while standing beside her. "Okay, let me finish this plate and I'll bring you both back to your house and we'll have a look around."

Kim bit her lip. "Um, is it okay if we just stay with you?"

"I guess you could, I'll just have to clear one of the other rooms out," Paul said. "Did my neighbor Clint talk to you at all? He's been quite helpful to me since I got back here."

Kim shrugged. "He was okay. A couple of days ago, he gave us a couple of cans of beef stew and suggested that we could stay at his house, but we said no."

"Why didn't you?"

"Every time we walked near his house, we could hear a woman scream, that's his wife, I think. Troy didn't want to move in with them because he was scared of her and so was I so we just stayed put in our house until the last of the food and the candles were gone."

"When your parents left to find food, did they say where they were going?"

"Not really, no. They just told us that they would be back. I didn't think it would be that important, I figured they were just running an errand since we were running out of food."

"Well, Clint told me there was a food bank set up near the medical school so I guess I'll drive over there in a bit. Maybe the people who run that place saw them."

Kim sighed. "They say the whole world is ending. Is that true?"

"Well, we're still here," Paul said. "Everybody just needs to stick together and we ought to be okay."

"Other than your neighbor, we're the only ones left on this whole street," Kim said. "Is it like that in the other parts of the country?"

Paul looked at her. Kim seemed pretty philosophical about the whole thing. He figured it best not to sugarcoat the truth. "A lot of people have died and if the Aztec gods decide to attack across our southern border, we'd all be in even bigger trouble."

Kim looked down. "So it's just a matter of time then till we all die then."

"I'd like to think that there is still some hope left in the world," Paul said. "When I was in New York for the past few months, I thought we were doomed when an American Indian god of evil tried to enter into our world, but something or someone stopped it at the last minute. I'm not sure what it was, or who it was that saved us, but it gave me some much needed optimism to keep on living. Maybe we just need to hold on a little bit longer and so we can come out of this alright."

"Do you think it was Jesus that saved us?"

"I don't know."

"If all these other gods just reappeared then why didn't Jesus come back too?"

"I don't know that either."

"What do we do then?"

"Well, one thing at a time," Paul said as he placed his now empty plate in the sink. "Let me wash these plates and then I'm heading over to the food bank to ask them about your parents."

The drive to the food bank took less than fifteen minutes. Paul had suggested that they both wait for him in the house so it would be safer, but Kim insisted they tag along and so all three of them stood outside of the old Harvard Medical School's main building. The structure always reminded Paul of the Capitol Building due to its Greco-Roman design, although the medical school's columns and facade was that of a deep grey color rather than the white-painted front used by congress in Washington DC. As the three of them came out of the car and walked around the compound, they noticed that it was mostly deserted. A number of wrecked and abandoned cars were nearby while a small group of people were near the entrance. The trees that once adorned the sides of the building were now gone and heaps of garbage were all over the area.

As they walked into the shattered lobby there were long folding tables spread out with piled boxes of foodstuff. A few civilian volunteers were distributing the boxes while being watched by a small group of National Guardsmen. Paul was surprised there weren't more people around.

Paul walked up to a black middle-aged woman in a fake fur coat who was writing on a clipboard. "Excuse me, are you the one in charge here?" he asked.

She barely glanced at him while continuing her scribbling. "If you want a box of food, you're gonna need to register first. Fill out that form by the table at the right and I'm gonna need to see some ID."

"Sorry, but I'm not here for a handout. I'm looking for two people who are missing and I wanted to ask you if you've seen them at all, we believe they might have come here about six days ago looking for food," Paul said as he took out a picture of Kim's parents and showed it to the woman. He had made a brief stop to the kid's house to get the photograph.

The woman didn't even look at the picture. "We get a lot of people coming in here all the time so I couldn't tell you."

Paul sighed. "Is there anyone here who might be able to help us?"

"Sorry, this line is for food packages. Next"

"Look, can I maybe just see your records? Perhaps they might have registered to get a handout a few days ago."

"Our distribution logs are sent over to the government, we don't keep 'em here."

Paul was beginning to lose his patience. "Can I talk to your supervisor, please?"

The woman pointed to the far side of the lobby. "Go look over there. Next."

Paul seethed as he tried to put the photograph in front of the woman's face, but she backed away and looked at the soldiers. "You didn't even look at the picture," he said.

A guardsman walked over to them. He was in full battle gear and cradling an M16A2 assault rifle. "Move along, sir."

Paul snorted as he took Troy's hand and walked to the side of the hall. All along the massive right wall of the lobby were thousands of pictures of men, women and children on billboards. A large sign was titled MISSING. Kim gasped as she realized just how many people had disappeared in the past few months. Tens of thousands of smiling faces stared back at them. Paul glanced at some of the pictures and then drew back, he knew at least a dozen people e on that wall. Troy just stared at one picture of a boy his age who was cuddling a puppy. There were telephone numbers and addresses written alongside many of the photos with urgent pleas for contacting the ones who inquired about them.

"I wouldn't be puttin' yo pictures on that wall cuz it's a dead man's wall," a nearby voice said.

They all turned and noticed a middle-aged black man mopping the floor a few yards away from them. His rusty pail had some melting ice water and his black wool coat was torn in a few places. The man glanced at them briefly before dunking the mop back in the pail and resuming his task.

Paul moved closer to the man. "I'm sorry, but what do you mean it's a dead man's wall?"

The man shrugged and didn't look at him while he continued his mopping. "All's I can say is, that nobody ever found the people that are on that wall, so it's bad luck to put anythin' on it."

Paul nodded. He wasn't the superstitious type. "I see. Have you worked here for long?"

"Only after this here apocalypse started. They gimme me some free food packets in exchange for keepin' the place tidy and all."

Paul moved closer and showed the picture to him. "Maybe you might have seen these two people. They're good friends of mine. They went out looking for food about six days ago and haven't come back," he said before pointing to Kim and Troy. "That's their kids and they are really worried about them."

The man glanced at the picture briefly before continuing his cleaning. "I might've seen 'em."

"When? About six days ago?"

The man nodded. "Yeah, it could have been them. I was cleaning the tables and they walked over and gave me a few cans of food from the box they took when they signed up. Mighty nice of 'em."

"Then what happened?"

The man shrugged. "I saw another man walk up to them just before they about to leave. I saw all three of 'em talk and they all left together."

Paul adjusted his glasses. "This other man, what did he look like?"

"He was a white man, like them and you, only older."

"Can you describe him a bit more?"

The man shook his head. "Y'all look the same to me. From the way they were talking, it seemed like they knew each other. That's about all I know."

So it must have been somebody they knew, he thought. Paul thanked him and walked over to Troy and Kim. "He says he might have seen your parents, they were here but they talked to another man they knew and then they all left. What kind of work did your parents do?"

"My dad was a software engineer. He had a small office with his partner in Somerville, but that's been closed since this end of the world thing started," Kim said. "My mom's an accountant and she worked near the airport, but she stopped going to her office when the lights went out a few months back."

"What about your mom and dad's friends, do they live nearby?"

"Dad's partner Blain always used to come over to our house before everything went belly up, but he went missing along with his family over a month ago. My mom brought her boss over for dinner once, he seemed like a boring guy, I think his name was John or something, but I don't think my dad knew him very well," Kim said.

"Okay, what about your relatives?"

Kim looked down. "My dad was an only child, and gramps and granny were in one of the planes that went down in the first few days. My mom's mom was still alive and living with our uncle Gus and his family near Rochester. They said they would try to come over to us, but we haven't heard anything about them for like a month."

"Sorry to hear about your grandparents," Paul said softly. "Do you know where your dad's office is?"

"Yeah, he took me there to visit a few times, why?"

"Let's go take a look."

The bridges were still intact so the drive took less than ten minutes. Paul noticed that gas tank on his car was already half empty and made a silent curse for not thinking about getting some fuel from New York before coming back up to Boston. The office building where Kim's father worked at was a small suite on the second floor and the whole place looked deserted. The only other clue that Paul found when he rummaged the inside of the place was Blain's home address near Tufts Park.

By the time they had arrived in the sidewalk facing Blain's house, Troy had fallen asleep in the back seat. Paul instructed Kim to remain with her brother as he got out of the car and walked over to the front door before knocking. It was then he noticed that the door was slightly open.

Paul knocked on the wooden part of the door before peering in. "Hello, anybody home?"

The whole living room area was in shambles. Overturned shelves and broken furniture greeted him as he slowly stepped inside. A rotten, pungent smell was coming from upstairs. As Paul slowly walked up the stairs, he noticed there were bloodstains on the wooden steps. When he got to the top of the staircase, he saw two bodies lying in the corridor. From their clothes, it seemed like they were a man and a woman, both had been eviscerated and much of their flesh had been gouged out. They must have been dead for weeks. He drew back down the stairs and began to retch. The bodies were heavyset and didn't resemble Kim's parents at all. When Paul noticed Blain's photographs in the living room, he concluded it was probably him along with his wife up there- they had the same hair color and facial features.

After spending a few more minutes composing himself and wiping off the vomit from his mouth, Paul walked back out into the street and got back in his car.

Kim gave him a quizzical look. "Did you find anything?"

Paul shook his head. "No, nothing, the house was deserted."

Since they were already on the other side of the city, Paul decided to drive southwards and make his way through Cambridge as he once more passed by the now closed Harvard University. He sighed when he remembered that this was the most prestigious place of learning until the whole god crisis began. *Now we would have to start from scratch again once this is all over*, he thought as he steered the car past Harvard square and onto the bridge until they were once again past the Charles River and heading back to Brookline.

Just as they had gone past Beacon Street and were close to the main village square, Kim immediately turned her head and started pointing at a row of abandoned cars along the other side of the street. "Look! Over there! That's dad's car!"

Paul instinctively applied the brakes. "Are you sure?"

"Yes, I'm sure! That's the car!"

Paul maneuvered the Volvo until it was parallel to the maroon colored BMW parked beside a row of other cars. Before he could say anything, Kim opened the front seat door and leapt out. "Kim, wait!" he said to no avail.

Kim somehow got BMW's car door opened and looked inside as Paul placed his own car on park and got out. By the time he walked over to the BMW, he saw Kim just sitting the front seat looking dejected. "It wasn't even locked. They left the keys inside," she said while pointing to the car key still sticking in the ignition lock.

Paul walked over to the driver's side of the BMW and opened the door before sitting down. As he started to look around for clues, Kim stood up and started to walk back to his Volvo. It was clear she was devastated and there was not much he could do to comfort her, except maybe give the kid some time to herself. Paul shifted his head from side to side as he got up and then bent over and used his hands to feel the flooring to see if there was anything in the car's interior that might yield any information as to where they might have gone to. The glove compartment was empty so Paul made one last glance before seeing something shiny embedded in the leather folds of the driver's chair. As he squeezed his fingers into the upholstery, he felt something thin and solid and pulled it out. Paul examined the object. It was a Red Sox pendant that somehow got stuck in the driver's seat.

When he got back into the driver's side of the Volvo, he noticed Kim was crying a little while Troy continued his snoring at the back seat. Paul turned to look at her. "It's okay," he said. "There must be a reason why they just parked the car and left it. Don't worry, we'll keep looking, okay?"

Kim wiped away the tears with some tissue paper from the glove box. "I watched this cop show on TV last year. They said that if someone just left the key inside like that, they did it voluntarily. Maybe they just decided to leave us behind on purpose."

Paul shook his head. "Come on, why would they do that? That's not what a parent would ever do to their children, especially in a time like this. There's a reason as to what happened and we'll find it out soon enough. I've got some cocoa powder at home and I'll make some hot chocolate for all of us."

"Is it too much to ask if we could all sleep in the same room together tonight? I don't want to be alone," she said softly.

"No problem," Paul said as he shifted the automatic transmission back to drive as the Volvo started to move again. "By the way, I found a Red Sox pendant in the driver's seat, it must have been your dad's," he said as he pulled it out of his pocket and showed it to Kim.

Kim shook her head and refused to take it. "That can't be my dad's. He hates the Sox. He hates baseball period. He prefers to just watch football and the Patriots."

Paul frowned as he drove the car back to his house. Was there a killer or an abductor on the loose?

7. White Tops Down

Colorado

John Smalley, the White House Chief of Staff, was with the president in the small briefing room inside Peterson Air Force Base when suddenly, the whole place shook as if a small earthquake had hit and the lights in the ceiling started to flicker. Several senior officers stood up in shock and began to look around in apparent confusion. The two Secret Service agents in the room instantly drew their weapons and stood by the door before one of them started talking in his radio headset.

Admiral Charles Zimmerman sat back down on his chair. The commanding officer of NORTHCOM began to sweat. "What in the hell was that?"

"Take it easy, Charlie," the president said. "I'm sure the staff will let us know what happened."

Within less than a minute after the room had shook, everyone jumped at the sounds of multiple explosions that sounded uncomfortably close. The door leading from the outside instantly opened and two more Secret Service agents ran inside, one of them was Andrew Mullins, the team leader.

The president looked up at them. "What's happened?"

"Mr. President, we have to move now," Agent Mullins said as everyone immediately stood up and started grabbing their papers and briefcases. "There was a possible thermonuclear explosion inside the Cheyenne Mountain

Complex, and reports of explosions within the perimeter of this base."

With that, the president was immediately ushered away by the Secret Service team as Admiral Zimmerman and John Smalley followed. They started to run as fast as they could. The team soon led them towards the empty parking lot, where the helicopters of Marine One were sitting.

John Smalley was starting to lose his breath as he kept running. His asthma was beginning to flare up again. "Any word on the Defense Secretary? He was in Cheyenne Mountain."

Agent Mullins didn't break his stride and his voice was calm. "No, sir."

Admiral Zimmerman was the oldest, but he still kept in regular shape and so the sprint wasn't too taxing for him, but he started to breathe heavily. "Why not take Marine One? I say we forget the motorcade convoy."

As they started to run across the nearly empty parking lot, a few more explosions could be seen just south of them as numerous detonations clouds ripped through the base. The Secret Service team pushed the president to the ground and surrounded him as they looked around. The Marine contingent near the helicopters began to run towards them with weapons on the ready. Admiral Zimmerman noticed that there were numerous wrecked and burning cars at the nearby highway to the north of them. He realized the helicopters were indeed the best alternative.

With two squads of Marines now surrounding them like a group of human shields, the Secret Service team got the president back on his feet. They continued moving until they got to the sides of the two Sikorsky VH-3D Sea King helicopters. Each chopper was specially modified to ferry the president and his staff whenever he needed it and with the best protection possible. With its olive drab colored sides and white-painted upper fuselage, the helicopters were nicknamed "white tops" by the Marines who flew them. Each Sea King had a crew of three, with two pilots in the cockpit and a crew chief who normally had the ceremonial duty of opening and closing the chopper doors while wearing a Marine dress uniform. But this time, everyone was in battle fatigues as there was no longer any pretense for show.

As the crew chief hustled them in quickly, the president sat down beside John Smalley and began to buckle his seat belt. Andrew Mullins along with his three man Secret service team followed them inside. Admiral Zimmerman was the last person to be brought into the cabin before the crew chief went inside and closed the door behind him. Both Sea Kings already had their rotors running, and within less than a minute, they were airborne and headed east. There would be a rendezvous with an alternate motorcade that would return the president back to Virginia. Two CH-47 Chinooks carrying the Marine platoon assigned to guard them were also sitting beside the Sea Kings and were now starting to lift off as well. Although the threat against aerial attack by the thunderbirds was very possible, the military had learned through a painful process of trial and error that these mythical monsters would usually appear only when aircraft would fly above two thousand feet; so therefore it was still practical to use helicopters for low level airborne transport.

The president shook his head. He was still in shock. "They nuked Cheyenne Mountain? Who are they?"

Smalley looked out of the small porthole along the sides of the helicopter. The Marine pilots began to rapidly jink the aircraft in order to perform basic evasion maneuvering just a few hundred feet off the ground. "We don't know at this point. Could be the Texan separatists or maybe some other group that wants to secede would be my best guess, Mr. President."

"It must have been an inside job," Admiral Zimmerman said as he griped the armrest on his own seat. "Our security was airtight."

One of the Marine pilots called out to them from the open cockpit door. "Everybody hang on, we have unauthenticated aircraft in the area."

As Smalley looked out of the small porthole once more he gasped. No more than a few miles away were two other helicopters and they were closing in on the aerial convoy. As the intruders closed in on them, he noticed that they were two Boeing AH-64 Apache gunships. "Hey, those are supposed to be two of our own," he said.

Admiral Zimmerman was in the opposite side of the fuselage so he couldn't see them from his side. "What are they?"

"Two Apaches," Smalley said as he kept peering outside. "Closing in fast."

As soon as they got to within a mile, the Apaches immediately engaged the two Chinooks that were at the rear of the group. Although the Chinooks were much larger twin-rotor helicopters, they were configured as transports and did not have any defensive weapons mounted on them. Like two predatory sharks attacking a pair of hapless whales, the lead Apache maneuvered in behind them and opened fire with its 30mm M230 chain gun. The burst of automatic fire instantly destroyed one Chinook's rear rotor and sent it crashing down into the barren plains of Eastern Colorado. The downed Chinook exploded into a large fireball upon impact. The second Chinook attempted to evade the gunships but its pilot overcompensated, tilting the large transport helicopter too quickly as it attempted to make a quick turn. The second Chinook crashed sideways as its twin rotors were sheared off by contact with the ground, its lozenge-shaped fuselage crumpled into a heap as it rolled onto the earth in a cloud of dust.

The sacrifice of the two Chinooks enabled both Sea Kings to gain some distance from their attackers. The Sea Kings accelerated to full speed, as they began their shell game by veering back and forth with each other in order to confuse the enemy as to which helicopter actually contained the president. The Marine pilots instantly concluded that the renegade Apaches were looking to abduct the president rather than kill him because of the strict use of their chain guns. They could see that the attack helicopters carried rockets and Hellfire missiles in their wing pods. Despite the Sea Kings flying at full throttle, the Apache gunships slowly began to close the gap in order to try to get within less than a mile for their chain gun's optimum range.

Smalley heard the Marine pilots screaming in their headsets, calling anyone who was listening in on their frequency for help. As the seconds ticked by, it felt like years as the enemy Apaches got ever closer. Admiral Zimmerman grimaced helplessly as he lay strapped in his chair on the opposite side of the cabin. Agent Mullins and his Secret Service team seemed to be whispering to each other, but Smalley couldn't hear what they were saying.

As the Apaches got to within optimum distance for their chain guns, the other Sea King helicopter quickly turned and charged straight at them, hoping to confuse the gunships for a few more seconds to give the chopper with the president some more time in which to escape. However, the Apaches instantly realized the desperate tactic that had been employed against them as the lead gunship instantly fired its Hydra 70 rockets at the charging Sea King. The rockets exploded on the front part of the Marine helicopter's cockpit and sent it crashing down in flames.

Now that Marine One had been stripped of all her escorts, the Sea King was flying just above ground level and jinking in every direction, its pilots were doing everything they could think of to evade the relentless gunships now tailing them. The Apaches had advanced target acquisition sights and the lead gunship took its time to carefully aim for the rear rotor before opening up with its 30mm cannon. Within seconds, close to a half dozen high-explosive dual purpose rounds began to impact the Sea King's rear rotor. Even though Marine One had special armor protection and electronic countermeasures, it did little against two barrages of 30mm rounds that nearly tore off the back rotor. The Sea King pilots tried as best as they could, but the loss of the tail rotor sent the helicopter on a downward spiral.

"Marine One going down," the Sea King pilot said just seconds before impact.

Smalley screamed as the crash crumpled the front part of the cockpit. The Marine pilot lowered the nose of the helicopter down at the last second in order to lessen the impact on the passenger cabin. The intense collision combined with the sudden stop upended the fuselage as the wreckage flipped over and it rolled a few times before settling on its side. Admiral Zimmerman had leaned forward and placed his head in between his knees just before the crash so he was lucid and able to act as soon as the helicopter had stopped. The Secret Service team had also braced themselves for impact and even now they were taking off their seatbelts before moving over to where the president was.

As he felt the warm blood running down his forehead, Smalley shook himself awake as he saw Agent Mullins and his team beside the president. Smalley groaned as he unbuckled his own seatbelt.

Agent Mullins unbuckled the president's seatbelt as the rest of his team began to examine the Commander in Chief to see if he was injured. "Mr. President, are you okay, sir?"

The president was in a daze. He had a pounding headache but other than that he didn't feel any pain in the rest of his body. "I-I think I'm okay."

Marine One's crew chief crawled from the rear of the cockpit. His right arm hung limply on his shoulder. "Both pilots are dead."

Admiral Zimmerman looked out of the side porthole of the fuselage that had ended up as the ceiling. "Those two Apaches are still circling around, if we get out of, we'll all be sitting ducks."

As he said those words, the two gunships instantly veered away and flew off into the horizon.

As his team helped the president off of his chair, Agent Mullins checked to see if there was a fire of some sort within the cockpit. The whole wreckage smelled of burned rubber and jet fuel. "We need to go," he said tersely.

One of the Secret Service agents was able to push out the side door of the helicopter. Using his arms, the agent pulled himself up and stood on top of the wreck as he started to help the others in getting out. Agent Mullins was the second person to get into the open as he helped the president through the door before jumping down onto the dusty ground. Just as he got the Commander in Chief to sit down alongside the fuselage, he immediately saw four dark spots in the sky that were slowly getting bigger. As he squinted his eyes for a closer look, he realized they were Blackhawk helicopters.

Admiral Zimmerman was crouched on top of the wreck and he saw them too. "Four choppers inbound," he said, stating the obvious.

Agent Mullins looked around. He noticed a copse of bare trees about half a mile away. "Mr. President, we need to move. Now."

The president said nothing and just nodded. John Smalley realized they needed to buy some time. "The rest of us will stay here, Mr. President. We'll try to delay them as long as we can."

"Then may the Lord be with you," the president said as he was led away by the four Secret Service Agents. Then they started to make a run towards the trees. One of the agents was limping but he kept up as much as he could while the others half-carried the Commander in Chief.

Just as the five of them got halfway between the wrecked Sea King and the trees, the two lead Blackhawks flew around the small group of Secret Service men who used their bodies to shield the president. The pair of transport helicopters circled them before touching on the ground, one in front and the other behind them. Almost instantly, the side doors of the Blackhawks slid open and men wearing black body armor poured out, aiming their assault rifles at the group. Another pair of Blackhawks started to circle the wrecked Marine One helicopter as Admiral Zimmerman noticed their side doors were also open and men with scoped rifles were aiming at him.

Knowing that further resistance was useless, the president pushed Agent Mullins back and stood up before straightening his tie and brushing the dust off from his dark blue suit. "You've done your job well, Andrew. It's time to give up," he said softly.

All four Secret service agents grimaced as they realized their Commander in Chief was right. They all placed their SIG Sauer P226 pistols on the ground and put their hands up but they continued to surround the President.

One of the men in black lowered his M4 rifle and pointed a finger at them. "Mr. President, come out here. Right now!"

The president pushed his way past his bodyguards as he kept his arms up in the air. "Don't hurt my men," he said as he took a few steps forward.

Within seconds the other black clad men grabbed the president and ushered him into the second Blackhawk. At that instant, one of the Secret Service men dove for his pistol and was instantly cut down by rifle fire. The other black clad troopers instantly reacted, shooting down the remaining three Secret Service agents. The last thoughts of Agent Mullins were about his wife and how he failed the president before he lost consciousness while bleeding out.

The president turned his head back as soon as he heard the rifle fire and let out a cry of anguish as he saw his bodyguards slaughtered. He tried to break free from the grip of the two men who were holding him but they held him fast. Another trooper who was following from behind drew a taser from his hip holster and fired it at the president, who then instantly fell onto the ground and lay stunned. The other two troopers picked him up by his shoulders and legs and started to carry him onto the waiting chopper.

A hundred yards away, John Smalley saw what had happened and he started to make a run towards them. "They've got the president!"

"John, wait!" Admiral Zimmerman shouted as he lay crouched down beside the wreckage of the Sea King. Beside him was the injured crew chief whose arm was in a makeshift splint.

The third Blackhawk that was still airborne instantly pivoted and hovered alongside Smalley, as one of the door gunners aimed his M4 rifle and fired. The president's Chief of Staff took a bullet to the throat and instantly went down.

Steve Van Dyke tore his helmet off in disgust as he keyed in his walkie-talkie. He was standing beside one of the Blackhawks on the ground as he saw the president being carried into the fuselage. "Goddamn it, cease fire! We got what we wanted."

"Sir," the voice on his walkie-talkie said. "I recognize Admiral Zimmerman, the NORTHCOM commanding officer is down there hiding in the Marine One wreckage. Do we have permission to take him out?"

"Negative," Steve growled. "There's no need to slaughter these people. Just take him with us."

"Affirmative."

Steve shook his head in disgust while he climbed onboard the Blackhawk as it prepared to take off. His men were only partially trained as a unit and way too eager to kill everything. It was a blemish to an otherwise flawless operation so far. The Soldiers of the Lord had now struck three times today. First was the hidden nuke inside Cheyenne Mountain. Then the series of bomb attacks in Peterson, and finally the successful downing of Marine One, taking President of the United States as their hostage.

God is with us, he thought while he made a silent prayer of thanks just as the helicopter lifted off from the ground.

8. The Prisoner

Siberia

Even though the time of day was high noon, the entire city was bathed in a twilit night as the convoy of military vehicles made its way into the Novosibirsk army garrison compound. The snowfall had been continuous since the Glooming had started and by now almost the entire country was blanketed in an ice-cold hell of biblical proportions. The two lead vehicles were GAZ Tigr light reconnaissance trucks, followed closely by a half dozen BMP-3 infantry fighting vehicles and a dozen Ural-5323 heavy cargo trucks brought up the rear. As soon as the convoy entered the compound, soldiers in winter coats immediately alighted from the nearby barracks and began to cheer. This was the first supply run the city had received in over a month.

General Dmitri Klimov stood outside of the front door of the headquarters building as his aide passed him a lit cigarette. He was nearly sixty years of age and his balding forehead and wispy grey hair was partly covered by his military cap. Klimov was the commanding officer of the 41st Army, the main contingent of the Siberian Military District. Normally a taciturn man, Klimov knew he had to turn on the charm and just tell the truth in order to survive in these perilous times, for he knew who was in charge of this convoy even though he wasn't sure why this particular man was sent over to him.

The fourth BMP-3 in the line turned sharply left and veered away from the rest of the convoy, it then drove up to the front of the building where

Klimov was waiting. As soon as the infantry fighting vehicle stopped, its four rear hatches opened; two were along the back of the IFV while the upper ones beside them were opened afterwards. Almost immediately, four men wearing black military fatigues and hooded masks instantly jumped out. Klimov could tell that they were Spetsnaz Alpha Group troopers, the top-tier of the Russian special forces. After they formed a protective cordon, a fifth man popped out from the top hatch and jumped down onto the snowy ground in front of them. Unlike the heavily-armed soldiers who were guarding him, this man was dressed in a black civilian parka and wore heavy boots as he made his way over to where the general and is aide was standing.

As the man got to the front porch, Klimov moved forward to meet him and held out his hand. "Colonel, it is a pleasure to see you, welcome to Novosibirsk!"

The man took off his right winter glove before shaking the general's hand. "General Klimov, I am honored that you would actually meet me out here when we could have been introduced in the warming comforts of your office instead."

Klimov shrugged. "Since your convoy is the first supply run we've had in almost a month, I felt honored to meet you out here, Pasha. Follow me inside, if you please."

With his aide walking discretely behind them, Klimov led the younger man down the dimly lit corridor as they headed for the commander's office. As the still functioning heaters of the building began to make him feel more comfortable, the man took off his heavy parka before handing it off to the aide behind him who quickly ran up and took it. Although Klimov affectionately called him Pasha, his full name was Colonel Pavel Denikin, and he was a deputy director in Russia's Federal Security Service, or FSB for short. Not even forty years of age, everyone within the government had already heard of Denikin's meteoric rise from obscure junior officer to newly promoted full colonel. It was said that he was the personal protégé of the Russian president and as such needed to be held in the utmost respect, lest anyone incur the head of state's enmity and subsequent wrath. Even though he had a higher rank than Denikin, Klimov knew it was better for his sake to treat the younger man as his superior.

Klimov's personal office was the only room in the building with its own fireplace. As both men sat down on the antique leather chairs beside the crackling embers, Klimov's aide quickly placed Denikin's parka on the coat rack by the door before heading off to the kitchens to make some tea as he closed the door behind him.

"My assistant is very efficient," Klimov said as he took his cap off and placed it on the coffee table in between them, "the tea should be here in less than five minutes."

Denikin ran his hand along his slick black hair to make sure it was in place. "Actually, I wouldn't mind a shot or two of vodka right now. I feel better drinking it than tea these days."

The general chuckled as he reached over and opened a bottle of clear liquid sitting on the table before pouring it into two shot glasses. "This is homemade vodka. One of the cooks has been using potato peels since we ran out of the commercial stuff weeks ago."

Denikin titled his head upwards and downed the shot of vodka in one gulp. Already, the fiery spirit had begun to give him a warm feeling that cascaded all over his body. "It's good to see you again, General. It's been a long time as I recall."

"Yes, five years or thereabouts since the last time I saw you, Pasha. You were just a young lieutenant then when your father introduced us. Now look at you: a colonel in the FSB and not even middle age yet. You are clearly destined for great things."

"Six years, actually. And I assure you I have earned my position within the service through merit, not because of who I know."

Klimov smiled. "Of course, Pasha. I didn't mean anything about that remark. You are a talented man and richly deserving of your rank. In fact, I admire you and your achievements."

Denikin looked away and snorted. The general was clearly licking his boots now. Most probably because of some sort of screw up in this last operation, no doubt. *Best to get to the truth right away*, he thought. "I'm sure you have been briefed as to why I am here?"

Klimov straightened his back. "I was able to receive a message by both courier and radio relay. My orders are to assist you and your men in any way possible. I was told to expect at least two companies of reinforcements. That is all, Pasha."

"The truth is only half of this convoy made it. The journey took almost two weeks and we were attacked three days ago. I lost half my men," Denikin said.

Klimov's eyes widened. "What? Who attacked you?"

"I'm not sure. We only saw glimpses of them in the snow. There must have been dozens of them. One of the men with me called them chorts- which is our word for devil. The one thing I remember about that word and what we saw is it denotes some sort of pig-faced demon from our classic folk tales. Nevertheless, they started ripping through the infantry fighting vehicles as if they were made of paper. My men reacted and we fired on them with everything we had. I think we might have hit a few, but it didn't seem to matter so I told everyone to accelerate and keep going. Those demons disabled at least a dozen vehicles that we had to leave behind. God only knows what happened to the men that were in them."

"I see ... should we conduct a rescue operation?"

Denikin shook his head. "No, those men are probably dead by now anyway, so why risk more? From the looks of things, we may need every soldier we have here. Things are getting worse and we are losing too many men across the country. Have there been any attacks within the city as of yet?"

"Field reports are not very accurate. Although we've had no reported attacks that were verified by my men there have been many disappearances but I cannot give you a definite number. It seems both the city and my troops are slowly being decimated by an unknown force. Some of my men are now openly complaining when they are being ordered to patrol the city since the police units have all but either fled or have disappeared. Four of my divisions are now at half strength based on the last roll call. The one good thing about this cold is that people are too weak to mount a protest- if the weather was any hotter, we would have riots all over the city right now because people are starving. We haven't been able to get much news from the outside since this nationwide blizzard began so what is the situation with the rest of Russia?"

"Not much better, I'm afraid," Denikin said. "The government has evacuated Moscow because it is too dangerous. The borders with the West are in flux because of events that are occurring in the EU. All the events that are happening seem to parallel the great Patriotic War. The government has begun a draft of all able-bodied men, but I doubt we have the time to train or even recruit them. The president and his cabinet are heading eastwards as we speak."

"To the underground bunker complex in Kosvinsky Kamen?"

"I'm not at liberty to discuss it, General."

"Of course, Pasha. My apologies for asking too much about it."

A knock on the door made both men silent as Klimov's aide came inside bearing a tray with two tall glasses of hot, steaming tea which he quickly placed on the coffee table before departing. Denikin helped himself to another shot of the homemade vodka before he began to sip his tea.

"As you can see," Klimov said, "all my men and facilities are at your disposal. So what is it that you need?"

"Let's start from the beginning. You sent Moscow a hand-delivered report about two children that you found in the forests just outside of the city."

"Ah, so that's why you are here then? I thought this was strictly a supply run with reinforcements."

Denikin looked at him seriously. "No more chit-chat, General. Let's get down to business. Your report said you found two children who may or may not have been able to somehow travel to another world."

"Yes, Major Bulgakov and myself planned the operation. I was surprised it went exactly according to plan since the source of the intelligence regarding the children was somewhat vague."

"Major Pyotr Bulgakov? Of the Twenty-Fourth Spetsnaz Brigade?"

"Yes. Do you know of him?"

Denikin nodded. "We planned and executed a number of operations in both the Caucasus and in Ukraine. A very competent commander."

"I agree, he was pretty good and we captured the children without any difficulty."

"Wait, go back from the beginning. How did your unit get wind of these children?"

"We received a coded transmission from Moscow that claimed that two children would appear at the exact coordinates in the forest outside of Novosibirsk. It was pretty surprising that we even got a radio message during that time since we had thought that all wireless communications had been cut off since the snow started to fall this summer. Since my headquarters always has two radio operators manning the communications channel at all times, we were lucky to get that single message," Klimov said.

"No such message originated from Moscow."

Klimov's eyes widened again. "What? But that's impossible! The codes were authenticated."

"Whoever sent that message to you was somebody else," Denikin said. "I saw a copy of that message that you sent in with your report, and I can confirm that no such order came from the Ministry of Defense. I don't blame you for following orders since it seemed to give us a clue as to what's going on and that's why I am here. I need to ascertain any sort of information so that I can report this to the president and find a way to save our country before it collapses."

Klimov sighed. "I see, Pasha. If I ever find the perpetrators of this subterfuge I will execute them myself."

"Moscow is working on it," Denikin said. "But in the meantime we have more pressing matters here. It said on your report that you were able to identify one of the two children and that he is Russian."

"Yes," Klimov said as he took out a folder from a stack of papers sitting on the coffee table and handed it to him. "The boy's name is Ilya Volkhov. Ten years old and residing in Orphanage Number Two before his disappearance in the two months leading before the operation."

Denikin leafed through the folder. There wasn't a whole lot of information in the files since the subject was just a child. "Typical orphan: abandoned by his mother and raised by the state. Father unknown. What makes him so special?"

"When we questioned him, the boy claimed to have traveled across a sort of imaginary world after he escaped from the clutches of Baba Yaga."

"Baba Yaga? The so-called witch of Slavic folklore?"

"Yes. Or so he says. The boy claimed that many other children were abducted and killed by this witch, but he was somehow able to escape."

"What else did he say?"

"He says this snow storm and everything else that is happening within the country is being caused by Chernobog, some sort of god, I believe."

Denikin nodded. "Yes, the god of evil- according to our old folklore."

"You believe all of this too, Pasha?"

Denikin placed the now empty tea glass on the table and leaned back in the leather chair. The flickering firelight cast yellow and orange shadows across his face. "That is consistent with the other reports we have been receiving. It seems that the gods of old have returned and are staking out their original territories. Russia would indeed fall under Chernobog's influence if this was true."

Klimov sighed once more. "I can still hardly believe it. Back in the Soviet era, we used to suppress the Eastern Orthodox Church, now it seems we have been wrong about which gods we should have been worried about. All our weapons are largely useless."

"Thinking of surrendering to these gods, General?"

Klimov shook his head. "Of course not. I have a duty as a soldier to serve the country. Until I am told otherwise, I shall follow my orders even if it means losing my life."

"That is good to hear. Now what about the other child?"

"She was a girl of about fifteen or sixteen years of age, I believe," Klimov said as he took out another folder from the table and handed it to the FSB deputy director. "Her name is Tara Weiss and she is an American."

Denikin started going through the file. The firelight was not the best illumination for reading, but his eyes were like an owl's. "Not much information here either. It says she is from the state of Arizona and she ran away from home? How did she make it all the way to Siberia?"

"We initially had a hard time getting a proper translator since she spoke only English, but one of the Spetsnaz troopers who was trained in her language was actually able to communicate with her," Klimov said. "She did not have a passport or any means of travel so we were confused on how she got here, but her story was the same as the orphaned boy, she claims she traveled across this other dimension or some sort of spirit world from America and over to us here."

"Did either of them say what the reason was as to why they came to Siberia?"

"Apparently both children were here to find information about the boy's mother from the orphanage."

"Did they explain as to how they were able to travel from this other dimension over to the real world?"

"That they did not explain," Klimov said. "When the Spetsnaz asked the girl, she broke down crying, saying they killed her pet dog or something like that. The boy was questioned separately, but he has refused to answer to this very day."

"So the commandos opened fire on a pet dog during the operation?"

"I wasn't there so I asked Major Bulgakov, he told me two of his men opened fire on a small dog when they thought it was a stray or something. I didn't mention it on the report since I didn't think it was important."

Denikin frowned. "I'm afraid every minute detail is important now, General. The Spetsnaz operators should have attempted to capture this pet dog instead of shooting at it."

"My apologies, Deputy Director," Klimov said, this time using the formal position of the man who was questioning him. "But the now fake cable from Moscow had stated that any stray animals in the operations area were to be shot dead."

"Yes, yes, I understand you were misled by that damned message. Moscow has so far been unable to trace who originated it despite the fact that the president had every single radio operator court-martialed and imprisoned."

"We were only following orders that we perceived to be genuine at that time, Pasha."

Denikin was clearly irritated. "Very well. Did they kill it by the way? I haven't seen a report to confirm it."

"The Spetsnaz did report that they shot at it but they failed to find it. It's possible that the animal is either wounded or…"

"Or it survived," Denikin added. "I want you to deploy a team back to that area and try to either find it or its remains."

"I shall do that at once but I hardly think the animal would still be alive. Spetsnaz operatives are highly skilled marksmen and it's doubtful they would have missed. The dog's corpse is probably underneath a blanket of snow," Klimov said.

"Nevertheless, I want the area searched. The president has confided his worries to me that we may not last long if this keeps up so any clue as to a possible cause to this crisis must be thoroughly investigated."

"A search team will be deployed at once, Deputy Director."

"Now, tell me what happened to the girl."

"After our preliminary questioning we thought it best to send her to Moscow. Major Bulgakov commanded the convoy himself. They left over a month ago and I'm pretty sure you received them. But you know this already."

"Word did get to Moscow that a convoy was on its way, but they never reached us."

"What? Is this some sort of joke, Pasha?"

"I wish it were. But no sign of a convoy from Novosibirsk ever reached Moscow."

Klimov's face was contorted in frustration. "Chort vozmi! There was at least a platoon of soldiers that we sent to escort that girl. So this means we lost her and Major Bulgakov as well. This is not good."

"That is why I was sent here, General," Denikin said calmly. "To determine whether there is any foundation to the president's suspicions as to whether your report was one hundred percent truthful."

Despite the roaring fire, the tea, and the vodka, an ice-cold feeling of dread began to creep over Klimov's body. "Surely you cannot suspect me of conniving with the enemy, Deputy Director? I have been completely loyal to the president and to Russia. My record speaks for itself."

"To your credit, I feel you have answered my questions truthfully thus far," Denikin said. "Other than the dog, are you certain you have included everything else that had happened in your report?"

"Yes. I give you my word as an officer of the Russian Army."

Denikin's face remained impassive. "Alright. You did well in assigning Major Bulgakov for the convoy. I knew him and trusted him like my brother. That would only mean then that whoever intercepted that convoy must have been behind the bogus radio transmission as well. Where is the boy right now?"

"Right here in this very building," Klimov said. "He is in one of the officer's quarters. I have a pair of men watching him day and night."

"Has he said anything to you lately?"

"No, ever since he found out that the girl was escorted out of the city, he has become defiant and would answer no more questions."

"Have you used enhanced interrogation techniques on him yet?"

Klimov winced at the words. What the Deputy Director meant was physical and psychological torture. Even as a general, he did not like that aspect of information gathering, Klimov preferred that others do it whenever the situation arose. "No, I felt that he had already answered the preliminary questions we had asked of him even though we didn't believe it was the truth. I don't know what else we could interrogate him on. I didn't want to use enhanced techniques either, at least not until you got here."

Denikin stood up and stretched his aching back. Despite having just rode in a steel tank all the way to Siberia, there was no time for rest. Time was too important. "Let's go see him then."

Despite being held in a small room with only a bed and an old wooden table with a creaky chair to furnish it, Ilya Volkhov wasn't complaining. It wasn't much worse than the dormitory hall that he lived in when he was at the orphanage. The soldiers detaining him had made a square sized hole in the door to the room before placing a metal slot in place of it so that they could observe him. Ilya thought it was annoying at first because when he would get ready for bed, he could see eyes looking at him from the opened slot, but he slowly got used to it. The young boy was allowed onto the building grounds two hours every day for some exercise. Ilya made the best use of it by constantly running and jumping from one end of the enclosed courtyard to the other until he could no longer catch his breath. On the whole, the soldiers of the army base treated him with indifference, but he had grown to like one of them: Private Anosov because he always smiled at Ilya and would even share some chewing gum whenever the boy would ask for it. Anosov had the day shift and so Ilya would sometimes play chess with him. They would have many bouts in his room since there was hardly anything else to do. Ilya had lost a dozen matches until he went on a winning streak before realizing Anosov was just letting him win, so he demanded that the young private play to the best of his ability from then on. As the weeks passed, Ilya still continued to lose at chess since he had never been very good at it to begin with, but he felt he was slowly getting better.

It was during one of their chess matches that the two very senior commanders opened the door and walked inside. Private Anosov had been sitting in the chair and to the opposite end of the small table was Ilya who had been using his bed to sit on. They both instantly leapt up onto their feet the moment the door opened. The young private instantly stood to attention and saluted as Klimov and Denikin walked into the room.

Anosov immediately snapped to attention and made a salute. "General Klimov, sir! I-I'm sorry I was just engaging our guest in a little game of chess, sir."

Klimov grinned and waved for him to be calm. "Do not be alarmed, Private. We are here simply to chat with our guest. With me is Deputy Director Denikin of the FSB."

Anosov turned while still in attention and saluted Denikin as well. "I-I am sorry for this, Deputy Director. I know I am not suppose to fraternize with prisoners- I m-mean guests without proper authorization, sir!"

Denikin returned his salute. "At ease, Private. You did an amazing job in using your own initiative to make our guest feel more comfortable. If you don't mind waiting outside, we would like to play some chess with our honored guest here."

Anosov saluted them both for a third time before hurriedly walking out of the room and closing the door behind him. Klimov motioned for Ilya to sit back down on his bed but the boy continued to just stare at the both of them, his face was a mixture of surprise and quiet defiance.

"Do not be alarmed, my young friend," Denikin said. "We mean you no harm."

Ilya looked up at him. "Then why am I being held prisoner here?"

"You are not a prisoner, Ilya, otherwise you would be in a cell," Klimov said as he sat down on the chair. "You are a guest here."

Ilya frowned. "If I am a guest, then why am I not being allowed to leave?"

"It's for your protection," Denikin said. "Baba Yaga is looking for you and therefore it's best you stay here so we can defend you if she arrives."

Ilya sat down at the edge of the bed and shook his head. "You cannot protect me. You will all be killed if she comes here."

Denikin furrowed his brow. "Oh? You're saying she is capable of destroying an entire Russian Army command? Is she truly that powerful? Then why hasn't she come then?"

Ilya shrugged. "She has her own reasons, maybe she doesn't know I'm even here. But all you're doing is putting yourselves at risk by keeping me here."

Klimov looked at the pieces on the chessboard. "And if we let you go how safe would you be? If we cannot protect you, then how could a little boy like you even fight her off?"

"I will not fight her, I can trick her."

Denikin crossed his arms. The boy was either delusional or he was the key to everything. "How did you trick her the last time, Ilya? How did you escape after she abducted you?"

Ilya looked out of the window. "I had some chewing gum in my pocket. When she opened the cage to examine me, I stuck the gum in the lock and opened the cage after she went to sleep."

Klimov moved one of the chess pieces on the board. "And that's how you escaped back to Novosibirsk, right?"

Ilya shook his head again. "No, when I got out of her hut I was in the Spirit World."

Denikin was taking mental notes. Based on his own experiences in interrogation, he concluded that the boy was sure of himself and it didn't seem like he was lying. "So she made you travel to her dimension because you were her prisoner then? Ah, that makes sense."

Klimov looked quizzically at the deputy director who merely winked back at him.

Denikin took out a small picture from his pocket and gave it to the boy. "We need your help, Ilya. Help us to understand what is going on so you can be reunited with this woman."

Ilya looked at the picture and gasped. "That is my mother!"

"Yes," Denikin said. "She is safe and sound with us and I promise that you will be reunited with her if you cooperate with us and tell us how to travel back and forth to the Spirit World."

Ilya grimaced. "You're lying, you do not have her."

Klimov continued to play with the pieces on the chessboard. "What makes you say we are lying to you, Ilya? Why should we lie?"

"I know you don't have her," Ilya said. "They told me so."

Denikin sat down on the bed beside the boy and looked at him. "Who told you this, Ilya?"

"Radegast and Ozwiena," Ilya said.

"I know of a Radegast, the old Slavic god," Denikin said. "I'm not familiar with the other one, is she a goddess too?"

"Yes."

"And what did she tell you as to where your mother was?"

"She said that Chernobog has her prisoner."

"And how will you get her away from a god like Chernobog?"

"With my friends," Ilya said. "The girl you took away. Tara. Where is she?"

Klimov said nothing as he looked at Denikin. He was the lead in this interrogation and the boy was already telling them many things that he had not previously heard. This was all just strange to him. In his years in service to the country, it just didn't make any sense but the FSB Deputy Director seemed to know what he was doing, so it was better for him to take the lead in all of this.

Denikin figured it was better to tell the truth this time. "We had her sent on a convoy back to Moscow so that she could return to America. But we never heard from them again. The source that told us where you would be appearing when we found you in the forest outside of the city. They must be the same people who ambushed your friend's convoy. She is missing but if she is like you, I assume she must still be alive somewhere."

Ilya frowned. "What about the dog? Your people started to shoot at it the moment you ambushed us. Where is it?"

"We don't know what happened to it," Denikin said. "I assure you that I didn't give any orders to shoot it."

Ilya didn't answer. He just looked down at the floor.

Denikin leaned back on the wall. "Did you need this dog to travel to this Spirit World? What's so special about this dog?"

Ilya just stared at the window.

"In order for us to help you, you must answer our questions," Klimov said. "How can we let you go if you don't tell us more?"

Ilya looked at the general first, then turned to look at Denikin. "You must let me go. If you want me to stop Chernobog, you must let me go."

Denikin put his hands in his pockets. "Not until we know more, Ilya. Do you know who it was that might have told us where and when you would return to this world?"

Ilya shook his head. "No."

"Why would they try to take the girl but not you? Is Tara more important to them? What can she do that you cannot do?"

"I don't know. The dog is hers."

"Where did she get the dog from? Is it some sort of American military dog that's specially trained or something?"

Ilya looked at the Deputy Director. Was he stupid or something? "This dog is not part of the American military. That is all I can say."

Klimov had had enough. He immediately stood up and grabbed Ilya by his shirt collar as he pulled the boy up on his feet. "You will tell us about this dog now! I can beat you to death and no one will care! You are a ward of the state and we can do anything we want to you."

Denikin immediately reacted by taking hold of Klimov's arm and forced the general to let go of the boy. "That's enough, General," he said before turning to face Ilya. "I apologize for that outburst. But we have lost a lot of good men because of Chernobog's machinations. Our cities are either being turned into defensive enclaves or are being abandoned. If you do not help us, our country will surely cease to exist. I beg of you, tell us about this dog."

Ilya trembled from the momentary fright. He was barely able to resist the urge to cry. "It says it's a god."

Denikin placed his hands on the boy's thin shoulders. "What type of a god? An animal god of some sort?"

"I-It said that it was a trickster god."

Denikin's eyes narrowed. "So it is this god that allows you to travel between worlds?"

Ilya slumped back down on the side of the bed. "I don't know. I was able to go into the Spirit World before I met the dog."

"How were you able to do that? Oh, I just remembered, you were in Baba Yaga's hut when it traveled across the worlds. But if you don't have the dog or the hut, then how can you go back to that magical land?"

Ilya looked away. "I will find a way. If I could do it before then I can do it again."

"Very well, Ilya," Denikin said. "You will stay a few more days and answer more questions for us tomorrow. I'm sure you must be tired now. We shall call back Private Anosov and you can resume your chess game with him, alright?"

"I just want to be alone right now," Ilya said softly.

"Very well, I will have the mess hall cooks make you a special meal in a little while," Denikin said as he made for the door. "You've earned it. Then we talk some more tomorrow. Enjoy what's left of the day."

With that, both men left and closed the door behind them. Once more, Ilya was alone in his cell as the dim light above him gave the whole room an orange look. He had told them too much. That general was pretty dumb but the dark-haired FSB Director might be very dangerous. From what they told him, he began to realize that there were enemies that wanted Tara. That was how they got ambushed in the forest when they returned after they helped to transform Okeus into Ahone. But that also meant that while the enemy had Tara, it didn't have Coyote the Trickster God. The trickster was the being that made travel to the other worlds possible. Even though the soldiers fired at the dog, Ilya had a feeling that it was still alive somewhere. So his first plan was to escape from this building and then go find the dog. From there, he would then find out where the enemy took Tara and then he would rescue her.

Ilya lay down sideways on the bed as he faced the wall and pretended he was asleep. He knew they were still watching him. If not through the metal slot then probably a hidden camera somewhere in the room. He needed to think up an escape plan by tonight.

9. Cabal

Germany

Built during the early 17th Century as an auxiliary residence for the local princes of the area, Wewelsburg Castle stood on a small hill like an ominous stone monolith over the abandoned town that surrounded it. The castle itself was shaped like that of a gigantic triangle, and it had fascinated the Nazi Party when they came to power, most notably the head of the SS, Heinrich Himmler. A former office worker who quickly gained Hitler's favor and became the leader of his personal guard, Himmler became preoccupied with the occult and old pagan religions, incorporating many rituals and runes of his own devising into the spiritual culture of Hitler's private army. When one of his acquaintances recommended the old crumbling castle located in Germany's Westphalia region as a possible headquarters, Himmler instantly saw a unique opportunity to implement his strange obsessions. Under his influence, Wewelsburg became an SS training school as well as a kind of temple in which rituals would be conducted to heighten the mystical aspects of Hitler's Third Reich. To that end, the Nazis constructed several additions to the castle and added occult symbols within the interior in order to turn the place into a spiritual enclave of pagan myth.

As the Nazis began to face defeat at the end of World War II, Himmler ordered the castle's destruction, but his henchman lacked the means to completely obliterate it. In the end, the SS officers in charge of the demolition used converted anti-tank mines that only succeeded in destroying a part of the structure before they fled. In the succeeding years, the local government took over the castle, turning it into a museum and youth hostel until the recent arrival of a new religious order called the Temple. Just two years before the Glooming began, this mysterious organization made a startling bid to rent out the entire castle and the cash-strapped local government could not refuse, despite the protests of the youth groups and the historical society that maintained a museum. The Temple quickly silenced their critics by constructing another youth hostel not far from the town as well as a brand new museum building in order to placate the historical society.

As calm settled in the town once more, there were soon disturbing rumors that had begun about the new owners of Wewelsburg Castle. Less than two months after they had acquired the place, the Temple began to hire foreign contractors to renovate the interior of the castle and when the local council inquired about it, they were quickly rebuffed and set upon by an army of lawyers who told them that according to the contracts they themselves approved, the Temple could do whatever it wished so long as it did not damage the castle in any way. Small protests had started over this but there was nothing that the local government could do, citing reasons that the criticism was unfounded since the entire castle was in private hands now, and whatever they were doing inside was their own business and no one else's.

However, this did not quell the concerns of the locals nearby as their pets began to disappear from their homes just a mere six months after the castle was newly refurbished. The townspeople became somewhat alarmed when their remaining dogs would face the castle and howl all night, and their surviving cats soon turned hostile to their owners, hissing and attacking other pets as well as their own children until they were thrown out. Their fears were heightened even more when they would see convoys of black-tinted vehicles that would come and go from the castle late at night as the inhabitants of that fortress never bothered to associate themselves with the locals. The few that did show up in the town's stores and food markets always wore black robes; they refused to communicate other than just to inquire about prices for goods and they would always pay in cash before immediately returning back to the castle. When the Glooming began, things became even worse when people started to disappear from either walking the streets at night or from their own homes; whole families just seemed to vanish into thin air. A few of the more courageous people in the town organized a march onto the entrance of the castle to demand that the people inside leave the area, but there were too few of them now so in the end, almost everyone in the surrounding town had left for fear that they would be the next to disappear in the night and fog.

As most of the locals finally left, a number of small, mysterious groups of people began to converge into the area; they were followers of the Temple and they soon took over a number of abandoned houses and began to fortify these dwellings while conducting strange rituals at night within them. The remaining townspeople sought help from the German government but to no avail, Berlin and the military seemed powerless as they concentrated their remaining forces on the border with France due to the threat of invasion by the Fomorians. In the end, anyone who still considered themselves to be decent human beings completely abandoned the area and now the Temple and its followers stood alone and unchallenged.

The Grand Magus of the Temple of the Black Sun was Kurt Orlok. He was sitting in the castle's newly built divination room as he continued to stare into a black bowl of water. He was nearly eighty, the son of an SS major and one of his mistresses. Orlok never knew his father. All he had was an old photograph of him in his black uniform and proudly wearing his death's head cap. By the time the war had ended Orlok and his mother lived in virtual poverty. But after graduating from university he succeeded in creating a multi-million dollar export company through his sheer will when the country's economy began to right itself during the 1960's. During his free time, Orlok became obsessed with finding his father even though he had a feeling that he was no longer alive. Sure enough, by using his money and influence, Orlok eventually tracked down the remains of his father who had died on the Eastern Front against the Bolsheviks. He had also learned that his father's death head ring, an ornate symbol of the SS, was supposed to be interred in a special crypt in Wewelsburg Castle but was stolen by American soldiers when they occupied the country after the Nazis had surrendered.

With a ruthlessness born of anger and neglect, Orlok used everything he could in order to find the man who stole his father's ring, eventually tracking the thief down in New York. The American who kept the ring was by now an invalid living with his sister in an old, dilapidated house. Orlok pretended to be a German reporter researching the war and when the old man had his back turned, Orlok strangled him with a telephone cord before killing the man's sister sleeping in her room upstairs. After avenging his father's honor, Orlok took the ring with him back to West Germany and later found out that his father was formerly assigned to Wewelsburg as a researcher for one of Himmler's occult projects- finding the Spear of Destiny, the Roman lance that had been used to pierce Jesus Christ's heart when he was being crucified.

It was at this next phase of his life that Kurt Orlok began to have a growing obsession with the occult. He had learned that his father had abandoned his Catholic faith when he joined the SS and therefore as his son, he needed to follow in his footsteps. The Temple of the Black Sun started out as just another New Age pagan hobby group led by an unemployed drug user named Bruno Muller out of Berlin forty years ago. But the moment Orlok became a member he slowly gathered support until the was able to throw out the original founder since Muller treated the order as nothing more than a false front, purely for his drug use and womanizing. Once he became leader of the Temple, Orlok immediately began to dismiss the ones who did not take to his esoteric directives as the organization began to embrace a new kind of religious paganism, one devoted to finding obscure artifacts and to engage in magical rituals to bring forth spirits and otherworldly beings. As the Temple's membership grew, Orlok styled himself as the Grand Magus and created an inner circle of his most carefully chosen disciples. Hidden from both the public and the general membership, this small cabal of twelve declared themselves as wizards and dedicated their entire lives in the pursuit to gain power through supernatural means.

Using his business acumen, Orlok also created a corporation and numerous charitable fronts to hide the Temple's finances. The German government attempted to label the organization as a cult and began an investigation into its tax avoidance schemes. But Orlok's army of lawyers and influence among the federal politicians (some of whom were members of the order) were able to successfully quash any sort of bad publicity and the investigations were quietly dropped a few years later. What spurred Orlok on was that he had a vision of the coming apocalypse, though very much different as compared to the Christians who believed that Jesus Christ would return but rather a bleaker, more sinister end to the world in which only the strongest humans would survive and not their through faith, but with their own magical powers in order to live indifferently among the monsters and demons who would inhabit this new, darkened world. His last vision compelled him to purchase Wewelsburg Castle at all cost and he did everything in his power to convert it into his seat of authority. As the Glooming began he realized that he was now vindicated. His foresight had at last come to fruition as he gleefully watched all those that had doubted him suffer and die.

As time moved back to the present, Orlok stood up from the stone chair and then looked away from the witching bowl; he had sensed the one he was waiting for had arrived. He walked over to the ornate mirror in the other side of the chamber and adjusted his black robes. The Grand Magus had numerous ailments and he could hardly stand but an old enemy was coming to see him and he needed to put up a powerful front. Orlok believed in never showing weakness, especially to one's nemesis. His forehead and the top of his skull was now bald leaving only the pale white strands on the sides and back of his head that covered his ears. Orlok's swollen cheeks had been pockmarked by acne since he was in his teens, and his portly girth continued to put undue strain on his back since he could no longer control his metabolism. Just as he took the cane from the nearby table and used it to balance himself, he heard a knock on the door.

A tall, well-built man came in. He was also dressed in black robes and had a military haircut. "Grand Magus, the one you expected is here."

Orlok turned to look at him. "Thank you, Helmut. Where is he?"

"He somehow appeared in the center of the Crypt, Magus. The other fraters and sorores are watching him carefully," Helmut said.

"Then let us go meet him."

Both men made their way to the North Tower. Before the Temple was able to acquire the castle, the Crypt, which contained a sunken, circular floor underneath a stylized stone symbol of the swastika that was carved high up in the tower ceiling, was nothing more than a display room for paintings and other exhibits. Once it all came under his control, Orlok immediately had the entire area refurbished and it was now used by the Temple as both a meeting room for the inner circle as well as a sacrificial altar. The sunken stage in the center was very convenient in order to prevent the spillover of blood when the victims were killed. They first began to ritually sacrifice small animals like dogs and cats but once the Glooming had started, they were soon able to abduct people with no legal or criminal ramifications. The Temple had secretly constructed an additional series of subterranean dungeons underneath the castle and it was there that they would keep the prisoners until such time as they were ready to be sacrificed. The rituals continued day and night until there were hardly any people left in the area.

By the time they got to the Crypt, they saw half a dozen robed men and women standing in a ring around the sunken center, weapons drawn and at the ready. An old man wearing a dark suit stood in the center of the depressed circle. Orlok waved his hands and the other fraters and sorores turned and left the Mourning Hall until it was just the three of them.

The man with the suit turned to look at him and smiled. His gaunt appearance and yellow stained teeth made him the stuff of nightmares. "Ah, it is nice to meet you again, Grand Magus. It has been so many years."

Orlok scoffed as he griped his cane tightly just in case the other man would attack. "How did you get through the wards I placed on this castle?"

The man held up his right hand so the other two could see the ornate brass ring he wore on it. "With this, of course."

Orlok still had good eyesight as he could see the ornate symbols that were carved on the ring. "You have a lot of nerve to come back, Solomon. And to proudly show off the seal that you have stolen from the temple piles insult upon insult."

Seth Solomon continued to smile. He knew he had the upper hand. For the moment anyway. "Your one time apprentices willingly gave the seal to me, Grand Magus. I would hardly call it stealing."

"It was not theirs to give!" Orlok hissed. "You were banished from the Temple because you stole sacred artifacts like the seal of King Solomon and murdered our fellow members. For you to return now either implies that you either wish to surrender and plead for my mercy, or you lack the courage to kill yourself."

Solomon laughed. "Did you know what this hall was once constructed for? It was known as the Trauerhalle, the mourning hall for the SS. Every time a senior SS officer died, his ashes were placed in an urn beside this well, right where I'm standing now. It was then that his coat of arms was burned and its ashes were interred into this well here to conclude the ritual," he said as he pointed downwards to a depressed stone pillar in the center of the circle. "But now I can see bloodstains all over this little sunken stage. My, my, you must have been quite busy lately."

Orlok gripped his cane tighter as tiny blue sparks began to emanate from the entwined metal snakes that were carved around it. "You will answer for the crimes you have committed against this order, you Jewish swine."

Solomon wagged a bony finger at him. "Ah, so your anti-Semitism now reveals itself. You're really not too dissimilar from your father, but I have not come here to insult you, I have come for a truce."

Helmut took out a 9mm SIG Sauer pistol from underneath his robes and aimed it at the interloper. "You talk as if you had anything to negotiate with. You are here in our sanctum and we can easily kill you right now and be done with it."

Solomon's eyes flicked over to the younger man. "Ah, Helmut Krause is your name. You were indoctrinated in the Temple a scant ten years ago after being discharged from the military due to sexual liaisons with a number of children. Now you are but a bodyguard in the inner circle. A step down, don't you think?"

Helmut's index finger began to squeeze the trigger of the pistol. "How dare you! How did you know all this?"

The other man instantly froze when a mist-like form began to coalesce beside Solomon. "This ring gives me power over seventy-two geotic demons and they tell me all sorts of things," he said before turning to face Orlok once more. "However, with what has happened in the world, it seems that it is better that we all put the past behind us since we now have a golden opportunity, not just to revel in our own power, but to rule over these lands as well."

"Explain yourself," Orlok said. "You cannot expect me to forgive and forget about what you've done when you still have the seal of King Solomon in your possession. Return it to me and perhaps I will then hear you out."

Solomon shook his head. "You do not need the ring. As I have been told, it seems you have found your own pathway to power. I am aware that you have the Book of Toth in your possession, and it has enabled you to construct that staff you are holding onto."

Orlok was taken aback. "Your... sources are very good. You have become a powerful sorcerer indeed. In fact, you may even have us at a disadvantage right now."

Helmut Krause realized it as well as he said nothing while putting the gun back underneath his robes.

Solomon chuckled. "Ah, well when you have the ear of all these demons it does get noisy at times. Do you realize how hard it is to listen to anyone when there are a million droning and chattering insects trying to eat their way into your ear?"

"If you have come here to destroy or take over the Temple, all my followers are prepared to sell their lives dearly to protect me," Orlok said.

"Actually, I would say only half of the twelve in your inner-circle would be willing to do that," Solomon said wistfully. "The other six, especially Lear, Campos, and Real, will be more than willing to sacrifice you in order to spare their own lives if there was an opportunity for advancement as well."

Orlok looked up at the ornately carved swastika in the high ceiling of the tower. "I... thank you for this piece of information. Perhaps I may now have to do some culling within my own order after this meeting. It seems I may now have to relinquish my claim to the seal of Solomon in order to make peace with you, is that your offer?"

"I am willing to make restitution for taking this ring, Grand Magus," Solomon said. "If we are to agree on this truce, then I will give you a gift in return—a most powerful present with which to build your powerbase in this country so that even the government itself would not dare to act against you."

"The German government is already powerless to act. With the threats of the Fomorians in the west and the giants in the frozen north, they have too much to worry about rather than having to deal with me."

Solomon shook his head again. "Ah, that is where you are wrong, Orlok. Already there is talk within the chancellor's office of conducting a heavily armed raid on this castle. They know about you and your magical order. You may be able to resist the first wave but not the next. Many of your followers will die."

"And how do I know what you are telling me is the truth? Perhaps this is just one of your little tricks in order to leverage this negotiation on your terms?"

"Look at me, Orlok," Solomon said. "Do I not look younger than the last time we met?"

"So you had plastic surgery. So what?"

Solomon began to lose his patience. "This is not plastic surgery! My infernal servants have granted me newfound youth and power! This can be yours as well. I know for a fact that you are dying. A stroke will incapacitate you within the next month and your beloved Temple will wither and die without your magical guidance. I have foreseen this."

Orlok took a deep breath. There were times in the past year that he felt pain in his forehead and a growing fear that something was going to happen to him. "Perhaps there may be some truth in your words after all. What is it that you propose?"

"I offer you a gift for compensation, but I must have your word and solemn oath that this magical war of ours is finished," Solomon said. "Germany shall be yours. I will take over southern Europe."

"I have heard that the Pope is now speaking in blasphemous tongues and scaring his followers at the Vatican with his strange behavior. Is that any of your doing?"

"Yes, I paid him a visit a few weeks ago and converted the entire Holy See to do my bidding. I would say he has about three or four of my demons inside of him now so that would explain his mood swings and differing personalities depending on the time of day. The Vatican will be my seat of power here on Earth. Yours is right here in the Wewelsburg. Together as allies, we will be unassailable against the last remaining governments of Europe. I could destroy you as easily as I did the Catholics, but I would rather have you on my side as per an alliance of mutual defense. We have the same outlook, after all."

Helmut snorted in disgust. "You want the Temple as a bulwark against an attack from your north, is that it? I bet you would sacrifice us the moment things turned against you."

Solomon shrugged. "I have no doubt the Temple would do the same to me if faced with a similar predicament. However, I can give you the means with which to protect yourselves further if you decide on this alliance. But I want your answer now, Grand Magus."

"I would first like to know about this gift of yours," Orlok said. "You seem to know that I do not have much time left in this world even though the events have finally favored our kind, so if you wish to be an ally, you must help me extend my life and then you will have the bargain that you seek."

Solomon snapped his fingers. A rectangular stone box began to materialize near the edge of the sunken stage. Helmut gasped. Orlok noticed that it looked like a coffin of some sort. Within a few minutes, the shadowy sarcophagus fully coalesced and settled down gently on the stone floor. Helmut walked over to it and started to examine it. The receptacle itself seemed to be made of polished black stone and there was a heavy lid on top of it.

Orlok turned quizzically to Solomon. "What is that thing?"

Solomon smiled slightly. "Have your manservant open it and find out."

With a nod from the Grand Magus, Helmut's muscular arms grasped the lid and he tried to lift it, but it was much too heavy so the former soldier began to push the lid sideways so it would just slide off. After a few minutes of pushing and grunting, the top of the box finally moved and the black stone lid fell off over the side, shattering into a million pieces on the stone floor of the Crypt. Orlok moved as quickly as he could while using his magical staff as a cane. The Grand Magus of the Temple let out a soft cry of surprise as he peered into the contents of the box.

It was a teenage girl. She looked to be around fifteen or sixteen, and was wearing a white gown of some sort. She appeared to be in a deep slumber as she lay inside the stone box.

Orlok turned to look at Solomon once more. "Who is she?"

"Her name is Tara Weiss," Solomon said. "She is an American from Arizona and my gift to you."

"Your gift? This girl is to be exchanged for the seal of Solomon? Is this some sort of joke? We have two other girls just like her chained in the dungeons underneath this castle, waiting for their time to be sacrificed!"

Solomon rolled his eyes. "That girl is special. She has traveled to the Otherworld and she can converse with the gods. In fact, both her and another child were able to defeat the machinations of Okeus and prevented him from being reborn in New York City."

Orlok nodded. "Wait, I had observed that incident in my witching bowl. So this is the child that tricked Okeus? Then she is quite powerful indeed. How did you capture her?"

"One of my demons told me of their imminent arrival back to Siberia, where the other child was from. I merely alerted the authorities there and they were the ones who seized her. A few days later, they attempted to transport her by land to Moscow, but I had several of my demons intercept that convoy and bring her to me."

"I see. What about the other child?"

"The other child is a Russian orphan named Ilya Volkhov. I believe he is still in the custody of the Russian government. Either way, he is out of the picture."

"Very well. Then her life essences must be very powerful if she has traveled to the other side, yes?"

"Yes, I have had my demons extract a portion of her life power and I have fed on it," Solomon said. "It has made me even more powerful as of late. Once you have extracted but a tiny portion, I can guarantee that your medical symptoms will disappear and you shall have years added to your lifespan."

Orlok tapped the sides of the stone coffin. A smile had finally made its way to his face. "You have proven your worthiness to the Temple, Solomon. You can count on us as your ally from here on. The magical war between us is over. You have my word and my oath as Grand Magus of the Temple of the Black Sun."

"That is good. Then our business here is concluded."

"Wait, I have a few more questions for you."

"Then speak them now for my time is short," Solomon said.

"If this girl is that powerful as you say, why relinquish her to me?"

"A few reasons. The first is for safekeeping. I do not yet have a secure abode with which to keep her so I figured that this is the best place to do so. She must be watched carefully at all times by a pair of your most trusted followers to make sure she does not wake from the spell I placed on her."

"I will see to it," Orlok said. "What are the other reasons?"

"The second is already obvious. I wanted to placate you for the loss of the seal so I exchanged her for that. I need your body to be strong again, Orlok. She will give you the means to do that. I will need as many allies as I can to stave off the other gods in order to hold on to my territory."

Orlok nodded. "Then you have my thanks. From now on, you are welcome here."

A fog began to form around Solomon as his body began to dematerialize. "Good. I may call upon you in the future as I'm sure you will me as well."

"I look forward to our next meeting," Orlok said. "Goodbye."

Within minutes, Solomon's form quickly faded from view until there were only a few wisps of rapidly disappearing smoke. Orlok wondered if the person they spoke to was nothing more than a simulacrum of Solomon just in case they made an attempt to kill him. Either way, he needed to consult with the book of Toth again. This time, he needed to strengthen the magical wards around the castle to prevent spirits from entering as well.

Helmut walked over and stood beside him once more. "What shall we do now, Grand Magus?"

Orlok crossed his arms. "First, you are to summon the inner circle here. Right now. We have to make another culling. Upon my word, you will execute Lear, Campos, and Real. One shot each to the head will suffice. The other three in the circle who are disloyal to me will be sacrificed along with the rest of the virgins by midnight. If they protest, rip out their tongues. I shall have no disloyalty to my leadership."

"Very well, Grand Magus," Helmut said. "Did you believe Solomon as to his reasons why he has gifted this girl to us?"

Orlok shook his head. "Not all of it. I'm sure he might be using this Tara as a sort of weapon that could be used against us should our alliance begin to fray. Either way, we must enact additional rituals and spells to make sure she does not wake. In fact, I think I may try to turn her to our side."

"That is a good idea, Grand Magus."

Orlok laughed. It was just a matter of time before he would be young again. Already, he could feel the sense of power beginning to course through him. "Yes, we will make our own plans. Even though Solomon knows we possess the Book of Toth, I don't think he knows all the spells that I have studied, nor does he know that we posses one other artifact that can turn the tide for us. There is one particular spell that I think will prove very useful for us now."

"What spell is that, Grand Magus?"

"I shall tell you soon enough. In the meantime, ready your pistol. There are a number of people in our order that will need to be sacrificed tonight."

10. Independence

Kansas

"My fellow Americans, it is with heavy heart that I must tell you of this sad but hopeful news. It is with great regret that I announce the formal secession of the State of Kansas from the United States of America. Along with Governor Lloyd Mallory, the moral people of this once great country have chosen me to lead this very Christian state to become an independent and sovereign nation because of the corruption and vile godlessness of the Federal Government. We did try our best to work with the politicians in Washington but it is through their utter rejection of the values that we have held on to so dear as God fearing Christians that we make this most drastic but inevitable of decisions. The apocalypse that is all around us is a direct result of our Federal government's rejection of the fundamental principles of Christianity, the one tenet that will save all our souls from the hell that has manifested itself on Earth. Only through our Lord Jesus Christ can any of us find salvation and redemption from the forces of Satan. Only through the full faith in the Lord can we all be saved."

Pastor Erik Burnley was standing at the podium as he looked directly into the camera. The sound stage was brightly lit, and he could barely keep himself from sweating as the makeup crew would dab his forehead with tissues and handkerchiefs in between takes. The building's air conditioning system had been on the blink for the past two weeks but there were more pressing concerns for the few qualified electrical technicians that they had in the compound. Although the dress shirt underneath his royal blue suit was freshly pressed and starched to the stiffness of cardboard, the sweat pouring down his neck was beginning to stain the collar.

"The Rock of God Church has stood alone as the vanguard against the forces of evil and we are now in command of all military and police forces in the state of Kansas. We have recently formed our own military organization called the Soldiers of the Lord, or SOL for short. This brave army of fully qualified volunteers, many of whom have had previous military and police experience, will serve as the backbone and the protectors of this great new country of ours, the sovereign independent country of Christian Kansas. I must also tell you that we have been in constant negotiations with the Federal Government, but they refuse to heed our calls for secession and subsequent independence, and so it was with great reluctance that myself and Governor Mallory initiated a military operation to secure a small stockpile of nuclear warheads in order to defend our holy state against those that wish to persecute our religious beliefs. To this end, our small but glorious country now has a powerful nuclear deterrent that we shall only ever use as a last resort should the enemy attempt to conquer us. To those that wish us harm, I shall say this: leave us alone and leave us in peace to await our Lord Jesus Christ's return. We are the Lord's chosen children and we will fight in his name if need be for we are not afraid because he is with us!"

Pastor Erik paused for a moment in order to let the words sink in.

"To this end our church leadership has agreed through mutual consent, that I shall serve as this country's president for the time being. This so-called Glooming is an extraordinary crisis that has affected the entire world and we are living in the most perilous of times. Governor Lloyd Mallory has graciously accepted the dual positions of vice president and Secretary of Defense in order to streamline the functions of our new government so that we can make rapid and informed decisions in order to properly govern and defend this new country of ours to the best of our abilities. There are no plans to set up a congressional body at this time so any new laws that we create will be through mutual agreement with the church leadership committee. The fundamental principles that our country's new constitution will be based on is the teachings of the bible: namely that the Ten Commandments as well as all the teachings of our Lord Jesus Christ will be part of our country's laws; the Rock of God Church and the government of Kansas will be one and the same, just as our lord intended it to be. The Kansas sovereign government shall be handing out copies of our new constitution in the next few days to anyone who wishes to look at it. We will be posting the articles of government on all the public billboards throughout the state for our citizen's perusal very shortly."

Governor Lloyd Mallory and his wife stood in front of the small crowd of people just behind the cameras. They clasped each other's arms and silently wept with joy as the fruits of their faith were at last being brought forth and into the reality of the world. Pastor Erik smiled slightly as he resisted the urge to wink at them since the video was still recording his speech live.

"Our new country's leadership will now be taking steps to secure this new sovereign land under the guidance of our unshakable faith. The first declaration is that anyone who is not of the Christian denomination must leave the state within forty-eight hours or face arrest and forced deportation. The same goes for all homosexuals. We are now a united people under one faith and that one true faith is Christianity. If there are others of a different faith that wish to convert to the one true religion of our Lord Jesus Christ, then please go to the nearest state church and request baptism for yourself and any other members of your family who would be willing to bare their souls for our Lord. All state churches will be open all day and all night for you, all you have to do is to surrender to the Lord and your soul will be saved from the hellfire that is spreading all over this world. The second declaration is the complete outlawing of all abortions; all of these murder clinics are to be closed down effective immediately. As to the doctors and nurses who perform these murderous deeds they have but less than a day to leave the confines of our country or they shall face the Lord's immediate and implacable wrath. The third declaration is the establishment of morality councils- these committees will be staffed by the most pious of all our Christian brothers and they are to determine whether one's individual actions are sinful or not. Each county will have several morality councils in order to make sure that each and every one of us follows the Lord's teachings and not to stray from it; although I have said that our Lord would return quite soon, I cannot tell you the exact moment when that will happen so we must still remain vigilant and obey his teachings lest we sin and get cast out of his kingdom before the final battle."

Pastor Erik paused once more as he took a short sip from a glass of water that had been placed on the podium. He needed to spell out a few more matters and that would be the end of this truly historic speech. With so many other things to do, he needed to make sure that the entire state was in agreement and loyal to him. So far everything was going according to plan. *That only meant that God was on his side for the proof was now undeniable*, he thought.

"As to the seat of our new country, the Rock of God Church compound here in McPherson County will serve as the temporary capital of our new government for the time being. Depending on how long it takes for our Lord Jesus Christ to return from heaven to guide us back to eternal salvation, we may reopen the Kansas Statehouse in Topeka in the near future. Our new government is racing against time to make sure that the local power stations as well as every water and sewage treatment plant remains functioning and will be fully nationalized under government control in the next few days. Our church membership over the past few months has now grown close to almost three million and we will start to bus a number of our constituents over to the once abandoned areas of Wichita and Topeka in order to ease overcrowding here in the church compound. I can assure all of our current church members that there will be ample housing that will be found, you can trust us on that. While I understand that the oil shortage has been acute these past few weeks, we will be taking steps to bring our supply of oil and gas back to normal levels, but I still must reiterate that our citizens to only use electric power as well as gasoline for their cars in the most conservative of manners as possible in order to safeguard what we have. Also, instead of just sitting by in an idle conduct, I ask each and every citizen of our new country to volunteer your time and your services. We have great need for engineers, carpenters, mechanics, electricians, and doctors. So if you have any spare time, do not let it go to waste for the Lord hates slothfulness. At the same time, if you have any previous experience as a member of the US armed forces or police force, please volunteer and sign up for the Soldiers of the Lord, we need all the able bodied men we can get. As you well know, we are surrounded by evil but our faith and our leadership will guarantee our victory over the forces of darkness in the times to come."

Neda Mallory was the governor's wife and she was wearing a silvery white dress for this occasion. She stood beside her husband along with Janet Clancey as they continued to watch, mesmerized by the extraordinary events occurring all around them. Pastor Erik took one last breath, needing to finish the speech.

"To those on the outside looking in, the new sovereign country of Christian Kansas is not a threat to you. As I said before, all we want is to be left alone. We ask that the Federals weigh any military option against us carefully for we are more than prepared to give up our lives in the service of the Lord. As to the rumors of what happened to the President of the United States, I can now admit to all of you that he is a guest here in our compound along with Admiral Charles Zimmerman, the commanding officer of NORTHCOM. The two men will remain for the time being until we can get full and written assurances from the US government that they will recognize our country's sovereignty, and they will take no steps to forcefully invade us. It was a sad decision that led to this, but it was a justified one. As the new President of Kansas, I have an obligation to protect my citizens by any means possible. Also, I would like to add that if there are any true Christians left in the other parts of the country to go ahead, and come and join us here in Christian Kansas. Our immigration policy is open to anyone who is of the European race and of the Christian denomination. As for other races, we will either accept them as new citizens or reject them on a case by case basis. While I admit that the Lord does not discriminate between people of skin color, we must be pragmatic since we feel that those of European descent would be best suited to becoming productive citizens of our new country. That is all I can say for now. Thank you and God bless our great new holy nation of Christian Kansas!"

As soon as the director yelled cut the small crowd erupted in cheers and made a thunderous applause. Neda Mallory wiped away the tears from her eyes as she embraced Pastor Erik the moment he walked off the stage as the crowd surged around him and shook his hand. A few more minutes of hugs and hearty congratulations commenced before the crowd slowly began to disperse as there was still a lot of work to be done.

Janet Clancey kissed Pastor Erik on the cheek. "That was an amazing speech, Pastor."

Pastor Erik smiled back. "Thank you, Janet. My only regret is you weren't there to share the limelight with me. Everybody knows you are my co-host on our daily program so it was rather awkward for me to be there on that stage all by my lonesome."

Janet nodded. "I just wanted to ask you, Erik. About the country's official stance on atheists that you just mentioned. You see, my brother in law is here and he's served us wonderfully as a volunteer doctor over at the hospital in Topeka. I introduced him to you a few years back."

Pastor Erik continued to smile as he shook hands with the remaining well-wishers. "Yes, I remember him. What about him?"

Janet shrugged in mild resignation. "Well, you see, he has been outspoken in his atheism and well, after this speech you just gave, I mean, is it possible I could get a deferment for him to prevent him from being thrown out, I mean?"

Neda Mallory had been listening as she placed her hands on her hips. "Oh come now, Janet. After all that's happened, your brother in law's still an atheist? Why, he ought to be one of the first people getting baptized as a Christian right now. I don't know how anyone could still profess a disbelief in gods with all these other evil gods out there."

Janet frowned as she acknowledged the governor's wife before looking back at Erik. "Well, he hasn't made up his mind yet and if you could just give a deferment for a few more days so that I could convince him, Erik? I've never asked a favor from you before but I would just like a little bit mercy and patience if that's alright."

Pastor Erik placed an assuring hand on his co-host's elbow. "Janet, I'm afraid Mrs. Mallory here is right. There's no reason for your brother in law to hold off on being converted to Christianity now. I'm sorry but these new laws will take effect immediately. We have to secure our spiritual power in order for the entire country to protect ourselves from the multitude of devils that are slowly surrounding us."

"But…"

"Janet, now is not the time for this and I've made my decision. I'm very busy, so let's talk later," Pastor Erik said as he started to walk towards the other members of the Holy Committee that were standing near the exit.

General Ken O'Neill along with Governor Lloyd Mallory shook Erik's hands as soon as he joined them. Steve Van Dyke saluted them all just as he walked in through the studio exit. Neda started to walk towards them but was waved away by her husband. She quickly realized that it wasn't her business to butt in on their conversation so she quickly turned and started to offer more advice to Janet who ignored her out of spite. The governor's insufferable wife then latched onto one of the stage hands and started another conversation.

"Follow me, gentlemen, I think it's better we talk while we head to the guest rooms," Pastor Erik said as he started walking towards the exit.

"I'm sorry I missed most of your speech, Mr. President," Steve said as he walked alongside. He was dressed in military fatigues with the new flag of Christian Kansas that was stitched on its side. "But things have been very hectic lately."

Pastor Erik laughed. "You are absolved, Steve. I regret that I can just only congratulate you right now on a job well done. It's a pity that we've both been so busy that this is our first face to face meeting in weeks. And please, just call me Erik. You are part of my inner circle of advisers now."

"You did a fine job, Steve," General O'Neill said as they all rounded a corner and were now along a glass walkway overlooking the inner compound. "General Teller has been telling me that even though you requested to be included in the boot camp for new recruits in SOL because you were formerly a SWAT officer instead of a soldier, he assured me that you don't need to take that course at all. In fact, you are putting some of our veteran soldiers to shame with your skills."

Steve smiled. "Thanks, General. I owe it all to the Lord's grace and mercy."

Governor Lloyd Mallory took off his cowboy hat as he tried to keep up with the fast paced walking. "So I take it that since we have now played our hand with this declaration of independence that we have all our defenses in place now?"

"Yes and no," General O'Neill said. "The north is pretty much secure. Iowa and Nebraska are getting snowed under and nobody wants to make a move- too many weather problems for any large scale maneuvering. The east is a bit more chaotic, there's plenty of riots in Missouri so we're still trying to get a clearer picture and that'll take some time. In the south, Governor Bierly of Oklahoma wants to secede too, but he's hampered because just below him in Dallas is one of the main staging areas for US Army North and he doesn't have the full loyalty of his National Guard troops. All he can do for now is act as an early warning asset in case NORTHCOM attempts to make a move against us from what's left of Texas, but I doubt they would since they need all the troops they have to protect against the Aztec gods below them. The real question mark though is over to the west. Our little stunt in Colorado Springs hasn't gone unnoticed. While the US Government is still in shock over what happened, there would be a flashpoint over there if they start massing troops along the border with us."

Pastor Erik nodded as they all started to walk down a flight of stairs into the building's bunker level. "What worries me is that the Feds might retaliate using their own nukes. Could they do that?"

General O'Neill answered almost right away. "It's possible, depending on who they put in charge. The President of the United States was still in the process of selecting his vice when we grabbed him and we got the 'football' as well so to speak because they were with Admiral Zimmerman when Marine One went down."

Pastor Erik arched his brow. "Football?"

"The nuclear launch codes," Steve said. "It's in a small briefcase and is close to the president at all times when he travels. They call it the football."

"Exactly," General O'Neill said. "We have the case and all the current codes. With the confusion in their government right now, we have ample reason to believe that the codes have not yet been changed since nobody knows who's in charge right now. The Speaker of the House is in Virginia but he hasn't done anything beyond diverting some troops in Colorado to find out what had happened. And since Zimmerman is or was the commanding officer of NORTHCOM then we still have the advantage in that both their military and civilian leadership are in a state of confusion."

Governor Mallory was trying to catch his breath from the non-stop walking. "So now it all depends on the Speaker then, I hope he isn't a hardnosed sonuva bitch or else our independence might be very short-lived."

General O'Neill chuckled as the group was waved through an underground guard post. "I've met the Speaker of the House a few times. I can tell you the guy's a fence-sitting political wuss. He's probably crapping in his pants right now trying to figure out what's going on."

Pastor Erik turned to look at them as they stood in front of a metal door. There were two armed soldiers standing guard beside it. "Let us remain vigilant, gentlemen," he said before gesturing the guards to open the door with their keys. "The US Government is still a very dangerous beast and we must play our cards carefully lest we slip up and lose this golden opportunity."

The guards unlocked the door and they swung it open. The room inside was much larger than an ordinary cell block. It had a metal table and chair which were bolted onto the bare concrete floor. The President of the United States had been lying in a cot along the side of the cell but he immediately sat up as soon as the door was unlocked. They had taken away his coat jacket, shoes, belt and his tie but he still had his button dress shirt that was partly torn and wore his wrinkled trousers.

Pastor Erik walked over to him and held out his hand. The president merely turned away and crossed his arms. A flash of anger raced over the pastor's face but he soon realized that their guest had every right to be in a bad mood so he let the wanton act of disrespect go as he sat down on top of the table while Governor Mallory placed himself on the chair with a groan. Steve and General O'Neill merely leaned on the walls of the cell as they motioned the guards to leave the room.

"This is a blatant act of treason," the president said softly. He'd barely had any rest in the past few days as he was thoroughly searched and examined by medical personnel before being shuffled off into this cell and placed on a twenty-four hour watch. "Do you know what the penalty for that is?"

Pastor Erik wiped off a speck of dust from his suit coat. "We have declared our independence so your government has no jurisdiction over us. I'm sure the guards allowed you to watch from the TV set in this room. I am here to ask you to be reasonable and not to let your emotions get the better of you. Both sides are in a precarious situation as you well know…"

"Only because you put us there! You committed a terrorist act against not one, but two US military bases, one of which was a detonated a nuclear device detonated. You've also kidnapped me, the head of state for this country! You have just royally screwed everything up and you've just about opened the way for those Aztec gods to overwhelm the United States."

Pastor Erik stood up and glared at him. "No, Mr. President, it is you and your lack of leadership that is the true cause of destroying this country! All you godless people in Washington and Virginia and your embrace for these blasphemous values that separate church and state and the oppression of the one true faith is what caused these minions of Satan to rise in the first place! What I am doing now is saving as many good Christians as I can since you have so clearly failed in this task. So do not take this tone with me!"

The president shook his head and sighed. "You are clearly insane, do you know that?"

"How dare you!" Pastor Erik growled. "Can you not see that the reason why these demons have come forth is because the apocalypse is here? Don't you realize that your very actions of supporting the homosexuals and these horrific and godless liberal values are what's actually causing God to punish the world right now?"

"I can't believe I'm hearing this."

Pastor Erik wagged a disapproving finger. "I can't believe that you're still denying the truth! I have been vindicated by this apocalypse! I was on air making this very prediction all those years ago and now it's come true! This is the evidence that you refuse to believe in and this is why the state of Kansas has seceded and is now a blessed bulwark of good against the forces of evil."

The president said nothing as he merely stared back at him.

Pastor Erik took a deep breath before continuing. "If you do not believe, that is your choice for it will be your soul that will be damned in the end. Neither myself nor my followers will go to hell because we are faithful servants of the true Lord, Jesus Christ. Now, all that I ask you is that we need to begin negotiations and we need to do this right away. You are well aware that we have a stockpile of nuclear weapons. We regretfully had to use one of these nukes in order to make a statement—"

"You made a statement alright. You've proven to the world just how crazy you all are."

"If you don't wish to believe what we believe in, that's your choice," Governor Mallory said. "But we have nuclear weapons now and we will defend our newly independent country should any US military forces make any attempt to invade us. I hope you realize that."

The president looked at them one by one before answering. "I represent the US government, a body that was elected by the people of this entire country. And I will tell you all this, the United States does not give in to terrorists. There is nothing to negotiate here. I demand you let me and Admiral Zimmerman go, and surrender unconditionally. I'll give you my sworn promise that you all will be given a fair trial. That is all I have to say to you."

Pastor Erik made a slight smile. "You still cling to this outdated notion that what you do as a secular head of state somehow matters, as if all this is just a temporary crisis and everything will be back to normal once it's over. But guess what? The world has changed irrevocably. Mankind isn't alone anymore. We are not the Lords of this Earth after all. There are other, more powerful beings than us out there. The gods are real and we need to choose sides. Are you with the devil or are you with us?"

"Let me go first and then we'll talk," the president said.

Governor Mallory chuckled as he put his cowboy hat back on. "Gosh darn it, you are one hell of a stubborn mule."

"Seems that the President of the United States is still not convinced that this apocalypse is happening," Pastor Erik said as he stood up. "Well in that case, he shall remain as our guest until he decides to finally face reality. Mark my words, Mr. President. We will fight back with everything we've got if your forces attack. Only you have the power to prevent the destruction of America but like Lloyd said, you're too stubborn to realize it. Let's go, boys."

As the four of them walked out of the president's cell, they started to make their way back upstairs.

Pastor Erik shook his head as he led the way for the others. "Stubborn old man, it seems that he's blind to what's all around him."

"You can say that again," Governor Mallory said. "What worries me is that the Federal government will try something if they think he's dead."

"Talk to Governor Bierly, see if he can act as a go-between between our country and whoever is in charge of the US right now," Pastor Erik said to him before turning his head over to General O'Neill's direction. "How soon can we begin stage one for Operation Valhalla?"

General O'Neill stopped dead in his tracks. "Operation Valhalla? You want to initiate that now?"

Pastor Erik crossed his arms as he stopped as well. "Yes, it's the one thing we can do in case the United States decides to initiate hostilities. Get it started immediately. Put Steve in charge of it."

"We'll get it done, Pastor," Steve Van Dyke said. "I swear to the almighty God we all worship that I won't fail."

11. The Siberian Break

Siberia

It was about an hour after midnight when Ilya Volkhov finally sat up on the bed. He shook the sleep from his eyes and began to slowly and deliberately put his clothes on. When the Spetsnaz abducted him and Tara a few months ago, they only did a cursory search of his clothing and had largely left the bits of raskovnik alone in the pockets of his winter jacket, thinking they were nothing more than just pieces of plant material. Ilya smiled in the twilit darkness as he placed his hands into his coat pocket and pulled out a few clovers of the raskovnik. With the help of Tara and the trickster god, he had found bits of that magical plant in the Otherworld and they used it to defeat the rebirth of an evil god called Okeus by feeding the Native American deity's larval form with some of the magical herb. What he didn't tell the general and the other interrogators who questioned him was that this magical plant could open any lock, and reveal the truth behind any secret that a person had hidden away in their minds. Ilya could have escaped months ago, but he waited until he learned that Tara had been kidnapped by an unknown enemy, and that the trickster god was either hurt, or on the loose somewhere in the city. His plan was to escape from the military compound and then hopefully find the talking dog, assuming it was still around. The young boy knew for a fact that the trickster was probably still alive, since ordinary weapons of any kind would not have affected it.

As he finished putting on his snow boots, Ilya crept up to the front of the door and placed his right ear on it. It was usually at this time the evening guard shift had settled down and the lone guard would usually start to doze off. He had hoped it would be one of the older men who would be assigned for the night since they tended to be more lethargic. The more senior ones would sometimes bring along a small container of homemade vodka that would get them to doze off for a bit. If he could time it properly, he should be able to open the door without alerting the guard and then sneak away before they knew he was gone. With his ear now pressed tightly against the door, Ilya closed his eyes and concentrated on the sounds in the corridor.

The boy's smile became a big grin when he predictably heard the snoring of the lone guard outside. Just as he got ready to place some of the bits of the magical plant near the lock on the door however, he soon heard a series of footsteps coming from the other end of the corridor. As his confidence turned into shocked disappointment, Ilya put the raskovnik back into his jacket and listened harder.

Two pairs of footsteps stopped just outside of the door.

"Get up, you lazy good for nothing idiot!" someone screamed.

"I-I'm sorry, Lieutenant, I must have dozed off!"

"You are a complete imbecile! I should have you arrested for dereliction of duty! Is that what you want?"

"N-No, sir! I think someone must have drugged my coffee."

"Do you think I am stupid? Are you insulting my intelligence now?"

"No, sir! I-I am just saying that someone else might have—"

"Shut up! I am assigning these two other privates to assist you and I will come back again sometime this evening. If I see any of you three not at full alert guarding our guest, you will all be arrested, is that clear?"

"Yes, sir!" all three voices said in unison.

Ilya's heart sank as he heard the officer outside curse a few more times before he walked away. As the lieutenant's footsteps faded into the background, he could hear the three guards murmuring to themselves.

"Yevgeny, you are so stupid! How could you fall asleep?"

"Don't blame me, Vlad, I was cleaning the toilets this morning and I haven't had any rest for the whole day, then they assigned me for guard duty at the last minute. I haven't even gotten my coffee ration yet."

"You two stop arguing, it's over now. You know how much of a tough bastard that Lieutenant Guskov can be."

"I don't understand," the soldier named Yevgeny said. "Why are there three of us assigned for guard duty now?"

"I heard that the new commander who came in with the convoy, his name is Denikin I believe, is planning to take the kid out of here tomorrow so he ordered the general to triple the guards for the rest of the evening," the third soldier said.

"How come he is able to order General Klimov like that? He looked to be nothing more than a colonel to me, that means our commander would outrank him," Yevgeny said.

"You really are clueless, Yevgeny. That man Denikin is a deputy director of the FSB and I heard he is a personal favorite of the president. You would be wise never to cross him," Vlad said.

Ilya fought the urge to cry. All his previous planning was now pointless. He would have been able to sneak past one sleepy guard but now he was up against three very alert sentinels who would keep themselves awake all night in order not to displease their wary superiors. Even worse was the news that they were taking him away to somewhere unknown and possibly even more secure. He needed to escape right now, but how?

"Vlad, check our guest and make sure he's still sleeping," the third man said.

At that moment, Ilya curled up just below the door as he heard the metal slot above the doorknob slide open. A ray of yellow light partly illuminated the room as the guard outside looked at the mound of clothes shaped like a person sleeping underneath the thick blanket. For a few seconds Ilya thought that the guard might have seen through the ruse, but then the slot closed shut again and he heard the footsteps walking back over to the guard desk. One soldier telling the others that the boy was fast asleep and there was nothing to worry about.

Ilya slowly got up and moved silently over to the window. It wasn't barred but the boy knew it didn't have to be since the room he was being held in was three stories up and it would be a long way down. As he unlatched the window and pushed the double panes outwards, a chill wind blew into the room. Looking down, he could see the snow in inner courtyard below. If he jumped, he would most certainly kill himself, or at the very least, break every bone in his body the moment he landed on the cobbled stone ground below. As he looked up, Ilya noticed a small ledge just below the overhanging roof above the window. It definitely was too small for him to sit on but there was another, albeit riskier possibility if he dared.

As he decided right then and there to get on with it, Ilya immediately grabbed the blanket from his bed and began to tie a knot on its ends along with the clothes that he had placed underneath it. Within a few minutes, he had a makeshift rope that wasn't even close to ten feet long. He would have to time this properly if he was going to pull it off. The risks were immense and if he slipped and fell that would be the end of him. There was a narrow steel divider in the center of the window frame that served as a base for the latches of the window panes, so he tied the end of the improvised rope around it and let the other end fall out of the window. As he down looked below one more time, he could see that the rope wasn't even halfway down the walls of the building. Ilya grabbed the pile of clothes on this bed and threw them out of the window, making sure that the heap landed in a pile down below. Taking the bits of raskovnik from his pocket, he turned and silently made for the door.

The solider named Yevgeny frowned as he once again sat down with the other two. He was both scared and ashamed after being caught by the lieutenant for sleeping while on sentry duty and he had the distinct feeling he was in deep trouble. He knew that his country was in a state of emergency and he could be severely punished for incompetence. As he drummed his fingers on the table, he noticed there was a cold draft coming from somewhere.

Yevgeny looked up. "Did it get cold all of a sudden?"

The other two privates looked at him. That was when Vlad noticed that the door to the boy's room was ajar as he got up and pointed at it.

Yevgeny turned his head, saw the slightly opened door and instantly jumped up and ran towards it. The other two men quickly followed. As all three of them pushed the door open even further and peered inside, they noticed that the windows had been thrown wide open and there was a makeshift rope tied to the divider of the window frame.

Vlad let out a startled cry. "Oh, he's escaped!"

Yevgeny ran over to the window and looked down below. "His rope was too short and it looked like he fell! I think he's probably dead."

The third soldier stood next to Vlad as they all looked down. "The stupid boy, why would he try to escape with only half a rope? That's at least another thirty feet to the ground. He's killed himself."

As the three guards were arguing as to how he had died, Ilya was in acute pain as he strained to keep himself from falling off the roof. After unlocking the door, he immediately ran over to the window and prepared to grab onto the roof overhang so that he would lift himself up on top of it as soon as the guards were alerted. The moment he heard them shouting an alarm, Ilya immediately grabbed hold of the edge of the roof with his hands and then he tried to pull himself up on top of the overhang. From there, he would wait until the guards would think that he went by way of the makeshift rope and they would therefore run downstairs to the inner courtyard, thereby leaving him free to get back down from the roof and escape. However, it didn't work out the way he thought it would; just as he launched himself out through the window, his arms buckled from the strain and he ended up just above the protruding niche above the window frame. His body was now wedged sideways and due to the icy sheen on the side of the walls, he was starting to slip.

Ilya looked down and he could see the three bobbing heads of the guards just inches below his thigh as they kept arguing as to who was responsible for what had happened. The boy's legs were pushing against the upper part of the frame, while his body was nearly horizontal as his arms held on to the edge of the overhang. The pain was practically unbearable as he hoped that they would not look up and see him. The passing moments seemed like an eternity and Ilya was almost ready to cry out from the agony of keeping himself aloft, but he finally saw that the three guards withdrew their heads from the window and he heard the sounds of their boots as they ran out of the room.

Now came the hard part. Ilya let out a small whimper as he got ready to push off from the top of the window frame and shift his body so that he could swing himself back into the room. It was going to be a tricky maneuver and if he failed he would probably fall off the roof and plunge down into the cobbled stone ground but now he had no choice. He remembered taking a few gymnastics lessons from a passing instructor in the orphanage; all he needed to do was to shove off with his legs and let go with his arms while turning his torso. As his strength was practically gone, Ilya pushed off with his legs as he quickly shifted his weight and thrust himself back through the window.

The ensuing maneuver worked as the boy was able to land his feet at the bottom of the window frame, but Ilya arched his torso too soon, and his forehead hit the top part of the windowsill. The ensuing pain on his brow and the subsequent flashes of light in his eyes was intense as he almost fell backwards, but he was able to bend his knees and push off one more time as he dived back into the room. For the next few seconds, he just lay there, writhing in pain from both his arms and from where the window had connected to his forehead. When his vision finally cleared, he heard the alarms go off all over the base. Ilya rapidly got up and ran out of the room.

As he dashed across the corridor and made a quick turn, Ilya collided with Private Anosov as the latter was just about to see what had happened after the alert sounded. The boy's momentum pushed Anosov so hard he almost fell, but he was able to maintain his balance as he rapidly placed one foot back to absorb the inertia. Ilya tried to push past him but Anosov grabbed onto the boy's left elbow and wouldn't let go.

Ilya cried out in pain and frustration. "You've got to let me go! I can save Russia if you let me go!"

Anosov placed a hand over the boy's mouth to stop him from screaming. "Ilya, I believe you. I want to get you out but you have to trust me."

Ilya immediately stopped struggling. "Why would you want to help me?"

"Because I know you are the one hope our country has," Anosov said. "But you must do as I say. If you keep going through this corridor, they will catch you and put you back in your room."

"What do I do then?"

"Follow me."

Anosov led the boy down the stairs to the floor just below them as they noticed a squad of soldiers making their way up. The two of them ran into an adjoining corridor and then stopped in front of a door labeled Supply. That was when they both heard the sound of footsteps coming down the passageway.

As he pulled out a set of keys from his pocket, Anosov had to carefully pick through them as he barely remembered which key it was.

Ilya kept alternately looking down the corridor as well as the door leading to the stairwell. "Hurry up," he whispered.

Anosov finally found the correct key for the door as he placed it in the lock and got it open, just as the sound of footsteps were around the corner. He pushed the boy through the slightly opened door and locked it just as two fully-armed Alpha Group commandos ran into the corridor.

One of the Spetsnaz commandos ran up to him. "What are you doing there, Private?"

Anosov stood up straight and saluted him. "I was about to go into this room to get some supplies when the alarm sounded, sir."

"Did you see a little boy in this corridor at all?"

"No, sir. There's nobody here at this time of the evening."

The two commandos didn't seem convinced. "Open the door," the other one said.

"Yes, sir," Anosov said as he turned and used the keys a second time to open the door.

Both Spetsnaz commandos quickly pushed past him and turned on the lights as they walked into the area. The supply room had very tight spaces, and they could see that boxes as well as shelves were stacked from floor to ceiling. One of the commandos started making his way around the gaps to make sure no one was hiding there. Anosov held his breath as he hoped the boy was doing his best to hide from these special forces operators.

Ilya was wedged in between two stacks of boxes as the commando came close to him. The boy was able to evade him the first time, slipping quietly to his right while the commando was looking the other way and then he quickly dashed into another gap, but now he had reached a dead end as there were tall stacks of papers on all three sides.

Just as the commando was about to turn into the last space, the Spetsnaz soldier was instantly startled by a loud caw coming from where the window was. As the commando instantly reacted by aiming his rifle at where the sound was coming from, he saw the black raven perched beside the cracked windowsill. The Spetsnaz had thought about shooting the bird for making him jumpy, but decided against it at the last minute as he made his way out of the room.

Anosov waited until both commandos had gone through the stairwell door and had closed it behind them before unlocking the office supply room once more. Ilya poked his head out as he once again noticed the coast was clear, but Anosov pushed him back into the interior of the room.

The boy was angry. "What are you doing?"

Anosov just shook his head. "Better for you to stay in there for now, I will get you out in a few hours, so just stay hidden in there, okay?"

Ilya frowned but he realized it was a good idea. "Fine then, don't be too long."

As Anosov locked him inside once more, Ilya wedged himself behind a stack of boxes and sat down. He noticed that two of his fingernails were cracked and bleeding as he felt the bump on his forehead. Other than the bruises, he was otherwise okay.

About an hour later, Anosov came back just outside the door as he wheeled a laundry cart. Unlocking the office door one more time, he motioned to Ilya to get into the cart. As the boy buried himself between heaps of dirty blankets and clothes, Anosov took the service elevator down as he pushed the cart out past through the preliminary checkpoints and they soon made it to the outer barracks. From there it was just a matter of passing through the final sentries to head over to the laundry area, which was just outside of the base.

When the cart was finally stopped just outside of the front entrance to the laundry room, Ilya pushed his way past the soiled fabrics as he peered through the slightly open top of the cart. From the looks of things, it was early morning and he could see the steam coming from the nearby chimneys. Anosov gave him a piece of paper containing an address where he could hole up and rest before attempting to make his way out of the city.

The boy finally pushed himself out of the laundry cart, and then ran across another street. Before jumping into an alleyway, he noticed a passing car nearby. Once the main street was quiet again, he buttoned up his winter jacket and then started moving along the sidewalk. The address that Private Anosov had given him was past the river, and he needed to find a way to cross its icy waters without detection.

12. The Children of Ammon

Zarqa Governorate

David Zim continued to look at the remote display on his tablet as he crouched down in the makeshift forward observation post. There were three other Mossad operatives in the remote farmhouse with him. One of them was manning the portable radio, another one was behind the wheel of the Granite field intelligence vehicle that was hidden way at the back of the house, ready to start it up and get moving at a moment's notice. The third man was sleeping on a folding cot in the main room.

David made a brief glance at his snoring colleague before returning his concentration on the tablet he was holding. The small mini-laptop was giving him a constant video feed from the remote Ground Target Acquisition System cameras that they had set up to the north of the area just before dawn. They were in the northern outskirts of Qasr al Hallabat, a small desert town to the north-east of the Jordanian capital of Amman. The next few hours could very well decide the fate of not just the Hashemite Kingdom of Jordan, but the country of Israel as well.

He remembered the night before, after arriving as part of the advance team that had been rushed into the area just less than six hours ago. That was when the latest intelligence estimates confirmed that the Babylonian Army would be passing through the area on their way south. Months of planning by the IDF and the remnants of the Jordanian military would finally be put to the test in this desolate place.

David took his eye away from the video feed for a brief minute. He grabbed a plastic water bottle from a nearby backpack lying on a table and sipped at it. From his time in the university he had remembered that this whole area was once the biblical land of the Ammonites, an ancient kingdom from the Bronze Age that took their name from Ammon, a legendary king who was born from an incestuous union of Lot and his daughters. The old myth was that Lot and his children were the only survivors of the Lord's destruction of the legendary city of Sodom. After his wife had been turned into a pillar of salt for disobeying God's direct command that she not look back when the city was ground to dust, Lot and his daughters thought the world had finally ended and they inhabited a desolate cave for a number of years. Sensing a need to repopulate the Earth, Lot's daughters seduced their old father. It was rumored that the Ammonites descended from that unholy union and ruled the surrounding lands before being exterminated by King David and the Israelites. How ironic it was that the old biblical stories were once again being played out in the present.

After a few minutes, David noticed that the distant horizon on the video feed began to blur. The massive sandstorm that always preceded the Babylonians was coming. Since they had placed the GTAS sensors ten miles to the north of their position at the farmhouse, it meant that the enemy was no more than a few minutes away.

After getting up from his chair, David kicked the side of the cot where his colleague was sleeping before turning his head to look at his radio operator. "Benny, alert Hippo One. Tell them that the enemy is in visual range."

As his radio operator started talking on his receiver. David's other colleague instantly got up from the cot, ran a hand along his scalp to straighten his hair before grabbing an assault rifle that was propped up by the wall. "What did I miss?"

"The operation is about to begin," David said as he kept his eyes on the tablet. "Man your station, Omri."

A very large and special Israeli Defense Forces unit along with what was left of the Royal Jordanian Army had been carefully concealed in the abandoned town of Qasr Al-Hallabat. In the months since the Glooming began, a new faction that they labeled as the Babylonian Army had swept through Iraq. In a territory once claimed by an Islamic extremist faction and the Iraqi government, it was now being dominated by legendary gods who were once thought of as no more than mere stories. Sandstorms had swept across the entire area while legions of demons killed anyone who resisted. 21st Century weaponry was no match against the waves of sand and dust of the monsters that lurked within them. The Western powers had been utterly defeated and now all that stood between the resurgent gods of old was a hastily formed military alliance between Israel and Jordan. As the days passed, the situation became more and more desperate. Syria, eastern Lebanon, and the whole of southern Turkey had now been largely overrun as the Babylonians spilled across the Jordanian border and if left unchecked, would soon threaten Israel itself. The Saudis had retreated across their own desert and were making a last stand in Mecca, their holiest Islamic city. Iran had also been battered to the point where they had lost half their country.

As his colleagues continued to relay information to their headquarters, David saw that the sandstorm ahead had picked up in intensity. He hoped that the remote sensors they buried would hold, as they needed every observation point that they could get.

In the town's headquarters, General Boris Siegel looked up and saw the reports that were coming in. All of his radio operators, who were once staring silently at their computer monitors just minutes before, were now in nonstop conversations with the unit commanders. The flap leading to the outside had opened and his, aide, Colonel Dan Tzur came in, followed closely by the Royal Jordanian Army field commander, General Saeed Ali.

"You are just in time," General Siegel said. "I am about to initiate Operation Megiddo."

General Ali frowned. He didn't like that particular name for the operation and he had protested somewhat, but he had kept quiet after the King of Jordan agreed with the Israelis on it. "Are you sure this will work?"

General Siegel looked down at the dusty floor of the tent. "I am not sure, but it is the only chance we have."

"I have seen a small demonstration of it when I was being briefed about it," Colonel Tzur said to his Jordanian counterpart. "I think it will work."

General Ali was still skeptical as he crossed his arms. "The king has told me that along with his men, he will fight to the death if those demons reach Amman. If that happens, I will probably be dead anyway so we might as well proceed."

General Siegel pointed at one of the video monitors that were situated at the far side of the command tent. "Keep your eyes on that video feed, General."

As the Jordanian CO started to watch, he noticed that it seemed to be nothing more than an elevated platform near the center of town. Within minutes, a heavyset man with a full beard, thick eyeglasses and wearing a rabbinic prayer shawl over the shoulders of his black robes, made his way to the center of the platform. Beneath the stage, there were a number of IDF soldiers who seemed to be wheeling in what looked to be a large wooden crate. A few minutes later, the soldiers dismantled the crate and revealed what looked like a glass aquarium that seemed to be more than ten feet tall. There was something moving in the bottom of the glass enclosure. As General Ali strained his eyes for a closer look, he almost recoiled in horror.

Rabbi Elijah Ba'al looked down at the glass enclosure and saw that the little creature it contained had begun to stir from its long slumber. The former exiled rabbi gestured at one of his assistants, an IDF soldier who carried a sealed ceramic pot with arcane symbols on it, to join him at the raised platform. The soldier walked up to Rabbi Ba'al as he noticed that the creature down below was staring at them with slitted eyes.

"Don't be afraid of it," Rabbi Ba'al said as he took the ceramic pot from his assistant's trembling hands. "That homunculus is under my control."

The misshapen creature looked vaguely human in that it had a pair of arms, legs and even a torso, but its head didn't seem to have a neck as it was fused to its tiny, uneven shoulders. Its head was malformed, with a bulging forehead, a snout for a nose, and a gash for a mouth. One arm was shorter than another and one leg seemed to be shaped like a stump. It had pale grey skin and was completely hairless, like that of a newborn rat. The creature snarled at the terrified soldiers that were guarding it with its malformed little teeth.

Rabbi Ba'al began an ancient chant as he held the old pot above his head. The homunculus began to get agitated as it pranced up and down along its glass enclosure. The creature tried to reach the open top of the aquarium, but its leaps were too short to get over the edge. The IDF soldiers glanced nervously with their Tavor assault rifles at the ready; they were under strict instructions not to kill the creature unless it had somehow got out of its pen. One soldier almost pulled the on trigger of his rifle but an IDF lieutenant spotted him in time as he pushed the rifle's barrel upwards to the sky as he tried to calm the terrified guard down.

As the rabbi continued his chant, the wind started to pick up as black storm clouds began to form above the town. The gusts of wind began to dissipate the incoming sandstorm as the water vapor in the air latched onto the dust particles and pulled them down into the sandy ground. A few more minutes passed as the rabbi's chants became louder while the entire scene began to reach a fever pitch.

Suddenly, everyone was startled by the multiple cracks of thunder overhead as Rabbi Ba'al let out a shout while throwing the ceramic pot into the aquarium. The pot shattered as it impacted right beside the homunculus. A strange red and greenish mist emanated from the broken pottery shards as it surrounded the little creature. The homunculus let out a shrill scream that terrified everyone as its body began to somehow shimmer and transform itself into a grey mist that melded with the gas that was already in its enclosure. Within moments, all that remained within the glass pen was a swirling, multicolored mist that resembled a miniature tornado.

Rabbi Ba'al raised his arms up to the sky. "Now, I command you to banish the sandstorm! Release your power! Now!"

At that moment, the miniature tornado smashed through its glass confines as it flew upwards into the sky. The strange, swirling vortex soon met up with the storm clouds above the town as the whole phenomena began to transform into a mile high, twisting tornado that seemed to be confined to the upper atmosphere. Even though they were a veteran IDF unit, a number of soldiers panicked and had to be restrained by their squad leaders.

General Ali had been watching the whole event through the video monitor. His eyes were as wide as saucers. "May Allah protect us!"

"Stage one of the operation is successful. Proceed to stage two," Colonel Tzur said to one of the radio operators who almost instantly relayed it.

General Seigel said nothing. Now it all depended on that crazy rabbi of theirs.

The tornado swirling above the town began to pick up in intensity as it started to move towards the incoming sandstorm. Within less than a minute, the two gargantuan weather anomalies collided as the mystical forces on both sides began a titanic struggle to control the skies above. The dust clouds were much larger, as the meteorological phenomenon stretched across the entire region and had been steadily expanding for the past several months, but the gigantic tornado was more concentrated as it swept through the edges of the dust storm. Even though the swirling clouds of sand seemed to have a mind of its own as it attempted to break past the tornado, the violently rotating column of air soon overcame the more dispersed masses of dust and swept it all aside as the skies around the town began to clear.

David Zim could see clearly now as his remote cameras observed the enemy that were once hidden behind the rapidly dissipating dust clouds. "Enemy contact at grid one-one, seventy-five-four. Call it in."

The Mossad radio operator began to rapidly relay the coordinates back to the town headquarters.

Omri was using his binoculars as he peered just outside of the window. The enemy was less than a mile away from their observation post. He prayed that they would not be detected.

The horde of creatures looked like an army from hell as they advanced across the open desert and headed towards to the town. Wild-eyed men rode in commandeered M1A1 Abrams and T-72 battle tanks that had once belonged to the now defunct Syrian and Iraqi armies. Human fighters wearing a hodgepodge of clothing and carrying assault rifles were advancing beside gigantic hybrid creatures that had the bodies of winged bulls but with the heads of bearded madmen. Thirty-foot tall giants wielding gargantuan stone clubs towered over their smaller counterparts as little imp-like creatures darted back and forth within the ranks of monsters and men.

Over at the command tent, General Siegel made a silent prayer of thanks as he saw that the skies were clear and he immediately nodded to his aide.

Colonel Tzur placed a hand on the shoulder of his most trusted radio operator. "Stage two successful. Initiate Stage three … now!"

David Zim's colleague, who had been manning the portable radio in the farmhouse, immediately jerked his head up. "Hand of God has been initiated! Air strike will commence in less than a minute."

"Everybody, take cover," David said calmly as he put down the mini laptop on the table before crouching down with the others in the makeshift foxhole they had dug in the middle of the room before placing a lead-lined tarp over themselves. All four men closed their eyes as they scrambled to put on their CBRN suits.

A pair of Israeli F-16s flew in a lazy circle over Al Zarqa, less than 20 miles away when a radio message was relayed to them. Almost immediately, both fighter bombers banked eastwards and went to full afterburners while arming their special payloads. Each F-16 had been modified by the Israelis over the years to maximize their strike role capability.

Within less than a minute, both fighter bombers had already sighted the advancing horde and were beginning their bombing run as they initiated a high angle of attack right at the center of the enemy army. Without warning, the enemy somehow detected them. Winged creatures of all shapes and sizes flew out from the edges of the surviving dust clouds and began to close with them.

One of the F-16 pilots started to panic as he saw the swarm of flying monsters bearing down on them at impossible speeds. He immediately banked right at full throttle in an attempt to evade their attacks. A winged griffon with a lion-like head smashed through the fighter's cockpit while a second monster tore off its wing. The lead F-16 tumbled out of the sky.

The remaining F-16 did not waver as it continued its angle of attack. The pilot of the aircraft had sensed that this would be a one-way trip so he maintained his calm and waited for his counterpart to initiate the release of the weapon. Sitting in the back seat of the F-16 was the weapons systems officer, who coolly looked at his heads up display as he finally found the right coordinates for the target. Just as the swarm of creatures got to within a few feet of the aircraft, it was able to detach its bomb. The single black lozenge-shaped object barreled through the air and fell right into the middle of the enemy ground troops below. The pilot and his weapons officer never got to see the bomb land on its target as their aircraft was torn to shreds in midair a split second after release.

For a few tense moments, there was silence as David Zim opened his eyes and noticed that they were still underneath the protective tarp covering the foxhole. "Did any of you guys hear anything?"

Benny, his radio operator, kept looking at his wristwatch. "It's been over two minutes. The bombing run should have been over already."

Omri looked around at the edge of the tarp as he kept his rifle on the ready. "Did it go off?"

"Wait here," David said as he stood up, pushed the tarp aside and scrambled back up to the floor of the room. As he looked out of the broken windows of the farmhouse, he could still see the horde of creatures.

Benny was the second person to lift himself out of the foxhole. "What happened?"

David had taken off his gas mask and was looking at his remote video display once again. "Radio HQ, tell them the weapon did not go off. Repeat, the weapon did not detonate. Reason unknown at this time."

The communications officer at the command tent in Qasr Al-Hallabat listened in on his headset for a few seconds before turning to look at the general. "Sir, observation posts confirm that at least one bomb was dropped onto the enemy positions but it failed to detonate. Reason unknown."

General Siegel cursed. The 20-kiloton nuclear bombs they had dropped onto the army of creatures had somehow failed to explode. What could have caused this?

General Ali crossed his arms. "Now what?"

Colonel Tzur sighed as he subconsciously kept a hand on the pistol in his side holster. "Now we fight."

General Siegel said nothing as he just nodded. Now it would be up to the troops they had defending the town and that damned rabbi. It was all out of his hands as he made another silent prayer now that his junior officers would be in charge leading the troops. He hoped that their discipline and training would prevail and would enable them to fight on.

As the horde of monsters and men began to advance only a few miles from the town, more than a hundred wire-guided missiles flew out from specially prepared positions and impacted their front ranks. Within seconds, more than three dozen enemy tanks were burning from the initial salvo. The horde refused to waver however, as they kept on advancing as more missiles were being fired at them.

Less than a minute later, over a dozen Apache gunships popped out of the open from their hiding places behind the town buildings and began to use rockets, missiles, and machine guns in a desperate attempt to cause as much damage to the enemy ranks as possible. In addition to the helicopter gunships, the Jordanians had several batteries of M114 Howitzer artillery pieces that began to fire at their pre-designated kill zones as the Babylonians advanced right into them. The army of monsters took a lot of casualties as great gouges began to form in the front and middle of their ranks, but they kept on coming as their own contingent of flying creatures began to engage the helicopters. The Apache gunships by this time had largely run out of ammunition and were forced to evade the swarms of winged creatures trying to bring them down. Sheer numbers prevailed as one by one, the helicopters were either driven into the ground or they retreated westwards at full throttle. By the time the air battle was over, only a pair of Apaches had survived and were on their way back to Amman for repairs and rearming. Many of the artillery crews manning the Howitzers were killed when the swarms of flying creatures descended on them, now that the helicopters were out of the picture.

Deprived of their air support, the IDF task force and the Jordanians began to use their main battle tanks from prepared positions as the horde of monsters reached the town's outer defensive perimeter. Israeli Merkavas fought side by side with modified Jordanian Challenger tanks as the battle was now hand to hand. Ground troops situated in bunkers began to use machineguns, grenades, and rifle fire to fend off the seemingly endless swarms of monsters and enemy humans who had joined in with the enemy. Thousands of prepared land mines detonated as the creatures seemingly walked right through where they lay without any sense of fear. Within minutes, the entire town was surrounded by a massive horde of supernatural creatures and attacks began to occur from all sides.

Rabbi Elijah Ba'al saw the things flying above him. That meant that the enemy had now penetrated the town's defenses and they were about to be overrun. He calmly remembered the words to the incantations that he had prepared for this very occasion. Now it all depended on him.

The rabbi raised his hands into the air as the screams and gunfire raged all around him. "Arise, protectors of the chosen people! Arise and fight!"

At that moment, there was a rumbling all around them as if there was an earthquake out in the middle of the desert. Both men and monsters hesitated for a brief instance as the unexpected erupted.

It was then that the earth shook as if the soil all around them was being tilled by the gods themselves. Gigantic hands made of hardened clay clawed their way out from underneath the ground as the newly created golems broke through the sands and concrete streets surrounding the town. Looking like hulking gorillas made of hardened clay, these massive creatures now joined in the battle.

Rabbi Ba'al's eyes were now glowing with a strange fire as he screamed from the top of his lungs, commanding the creatures he had created from clay and the essences of his prisoners. "Fight the enemy, my golems! Fight them and destroy them all!"

The battle was now joined. Both the Israelis and the Jordanians hesitated and nearly wavered as they saw a new horde of clay monsters bearing down on them. But soon, their newly found fears turned into hope as they renewed their courage and fought side by side with the golems. A large number of the flying creatures were thrown to the ground and trampled over by the golems as they ignored the fangs and claws that scratched at them. Several squads of IDF soldiers began to use their golem allies as both cover and as battering rams while they maneuvered and fought behind the construct's protective clay bodies. Two dozen giants from the enemy horde were able to smash a few of the golems with their massive clubs, but they were taken down by accurate sniper fire from Israelis and Jordanians stationed on the rooftops. It took awhile to hit the monster's brains with their aimed shots since they were so much smaller compared to the size of the gigantic heads they were encased in.

It had now descended into a swirling melee as both sides threw everything they had into the town. The defenders were taking enormous casualties, but the monstrous horde incurred even greater losses as they seemingly fought without tactics or subterfuge. The golems targeted the most powerful of the enemy beasts as they fought the lamassu and the griffons to a standstill, while the defending soldiers were busy shooting at their human counterparts. Slowly but surely, the tide of battle began to turn as the golem reinforcements began to beat back the horde.

One of the giants in the outskirts of town made a shrill whistle and then turned around as it started to run back across the desert. Pretty soon, the rest of the monstrous swarm had begun to retreat towards the safety of the dust storms in the distant horizon. As the fighting began to die down, loud cheers began to emanate from the surviving troops.

General Siegel wiped the blood from his forehead as he surveyed the wrecked command tent. Two of the flying creatures tore through the HQ and the command staff was forced to defend themselves. General Ali and Colonel

Tzur were both lying dead on the ground, having fought till the bitter end.

Two Jordanian medics came over and began to administer first aid to the survivors. General Siegel waved them away when they asked if he needed assistance. His head had a vicious cut from the claw of the flying thing that tore Colonel Tzur's head off, but he had killed the creature with his pistol. Within minutes after it had died, the dead creature's corpse had somehow shriveled up into a pile of dust that got carried away by the slight breeze in the wind. It was like black magic.

An IDF major came running into the area, the barrel of his Tavor assault rifle was still smoking after prolonged use. "General, Colonel Livni reports that the enemy has withdrawn back into the sandstorm out in the distance. Should we pursue?"

"Negative," General Siegel said softly. "I don't think we have enough men left to do that. Do you have a casualty report?"

The major handed him a clipboard. "Yes sir. We took casualties but those golems turned the tide for us. This is the first battle that I know of that the humans have won! Israel is saved!"

General Siegel looked around sullenly while glancing at the numbers on the report. The defenders had taken over sixty percent casualties and their air support and artillery were all but gone, along with most of their armored fighting vehicles. The special Golem Brigade had also taken serious losses and was down to less than a quarter of its original strength.

This was supposed to be a victory?

13. The Wendigo

Greater Boston

It was half past midnight and Dr. Paul Dane lay awake in his bed. As he sat up, he looked to his left and noticed that the two children were fast asleep on the bedroom floor. He had tried to prepare one of the spare rooms so that they could use it, but Kim and Troy had insisted on sleeping in the same room as him. Both kids lay huddled in a mass of thick blankets and pillows that served as a makeshift sleeping bag. Even as she slept, Kim seemed to be subconsciously holding onto her brother as her arms were wrapped protectively around him as she snored softly.

Paul silently placed his socked feet onto the floor as he took the flashlight from the night table beside the bed. As he got up, he put his glasses on and slowly made his way over to the window so as not to disturb the kids. He flipped the switch on the handheld flashlight as he pointed it down to the floor. The artificial beam of light had started to dim and he had no more spare batteries left so he turned it off. There were perhaps a dozen candles left around the house and there was still the old kerosene lantern so he only used the flashlight as a backup now. The few days that had gone went by slowly. There was still plenty of firewood to scavenge since the neighborhood was all but abandoned now. The last trip to the food bank had been a grim affair since there seemed to be only a handful of volunteers left. There were even less people who came over to get what little of the food packages that

139

remained. Paul frowned in the darkness as he remembered that the car had maybe a quarter tank of gas left. In a few weeks, he would need to either siphon gas from some of the abandoned cars in the area, or he would have to start walking if he needed to get around.

A muffled thump coming from the outside made Paul instinctively look out of the window. Right across the street was his neighbor, Clinton Taylor who had apparently just closed the trunk of his car before getting into the driver's seat and then starting it up. Paul noticed that Clint always seemed to have plenty of gas for his car because this was the fifth time in a row that he noticed him going out for a drive in the middle of the night. Last evening, Paul had stayed awake to observe and it was only at the crack of dawn that Clint's car had finally pulled up in his driveway. Where had he been going to at night?

There was a growing sense of foreboding about this whole place. His old neighborhood didn't feel the same way anymore. It wasn't just the country being in a state of siege from the Aztec gods in the southern borders, it felt like the nation was collapsing in on itself. He had heard about the religious secessionists in Kansas over the radio and of the flooded areas of the southeastern states and it all seemed to be coming to a head. Paul was beginning to regret leaving New York City, especially when the one person who understood him was still there.

That was the moment when he decided it would be best to leave for Brooklyn tomorrow. He would take the kids with him since it was obvious that their parents were probably dead. Detective Valerie Mendoza would welcome him with open arms.

But there was still one thing that bothered him about being where he was. It was the mystery about Kim and Troy's missing parents. What had happened to them? Would the kids go with him to New York without the peace of mind of knowing what happened to their parents?? Could he leave them behind if they chose instead to stay and wait it out for a little while longer? He knew he had to find the answers because it was bothering him too.

Paul slowly made his way over to the master bathroom and put on a pair of slacks over his thermal underwear. After putting his soft walking shoes on, he slowly took a thick jacket from the coat hanger and slipped into it as he made his way to the door. He glanced at the kids one last time before closing the door behind him. Then he made his way to the ground floor of the house. The dying embers from the fireplace were still visible as Paul opened the front door and peeked outside. As expected, there was no one around.

Paul left the house as he silently made his way to the front of Clint Taylor's home. Unlike Paul's residence, Clint's place was an A-frame, colonial style three-storied home made almost entirely of wood. It had an elevated front porch with white picket fences and its surrounding walls were painted grey with white trim. The tall, narrow windows seemed to have been covered up from the inside. As he slowly made his way up to the porch, Paul tried the knob on the front door but it was evidently locked. He tried to peer through the windows, but the pulled blinds were impossible to see through. As he made his way around to the back of the house, Paul kept hoping he was wrong in suspecting his neighbor was up to something, but he was almost certain that something just wasn't right with him and he had to make sure.

He had known Clint for years, almost two decades in fact, but from the moment he had returned, he had sensed that his old friend was no longer the man he had known for all that time. Paul had gone over to his house a few days back and asked about Clint's wife Donna to see if there was anything he could do, but his old neighbor was evasive and told him not to worry. Just by talking to him, Paul felt that the old neurologist was hiding something. Clint just wasn't a very convincing liar and it was clear something was wrong with Donna but he refused to reveal what it was.

As he made his way to the back door, Paul remembered Donna. Clint's wife was more of the quiet type. She had been working as an accountant for Harvard University but she mostly kept to herself and would only come alive when she and her husband were watching baseball games. Beyond that, he didn't know much else about her other than the fact that she once had been a nun and was deeply religious. Donna had been a frequent volunteer in the local church when it came to all sorts of activities. After his return from New York, Paul would sometimes hear distant screaming from Clint's house in the middle of the day. Kim was apparently so scared of the woman, she steered clear of the house every time she needed to walk past it. The only thing that Clint mentioned was that Donna had somehow become unhinged when the old gods returned. She had seemingly lost her mind and her will to live and he was treating her as an invalid. Paul felt that more could have been done but with the country in crisis, it would be impossible to find a psychologist who would be able to treat her..

When Paul finally twisted the knob on the back door, it opened with a slight squeak. Clint must have apparently forgotten to lock his rear door but with the area pretty much deserted, he probably felt secure enough to not even bother with it. As he pushed at the inner screen door, Paul slowly made his way inside while turning on his flashlight.

The back door had led into the kitchen and it was a mess. The once gleaming stainless steel countertop was stained in a deep brown. Paul noticed that there was a pile of dirty chef knives in the sink. The table in the center of the kitchen seemed to have deep groves along its grimy top and there were two cleavers lying side by side on it. The whole place smelled of rotting meat.

Paul silently cursed to himself as he shook the flashlight to try to get some more power out of it as its beam of light started to get dimmer. He had admonished Troy a few days ago when he noticed that the boy had been keeping the flashlight on for almost the entire night. After that, he always kept it by his side. Paul felt a pang of regret as he made his way through the narrow corridor that led to the living room. Troy couldn't speak and the last thing he wanted was to tell him off, but he did.

As he passed by a slightly opened door that led to a study, Paul noticed a number of things lying on the mahogany desk. He pushed the door inwards a little bit further so he could slip inside. There seemed to be a curious collection of old leather wallets and ladies handbags sitting at the top of the table. Paul stood behind the desk and picked up one wallet in particular then he started to examine it. The wallet contained a driver's license that belonged to a certain Alexander Fisher as well as a credit card. As he went through a few other wallets, the hairs at the back of Paul's neck began to rise. What happened to the people who owned these things? After examining over two dozen that belonged to different people from all walks of life, Paul started to rummage through the handbags.

As he looked through the second handbag, Paul let out a soft gasp. This particular one was black leather and it had a driver's license that belonged to Kim's mother. The rest of the contents consisted of a tube of lipstick, some coins, a silk handkerchief, a cell phone and a small picture of the entire family. It looked like a selfie picture taken in a water park; Kim and Troy were making faces as their smiling parents posed right behind them.

"I'm sorry," a voice said from across the room.

Paul dropped the photograph and shined the flashlight in front of him. Standing in the doorway was Clint Taylor. He still wore his dark blue suit and he had a cleaver in his hand. Paul said nothing as he looked around for a weapon.

"Look, Paul, we've been friends and neighbors a long, long time and I never had any intention of ever hurting you," Clint said calmly. "But you've got to understand my predicament."

Paul was breathing in short, nervous gasps. "And what predicament is that?"

Clint looked down on the floor. "Donna. My wife. She hasn't been well and this is the only way to keep her from transforming into one of those things out there."

Paul shook his head in disbelief. "What things, Clint?"

Clint sighed. "Come on, Paul. You're a world famous expert on mythology. I've read all your books. Heck, you even gave me free copies of them. Don't you remember the myth of the Wendigo?"

"The Wendigo?"

"Yes, you remember? The old Indian legend?"

"An evil, beast-like spirit that can transform into a man or some half animal monster," Paul said. "Legend says that anyone who eats human flesh can turn into one."

"Precisely," Clint said. "When this whole thing started, heck, people are now calling it the Glooming from what I've heard. Anyway, when it started, Donna became quiet and stopped eating. For weeks, I tried to figure out what was wrong with her but she just withdrew into herself. By this time the hospitals were full to bursting and I couldn't find a psychologist to treat her. Then I thought it may have been a seizure disorder or some other brain dysfunction but none of her symptoms fit so I figured it must have been some sort of mental illness. Then she started getting hysterical and violent. It all came to a head when Rachel from next door came in for a visit one evening."

"Rachel S-Sandborn?"

"Yes, our good 'ol neighbor, the one who had a husband in the oil business. Rachel came over to ask a favor, I don't even remember the details anymore. I only left them alone for a few seconds while I went upstairs to get something from my bedroom closet. The next thing I knew, there were screams coming from downstairs so I hurried back to the living room. Donna had torn her throat out and was taking huge chunks of flesh from her throat and shoulders. By the time I was able to get my wife off of her, Rachel was dead."

Paul didn't answer. All he could think about was that he would be Clint's next victim. He just stood there as he kept pointing the flashlight at him.

"I couldn't bring her to the cops. She was my wife and I still love her dearly," Clint said softly. "When the whole world is breaking down, all you've got left is family. Do you know what I mean?"

"Clint, I—"

"No, you don't know what I mean because your wife is dead. But if she was alive and she did this, would you have let them take her away? And since law and order had broken down they would probably kill her in the end since there aren't any more jails that are still going or any treatment centers out there anymore. Would you have let them do that to Elizabeth?"

Paul kept quiet.

"No, of course you won't answer because you haven't been in my shoes, Paul," Clint said. "So I did what I had to do, I got rid of Rachael's body and tried to cover it all up. But then her husband came snooping around the next day. So you can guess what happened then."

"You killed him too?"

"I had to do it. If he found out, that would have been it," Clint said softly.

Paul realized that his old friend had gone insane. "How?"

"Oh, just led him down the cellar to meet Donna. She distracted him and I smashed his head in with a hammer. He was a good man, we went sport fishing together a few times. It was the hardest thing I ever had o do," Clint said wistfully. "And before I could dispose of his body what does Donna do? She starts to eat him before he's even cold! I couldn't bear to watch so I just walked back upstairs and locked the basement door behind me. The next day, she sort of comes back to normal."

Paul was incredulous. "Normal?"

"Normal in that she didn't get violent and was pretty docile. Then she started to get hungry again. I told myself I couldn't kill anybody else and so I built a cage downstairs to keep her in. But then she started to change."

"Change?"

"Yeah. She grew thinner. Her rib cage started to show and her eyes became hollow. Her gums started to receded and her nails got longer. She started screaming and howling so much, the other neighbors started to notice. That's when I dug up Rachel's corpse to feed her with because she wouldn't eat anything else. And you know what?"

Paul tried to keep a straight face. "What?"

"She got better! Yes, she did. Her features began to switch back to normal. It was like she could somehow transform into something like a normal person if I could just keep feeding her human flesh. I began to experiment. I needed to find out the length of time she needed when it came to eating before she would change again. From my estimations now, it seems she needs to consume either an adult-sized body or two kids every three days or else she undergoes the metamorphosis."

"What happens if you wait too long?"

"Something terrible happens," Clint said. "It seems she gets thinner and gets taller.. She gets more violent and stronger so unless I allow her to feed, she could break out of the cage I built for her downstairs. If she keeps transforming, she could end up on the loose and could wipe out the rest of the city."

Paul raised his other hand in a gesture of peace. "Then we need to find a way to neutralize her, Clint. If she's been infected with the spirit of the

Wendigo, then she's already dead and it's too dangerous to keep her around."

Clint shook his head violently. "Kill my wife? No, no, no. She's all I got left. Can't you see that? The world is dead to me and she's all I got left!"

"She's already gone too," Paul said softly. "How many more people have to die? You know the Wendigo myth, that creature will never be satiated. It will just keep on eating and it will never stop."

"No! I don't believe you! There must be a way to cure her! We just have to hang on!"

"How did you kill Kim's parents?"

Clint looked at him quizzically. "Who are you talking about?"

"The kids, the ones who live in the blue house down the street! You must have killed so many people that you can't even remember them anymore!"

Clint thought about it for a brief minute. "Oh, them- they were the last ones I killed. They were a couple that I saw over at the food bank. I recognized them as our neighbors so I walked over and told them that I'd found a huge cache of food in one of the houses that was untouched and I invited them to share it with me. They seemed so trusting, I thought it was going to be easy but in the end it was so hard because they were so kind. I almost didn't go through with it."

"And yet you tried your best to cover it all up afterwards," Paul said. His friend was truly lost now and he pitied him. "You even drove their car and ditched it a few blocks away."

"H-How did you know that?"

Paul straightened his back and thrust out his chin. His fear began to subside and it was replaced by a growing sense of anger. "Their kids are staying with me. I looked for their parents and found the car. That's when I found this." He pulled out the Red Sox pendant from his pocket and threw it at his neighbor.

The pendant hit Clint on his shoulder and fell down on the floor. He bent over and picked it up with his left hand and he carefully held it up in front of his face. "Oh yeah, I lost this some time ago as I remember. This was Donna's and she always wore it on her blouse when we attended the games. I-it must have slipped out of my pocket when I was cleaning their car out."

Paul was adamant in his resolution. He needed to be stopped. Now. "This can't go on, Clint."

Clint was glassy eyed. "Yes, it's gotta keep going. I'm sorry, but my wife has to come first. We just have to hold on until it's over and then I can get some proper treatment for her."

Paul snorted. "So the kids in my house, are you going to kill them too?"

Clint's chin began to tremble. "I don't know if I can. I've never killed kids. But I think I'm going to have to. I think we can make it painless for them. Help me, Paul. They must trust you by now. Donna hasn't eaten in over a week and I'm afraid she could break out of that cage anytime now. I'm asking you as a neighbor and as an old friend. Help me with Donna and I'll do anything you want, I promise."

"You've gone nuts," Paul said. "This is all so insane!"

Clint looked away. "Will you help me, Paul? Please? I-I am not going to ask again. I'm begging you for the last time. Just say yes, please."

Paul grimaced. "No! I'm not a killer!"

Clint sighed as he tightened his grip on the cleaver. "Nothing personal, then. You were a friend and I will always consider you one. But my wife needs to feed. And I choose her well being over the rest of the world."

Paul panicked, and moved to the side of the desk, dropping the flashlight on the floor as Clint advanced on him. As Clint tried to get around the office table, Paul got behind the tall leather chair and pushed it against him. Clint screamed as he got pinned to the wall of the office and swung the cleaver, which caused a big gash on Paul's upper left arm just below his shoulder. Paul screamed in pain and had to let go of the chair as Clint pushed it aside and lifted the cleaver high over his head for a downward strike.

"For Donna!" Clint screamed at the top of his lungs as he swung the cleaver down, toward Paul's head.

Paul was able to get both hands on his neighbor's arm and the cleaver stopped inches away from his forehead. Clint kept screaming his wife's name over and over again, as if to give him strength for what he had to do as he pushed forward and both men fell on top of the desk.

As the two of them struggled, Clint's screams soon attracted a high pitched wail coming from the basement of the house that began to steadily get louder.

Paul gasped as he was pinned on his back while lying on top of the table. His neighbor was a heavyset man and he used his bulk to hold Paul down on the desk. Paul had both his hands gripping the wrist that held the cleaver and was barely keeping the heavy chopping blade from gashing his head. Clint kept on screaming as his other hand kept Paul's head in place for the mortal blow.

With his eyeglasses somewhere on the floor below, Paul groaned as Clint's fingers dug into his face as his neighbor kept his head pinned down on top of the desk. His strength was slowly draining away, and his arms were numb as the cleaver inched closer. With one final effort, Clint shifted the strength of his arm and brought the razor-sharp cleaver down to Paul's shoulder instead as he started slicing through Paul's winter jacket and began to draw blood.

Paul screamed in pain. With an animal-like desperation, the mythology professor used his teeth to clamp down on one of Clint's fingers that was pushing on his face and bit into it with all the strength his jaw could muster. Clint howled in pain as Paul nearly tore his finger off, and he instinctively pulled his hand away from Paul's face. Paul instantly pushed out with his forehead and head butted his neighbor on the chin.

The counter-attack was so ferocious that Clint moved back, stunned at the blow on his forehead as he became disorientated. Paul knew he had to finish this before his crazed neighbor could recover as he grabbed a granite ornament from the office desk and smashed it across Clint's head. His neighbor staggered a bit as he dropped the cleaver, but the second and third blows from the stone ashtray in Paul's hand finally took him out of the fight as he fell backwards and crashed in a heap on the floor.

Paul groaned as he clutched his shoulder in pain. As he looked at his arm he noticed that the gash didn't cut too deeply; he would recover but stitches might be needed to close the wide cut. As he stood there trying to recover his wits, a loud grating noise like the screeching of metal began to reverberate from the door leading to the basement. Within seconds, he was startled by a loud banging noise and an even more powerful scream coming from the basement just down the corridor.

ended in razor sharp claws. The creature's feet seemed to have been human once but now it seemed to have arched upwards into hoof-like protrusions, like that of a deformed deer's. Its worst aspect was its face, which resembled like a cross between a human being and a moose. A pair of small antlers seemed to be growing from the side of its head while its long, tousled hair resembled a lion's mane. The creature turned its snout upwards to the night sky and bellowed at the full moon above it.

Both children screamed. Paul kept pulling at Clint's shoulders as he started to drag him to the edge of the open door. "Get in the house now!"

The kids ran inside first and helped him get his neighbor past the door sill as the Wendigo began to charge forward at them. Paul gritted his teeth as he pulled Clint in further so he could get the door closed before the monster could reach them.

They finally got Clint's legs through the door just as the Wendigo made it to Paul's front porch. Troy reached into his pocket and threw a handful of pennies and quarters at the creature's face just as it started to poke its head in through the open door. The Wendigo howled in frustration, and it took a step back while brushing aside the coins from its bloodshot eyes just as Paul and Kim finally closed the front door and pushed the deadbolt in place.

Paul let out a brief sigh as he sat behind the door while trying to recover his breath. All of a sudden there was a loud crash as the front door nearly buckled but somehow held. He quickly got back up and started to drag the leather sofa to help barricade the entrance. The door continued to take a ferocious hammering as the creature outside screamed to get in.

Kim quickly ran behind one end of the couch and she started to help him push it into place as the relentless pounding on the door continued. "Oh my god! What is that thing?"

Paul gritted his teeth as they both pushed the sofa right behind the door. "It's a Wendigo. An evil Indian spirit that's cannibalistic."

Kim was wild eyed. She seemed almost hysterical. "W-What are we gonna do?"

The creature outside let out a roar of rage as it failed to get through the door and then everything became quite all of a sudden. The only thing all three of them heard was Clint's groaning as he stirred on the floor.

Paul knew that the ordeal wasn't over. He quickly looked around before pointing at the smoldering embers of the fireplace. "Get that fire started again, hurry!"

Kim ran over to the logs that they had placed beside the hearth. "T-There's only half a dozen logs here! We left the rest of them outside, by the porch!"

"It will have to do," Paul said as he grabbed a bunch of the wooden logs and threw them into the fireplace before relighting it with kerosene and the lighter in his pocket. "We need to keep the fire burning until dawn."

Kim sobbed as she knelt down on the floor with a sense of resignation. "But we don't have enough firewood. The fire's only going to last for a few hours! We're all gonna die here!"

Paul grabbed her by the shoulders and looked into her eyes. "Nobody is going to die! Don't give up on me!"

At that moment, the window from across the room shattered as they all saw a pale, gangly arm burst through the window pane but it was stopped by the metal bars of the frame. Kim screamed again as Troy grabbed a small ceramic pot from the top of a coffee table and threw it at the monster's arm. The vase shattered as it hit the side of the monstrous limb and the Wendigo withdrew it back with a frustrated roar.

Clint's groans had turned to coughing. It seemed that he was starting to regain consciousness. Paul quickly ran over to a standing floor lamp and tore out the electrical cord that was attached to it. He then quickly moved over to Clint's side as he began tying his neighbor's arms behind his back.

Kim had recovered somewhat as she stood up and looked at him. "What are you doing to Doctor Taylor?"

Paul made sure the knot he made on Clint's restraints was tight. "He tried to kill me. That Wendigo out there is Donna, his wife. He had been killing the people around here and feeding them to her."

Kim whimpered as she put two and two together. "D-Did he … kill my mom … and dad?"

Paul only nodded. A part of him felt that it was one shock too many for the kids to take, but he had a distinct feeling it was better to tell the truth now than hide it from them.

Kim screamed as she ran over to Clint and tried to hit him, but Paul got up and hugged her as she cried in his arms. Troy ran over to the fireplace and grabbed the poker as he tried to swing the hot metal rod at Clint, but Paul was able to knock it away as he took the little boy by the shoulder and held him tight as well.

For a brief moment, there was a sense of peace as the children kept crying in his arms and all Paul could hear was their pain and loss. His left arm felt numb but it was still functional. He needed time to think of a plan to escape but feared they were trapped. The car was right outside but it would be suicide to try and reach it with that monster on the loose.

As the children slowly began to relax, there was a loud crash coming from the kitchen. Kim let out a yell as Paul stepped away from them and ran into the kitchen area. The Wendigo had tried to smash through the back door but thankfully it too was locked tight. Paul gritted his teeth as he pushed the heavy wooden dining table to reinforce the back entrance.

With the help of the children, he barricaded the rear door was as well. Paul then moved over to the stove top and turned on two of the gas burners as he placed two large sauce pans on the counter. He quickly opened the cupboard and took out the remaining bottles of extra virgin olive oil that he had been storing and quickly poured their contents into the pans before placing them on the roaring burners.

Paul then turned to the two kids as he kept rummaging through the pantry. "Make sure all the windows upstairs are also locked tight. Go!"

Both Kim and Troy instantly turned and ran up the stairs. Paul kept trying to remember the things he had in the house that could be turned into some sort of weapon against the creature as he heard a loud crash and the children's screams coming from upstairs.

Paul quickly ran up the stairs. As he got to the corridor, he saw Kim backing out from one of the rooms.

Kim screamed as she pointed at the Wendigo smashing through the bedroom window. "It's t-trying to get in!"

The Wendigo had broken through the glass and was trying to twist the window latch from the inside in order to get in. Despite its savage nature, it still seemed to have some sort of rudimentary intelligence, which made it even more dangerous.

Paul noticed his umbrella by the side of the room and he grabbed it. He began thrusting it like a spear at the creature's arms as Kim kept screaming in terror. The umbrella's metal point scratched at the Wendigo's right arm and the creature made a grab at it as it bellowed.

As he kept trying to stab it with the pointed umbrella, Paul had an idea. "Get me the deodorant spray in the bathroom!"

Kim looked at him in disbelief. "What are you gonna do? Make it smell better?"

Paul grimaced as the creature got hold of his umbrella and the Wendigo snapped it in two with just one clawed hand. "Get it now or we're both dead!"

Troy ran into the bathroom, then reemerged holding the spray can of deodorant before placing it into Paul's hands. The mythology professor took out a lighter from his pocket and held it slightly in front of the spray nozzle just as the monster was able to unlock the latch on the window.

As the Wendigo started to push its head and shoulders through the window, Paul flicked the lighter on while spraying the creature's face with the deodorant. As the vaporized chemicals from the spray can flew past the lighter's flame, the mist instantly ignited as a jet of flame erupted from Paul's hands and right into the snarling face of the Wendigo.

The creature shrieked in pain as it was horribly burned while the curtains around it began to catch fire as well. The Wendigo backed out of the window and quickly disappeared away from sight. Paul hurriedly stamped out the flaming curtains. Then he twisted a wire hanger to reinforce the latch on the window before moving a large antique dresser as an additional barricade behind it.

"Do this to all the other windows as well," Paul said calmly to them. Kim stopped protesting as she dutifully obeyed, while he noticed that Troy's eyes had lit up as if he was some sort of hero to the boy. *Maybe he was finally coming out of his shell*, Paul thought.

As he propped up a shower rod on the folding door to the attic to keep it from opening downwards, Paul heard a loud, grating noise coming from downstairs. At that moment, the two kids joined him in the corridor.

It was then that he heard Clint's voice coming from the ground floor. "No more, Donna! Please!"

Paul ran down the stairs as the two kids followed. As he reached the foot of the stairs, he noticed Clint had somehow freed himself and had moved the barricade away from the front door. Before Paul could do anything, his neighbor unlocked the door and opened it.

The two children screamed as the Wendigo entered the house. Paul pushed them back up the stairs before turning to head into the smoke-filled kitchen.

As the creature that had once been his wife towered over him, Clint knelt down in front of it. He had a blank look on his bruised face. "I'm sorry, Donna," he said softly. "It's over now. Please, just take me and let's finish this."

Paul moved towards the blazing stovetops. The olive oil had reached its burning point and it had filled the entire kitchen with smoke. He instantly took the hand towels sitting on the countertop and wrapped it around his hands before grabbing the saucepot handles.

The creature snarled and quickly drove its snout into Clint's neck. Its razor sharp fangs began to chew through his jugular veins and windpipe. As he choked on his own blood, Clint tried to smile and think of the good times he had with her before he died. Just as the Wendigo gorged on her husband, Paul ran into the living room holding two pots of boiling oil.

As Paul swung his arms back to throw the oil, the creature looked at him. The Wendigo's mouth was covered in blood and entrails while its eyes sparkled and shimmered. For a brief moment, he saw that the creature had somehow transformed into the loving wife Clint was forever faithful to. Time seemed to stand still as Paul hesitated. The Wendigo seemed to look differently now as it seemed to have shrunk in size and its features became more human. He could see that the bloodshot eyes were no more and they now resembled Donna's deep brown pupils. It was as if Clint's wife had somehow wrestled control of her body from the beast that was inside of her.

But the moment soon passed and Paul could see that the creature standing in front of him had begun to transform back into a malevolent, supernatural entity once more. Out of the corner of his eye, he saw the two kids coming down the stairs and that was when the thoughts of their dead parents filled him with a sense of reality once more. With all his remaining strength, Paul threw the contents of both saucepans at the Wendigo.

The creature roared with pain as the smoldering oil covered most of its body. Its once pale skin glistened and began to blister as the oil burned through it. The Wendigo shrieked as it backed away into the living room. Paul followed as he dropped the pans and picked up the poker that was on the floor. As he swung the metal rod at the creature, it grabbed the side of the poker and tore it away from him. As Paul backed away, the creature tried to swing a claw at him but its eyes were still burning from the oil and it could hardly see so it missed.

As he tried to put some distance between them, Paul kept moving to make sure that the fireplace was beside him as he frantically looked around for another weapon. Just as the creature got close to the fireplace, Kim ran into the living room carrying a small white paper sack. As Paul tried to warn her away, she tore open the top of the pack and sprayed the Wendigo with a cloud of white powder. Paul realized it was white flour she had taken from the pantry. What happened next was totally unexpected. Part of the airborne white mist had touched the burning fireplace and it instantly engulfed the creature in flames as the dusty flour had ignited like gunpowder. Within seconds, the creature was screeching in terror as the fire had spread over its entire body, making it thrash around helplessly.

Paul grabbed the two kids by the arm as all three of them ran out of the house. Within minutes, the entire living room was on fire. Paul had taken the car keys by the front door mantelpiece as he ran out and they were now inside of the Volvo as Paul began to activate the ignition.

When the car finally started up a few seconds later, Paul shifted to reverse as he backed the car out from the front of the burning house. As the tires screeched, Paul accelerated as he drove the Volvo to the end of the block and then towards the highway on Boylston Street.

Kim calmly put on her seatbelt as she sat in the front passenger seat. "I saw a video about it on the internet. My science teacher in school told me the same thing. Flour dust is flammable."

Paul kept his eyes on the darkened street as he kept on driving. "Good to know."

Troy leaned forward from the backseat so that his face was in between them. "I don't know my way home."

Paul glanced at him briefly and smiled. "That's okay, I don't either."

14. Intolerance

Reverend Julius Jones adjusted his glasses before picking up the tray of plastic cups that were filled with water and fruit juice. He had been working non-stop for the past two days with hardly any rest, but he felt that this was the right thing to do. Julius made his way from the kitchen and headed for the nave. Just a few months ago, his parishioners numbered close to two thousand. As of last night, he figured there were now more than five thousand people he was giving aid and comfort to. Julius had taken over as lead pastor of this non-denominational Christian church over six years ago. He was only the second black priest in the church's history. The moment he started giving services, Julius's message stressed that everyone, regardless of what they did, was welcomed by God to his bosom and would be saved.

In his younger days, Julius had been involved with gangs and his own younger brother was killed in Chicago's south side. His father had had enough and brought the family over to Wichita a few months after that. His brother's death shocked him and under the tutelage of his grandmother, Julius had at last found salvation in religion as he wholeheartedly pursued his new calling as a priest. Every night, he would pray for his brother's soul and he would make a pledge to himself and to his god that he would never turn anyone away who would ask for help.

And so it came to pass that when the ancient gods revealed themselves to modern day society, and with so many of his parishioners were thinking that the Day of Judgment had finally arrived, Julius continued to stress calmness and the forgiveness of others. He lost many of his flock when hundreds of them packed up and left for the Rock of God Church in nearby McPherson County, but he continued to gain new adherents due to the fact he was willing to accept anyone. Pretty soon, a number of people from different faiths and even a few atheists began to work with him in order to stem the growing tide of intolerance as the Rock of God Church grew and eventually took over the city.

As he made it to the church nave, Julius noticed that the lights in the high ceiling had begun to flicker again. That meant that he might need to start the generator in order to provide auxiliary power, but he was worried they might not have enough gas left for the motor to run. Since he had converted the front of the chancel as a sort of distribution point, Julius walked over to the set of tables he had placed facing the nave and set the tray of water and juice cups on it. Julius and his volunteers had spent the past week moving the church pews to the side of the nave and that allowed the refugees to place their sleeping bags and mattresses in the center of the hallway. While some of his parishioners complained that the church nave was meant for services to the Eucharist and not as a sleeping area, he stressed to them that mass was not as important as sheltering the oppressed.

Michelle Kaplan, who was one of his volunteers, came through the entryway and ran up to him. She had winter gloves on and a scarf around her neck as a cold front was starting to move in. "Reverend Julius, there seems to be a convoy of cars that's coming down the street. I think it's the council."

Julius nodded as he adjusted his clerical collar. The so-called Morality Councils were a new creation by the Rock of God Church and they had the power to arrest anyone they deemed a "sinner". He had made sermons against their organization many times and he had a feeling that a reckoning was finally coming. "Tell all the volunteers to get ready. We need to get our people into the nave right now and hold each other's hands," he said softly.

As if on cue, the other volunteers began ushering in the people that were camped outside of the church and led them into the nave. The other refugees that had been sleeping on the floor of the church were being woken up as they all started to crowd the center. Julius reassured them as he shook a few nervous hands while walking over to the front of the vestibule. As more and more people flooded through the double doors, Julius continued to smile as he maintained a calm demeanor in order to prevent a panic. When the last of the refugees were helped inside, a half dozen of his volunteers stood beside him as they waited for the inevitable.

For a short minute, there was an absolute silence that hung over the nave, one so quiet one might hear the proverbial pin drop. But seconds later, the double doors leading to the outside were suddenly flung open as more than two dozen men dressed in tactical gear and carrying batons and transparent riot shields flooded the vestibule.

Reverend Julius smiled as he stepped forward and extended his hand. "Can I help you, gentlemen?"

One of the men in riot gear lifted up the transparent visor of his helmet as he walked up to Julius. He was fair-haired with a mustache. "You know why we're here, Reverend."

Julius just kept on smiling. "Art Davis, how nice of you to come by again. How is your family?"

Art shook his head. "I'm in no mood for small talk, Julius. Your church was declared to be unofficial almost a week ago by a unanimous vote from the Council. We gave you plenty of leeway and it looks like you've just abused our charity."

"Charity is an interesting word," Julius said. "It means giving help to those in need. And that is exactly what I am doing for these people. They needed help and I am giving it to them."

Art frowned. Just a few months ago he had been head of security for the Rock of God Church's compound up north, but he had been unceremoniously dumped in favor of that SWAT officer from Texas. Pastor Erik Burnley offered him a job in the Wichita Morality Council as a sort of goodwill gesture and he hated it. "You know as well as I do that we are an independent country now. We have new laws in place to ensure that everybody will be going to heaven when Jesus comes back. You know this."

"I am a believer in our Lord Jesus Christ just like the rest of you," Julius said softly. "But I believe that as long as people of different creeds ask for my help, I must give it to them. Our Lord would have done the same."

Art was starting to lose his patience. He didn't want a confrontation but he noticed that some of his men were obviously looking for trouble. "All these other creeds have been proven false, Reverend. Either you're with Jesus or you're with the devil. It's as simple as that."

"As I've told you, I am with Jesus and I am doing his work."

Art grimaced. "No, you're not! You are giving aid and comfort to the enemy!"

Julius waved his left hand to his side. "Look around you, Art. Are these people truly your enemy? They are human beings and they all deserve love and kindness."

Art waved an accusing finger at him. "You're wrong. You have got atheists and homosexuals as well as Jews and Muslims staying in this church of yours. They are not Christians and do not deserve to be in this country!"

"While I admit that we have some people of the gay persuasion here," Julius said. "Some of them also believe in Jesus Christ and they are therefore Christians as well. Jews and Muslims also believe in the same god as Jesus did, they are considered our brothers. As for the atheists, well, I believe that they can also be saved so long as they do no harm to anyone."

One of the other men wearing riot gear banged his baton on the shield he was holding. "Your kind doesn't belong in the country of Christian Kansas, you faggot loving nigger!"

Art held his hand up to calm his men before facing Julius again. "Look, let's be reasonable here. You were given days to vacate this church, and you could have taken all these people with you. The bottom line is you don't belong here with the true Christians anymore so why don't you just get going? I can give you some time, but you and all your followers must be out of here by this evening. Okay?"

Julius took a deep breath. "I appreciate you being diplomatic in this, Art, I really do. But me and my people have a right to stay as well. We're not bothering anyone. The fact is, we got nowhere else to go to. You know how the rest of the country is like. Just allow us to stay and I promise you, we won't cause any trouble."

A man stepped forward from the group of volunteers and stood beside Julius. He wore thin, steel rimmed glasses and a rumpled wool coat. "Art, you remember me don't you? I'm Janet Clancey's brother in law, Mike Thomas."

Art snorted in disgust. "I know who you are. I just can't believe you haven't converted yet. Where's Janet's sister?"

A woman walked to the front of the crowd and stood behind Mike. "I'm right here, Art," she said. "You can tell Janet that I'm standing here with my husband and I won't be leaving him."

Art rolled his eyes. "I can't believe this, Alice. You're a member of the Rock of God Church for chrissakes! What are you doing here with these gays and atheists?"

Alice held onto her husband's arm. "I don't want to be part of a church that discriminates against people just because they have a different religion or even if they don't have one. Can't you see that Erik has twisted the words of the Bible and is turning you people into animals?"

Another of the men in riot gear lifted up his visor and spat at their general direction. "Go to hell, you traitor. If you're not part of the One True Church then you're going down with the rest of them!"

Art held up his hand to his men for a second time. "Alright, everyone just calm down!"

But several of the Council members were raring to go as a few started to curse at the crowd while three others pointed their batons at the refugees as if they were marking their targets.

Julius held his arms up in a gesture of peace as he looked around. "Please, everyone, please! Let's all calm down here. We don't want any violence."

Art was getting agitated. The council had ordered him to either arrest the refugees or force their deportation. He was against the former but they were refusing to leave peacefully. "Julius, you need to leave and take all your people with you, this is your last warning. If you don't file out of here in a peaceful manner, we are going to arrest you and everybody else."

Several of the refugees got the message as a few dozen took what little possessions they had and started to make their way to the side doors. The majority of the crowd, however, sat down in the middle of the nave and locked their arms together.

Art's face was flushed. "Goddamn it, Julius. You're going to be responsible for what happens next."

"We have a right to be here," Julius said softly. "You can't force us out just because some people here have a different religion. We never even got a chance to vote if Kansas would secede or not. I'm sorry but we cannot follow a set of laws that was agreed upon by a church that promotes intolerance and bigotry."

Art pulled the transparent visor back down on his helmet as he signaled his men. "Alright boys, let's round them up!"

Alice was wild eyed. "You can't do this! No one but God can judge anybody else!"

Julius held up his hands as he knelt down. "No!"

Within seconds, the council troopers began pushing past the volunteers as they charged towards the sit-in at the nave. Alice and Mike Thomas attempted to hold hands with the others at the front of the crowd, but they were quickly beaten by men wielding truncheons. People began to scream as the troopers used their batons and the situation immediately descended into chaos. The side doors of the church began to open as additional troopers came in along with attack dogs that were barely controlled by their leashes. One Council member decided to just unhook the strap on his pit bull terrier. It immediately bit a screaming black woman in the arm and wouldn't let go.

Julius tried to get up and stop them but another trooper immediately hit him in the forehead with his baton before surging past him. The pastor fell backwards on the stone floor, blood streaming from the gash on his head. Mike attempted to protect his wife but he was beaten into a bloody pulp and he fell into a heap on the floor. Alice screamed as she tried to shield her fallen husband with her own body but was rapidly pushed aside.

Art used his shield to separate Alice as additional troopers came rushing through the main doors of the church. They had been friends before and Art was always invited to their parties. "Alice, stay down for God's sake!"

But Alice was in near hysterics as she saw them continuing to beat on her husband. "Mike! Miiike! No, they're killing him!"

As Art turned to see what the others were doing to Mike, Alice slipped past him to try and help her husband. Another trooper saw her coming and immediately smashed his truncheon on the ridge of her nose. Alice crumpled, the back of her head thudding on the tiled floor of the vestibule.

Art grabbed the other trooper by his collar. "Why did you do that? She was a member of ROG, goddamn it!"

The Council trooper pushed him away with his now bloody baton. "Shut up, Art. She's a traitor and she protected sinners. She got what was coming to her and her kind."

Art fumed as he knelt down beside Alice. She was barely conscious and coughing up blood. "Goddamn you! She was a woman! You just smashed her face in!"

The other guy merely shrugged as he walked past him to look for more people to beat on. "We're here to do our job, God will sort out the rest."

15. The Raven

Siberia

Since the crisis began, a strange weather pattern had developed all over Eastern Europe. Even though the fall season had barely started, the entire region was now only experiencing an average of three to four hours of daylight. It was as if the gods had somehow shifted the orbit of the Earth so that most of the day was now spent in either a gloom-filled twilight, or in the blackest of nights.

Ilya Volkhov crept out of his hiding place near the abandoned factory building as he squinted at the dying rays of the sun on his face. He had been on the run since yesterday afternoon. The night before, Private Anosov was able to smuggle him out of the military compound just a few miles away. There were a few times his pursuers had gotten close to him, but in the end he saw a team of four Spetsnaz commandos just walk past his hiding place. The soldiers were from the elite Alpha Group section and they even had a sniffer dog with them, but Ilya foiled the animal's scent by using a small container of black pepper to help cover his tracks. Anosov had given him the pepper shaker just before they had parted from the base perimeter and told him that he needed to use it against the dogs.

For a lowly private, he seemed pretty clever, Ilya thought as he just sat there near the rubble. The sun on his face was a blessed welcome, but he was just biding time until nightfall so he could rendezvous with Anosov at the address he had been given. As he silently observed the deserted, snow-filled streets from his vantage point, Ilya marveled at how quiet the city had now become. There was a time when all the children in the orphanage went out to see the museums around Novosibirsk and they encountered so many feral dogs; there were packs of strays on the loose all over the city back then. The boy had heard from his guards that all the dogs in the city had pretty much been rounded up and used for food, now that the convoys from Moscow had gotten less frequent. The situation became so acute, they said that not even pets were safe anymore. Ilya knew he was running out of time if he was going to fulfill his pledge to free his country from the clutches of the black god. If he didn't act against Chernobog soon, there wouldn't be any people left to save.

Ilya bit his lip as he thought about what to do next. Even though Private Anosov gave him an address to an old house where he could hole up in, he could not stay in there forever. He needed a plan to find out where Tara was and to try and rescue her. A goddess that he had met in the Otherworld had told him that he would need allies if he was to take on Chernobog, but the only friend he knew was Tara. If he was going to save Russia then he would need to get her back, but how?

That was when he thought about Tara's talking dog. It looked like nothing more than a little puppy even though it was fully grown. There was a growing doubt inside of him that felt that perhaps the dog was killed when they were abducted by the soldiers. If the dog was indeed dead, then how could he possibly make it back into the Otherworld, much less find Tara?

Ilya immediately turned and looked up when he heard a cawing noise out in the distance. Perched up on a broken lamppost about a half a mile away was a raven. It continued to caw for a bit before ruffling its feathers and then flew off. Ilya smiled. It was a raven that had somehow made it into the broken window of the supply room that had saved him the night before. Although he had been taught in school that ravens were bringers of bad luck, it seemed that every one of his recent encounters with those black birds had been doubly fortunate. The boy hoped that this latest encounter would bring him even more good fortune.

When the sun finally disappeared over the murky horizon and a twilight dusk settled onto the city once more, Ilya checked and made sure the street was deserted before making his way across. He had already crossed the bridge past the river and based on the handwritten map Private Anosov had given him, it looked like he was no more than a few blocks away from the rendezvous point.

Ilya noticed that a few houses in the block of nearby buildings still had people in them as he saw the faint, flickering candle lights from their windows. A few small chimneys still belched grayish smoke as the surviving people of the city were doing their best to stay alive. The boy moved deliberately as he sprinted from one cover to the next, making sure that the occasional car wouldn't notice him as he kept hiding in corners and alleyways.

His winter boots were muddy and starting to crack as he had been using them relentlessly for some time now. The fact that they were hand me downs from an older boy in the orphanage meant that they were old and he would need a new pair soon.

As he got close to his destination, Ilya noticed that it looked like a medium-sized factory building near the outskirts of a frozen park. There was a two-story building in the center and was connected to what looked like a pair of office bungalows. The main building had wooden sliding doors and it looked like a cross between a garage and a barn. As the boy moved closer, he noticed that there was some faint yellow light coming from the inside. A small chimney on the wooden roof gushed out a column of smoke.

The sliding door was ajar so he crept closer and peered inside. The floor within was concrete and there was a large crack that ran in the middle of it. At the far end of the hall was an old, rusting tractor. Near the side was an aged masonry stove with a fire burning in it. The tall stove radiated a comfortable heat that warmed Ilya's cheeks as he stared into the high-ceiling garage. As he continued to observe while crouching down near the edge of the entrance, Ilya noticed an old, heavy-set woman, bundled up in winter clothing, step out from a side door and walked over to the oven carrying two bowls.

Ilya hadn't eaten for almost a day and his stomach growled as he smelled the aroma of cooking coming from the inside. Since there didn't seem to be any soldiers about and this was the address that Private Anasov gave him, Ilya decided to reveal himself as he pushed at the door to widen its aperture so that he could step inside.

The old woman noticed him almost immediately but didn't betray a hint of emotion as he moved closer to the warmth of the stove. All she did was glance at him briefly before taking the lid of a pot sitting near the edge of the oven and using a ladle to stir its contents.

"Hello, I'm Ilya," the boy said as he stood a few feet away from the old woman. "My friend, Private Anosov, told me to come here."

The old woman had thick flushed cheeks behind an embroidered headscarf as she merely gestured at a wooden chair beside a nearby table. Ilya just stood there for a time but then he sighed and finally sat down. The old woman placed a bowl of steaming potato and cabbage soup in front of him along with a slice of thick bread.

"Thank you," Ilya said as a spoon was placed beside him so he picked it up and started eating. The hearty soup warmed his trembling body and sent a cascading sense of comfort that relaxed him. As he put the spoon down on the empty bowl, Ilya nearly burped out loud but he was able to place his hand over his mouth to stifle it. The old woman's stone-faced expression hardly changed at all as she placed a steaming mug of hot tea on the table and then took the bowl away.

As the boy started to sip the tea, there was a screeching noise that came from behind, surprising him. He instantly stood up and turned around. A middle aged man wearing a thick winter coat had gone through the entrance and then closed it again. He wore an ushanka, the traditional fur cap that had long ear flaps that he took off, revealing a bald head with wisps of grey hair on the sides of his scalp. The man smiled at Ilya as he held up a gloved hand in a gesture of peace. His face was gaunt and crisscrossed with wrinkles.

Ilya said nothing as he tensed up and got ready to run.

The man's smile widened into a buck-toothed grin. "You are the boy that my son said was coming here, yes?"

Ilya's brow was furrowed. "Your son? Who is your son?"

"Dmitri Anosov," the man said. "He is a private in the Forty-first Army here."

Ilya let out a sigh of relief. "Private Anosov? You are his father?"

The old man nodded. "Yes, I am Yuri. And you must be Ilya. Dmitri has told me a lot about you."

Ilya walked up to the old man and shook his hand. "I would like to thank you for your hospitality. I'm sure you know that I am on the run from the military."

"Yes, Dmitri told me as much and to prepare for your arrival," Yuri said as he walked over to where the table was. "Come and sit by the fire."

As Ilya sat down and finished his tea, the old woman served a second bowl of soup to Yuri. The old man placed his hat on the side of the table and looked at the boy closely as he started to eat. Even though he seemed agitated, Ilya was clearly exhausted as Yuri could see that the boy could barely keep his eyes open. The old woman had gone into one of the side doors and disappeared from sight.

The boy looked at the old man as he ate his meal. "What did your son tell you about me?"

Yuri bit off a piece of bread and swallowed it before spooning more soup in his mouth. "Nothing much, he simply told us that you were a very special boy. When I asked him why the authorities were keeping you prisoner, he simply stated that there was a rumor going around that you had somehow been to another world. A magical world, that is. And he said that you may hold the key to what is happening all over the country. Is that true?"

"I know things," Ilya said softly. "The weather is being controlled by Chernobog. He has my mother prisoner and I must rescue her."

Yuri nodded. "Ah, so that is what has happened. This is just like one of our folk tales, except that instead of a fair maiden on an adventure, it is a boy of about twelve that will be saving the day."

"I'm ten."

Yuri laughed. "Oh, I'm so sorry, remembering my own son as a boy was a long time ago, and so I am not very good at determining children's ages anymore. So tell me, boy, how are you going to save us against this god?"

"I'm not sure yet. I need the help of my friends."

"And who are these friends of yours?"

"One of them is a girl, an American, slightly older than me. The other is a talking dog. Though I don't think he really is a dog, but some sort of god."

"So you know of two gods already, that is remarkable."

"I've met two other gods while journeying into this Otherworld," the boy said. "I need the talking dog to bring me back there and then I will need to rescue my American friend."

Yuri arched his left eyebrow. "Rescue? Has she been abducted by Chernobog too?"

Ilya shook his head. "I don't think so. She was abducted by someone else, perhaps. But I know this dog can help me find her. All I need to do now is find the dog."

Yuri laughed. "You will have a hard time looking for dogs in this city right now! The people have been starving and the last street dog disappeared weeks ago. I have heard that many folks have even eaten their own pets."

"But this dog has a power. I doubt he would be eaten because it was no ordinary animal."

"Perhaps you are right. What does this dog look like?"

"A very little dog. Like a puppy, except that it is fully grown. Not much fur on its coat and it has very big ears. It was like one of those toy dogs that rich women carry around."

"Not much meat in a little toy dog like that," Yuri said as he finished off the last of his soup. "I can ask around but I doubt anyone would have seen it. If it doesn't have a thick coat of fur, it might have died from the cold already."

Ilya looked down. "I hope not. But I also think that because it is a god, it won't be harmed by the cold."

As soon as the boy said those words, there was a sound of a vehicle that stopped in front of the garage. Ilya instantly stood up while Yuri turned around and headed for the door. The boy slowly backed away towards where the oven was. Yuri opened a small viewing latch on the door before unlocking it and pushing it sideways. A large, heavyset man with a dark crew cut and black coat instantly stepped through the opened door. The man looked younger than Yuri and his clothes seemed to be made of better materials. Ilya could see an old van parked at the front from the opened doorway.

The boy stayed where he was when he saw the two men whisper to each other. The other man then walked over to where the table was. Just as Yuri was about to close the door, a black raven flew through the opening and flapped around the top of the ceiling for a short while before landing on top of the old tractor at the far end of the room.

"Looks like that bird was attracted to the warmth of the oven," Yuri said as he locked the bolt of the door into place. "I will probably catch it later. We haven't had much meat here in the past two weeks."

The other man looked up at the bird. "An old crow like that would taste horrible."

Yuri smiled as he walked back towards the table. "It's a raven. I've eaten a few of them before. If this winter keeps up, I may very well need the meat."

Ilya's curiosity won over his caution. "How can you tell the difference between a crow and a raven?"

Yuri sat back down on his chair. "Ravens have larger beaks, and they are curved. They also have pointed wings and a wedge-shaped tail. Crows are smaller birds with blunt wings and the caws they make have a higher pitch. I have lived near these woods for over fifty years and I can tell which bird is which just by a glance."

The other man kept standing as he looked at the boy. "You must be Ilya. I am Leonid. You asked for help, yes?"

Ilya nodded. "I just need some information and maybe a safe place away from the soldiers that are looking for me."

Yuri held up his arms. "You are safe here, lad. Nobody comes to this area. As far as the dog, you can tell Leonid all about it."

Ilya sat down beside the table and repeated what he had told Yuri a few minutes before. Leonid seemed to take it in slowly, but the boy was glad that they were taking his claims seriously.

After a few minutes of silence, Leonid looked up and stared at the boy. "I have a network of people around here. We could get you to Moscow so you could talk to my friends there."

Ilya frowned. "Why would I need to go to Moscow for?"

Without warning, Yuri reached over and grabbed the boy's wrist, pinning

A momentary fright seized him as he dropped the granite ashtray from his hands. Paul started to feel his way around the carpeted floor for his glasses. After a minute's worth of frantic searching, Paul's fingers triumphantly clasped the thin eyeglass frames as he stood up once more and put them back on. Right at that moment, he staggered in shock and surprise as he heard the noise of splintering wood coming from the basement door. Donna must have broken through her cage and was now trying to get out of the basement.

Paul was about to leave, when he saw that Clint began to stir his head, letting out a short groan as he lay stunned on the floor. Paul bit his lip and made a decision as he grabbed Clint by his shoulders and began to pull him out of the office and into the living room. As he dragged his neighbor past the darkened corridor, he saw that the basement door beside him was slowly giving way to whatever was inside.

Whether it was with the help of adrenaline or just sheer willpower, Paul was able to drag his neighbor out of the house as he closed the front door behind him before pulling at Clint's shoulders again. All he had to do now was to get him across the street. Just as he dragged Clint into the middle of the lane, the door to Paul's own house flew open and the two kids ran out to him.

"What's going on, Professor? I heard screams and crashing sounds," Kim said as she stood over him.

"Help me get him inside, quick," Paul said in between breaths as he kept on dragging his unconscious neighbor forward. Droplets of blood from his wounds fell on the street.

Troy instantly got beside Paul and started to pull as well. Kim sighed and got behind them as she grabbed Clint's legs and tried to pull them up so it would add less drag. But just as they made it to Paul's front porch, the door to Clint's house was violently ripped open and something tall and gangly stepped through as the three of them turned and looked.

It might have been human once, but now it was a creature from which the stuff of nightmares was made. It was close to eight feet tall and it had very thin arms and legs. One could see the exposed rib cage in its emancipated torso just underneath the creature's withered breasts. Its long, thin hands his right arm to the table. The boy cried out and tried to slip away but Leonid quickly moved over to where he was and held onto his shoulders.

Ilya struggled but the two grown men were too strong for him. "Hey! Let me go!"

Yuri just smiled as he kept a tight grip on the boy's arm. "Looks like we finally caught the other one. Will your superiors be pleased?"

"Very pleased," Leonid laughed. "Moscow told me that the Temple would pay a very high price for this boy. I don't know why, but he is important to them."

Ilya shrieked. "Let me go! Who are you people?"

Leonid kept on giggling. "Stop struggling, boy. You said you wanted to see your American friend, yes? Well, we will be bringing you to the people that have her. So that means that we are indeed helping you after all."

Ilya looked up at him. He was betrayed by everyone. "So you were the ones who took her then? You are a traitor! Let go of me, you dick!"

Leonid used the back of his hand and hit the boy across his face. The force of the blow sent Ilya sprawling to the ground. For a brief moment, the boy's head spun and he saw nothing but bright flashes in front of him. Then the pain sent him reeling on the dusty floor.

"Watch your tongue, you little shit," Leonid said.

Yuri crouched down and helped the boy back up on his feet. "Leonid, you're not suppose to hurt the boy like that. The Temple said that he must not be harmed. They could give us less money and food if he is not in one piece."

Leonid pointed a stubby finger at the boy. "Do not test me, lad. I have killed men three times your size."

"You won't be doing anymore beating today, that's for sure," a voice from across the room said.

Yuri and Leonid instantly turned around. All along the sides of the garage stood two dozen men in full battle gear. Most of them were carrying AS Val automatic rifles that were equipped with integrated suppressors. A few others had AN-94 assault rifles while one of them carried a Saiga-12 automatic shotgun. All of them wore black helmets and hoods.

As the three of them just stood there, two of the heavily armed men pushed open the door to the outside. A man with a chiseled jaw wearing identical battle gear stepped inside but he wore a beret instead of a ballistic helmet on his head. The man with the beret wasn't carrying a rifle, but he had a GSh-18 pistol strapped to his side holster.

Yuri instantly had his hands up as he backed away from the other two. "W-Who are you people?"

The man with the beret stepped forward but stayed away from melee range. "I am Major Andrei Zorin. We too have been looking for that boy."

Leonid grimaced as he held onto the boy and kept Ilya close to his body. "You can have this boy but you need to let me go!"

Major Zorin looked at him coldly. "You are surrounded. I may yet decide to let you live if you back away from the child. Do it now."

Yuri fell down on his knees as he began to crawl towards the major. "Please, don't shoot! It was him! It was Leonid who put me up to this! My son, he is in the army too!"

"We know all about your son," Major Zorin said. "I'm sorry, but he died while being interrogated."

Yuir's words became hysterical. "No! Why did you kill him?"

Major Zorin shrugged. "I was not in charge of the questioning. It seems our superiors were a little too eager to get the truth out of him."

Yuri got up and started to wail as he moved forward in a last desperate show of anger and defiance. Major Zorin instantly drew his pistol and shot the old man in the forehead. The gunshot reverberated across the room as Yuri's corpse fell backwards into the dusty concrete flooring.

Leonid backed up closer to where the oven was as he dragged Ilya in front of him. "If you shoot me, you will hit the boy! Do not shoot!"

Major Zorin calmly stepped over Yuri's corpse as he got closer. "You do not stand a chance. Give it up."

Leonid gasped as more than a dozen laser beams were pointed to his head. No matter which way he tried to duck and cover, the red tracers continued to follow and blinded his eyes. He cried out in despair as he used one free hand to try to wave the beams of red light away but to no avail. "Stop! Stop it!"

"This organization you work for," Major Zorin said. "It's called the Temple, right? What exactly is it about?"

"It's the Temple of the Black Sun," Leonid said tearfully as he pushed the boy away from him and held up his arms in the air. "They are supposed to be a group of magicians based in Germany. One of them was an American, he told us about the two children and made us forward information to the military here so they knew where the kids would be."

"So we captured the kids for your masters," Major Zorin said softly. "But what happened to the convoy with the American girl in it?"

"I don't know! All we did was relay the information to the Temple, and they said they would take care of the rest! The American's name was Solomon! The head magician is a German named Orlok! I don't know anything else!"

"Very interesting, thank you," Major Zorin said to him before looking up at his men. "Do it."

The moment he heard those final words, Leonid cried out in terror as several subsonic rounds instantly passed through his head and he fell forward, blood gushing from the multiple holes. Ilya whimpered as he crawled forward, away from the convulsing corpse.

Major Zorin walked over to the boy and held out his hand. "Let's go, boy."

But Ilya stayed down on the ground and merely looked up at him. "I'm not going back to Moscow with you, please let me go."

Major Zorin sighed as he holstered his pistol. "I've got my orders, either you get up now and come with us, or my men will grab you by your little balls and drag you with them back to the compound. Colonel Denikin wants you back right away, so let's go, you little shit."

"Such language, you shouldn't say such rude things to a child like that," a high-pitched voice from the far side of the room said.

The men of the elite Alpha Group were stunned as they started aiming their weapons in every direction, trying to find where the source of the voice was. Major Zorin instantly crouched down and grabbed Ilya by the shoulders. The boy struggled but the Spetsnaz officer was too strong for him as he started to drag the boy towards the entrance.

One of the commandos aimed his silenced battle rifle at the raven perched on top of the tractor. "It's that black bird!"

Most of the other soldiers laughed in apparent disbelief as several more of them aimed their weapons at the raven.

Major Zorin instantly put one arm up while keeping the other one on Ilya's shoulder. "Hold your fire!"

The raven didn't seem too concerned. It just kept on looking at them despite the multiple laser beams that were pointed all over its body.

One of the other commandos shook his head. "Is this a joke?"

The first soldier was adamant. "I'm telling you, it was the bird that was doing the talking!"

For a few seconds there was nothing but total silence other than the crackling fire in the oven. Nobody moved as they continued to stare at the black bird while it ruffled its feathers, still perched on top of the tractor.

The raven smoothed its wing feathers with its beak before looking at them. "Okay, you got me."

Major Zorin continued to gesture at his men to hold their fire. "We were expecting a talking dog but now we got a talking bird instead."

"A lot of birds talk," the raven said. "Perhaps you just weren't listening hard enough."

Ilya looked up at the bird. "Coyote? Is that you?"

"More or less," the raven said.

Even though the situation was serious, the boy couldn't help but smile a little. Despite all the betrayals and the odds, he had succeeded in meeting up with the trickster.

Major Zorin smirked as well. "So the magical, talking dog turned into a magical talking bird. I feel like I am back listening to my babushka tell her folk stories while I sat on her lap as a child."

"You should have listened more closely to her," the raven said. "There's a certain amount of truth to those stories."

Major Zorin gestured at one of his men and the door to the outside was quickly sealed shut. "This is fortunate for I have orders to take you with us as well, little black bird. Do not worry, my men will not harm you this time."

"Oh, I have no doubt of that," the raven said. "But we're not going anywhere."

Major Zorin looked confused. "You aim to take the boy with you? I don't think you realize that I have almost three squads of Spetsnaz, and their weapons are all pointed in your direction. Do you want this to end up like the last time?"

The raven shifted sideways slightly as it ruffled its feathers. "Yes, I must admit you surprised me the last time because we had just entered your world, so I wasn't expecting an ambush then. But this time I brought along some help."

Major Zorin and a few other men instantly began to look around the garage. A Spetsnaz trooper who was closest to the side of the tractor soon noticed that there was something near the back of the old vehicle, hidden in the shadows. As he raised his assault rifle and took a look through its night-vision optics, the soldier let out a cry of alarm as his finger squeezed the trigger of the gun.

But the soldier was too late as the creature closed in on him with a speed of a thunderbolt, using its clawed hands like a battering ram as the Spetsnaz commando was thrown backwards like a rag doll, his rifle flying across the room. At first glance, it seemed to resemble a man but its pale white skin was tough and leathery, like a crocodile's. It didn't seem to wear any clothes as they could see that its broad feet ended in talons. The creature's head was completely hairless; the nose was still somewhat visible while its mouth was filled with black, razor-sharp teeth. But the most inhuman aspect was its eyes; they were completely blood red and glowed in the semi-darkness.

The other Alpha Group troopers instantly reacted as they brought their weapons to bear on the intruder, but the creature was too fast as it began to systematically tear into them. A few commandos ended up getting shot by their own colleagues as the monster fought against them at point-blank range. The commandos in the other side of the room opened fire from the opposite direction but even their armor piercing, subsonic rounds only seemed to make the creature angrier as several more of their own went down.

Ilya watched in horror as the creature made short work of at least a dozen men before leaping up into the air and then landed on top of another group of soldiers at the opposite side. Within less than twenty seconds, almost all of the Spetsnaz commandos were either dead or incapacitated. As the boy tried getting up, somebody grabbed him from behind and held onto his shoulder.

Major Zorin drew his pistol and aimed it at the boy's head while standing behind him. "Stop you attacks or I'll kill the boy!"

The creature slowly turned in his direction as it wiped the blood from its maw using one of its wiry arms. Only the three of them were left standing.

"I wouldn't do that if I were you, Major," the raven said. "My friend you see, he is quite fast and you'll be dead before you can even squeeze that trigger on the halfway mark."

Major Zorin said nothing as the creature faced him and started moving in his direction. The Spetsnaz officer took a few steps back as he dragged Ilya along until his back hit the wooden garage door.

The raven kept staring at them. "Last chance, Major."

Major Zorin spat at the creature before he pushed Ilya to the ground and then aimed his pistol at his adversary. "I am a commander in Alpha Group, we never surrender!"

The creature's kick was a blur as its foot connected with Major Zorin's chest before he could even fire the pistol. The force of the blow sent the major flying into the air as his body smashed through the wooden entrance and flew back for almost thirty feet before landing near a distant copse of trees with a muffled thud.

Ilya's mouth was open as he saw the creature take a glance at him before moving through the man-sized hole in the door so it could take on the supporting troops that were outside. A few minutes later, the boy heard distant sounds of shouting, gunfire, and explosions before several loud crashes and then finally an eerie silence.

The raven flapped its wings and flew up into the ceiling for a bit before landing beside the boy. "We need to get going. Tara is in trouble and I need your help," it said.

Ilya got up and dusted himself off as he saw that the creature was heading back towards the entrance. "What is that thing? Is it some sort of a demon?"

"He used to be an American soldier," the raven said. "He goes by the name of Patrick Gyle."

16. Skyship

Germany

Achim Lange frowned when he noticed that his dark red beret had a tiny stain on it. He quickly took it from the table and placed it back on his head. After picking up his fork he resumed eating again. The mess hall was serving his favorite dish, a plate of currywurst and French fries, yet he didn't have much of an appetite because of what was happening in Europe. So instead of putting food in his mouth, he just started to stir the fork back and forth, making strange patterns with the curry sauce on the plate.

His co-pilot, Matthias Seidel, noticed what he was doing. "What is it, Achim?"

Lange looked up at him as he put the fork down again. "For the first time in weeks, you finally call me by my first name."

Unlike his colleague, Seidel had a hearty appetite as he kept on chewing. "We've been acting professionally for months now because of this crisis, but I think it's better if we take a little pressure off by calling each other by our first names again, don't you agree?"

Lange looked out into the window. The skies were overcast even though it was high noon. "What difference does it make? We're about to be overrun anyway. If not by those Fomorians in the west, then by hordes of giants and demons from the east. My grandfather fought in the war and he told me how he felt about it before he died. I have the same feelings now."

Seidel gave a low whistle. "Oh, don't be so glum! The Fomorians may have conquered most of France, Britain, and Ireland, but they have yet to cross our borders. It seems that they are not making any headway in Spain either. I think they have overstretched themselves and the tide is now turning."

"They are not advancing into Spain because that country has its own demons," Lange said. "I was in the Costa del Sol last year with my girlfriend, and I heard they are worshiping strange gods down there. Central Spain isn't any better because I heard there is a war between a group of witches and an army of Catholic fanatics."

"Fine, be that way. I won't join your sour graping. I will remain optimistic. How is your girlfriend, by the way?"

Lange's cheeks were beet red. "She and her family evacuated to Hannover weeks ago! I told you this already!"

Although the dining hall was half empty, a few heads turned in their direction. Both men looked away from each other and said nothing for the next few minutes.

Seidel smirked. "I'm sorry, Achim. I guess I just forgot. I was just trying to make you feel better, that's all."

"I wish I was gay like you, then I wouldn't have to worry about others so much."

Seidel frowned. "You think because I'm gay it means I don't care? You are so stupid."

"You don't have a steady relationship, nor do you seem too concerned about the casualties we've taken either."

"As I've said, I am just optimistic about all of this, that's all."

Lange sighed. "Believe what you want, I don't want to hear about it."

A lieutenant entered the NCO mess hall and walked up to the two of them. "Staff Sergeants Lange and Seidel report to the main briefing room immediately."

The two men stood up and saluted before heading out.

Lange continued to adjust his beret as he walked out the door. "What do you suppose they want us for now?"

"Perhaps they will tell us the war is over," Seidel said softly.

Colonel Anton Wegener ran his fingers through his close cropped silvery hair and looked at the map once more. The headquarters staff of the Rapid Force Division was woefully understaffed and would normally be commanded by General Langsdorf, but the CO and most of his command staff were missing after their helicopter went down last month near Poland. All attempts to recover the wreckage were met with failure due to reports of demonic attacks coming from the east as well as the ever encroaching cold front. Wegener was the commander of Kommando Spezialkrafte, the elite special forces unit of the German Army, and now he was placed in charge of protecting Berlin from an unknown threat.

His aide, Captain Paul Huff, walked into the headquarters room and handed him a piece of paper. "Colonel, I'm afraid we only have one Tiger gunship available for reconnaissance."

Colonel Wegener could barely hide his disappointment. "What about unmanned aircraft?"

"We have no drones left, Colonel. There is a squadron of Tornados near Stuttgart, but it is less than full strength. I could request that they-"

Colonel Wegener shook his head. "No, no. EUCOM needs that squadron against the Fomorians. We will have to make do with what we have."

EUCOM was the European Combat Command of the US military; they had been cut off from the American mainland so all remaining US forces in the European Union were transferred to their command and deployed along the French border with Germany. Most of the German Army along with the remnants of the French, Dutch, and Belgian forces were now under their control as well. The only major forces guarding Germany's eastern borders were centered around the 1st Panzer Division, less than 10 miles east of Berlin. The few reconnaissance units that had been sent into Poland had not returned.

The German government was in an acute sense of panic. Most of their parliament ministers in the Bundestag, along with the president, had been hastily transferred over to Hanover when the Fomorians overran Ireland, the United Kingdom, and most of France. Only the chancellor and his staff had stayed in the capital city of Berlin for it was too close to the eastern border.

Although Bonn was the seat of government during the days of the German partition, it was now considered too close to the French border to be secure. Refugees from all over Europe were fleeing towards the center of the country despite the fact that there were no safe areas to go to.

A staff member who was working the computer information systems uploaded the latest photographs onto the main monitor at the center of the room. It showed a very dense cloud formation that looked like a gigantic grey island in the sky.

Colonel Wegener crossed his arms as he stared at the pictures. "How close is that cloud from Berlin?"

"Based on our meteorological estimates, the formation should be skirting over the eastern edges of the city, sir, latest reports have it over Muncheburg," a staff sergeant said.

Colonel Wegener stared at his aide. "Can we get a remote camera feed from the gunship?"

Captain Huff nodded. "Yes, Colonel. We can have the live video feed up on the monitor."

"Okay, send the Tiger up," Colonel Wegener said softly.

Minutes later, a Tiger attack helicopter piloted by Sergeants Lange and Seidel had taken off from their base in the southern outskirts of Berlin and flew on a steady course towards a mysterious cloud formation that was nearing the city from the east. The Tiger gunship was Germany's answer to the US military's Apache; both helicopters had four blades on their rotors as well as dual turbo shaft engines and with an almost identical weapons system. Achim Lange was sitting in the forward pilot's position in the tandem cockpit while his colleague Matthias Seidel occupied the gunner's chair, which was slightly elevated behind him. Both men could operate either the weapons or the flight controls from their own respective chairs in the event of an emergency, though in most situations, Lange would handle the flying of the aircraft while Seidel concentrated on the weapons.

"Tiger One to Base," Lange said as he activated the Tiger's communications array. "Enabling live video feed now."

"Base to Tiger One," the voice from ground control said. "Affirmative, we are receiving your video feed, over."

Lange banked the control stick due east as the Tiger accelerated close to two hundred miles per hour. The skies were already overcast and had been for weeks. He could count the number of days in the past few months in which a few rays of the sun had actually shined over the city. Within minutes, both the pilots in the air and their regional headquarters could see the massive cloud formation floating less than three miles ahead of them.

"My god," Seidel said.

It looked like a gigantic, towering mass of grey cotton candy and was at least several miles in diameter. As the Tiger helicopter approached, it seemed to resemble a tiny gnat on a collision course towards a ghostly giant that floated in sky.

Lange kept his eyes on the display as he focused on the sensory data. "Range to target, less than two miles. Target altitude at eight thousand feet at its base and twenty thousand feet at the top of its formation."

"Twenty thousand? That's past our service ceiling for this helicopter," Seidel said.

"Shut up! I know that," Lange snapped at his designated gunner before keying his communications to ground control. "Tiger One to Base, what exactly are we looking at and how do you want us to proceed, over."

"Our meteorologist says it resembles a cumulonimbus cloud formation," ground control said. "Characteristics are thundercloud and other atmospheric instability. Tiger One, can you use your radar on it?"

"Affirmative, activating radar," Lange said as he activated the Tiger's Doppler radar system. The Tiger carried a microwave emitting system that bounced a signal off of a target to determine its velocity. Though normally used for ground attack, the radar also had meteorological uses.

As the pilot started to use the helicopter's sensors, the cloud seemed to have a life of its own as it started to turn darker grey. Seidel sensed something was wrong and he activated the helicopter's Osiris sensor that was mounted on the Tiger's mast, just above the quad rotors. The Osiris combined optical TV and thermal sensors along with a laser range finder.

Both of them couldn't believe the readings that came back on their cockpit displays.

Lange could barely keep his hands from shaking. "Are you seeing what I'm seeing?"

Seidel blinked several times as he assumed he was dreaming at first. "My god, there is something in that cloud formation!"

Back in the operations room, Colonel Wegener hard a hard time trying to piece together the flood of information that was being relayed from the Tiger gunship. He pointed to the staff meteorological officer. "What exactly does all this mean?"

The staff officer kept fiddling with a hand calculator while nervously adjusting his thick glasses from time to time. "Colonel, this may sound unbelievable but based on those readings it looks like there is an object within that aerosol formation."

Captain Huff's face turned white. "What do you mean? How big is it?"

"From the radar signal, we can't really be too sure since the system on the Tiger is designed for ground attack," the staff officer said. "We may need a visual confirmation."

"Order Tiger One for a closer look," Colonel Wegener said to the radio operator.

"Affirmative," Lange said as he banked the control stick to his left as the Tiger gunship flew slowly into the cloud cover. "Matthias, keep your eyes open, visibility is practically nothing in this cloud so let me know before we collide with whatever is in side of this."

Seidel chuckled. "You've finally called me by my first name! I guess we are making progress."

Lange said nothing as he used the radar indicator on the Osiris system to try and locate where the object was. As the helicopter climbed even higher, it entered what seemed to be a hollow pocket of clear air within the cloud itself. That was when they finally saw it.

Both men gasped at the same time as the Tiger gunship flew underneath the object. It was a cigar-shaped craft made of rusted metal that seemed to float within the cloud itself. As the helicopter flew less than a hundred feet from its side, they could see what looked like riveted sheets of iron haphazardly stamped along its massive hull with dents as well as numerous patches all along the aircraft's body.

"T-Tiger One to Base," Lange said nervously as he put the helicopter into a climb to see how high the object was. "We have contact with unknown object. It is some sort of aircraft made of metal. It's quite massive, three times the length of an American aircraft carrier. Are you getting this, over?"

Seidel kept blinking as if he was trying to wake up from a dream. "My god, it looks like an iron zeppelin!"

The operations room was completely silent as everyone stared at the live video feed coming from the helicopter. The only noises came from the humming of the electronics systems and the intermittent squawking on the radios.

Colonel Wegener broke the silence. "Can anyone tell me what that thing is?"

"I-it looks like an all-metal version of the Hindenburg," one of the radio operators said.

"It's much bigger than any airship ever put in the air," Captain Huff said. "How can it stay up in the sky like that, it's impossible!"

As the helicopter's camera panned around the unidentified aircraft, it focused on what looked like a painted symbol on the starboard side of its hull. The massive, black insignia resembled a sun wheel mosaic, with stylized, forked rays emanating from the innermost circle to the borders of the larger circle encompassing it.

"Sir," another radio operator said, "I've seen that symbol before!"

Colonel Wegner stood over him. "Where?"

The young man swallowed nervously before answering him. "I stayed at a youth hostel a few years ago before I joined the army, and I saw that very symbol in the castle where I stayed in. It's called the sun wheel and it's from Wewelsburg castle."

Colonel Wegener placed a hand on his chin. "Wewelsburg, why does that name seem familiar to me?"

Deep in the bowels of the airship, its mystical engines were humming to life as the craft lurched forward, ever closer to the capital city of Berlin. Near the top central portion of the hull was the vessel's bridge, it was composed of a number of platforms that were connected by metallic walkways and surrounded by swirling, mystical energy. In a number of the platforms were machinery with all sorts of levers, switches, and gauges with which to control the airship. Manning the bridge was a crew of impish-sized creatures, they resembled short humanoids but their skin color was that of polished obsidian and their hair and beards seemed silvery white. These strange, faerie-like beings wore goggles over their eyes and would continually adjust the levers and switches to make sure that the vessel was in working order.

Helmut Krause glanced around nervously as a number of the creatures darted to and from the upper platform where he was standing at. He kept one hand underneath his robes, ready to whip out his pistol in case these Dokkalfar would dare to try and push him off the platform and into the mystical energies that surrounded them.

Kurt Orlok was standing right beside his henchman as he looked at a gigantic glass ball that was seemingly suspended in front of them. "Stop fiddling with your gun, you fool."

Helmut nodded meekly as he took out his hands and clasped them in front of his body. "I-I'm sorry, Grand Magus. It's just that these creatures make me nervous to be around them."

Orlok sneered at his servant's cowardice. "They are operating this airship and that means that they are important to us so, you will either tolerate them or you will remove yourself from the bridge."

"Y-Yes, Grand Magus."

"Now be quiet. We shall begin the next phase," Orlok said as he raised his palm towards the crystal globe. Almost immediately, the ball began to glow and it soon projected a three-dimensional image of the outside within the confines of its circle, like some sort of mystical video feed. As the images of the outside of the ship's hull were being shown in real time, both men quickly noticed the small helicopter that was flying around the airship.

Helmut pointed at the Tiger gunship that was observing them. "Magus, look!"

"Yes, I see it," Orlok said. "It is of no consequence."

Helmut giggled. He knew what was going to happen next.

Orlok raised his arms. "Black elves, now is the time for vengeance! Prepare the lightning cannons for ground bombardment!"

As the Tiger gunship slowly circled the giant airship, both men noticed that a number of towering metallic spikes began to protrude from the lower sides of the craft's hull. The bottom portion of the ship now looked like a porcupine.

"Tiger One to Base," Lange said into his helmet microphone. "Something is happening! The unidentified airship has begun to deploy what we think are weapons!"

The helicopter pilot had barely said those words when massive bolts of lightning began to emanate from the protruding spiked towers and connected to the ground below. Whole sections of the city were soon bombarded by electrically charged, superheated plasma. Fires began to quickly rage as whole buildings collapsed from the onslaught. The country had not been bombarded like this since World War Two.

The operations room was now in a panic. A representative from the chancellor's staff had noticed what had been going on and immediately started to openly complain and condemn Colonel Wegener, accusing him of incompetence for not warning them about the unidentified aircraft. Captain Huff had to draw his pistol to force the man to leave the room.

"Prepare orders for general evacuation of the city," Colonel Wegener said to his radio operators before turning to look at Captain Huff. "What kind of air defenses do we have available?"

"We have Stinger missiles which are man portable anti-aircraft weapons. But those things are designed to take out fighter aircraft, not a flying metal battleship like that thing up there," Captain Huff said glumly.

Colonel Wegener looked on helplessly as the live video feed from the helicopter showed that the craft was moving closer to the center of the city. "There must be a weapon we could use against that thing!"

Captain Huff thought about it for a brief moment. "Colonel, we have an MLRS battery from the First Panzer Division nearby. Although they are used for ground artillery, we could just have them aim at the cloud. No guarantee we could hit anything with it though."

Colonel Wegener nodded. The M270 Multiple Launch Rocket System was a battery of rockets mounted on a vehicle. They were meant for ground support and there would be no guidance for the rockets at all. "Do what you can, and if we have any sort of anti-aircraft gun available, then have them shoot at that damned cloud too." he said.

The two men in the Tiger gunship watched helplessly as the airship continued its path of destruction as whole districts of the city disappeared in fire and explosions. The helicopter's electronic systems were going haywire from the nearby discharges of superheated lightning bolts emanating from the enemy airship. Both men knew the rockets they had mounted on their pods would do little damage to the flying battleship floating in the air just to the side of them.

Lange keyed in his microphone for cockpit voice only. "Matthias, what is our weapon load out?"

Seidel smiled underneath his helmet. He knew what his pilot was going to do. "We have four Stinger missiles and about eight available PARS," he said. The AIM-92 Stinger missiles were for air-to-air use while the PARS 3 LR were primarily for anti-tank ground use. None of the weapons they had in the helicopter were designed for use against the craft that they were facing at that moment. There was only one way that they could conceivably damage such a craft, but it would also be the end of them.

"Do your magic, Matthias," Lange said softly. "Then I will do the last bit."

Seidel made a loud whoop just before he started arming the weapons. "For Germany, and for all mankind!"

Orlok and Helmut had their eyes glued to the giant crystal ball in front of them. They could see entire neighborhoods on fire. Smoke and ash had obscured many parts of the city. Half of Berlin was already gone.

The Grand Magus of the Black Sun Temple had an aloof visage as he surveyed the damage. "How soon before we need to recharge the energy sphere?"

Helmut looked at a dial attached to the side of the platform. "We have enough power for another dozen strikes before we have to return to base, Grand Magus."

"Very well, let us fire a single salvo at the city center and then we prepare a portal to-"

But Orlok's words were interrupted when both of them heard clanging noises coming from the far side of the hull. Both men quickly scanned the ship using the gigantic scrying ball. Within seconds, they both saw that the helicopter that had been circling around them had fired all of its rockets and hit the airship.

Orlok scoffed. "Annoying little gnat."

Then the Tiger gunship did something unexpected after it had expended all of its missiles. It quickly banked right and accelerated before colliding nose first into one of the lower lightning gun batteries. There was a brief explosion as the whole bridge shuddered upon the impact.

Orlok was enraged. "Damage control!"

Helmut continued to read the gauges on the control panel. "It looks like two of the lightning gun batteries were slightly damaged."

Orlok rolled his eyes. "If that is the best that the German military can do, then this shall-"

The whole ship shuddered once again as multiple grinding and banging noises were heard coming from the outer hull. As Orlok and Helmut looked on, a half-dozen rockets that were seemingly fired from the ground had impacted along the base of the ship's fuselage. Based on the smoke contrails that had passed through the cloud cover surrounding the airship, dozens more had narrowly missed hitting the hull.

"Looks like rocket artillery from the ground, firing blindly at us," Helmut said. "It must have been by sheer luck that some of those things actually hit."

Orlok gripped the horizontal iron bars that ringed the main platform. The airship was so huge that even incidental attacks were able to score some hits on them. He needed to tell the builders to reinforce the hull against subsidiary hits when they returned to base. "How far are we from the center of Berlin?"

"We're just over Tempelhofer Park, coming up to Kreuzberg," Helmut said. "Perhaps another ten minutes."

"I don't want to wait any longer, order the remaining batteries to fire before we withdraw to recharge our guns and assess the damage they did to our ship," Orlok said.

"At once, Grand Magus."

Colonel Wegener had gotten out of the vehicle as soon as it stopped and began surveying the damaged street. Whole buildings had collapsed as their water pipes burst when the heat transformed the liquid into steam, Internal electrical cabling had caught fire and erupted in less than a second as well. The vast currents of electrified plasma had torn through the buildings and cracked their foundations, causing quite a number of them to collapse. The people that were inside of them fared worst of all. Although the statistics said that roughly ninety percent of human beings survived lightning strikes, these attacks were unique since the bodies that were lying in the rubble had apparently exploded from the inside out; the intense electrical surge heated their blood to the point that it had turned instantaneously into steam, shattering their bodies as their internal organs gave way.

Captain Huff stood next to his commander as he listened to a walkie-talkie that he was holding. "Several of our technicians estimate the strength of those lightning bolts surpassed any known natural discharge to date. They believe that the electrical currents that struck the city to be over two billion volts each. And there must have been at least several thousand of these strikes."

"Any word on the chancellor?"

"They were able to evacuate the Reichstag building just when the attack started. He is safe along with his staff. We recommended that they join the rest of the government in Hannover but he is insisting that he will not leave Berlin. We may not be so lucky next time."

Colonel Wegener merely nodded. The cloud had moved northwards towards the ice-covered Baltic Sea before dissipating and there was no sign of the airship that was hidden inside of it.

17. Crucible

The border was in complete chaos. Tens of thousands of people were fleeing after the battle of Amman, but the IDF refused to allow the refugees to bring their vehicles into the Israeli border. As a consequence, there were thousands of abandoned cars strewn all along the border crossing. The town of Jericho itself was firmly under Israeli control. A pair of IDF Cobra gunships, a type of helicopter that was hastily taken out of mothballs and pressed back into service, were patrolling the skies right at the crossing. Long lines of refugees stood just outside of the newly- built checkpoint as they waited their turn to be processed.

David Zim cursed as the Granite reconnaissance vehicle that he was driving could not find a clear lane as it maneuvered around the abandoned cars. He honked the car horn as he drove through a line of refugees, many of them hastily backing away with a dejected sense of desperation. Along with the three remaining men on his team, he still wore the Bedouin robe to hide their true professions as Mossad intelligence agents. The battle of Amman was a disaster since the King of Jordan had been killed while fighting with his remaining troops in the defense of the city. The surviving IDF expeditionary forces in Jordan had slowly been withdrawing back to their borders when it was deemed that the Golem Brigade was not yet ready to be redeployed. With the death of its king and the destruction of its capital, the Hashemite

Kingdom of Jordan had virtually ceased to exist. Israel now stood alone as it prepared for the coming onslaught.

The six-month old baby that the woman was carrying in the backseat started to cry. David briefly glanced back at the two before concentrating on getting the vehicle past the last pile of idle cars as the crossing was less than a mile away now. His radio operator was sitting in the front seat of the car while his two other men shared the backseat with the woman.

David finally found a lane in which he could drive the vehicle through as an IDF truck pushed its way past a pileup of two cars and he quickly followed. "We're almost at the border, Leyla," he said to the woman at the backseat in perfect Arabic. "I'm sure we could find some formula for your daughter once we get into Jericho proper."

Leyla smiled at him. "Thank you for everything, David. My husband would be honored that you're doing this," she said softly. Her husband was Major Ahmed Natsheh and he had been friends with David for a number of years. David had first met her future husband when he was a Jordanian exchange student in Ben-Gurion University and they had been friends ever since. Major Natsheh's final words to him were to ask if David could ensure that his wife and infant daughter would make it to safety if anything happened to him. David had promised him that he would. Major Natsheh's words had come to fruition when he fought and died by the King's side as the Babylonian forces broke through Amman's inner defenses. David's team had been serving as an observation unit, and they were one of the last Israeli units to pull out just as the demonic forces overran the city.

The mental image of the demon god Pazuzu was still fresh on David's mind as if it happened just a few minutes ago. The monster must have been several hundred feet tall as it rampaged through the city, brushing aside tank and missile fire as if they were nothing more than the sting of bees as it smashed through whole buildings. David and his team had been observing the giant demigod as it crushed everything in its path and they had barely got away in time. Even though Israel had been using the black magic of Rabbi Elijah Ba'al and his golems, what kind of defense could they possibly mount against a gigantic monster such as Pazuzu?

A tap on his shoulder made him come back to his senses as his colleague Benny was now pointing at the open crossing gate ahead of them. "David, let's get a move on," his radio operator said.

"Sorry," David said as he maneuvered the Granite to the rear, behind the line of Israeli vehicles that were being allowed in. "I haven't gotten any rest for the past forty-eight hours."

Leyla just smiled at him through the rear view mirror as she noticed that the two men sitting beside her were fast asleep. She was able to calm the baby down and it was now napping.

A squad of heavily-armed IDF soldiers surrounded the vehicle. Benny took out a piece of paper and held it out to an NCO. "We are a forward observer unit with the Institute."

The corporal took a look at the passengers. "You can go in, but you will need to drop off the woman and her baby over to the refugee processing center."

David was shocked. "What? She's the wife of an old friend. I'm taking her to stay with my wife in Beersheba."

The IDF soldier shook his head. "Sorry, orders. I cannot let you go through with her in the vehicle. She needs to get out now."

David's surprise turned to anger. "This is outrageous! Who is your commanding officer?"

Leyla glanced around nervously as she held onto the baby in her arms. "David, what's happening?"

The corporal sighed and pointed to a khaki colored tent behind the checkpoint. "Over there."

David got out of the driver's seat. His two other men had woken up. "Benny, take over. Do not let her out of the vehicle," he said to his radio operator before turning to look at Leyla. "Don't worry, I'll sort this out."

As Benny maneuvered the Granite to the side in order to let the cars behind them pass through the checkpoint, David headed over to the command tent. The heat and his lack of sleep was giving him a punishing headache. When he entered the tent, he noticed two IDF officers poring over a map.

David placed his hands on his hips. "Who is in charge here?"

A heavyset man in rumpled fatigues looked up at him. "I am. Major Shimon Shapira. Who are you?"

"David Zim, I'm with the Institute. I have a Jordanian friend with me in my vehicle but your border guards said that she must be taken to a processing center. I would like to ask you to make an exception with her."

Major Shapira looked down on the dusty floor. "I'm sorry, but I have strict orders to bring all non-Israelis to the refugee camp."

"Does that include women and children?"

The other IDF officer walked over to him. He had a lieutenant's rank. "Yes," he said. "That comes direct from IDF High Command. We cannot make any exceptions whatsoever."

That was when David realized he hadn't seen a single Arab at the outskirts of town at all. And Jericho was supposed to be administered by the Palestinians. "What is going on here? Where are all the Palestinians that were over here before we came?"

The lieutenant waved him away. "We cannot answer those questions. You can ask your own case officer about it when you get back to the Institute."

David didn't move. "I'm not going to give my friend's wife and her baby away just like that without an explanation."

Major Shapira sighed. Like David, he too was tired. "All non-Isrealis, and that includes the Palestinians, are being taken to a special camp outside of Jerusalem."

The lieutenant put his hand up in protest. "But, Major, you're not supposed to divulge this kind of-"

Major Shapira crossed his arms. "He has a right to know. I know who he is; his uncle is a member of the Knesset and he will find out about it sooner or later anyway," he said to his subordinate before turning his attention to David. "The IDF is now pretty much under the command of that damned rabbi. I don't like it anymore than you do, but he showed us in Qasr al Hallabat that we could win against these demonic creatures. So he pretty much gets what he wants these days."

David's mouth hung open. "Rabbi Elijah Ba'al? He's behind all of this?

Look, I was at Qasr al Hallabat and I can tell you it wasn't a victory for us, all it did was to delay the inevitable. Those golems he created were able to hold back the Babylonians, but those damned demons just gathered reinforcements and ultimately pushed us out of Jordan anyway."

"Perhaps you may be right," Major Shapira said tersely. "But the IDF general staff and the Israeli government believes that if he can create more golems, then it might be enough to turn the tide in our favor."

"That is insane! Do you know how Rabbi Ba'al creates those monstrosities? He uses Palestinian prisoners and then he…" David's voice trailed off as he realized the awful truth.

Major Shapira held both his hands up in a gesture of peace. "David, you need to calm down, son. It's not as bad as you think."

But David wasn't hearing him as he turned around and ran out of the tent. His legs were tired but he pushed on as he sprinted back towards the Granite reconnaissance vehicle. The soldiers at the checkpoint were just milling about as he opened the driver's side door and pushed Benny back to the front passenger seat.

"What gives, man?" Benny said as he slid over.

David closed the door as he started up the vehicle. "Everybody get ready and just do as I say."

Benny was suspicious, as were the other two. "I don't like this, what's going on, David?"

Omri leaned forward and stuck his face near David's shoulder. "Yeah, what's happening?"

David said nothing as he turned the vehicle and waited for the next car to pass through the checkpoint. The moment he saw a gap at the crossing, he immediately floored the accelerator and sped right through the checkpoint. One IDF soldier tried dive away to avoid being hit while the other Israelis aimed their weapons and shouted at them to stop.

With his three colleagues simultaneously screaming at him to stop the vehicle and to explain what he was doing, David noticed that Leyla had been fearfully staring at him while she gripped the crying baby even tighter. A machinegun emplacement just behind the checkpoint fired a short burst, aiming for the vehicle's tires, but David was able to veer slightly to the left as he narrowly dodged a parked army truck and drove into a deserted street at the edge of the town. Two M-242 Storm Commander utility vehicles that were parked near the crossing started their engines and were quickly in pursuit, sirens blazing.

David kept his eyes on the narrow road. He knew that the village itself was quite small. Once he got past the town center, the Granite would be able to maneuver around the barren fields and into the desert beyond.

"Enough of this," Omri said as he leaned over from the back seat and grabbed hold of David's arms. Leyla screamed as the Granite skidded and nearly fishtailed into a brick building. Benny grabbed onto the car's steering wheel and used his other hand to deactivate the ignition.

David snarled as he thrust his right elbow back, breaking the bridge of Omri's nose. He quickly leaned back to the side of the door and pulled out his Jericho pistol. Omri had fallen back to his seat as he moaned while clutching his face. The other Mossad agents were too shocked to react as David alternately pointed the gun at each of them.

Benny had his hands in the air. "David, have you gone insane?"

David grimaced as he kept pointing the pistol at them. "All of you, get out!"

With a curse, Benny turned and opened the front seat door and slid out. The third Mossad agent helped Omri out of the backseat. All the while, David kept pointing his pistol at all of them. The pursuing IDF vehicles had stopped twenty feet away, their sirens still blazing.

When the other agents were all out of the vehicle, David glanced at Leyla. "Get in the front seat, hurry!"

Leyla quickly moved over the top of the front seat and sat down beside him. She had left the baby at the back after she placed a seatbelt on her. "David, what is happening?"

David quickly restarted the ignition as he saw his own teammates running towards the IDF patrol vehicles, shouting at them. He floored the accelerator and the Granite quickly sped forward along the dusty, abandoned street. The other Mossad agents quickly got inside the other vehicles and they soon started after him again.

He kept the Granite's speed close to maximum, only taking his foot off the accelerator when he needed to make a turn. After a few minutes, they had made it past the town center and were now traveling across open farmlands. For a brief moment, he actually thought they were going to make it.

An IDF Cobra helicopter quickly spotted them and dove down in pursuit. As soon as it was in range, it began firing its M197 electric cannon. The 20mm rounds impacted the rear of the Granite and tore off the back portion of the vehicle. David immediately lost control as the car skidded and then rolled over as it lost its traction on the dusty farmlands.

David blinked his eyes as he woke up lying on the side of the vehicle. He must have lost consciousness for a few seconds but was woken up by Leyla's screams. She had thankfully put on her seatbelt and was now partly suspended sideways. Her baby had also woken up and was crying as well. He moved over to the backseat and found the baby was dangling but secure on her seatbelt. David disengaged the baby's seatbelt and cradled the child in his arms as he examined her for any injury. The baby didn't seem hurt but she was clearly upset as she continued to bawl.

"My daughter!" Leyla cried as she began to disengage herself from her own seatbelt.

David kept holding the baby as he stood up and started to reach for the passenger side door. "Leyla, go! I'll follow you, head for cover, we need to get to cover!"

With tears in her eyes, Leyla nodded as she started to climb out of the side of the tilted vehicle. David could hear the sounds of sirens as he started to open the door. He realized that the pursuit vehicles were already there. Just as Leyla was able to get her head and shoulders through the top part of the Granite, shots rang out and she instantly fell back into the vehicle compartment and collapsed.

"No!" David cried out as he crouched down and tried to examine her. Leyla's eyes were open and he could see a bloody hole at the back of her head. David roared with anger and frustration as he put the baby down near his side and began to pump Leyla's chest, hoping he could get her to start breathing again. The seconds seemed like an eternity as he kept alternating between pressing her chest and blowing air into her mouth. But it was no use, he soon realized that she was gone.

"You in there," a voice above him said. "Put your hands up or we will shoot!"

David looked up. Two IDF soldiers were standing on top of the Granite, pointing their M-16 rifles at him. He realized it was over. As they pulled him out of the vehicle, all he could remember were Leyla's eyes. They were deep brown and reminded him so much of his wife.

He could see a long, dust colored crack in the wall that had started from the concrete floor and forked its way up to the ceiling. David was sitting on a chair that was bolted to the ground and his right wrist was handcuffed to the metal armrest on its side. There was a metal table in front of him with a small plastic cup of water on it. He had been sitting there for hours after they had pried him loose from the vehicle. They had tried to question him about his motives but he just kept quiet and refused to answer. All he did since they left him alone was to stare at the cracks in the walls of the room.

A fly buzzed around and finally landed on the table near the cup of water. His left hand was inches away but he didn't make a move as he continued to observe the winged insect as it started to move towards the plastic cup. When it got close, the little bug buzzed its wings and flew up again before landing in the inside of the container as it balanced itself near the edge of the clear water. At that instant, David snapped his left arm up and brought his hand down over the rim of the cup, trapping the fly within it. As the insect buzzed around within the cup, trying desperately to find a way out, David soon heard footsteps just outside of the room. He could sense a woman's voice arguing with someone just beyond the door and he instantly recognized who it was. As he heard the door being unlocked, he pulled his left hand back, away from the cup. With its way clear, the buzzing fly flew off towards freedom.

When she entered the room he stood up, but his right shoulder slightly drooped because the handcuff chain was unable to give him enough of an extension. It didn't matter to David as his wife ran over and they hugged each other.

Tzipi Zim kissed her husband lightly on the lips before staring into his deep brown eyes. She wore the standard-issue olive green uniform of the IDF. "What happened, David? I have been told all sorts of stories on my way here."

David sighed as he kept his left arm over her shoulder. "They killed Major Ahmed's wife."

"Who did?"

He looked away momentarily. The memory was still painful. "Who else did but the IDF, of course."

"But I heard that was because you ran through the checkpoint so they opened fire."

"No! That wasn't what happened. We were clear of the checkpoint and she got out of the vehicle and started running, that's when they fired on her."

Two of her fingers twisted his chin until they saw each other's eyes again. "David, I am a warrant officer in the reserves. I have manned checkpoints myself. You must have done something to put them on alert. If you drove past the checkpoint, then they were within their rights to open fire."

David's chin trembled. "I-I was just trying to save her, and the baby. I couldn't turn her over to them. I know what they were going to do to them."

"What would they do to her? We were told that they would just be sent to the refugee center near Jerusalem, she would have been safe there."

He grimaced. "That is a lie! They would have executed her and the child in order to get their life force- their very souls! It's a fate worse than death, Tzipi!"

His wife's surprised look made him realize she didn't know. "But that's impossible! I can't believe what you're saying! Why would we take their souls? What for?"

He put his left arm to his side as he sat back down on the chair. "They need souls to power the golems, Tzipi. Without souls, the golems are just nothing but clay statues."

Tzipi just shook her head. "I-I can't believe that."

"You just don't want to believe it. I've seen them being created by that accursed rabbi. The government is saying that he is protecting us, but that man is worse than the demons out there."

"Rabbi Ba'al? But he is now one of the chief rabbis of Israel. Everyone says he's a national hero."

"The man is a disgrace! He isn't a rabbi, he's a murderer and a sorcerer, and he's selling our souls to the very demons we're fighting against! We are no longer the chosen people, not with what we've been doing to the Arabs and anyone who isn't a Jew here. His black magic has betrayed the teachings of our god and our very identity."

"What about the battle in Jordan? He's built the Golem Brigade for goodness sake."

"Dammit, Tzipi! Let me ask you, where are the Palestinians? Where are the other Arabs? Why are all non-Israelis in these camps?"

"Are you saying that he's sacrificing them to build these golems? How is that even possible?"

"Look around you! The gods have returned! Everything that we once knew is wrong!"

Tzipi placed her hand over her forehead and sighed. "What about Israel, David? Don't you remember what our grandparents went through to create this country? If we don't support what that rabbi is doing, if we don't support what our government is doing, then we're going to lose it all."

David stood up once more as he squeezed her arm with his free hand. "Do you want to be part of a state that uses large scale human sacrifice in order to defend itself? Is that the kind of country you want to live in?"

She had tears in her eyes as she hugged him once more. "But what is the alternative then? If not this, then what?"

David kissed her on the neck as he rested his chin on her slender shoulders. "I don't know. All I know is that what we're doing is wrong. I tried to make a difference and now both my best friend and his wife are dead. What do you want me to do?"

At that moment, there were more noises coming from the door, people talking.

David looked up. "Who is that outside?"

"It's Uncle Ariel, he picked me up and we rode in his car on the way here," Tzipi said softly.

The door opened and Ariel Weizman came limping in as he used his cane for balance. David noticed the two guards along with Major Shapira outside; they had evidently wanted to come in but Ariel waved them away with the back of his hand. The major glared at David for a few seconds before ordering the guards to shut the door.

"Well, Tzipi, you had your ten minutes," Ariel said as he moved over to a chair at the other side of the table and sat down. "I hope you've been able to talk some sense into your stubborn husband here."

David backed away and pointed an accusing finger at his uncle. "You've got a lot of nerve talking to me in third person even though I'm here."

Ariel sighed and put his right palm up as a gesture of peace. "Alright, David. I'm just glad that you're in one piece. You could have been killed by our own forces and I would have had to give Tzipi here the bad news. What you did was brash and insubordinate."

"I tried to save two lives from your infernal government camps," David said tersely. "You are in league with Satan. Our country has fallen so far that it's only a matter of time before God forsakes us utterly."

"Oh, stop deluding yourself, David," Ariel said. "You saw firsthand what the Golem Brigade was capable of doing. They enabled mankind to win its first ever battle against these demonic creatures. Not even the Americans were able to do that."

"We used demons to fight other demons," David said. "There is nothing noble about that. We sacrificed countless innocent lives in order to do that. Let me ask you, once we run out of Muslims and Arabs and Palestinians to sacrifice, who will be next? Will you be using Christians, then after that the Ethiopian Jews or the gays, anyone that doesn't explicitly follow Rabbi Ba'al's orders?"

Ariel frowned. "Now you are just being unreasonable. Rabbi Ba'al has assured us that we can stem the tide once the Golem Brigade is up to full strength."

"He's lying! I was at Qasr al Hallabat and I saw with my own eyes how much lives it took just to hold off a single attack from those things! What he is doing is not the answer!"

Ariel looked at him with tired eyes. "Then what is the answer, David? What else could we do?"

David pounded his fist on the table. "We had Noah! We could have asked him how to deal with these gods but what did we do instead? We held him prisoner and tried to drain his blood and take his soul! All that damned rabbi wanted to do was to make another golem with him!"

Tzipi looked at her uncle. "Is this true, Uncle Ariel? Did you really have Noah and you tried to sacrifice him to that rabbi as well?"

Ariel held both his hands up to try to calm them down. "Look, we've made mistakes but we're learning. The victory in Qasr al Hallabat was but the first step. We are making headway with this god problem, we just have to trust in Rabbi Ba'al and give him more time."

"You mean you want to give him more souls!" David hissed. "We are all damned if we keep following this rabbi!"

"David, you need to get a hold of yourself," Ariel said softly. "You are still held in high regard by the Institute after your recent missions but I can't keep covering for you. If it wasn't for my influence and your successes, you would already be in prison. You disobeyed a direct order during wartime. You know what the consequences are for that."

David didn't reply as he just looked away.

Tzipi walked over until she stood beside her uncle and placed a warm hand on his shoulder. "I would like to thank you for everything you've done for him, Uncle Ariel."

Ariel placed his hand on top of hers. "You're welcome. Your husband has been through a lot in the past forty-eight hours and needs some rest. I will take you both back to your apartment in Beersheba on the condition that you won't try a stunt like this again," he said, looking at David.

Tzipi smiled. "I can go back to Beersheba with him, but what about my unit? We've been tasked to reinforce the Golan Heights."

David knew better than to keep arguing so he continued to keep quiet.

"You've both been granted leave," Ariel said as he slowly got up. "Take care of your husband and see that he doesn't get into any more trouble. The situation is as serious enough as it is. You both get some rest because I have a feeling we will need you again very soon."

"I accept," David said. "But on one condition."

Ariel looked at him. "So I use up all my favors to get you out of trouble and you still demand a condition? What is it now?"

"Leyla's baby girl. She comes with us."

Ariel rolled his eyes. "Oh, come on! I pulled a lot of strings to keep you out of a prison cell, David! This is how you repay me? By making more demands?"

"Uncle Ariel, you know that David and I have been trying for a baby but because of our careers and that miscarriage, well it hasn't been a good year for us," Tzipi said. "Besides, you've always said you wanted to see us have children."

Ariel glared at them before making his way to the door. "I'll see what I can do, but no promises."

After their uncle left and the door had closed behind him, both David and Tzipi looked at each other and smiled.

18. The Recommencement

Brooklyn

After nearly dropping the casserole as he ascended up the stairs of the apartment, Dr. Paul Dane finally made it to the door and knocked twice. Within minutes, the door opened and Detective Valerie Mendoza smiled as she bade him to enter.

Paul stepped inside. "Sorry it took awhile, but I needed a bath since all that gardening really made me sweat."

Valerie kissed him on the cheek before taking the casserole from his hands. "Is this for me?"

"Of course," Paul said. "I figured that if you're going to invite me for dinner, it's only fair that I bring my share of the meal."

Valerie closed the door behind them and then took off the top of the deep serving dish. "Mmm, this looks good. Pasta?"

"With fresh tomatoes and basil from the garden, I made a big batch so I figured I'd bring some of it over," Paul said as he walked over to the small living room and sat down on the sofa. He winced a little as he inadvertently put too much pressure on his left arm.

Valerie moved over to the dining table and placed the casserole beside a plate of empanadas. "The wounds on your shoulder still hurt?"

"Yeah, it's still sore and with the planting and all that gardening, my entire body is aching. My palms have got blisters too."

Valerie laughed as she walked over to the stovetop at the other side of the room. "Serves you right, Professor. You haven't put in an honest day's work until a few days ago. Now you know how farmers feel at the end of the day. Get yourself seated down at the table, dinner's ready."

Paul groaned as he got up from the comfortable sofa and made his way to the dining table. It had been a few days since he drove the kids down to Brooklyn after his own home in Boston had caught fire while fighting the Wendigo that was once his neighbor's wife. His wounds were not serious and since there were plenty of empty apartments around, Paul and the two children had decided to stay. Kim's younger brother Troy would talk endlessly about the Wendigo while his sister became more withdrawn. With Valerie's help, Paul was able to acquire a nearby apartment its owners had abandoned to share with the two kids.

Valerie placed her own casserole beside the pasta dish on the table before she sat down. "Okay, dig in. Is my mama getting along with Kim and Troy?"

"Oh yeah, She's wonderful. Your mother has a way with kids. Troy couldn't even speak the first time I met him up in Boston, but now he's a motor mouth. It's Kim I'm worried about now, though."

"Why? What's wrong with her?"

"First time I met them, she was the talkative one, but ever since she found out what happened to her parents, she started to distance herself, withdraw from the world. I've been trying my best to engage her but she just seems to have a lack of motivation for anything."

Valerie took an empanada and placed it on her plate. "Just give her some time, Professor. People deal differently with loss. Her little brother may have moved on, but it must have impacted her a lot more. Plus she's the older one, so she's probably trying to find her place in the world."

Paul nodded. "That's true. Val, you know you don't have to keep calling me professor. Just Paul would be fine."

"I guess I'm just not used to being around people with doctorate degrees. I come from a middle class Puerto Rican Mexican family, and I'm one of only two children in the clan that even finished high school."

"Well, people with advanced degrees aren't much different from other folks," Paul said as he spooned some of the food from the steaming deep dish onto his plate. "What's this? I thought it was lasagna."

"It's called pastelon. It's a Puerto Rican version of lasagna except that it's made with plantains instead of pasta sheets. There's not much meat in it though, for obvious reasons, so there's more veggies and béchamel sauce."

"Delicious," Paul said as he ate some of it. New York City was now one of the safer areas of the country after that incident in the Museum of Natural History. A certain calmness had descended over the city as if it was blessed by some unknown, benevolent demigod. Demon attacks had largely died down although nobody dared venture down into the subways and most people stayed in at night. The city officials along with the police had begun to parcel out unused apartments to refugees from other parts of the country that were steadily streaming in. People started to work hand in hand as they used every available green space to grow vegetables to supplement the meager food convoys still coming in. There seemed to be a sense of hope blossoming in this place.

As the sun started to set, Valerie took out her lighter from her pants pocket and began to light the candles that were strewn all over the apartment. Of all the things that were now in short supply, a small set of wax candles were getting to be more expensive than fresh meat. "You ought to try the empanadas too," she said. "My mama made them."

"Well if she made them then how could I say no to that?"

"Are you saying that you'd rather eat her food than mine, Paul?"

Paul laughed as he shook his head. "No, not at all. I like both your cooking and I'll eat whatever you place on the table."

"That's better. Have you thought about the future at all?"

"What do you mean?"

"Well, it seems you've completely gotten away from your academic background and became a farmer," Valerie said. "Is that what you're planning to do from now on?"

Paul looked out into the distance. "To be honest, I don't know yet. I guess I'm just taking it one day at time for now. Those two kids are all I could think about right now, I've never been a parent before but it feels like I'm obligated to take care of them. I don't think they will like it very much if I put them up for adoption or something like that. Why do you ask?"

Valerie looked at the food on her plate. "Well it's just that we received a communication about you from the Feds."

Paul was surprised. "You did? When?"

"About a week ago while you were still up in Boston. I thought about maybe driving up there to give you the message, but then I figured that if the government wanted to talk to you badly enough, they would come to your doorstep."

"What did the message say?"

"Not much, they just wanted to get in touch with you. That's all they would say to me. I told them you went back to your place in Boston. They never tried to contact you there?"

"Nope. But then again all the phone lines were out, including the cell signal, so I couldn't have been able to call you either even though I really could have used your help against that Wendigo."

"My god, that must have been a terrifying experience. What made you think that fire would kill it?"

"I've always figured that the Wendigo was sort to like an animal spirit. And animals are always afraid of fire, it's a part of their basic instincts," Paul said. "Then again, I don't even know if it did die. It could still be wandering around Boston right now as far as I know. I just got the kids to the car and drove out of there as soon as soon as we had a clear path to the driveway."

"You were lucky, by the time you got to the police station. Your car was just about to give out. Do you really think that Wendigo is out there right now?"

"I've always thought of that monster as a manifestation of mankind's fear of cannibalism, just a symbol of an old taboo that the original native peoples of this land had. Perhaps I may have destroyed its physical aspect, but I have no doubt that it could return in some shape or form again."

"That's a very scary thought, Paul. You don't think it would follow you down here, do you?"

"I don't know. I don't think so. My neighbor apparently enabled it since he was killing people and feeding them to his wife. Perhaps it was that act that made its physical form even stronger. Whatever the case, we have to make sure that no one resorts to cannibalism, lest that creature manifests itself again."

Valerie frowned as she placed her fork down on the plate. "I shouldn't even have brought it up, now I've lost my appetite even though we got lots of food here."

"I'm sorry, Val. Let's change the subject then."

"Let's do that," Valerie said as she opened a paper bag that was sitting on the table and took out a bottle of wine. "Cabernet sauvignon. I've been saving this last bottle since this whole Glooming started. I figured we might as well open it."

Paul noticed the wine opener lying on the coffee table nearby. "Allow me."

An hour had passed and the wine bottle was practically empty. Valerie couldn't stand the dirty plates on the table, so she took them over to the kitchen sink while Paul relaxed on the sofa. The aches in his shoulder had turned to an itch where the stitches had begun to get annoying. With the dishes now immersed in lukewarm water, Valerie went over to the couch and sat down beside him.

Paul heard a slight beep from his phone so he took it out, read the text message on it before he put it back into his shirt pocket with a smile. Unlike up in Boston, New York had been able to reactivate a few cell sites so there was limited mobile phone coverage. The mayor even claimed that they might have the electrical grid back soon, but Paul doubted it. "Your mother said she was able to put the kids to sleep and will stay with them for the night. I didn't think she'd be able to win Kim over, but she sure proved me wrong."

Valerie laughed as she finished off the last of the wine in her glass. "Didn't you know? There were eleven of us and my mother raised the whole family mostly by herself. Trust me, Kim and her pouting would be small potatoes to her."

"That's good. I'm wondering if I'd be staying here with the kids though."

"What do you mean? Are you afraid that the owners of the apartment where you're at will come back? I'm sure we can find another place for all three of you here, the whole city has been so depopulated, there's a lot of room to spare."

"It's not that."

"The food situation then? I heard that it's not much better in the other cities either. Las Vegas is now uninhabited since there's no water over there. At least over here, we're close to the government food banks in Virginia and everybody is helping out by growing their own food."

"It's not really that either."

"What then?"

"It's the people around here. I can sense a change."

Valerie seemed confused. "What sort of change, Paul?"

He hesitated before answering. "Well, it's just that I've heard talk that quite a few people around here have begun to worship all sorts of gods. I mean the old pagan gods. When one of the guys invited me for a drink of water in his apartment yesterday, his whole place was filled with small wooden idols that he carved by himself. When I asked him about it, he said that he was now worshiping Ahone, a god that was once worshiped by the Algonquin natives in this area hundreds of years ago. But he also had idols of other gods and he sort of gave prayers to each one of them. The whole thing made me feel uneasy because it seems we are sliding backwards as a civilization."

"Reverend Beekman said the same thing to me," Valerie said. "He used to have a small church in Baruch Houses over at the Lower East Side. Since he moved to Brooklyn and tried to revitalize his church, he told me that very few people profess to be any sort of Christian now. They are mostly turning into pagan worshipers of different gods. It's a growing trend among people here. My mama is putting up all sorts of Aztec god stuff in her apartment."

"Doesn't it worry you, Val? I mean you are Christian, aren't you?"

Valerie took out an Aztec amulet that was hidden beneath her shirt and displayed it prominently below her neck. "This was given to me by Mama and I've worn it since I was a child. I thought it was just nothing but now I think it's what saved me when I was attacked and half my face was cut. We had crucifixes and all that, but she never really took me or my brothers and sisters to church on a regular basis, so I just didn't find the time to wonder what my faith ever was. Now that this whole thing started, I don't know what to believe in. What about you?"

"Well, my mother was Catholic and my father was Protestant but not totally religious in a going to church, every Sunday sort of way. I was exposed to a lot of New Age and Eastern religions during my college days but I can't say I ever got serious about any of it. That was when I fell in with Joseph Campbell's philosophy of the monomyth. It's been a big part of my life and that was why I ultimately started writing books on it. Elizabeth and I were big believers in it."

"Monomyth? What's that?"

"Mono is Latin for single or one, and it basically means that I believe all the myths of the world are just variations of one great story. It's about a journey of a person- it can be Jesus, Buddha, Moses, or any of the other mythic heroes like Hercules, for example. It's a template that's found in every part of the world. It's a journey of finding oneself. I also believe in a universality of myths; that there are similarities of gods and stories from all over the world because there are so many similar tales of gods and monsters, that it can't be just mere coincidence."

"You mean that these mythical beings that have now come to life in every part of the world have some sort of commonality?"

"Yes! If you look at the different gods of the world's major regions, you'll note that even though one set of mythology is in another part of the world, there are universal similarities," Paul said as he began gesturing. He was fully animated now that he was in his element. "Take the concept of the trickster god for example. One Native American tribe believes he takes the form of a rabbit, while another tribe believed he was a coyote, and yet other peoples in places like Siberia for example, thought of him as looking like a raven. But in every culture there is a trickster god with very slight variations. The Norse believed Loki was a trickster god before he turned completely evil and got them all killed at Ragnarok. The Native Americans on the other hand, believe the trickster to be responsible for the creation of the world. But if you look at it, Loki did bring about the world of ordinary men by destroying the Norse gods, so in a sense, he was responsible for the creation of the world as well. You see, it's all variations of the same story despite the fact that the names and the physical aspect of the god is different, the stories in the end are so similar that there is a connection between each of them."

"So what you're saying is that all these different trickster gods from different parts of the world are all just one being?"

"No, what I'm saying is that there is a shared human spirituality because the beliefs that came about in so many different parts of the world are very similar, they may all very well come from a single source."

"So what do you believe in, Paul?"

"I just told you," he said as he leaned back on the sofa. "I believe that we are all one people on a spiritual level."

"That doesn't answer my question though, do you believe in God? Are you Christian?"

"I was a Christian. But my belief was that God is just a metaphor, another myth that transcends the mere concepts of a god that takes the form of a man or an animal. I didn't believe in a supernatural being in a literal sense."

"Right, you believe in the stories, the myths that are universal. But what about now? You've seen gods and monsters walk the earth, and I mean literally. Doesn't that prove your theory of the monomyth is wrong?"

Paul looked away. "I-I thought of them as stories that could somehow prove that there are more similarities than differences between the peoples of the world, and we could have built on it. I had hoped that we could somehow create a more peaceful society of tolerance and understanding because we were bound by common stories of how the world was created, and of our place in it. Now I don't know what to believe."

Valerie placed a hand on his arm. "Most people I knew before this all came about, they believed in something, or at least wanted to believe in a god that could be there for them in times of need, but most of their lives were spent worrying about their family or their job. But now that we know these gods are real what do we do now?"

"I don't know. But this does help explain why people are starting to worship some of these gods. They view them as powerful beings and they are, but they also have the characteristics of flawed human beings. These gods take revenge and they kill people who anger them. I can't worship a god who does this, even when it's been proven that they exist."

"Can anyone still be an atheist with all these gods running around?"

Paul placed his own hand on top of hers. "I guess the word atheism needs to change now. Just a few months ago it meant not believing in the existence of gods, from now on it ought to mean a refusal to worship gods. There is a word just for that, it's called irreligious."

"Is that even possible? How can you not worship a being more powerful than humans since they've been proven to exist?"

"Would you worship an evil creature that threatens to kill you and those you love just because they would feel slighted at your attitude to them?"

"It's called avoiding trouble. A lot of people would say yes just to avert that kind of curse, Paul."

"I just can't do it. I can't worship a megalomaniac, even an all-powerful one. I know they came from different times when cultural values were different but I'm a man of the Twenty-First Century, not some primitive who thinks everything is magic and superstition," Paul said.

"Where has it gotten us, though? Our military or any other nation's military can't stand up to them."

"So what are you saying? We give up on the civilization that we've built on, just go back to the ways of ancient times and let the gods rule the Earth?"

"Do we have a choice? The Feds are almost at the breaking point. Let's not even include the separatists in Kansas in this argument."

"What? What's happening in Kansas? You mean that church that's taken over the state?"

"Oh, you didn't hear? They've got nukes and used it against the Feds in Cheyenne Mountain. Wiped out an entire underground base, along with the Secretary of Defense and a whole bunch of soldiers. Suicide bomb attack, from what I heard."

"Oh my god."

"That's not all," Valerie said. "They've got the president and the Commander of NORTHCOM as hostages. They said that if the Feds attempt an invasion into their territory they will kill them and just nuke everything."

Paul remembered having a high level meeting with the president and Admiral Zimmerman. Now the government would be powerless to make rapid decisions until a replacement was found or they mount a rescue. "So who's running the country now?"

Valerie rolled her eyes. "The Speaker of the House, from what I heard. But he doesn't seem to be doing anything. The military wants to fight back, but what's left of Congress is hesitating until there is a vice president that can lead the country. I heard they might appoint someone soon, but there's plenty of confusion from what we've heard up there. They aren't sure if a new president should be elected, or they should just appoint someone in a temporary position."

"Wow, what a mess. We've got the Aztecs ready to invade from the south and right in the center of the country there is a new separatist movement."

"Kansas is run by Pastor Erik Burnley. Do you think Jesus put him up to it? His congregation seems to think so. I personally know quite a few cops, and their families are on their way to join up with him. He's getting more powerful by the day."

"I don't know if the Christian god put him up to it or not," Paul said. "But if that was true, why would he need nukes to defend his territory?"

"Do you think the Christians in Kansas are just lying then? Why are so many people joining up with them?"

Paul put his hands up in exasperation. "I don't know. It would make things a whole lot less complicated if Jesus Christ did come back and show himself. At least many of us would be taking his side, but all we've seen so far are just the gods that came before him."

"So what are our alternatives? Either worship the ancient gods or just die then?"

"Whenever I came up against a big problem in the past, I found the only way to solve it is to find the source of the problem," Paul said. "If there was something that triggered the return of these gods, then maybe there's a way to make them leave us alone again. If they left us before, then they could leave us in peace a second time. I may need to study up on the monomyth a little further, perhaps it may have the answers as to what we need to do."

"Let's say we do find the cause to all of this and find a way to banish these gods and their creatures, would that really achieve a victory? Many countries have already gone down and the existence of these gods has been proven. So what I'm saying is, can we truly get back to normal ever again once this is all over?"

Paul slid two fingers underneath his glasses and rubbed his nose. "That's a great question. But there's no way the world will ever be the same again. I think we ought to tackle the problems we're facing one at a time. The world finds a way to carry on, we just have to be there when this is all good and done."

Valerie's head was now leaning on his shoulder. "Easier said than done," she said softly. "There must be dozens of gods out there right now, how do we banish them all?"

"One god at a time," Paul said. "We need to find out what exactly happened at the museum. If it wasn't us that defeated that giant worm, then we need to get in contact with whoever did."

Valerie couldn't help but kiss him on the cheek. "That's a problem for another day."

Paul turned his head, put his arms around her shoulders and gave her a deep kiss on the lips. "Is it okay if I stay here for the night?"

She grinned. "I was wondering when you'd be asking that question, Professor. I thought you didn't like me."

He gave her another long kiss. "Whatever gave you that idea?"

Valerie laughed. "Well, you took off to Boston for a few weeks even though I offered to put you up here."

Paul rested his chin on her head. "I'm sorry about that. I was selfish. Now I realize that I can't run away from my responsibilities. There just isn't a safe place anywhere on this planet, I know that now. I had to make a choice to find a way to get rid of these gods, or give up and just die. But with you and the kids on my mind, I now know I have to use the knowledge I've got to help everyone."

"There was another thing that worried me."

Paul looked at her. "What?"

Valerie ran a finger along her scar. "This. My face looks like it was stitched together."

Paul took her hand away as he started into her eyes. "Lady, you are one beautiful woman. And I could care less about that scar. I don't even see it."

"Thanks, Paul."

"No. Thank you."

It was early morning when Paul got up from the bed and walked into the bathroom. The day after his return to Brooklyn, he had decided to shave his beard off. Valerie had said his smooth chin made him look years younger and the two kids hardly recognized him. As he stared into the mirror, he wondered how he could have possibly been so selfish towards her. Of all the people he had known since the crisis had started, Valerie had always been there for him. She wasn't a fountain of knowledge like Elizabeth was, but she was feisty and had a lot of heart. Perhaps it was because he couldn't let go of the memory of his wife, which was the reason why it took him so long to finally acknowledge his attraction to Valerie. Whatever happened now, Paul had a feeling that he would no longer be alone. He had found a reason to rejoin the world instead of rejecting it.

A loud knock on the outside door made him jolt as he dropped the toothbrush into the sink. Less than a minute later, Valerie came out of the bedroom with her pistol in her hand as he joined her in the living room. He wore checkered pajama trousers and a white t-shirt while she had put on a bathrobe.

Paul dried his face with a hand towel as he heard more knocking. "Are you expecting someone this morning?"

"Nope," Valerie said as she checked to make sure there was a round in the gun's chamber before standing by the door. "Who is it?"

"Special Agent Lawrence Johnson, ma'am. FBI," the voice from the other side of the door said.

Valerie looked at Paul and winked at him. "Doesn't sound like a Wendigo. Should we let him in?"

Paul shrugged. "I don't see why not."

Valerie opened the door. Standing outside in the corridor were two large men wearing suits. They both had serious looks on their faces. She could see the bulges underneath their jackets, indicating that they were armed. Valerie kept her own pistol out of sight but she had a feeling both men knew about it.

"Ma'am, I can see that Professor Paul Dane is with you," Johnson said. He was the taller of the two. "We'd like to speak with him."

"Why don't you both just come in," Valerie said as she placed her Glock in the pocket of her bathrobe while the two men entered. "Would you like some coffee?"

"No thank you, ma'am, we can't stay for long," Johnson said before turning to look at Paul. "Professor Dane, we need you to come with us, please. We've been looking for you these past few days."

Paul adjusted the glasses on his nose. "Is this an order or a request?"

"We are aware that you tended your resignation with the DOD," Johnson said. "I would just like to request that you come with us because the Deputy Secretary of Defense would like to speak with you."

Valerie said nothing as she looked at Paul.

Paul returned her stare before turning to face the two agents again. "I'll have to think about it first," he said. Paul was wary of them after what had happened, and he was still somewhat defensive about meeting any of their type.

As the four of them were talking, the door to the outside was left open and a thin, middle-aged woman walked into the room before closing the door behind her. As Paul and Valerie stared at her in surprise, the two FBI agents moved back and flanked her. Agent Johnson had started to tense, he knew that Valerie was armed but he kept his cool and didn't draw his own weapon.

The woman was wearing an office suit. Her blonde hair was turning gray but it was combed neatly and barely touched her shoulders. "Sorry to barge in like this but there isn't much time so I had to use the direct approach," she said.

Valerie was leery at being surprised like that. Her hand had instinctively grabbed the pistol underneath her bathrobe, but she had managed to stay calm. "Who are you?"

"My name is Mary Arctor," the woman said. "I'm the Deputy Secretary of Defense. My superior was killed when the Kansas separatists attacked our bases in Colorado. So until they put someone in charge of the executive office that will replace him, then I guess I run things for the DOD for now."

"So you're the new Secretary of Defense until they decide to replace you," Paul said wistfully.

"Yes," Mary said. "On behalf of my organization, I would like to apologize at the way you were treated when my predecessor was in charge. When the team for the museum was being organized I voiced my opposition for the inclusion of the nuclear weapon, but I was overruled. I also wanted you to have full command over the operation, but again I was overruled and my suggestions were ignored."

"Apology accepted," Paul said. He was willing to help the government, but only if they didn't put the knuckleheads in charge. "So what do you want from me now?"

Mary kept a straight face as she stared directly at him. "Let's stop beating around the bush. The situation has been steadily getting worse all over the world, and I would like to reassemble this mythological task force before it's too late. What I can guarantee this time is that nothing will be kept from you, and you will be completely in charge, that I can promise. The military officers in the new task force will serve purely as advisers and not in a command capacity."

Paul crossed his arms. "That's all well and good, Ms. Arctor, but what if they decide to replace you? Will all the promises you've made go out of the window again?"

"You can always quit again if that should happen, or if I don't live up to my guarantees," Mary said. "But as long as I'm in charge, you will get what you need. The fact is we need you more than ever now. I could beg but I hope you won't force an old woman like me to get down on her knees because I will have a very hard time getting back up."

Paul smiled as he put his palms up in a gesture of reconciliation. "I'll accept under one condition. Well, a few conditions I mean."

Mary's face was impassive. "Name them."

Paul looked at Valerie. "I will need a police liaison and advisory so I would like Detective Mendoza as part of my team."

Mary didn't bat an eye. "Done."

"There's two young children who have recently been orphaned," Paul said. "I would like them to stay with me until we can find their closest relatives."

"Fine, anything else?"

Paul made a sweeping gesture with his hand. "I'd like the three of you to leave and wait outside while I put my pants on."

Valerie was giggling as the Deputy Secretary and her two FBI agents left the apartment. "That was a little mean, Paul," she said. "But why would you need me in this task force of yours? I'm nobody special."

Paul smiled as he kissed her for the first time that day. "You are pretty important. You were right there when that worm god manifested itself in the museum, and you encountered a possible Aztec cult and survived both times. You know how to speak Nahuatl too so that may come in handy when we have to deal with the threat down south. And of course, there's one other, very important thing."

"What's that?"

"I realized that can't live without you, Val. I need you with me. Whatever happens, I want us together."

She smiled and gave him a hug. Valerie knew as well that she needed him too. They were so much alike. Two lost souls looking for companionship and love. From now on, neither of them would be alone, not as long as they could help it.

19. The Seekers

Otherworld

"You seem to be in a very happy mood. I never saw you like this before," the ghost boy said. His name was Andrei Shokolov but almost every other boy had called him Buratino, the Russian version of Pinocchio.

"It's a good day for me," Ilya Volkhov said as he sat on a small boulder. The sun had been shining relentlessly on the windswept island, yet he neither felt warmth nor cold. "I am finally free after so many months, and I get to meet you one more time."

Andrei's physical form seemed to be made of mist and there was a faint greenish glow surrounding him. "You're lucky you can still feel something. I cannot feel anything anymore."

Ilya nodded solemnly. "So where is this place?"

"I think it's an island called Booyan. Our fairy tales says this is where the dead go to live happily ever after and sometimes to be reborn. Why did you tell the raven god to come here? You're not dead."

"I just wanted to see you again," Ilya said. "It would have made me really sad if you went to someplace like hell or something. I also wanted to say something to you."

"What?"

"I just wanted to say I was sorry for not trying to help you fight Baba, Yaga. I couldn't stop thinking about that day we went into her hut and what she did to you."

"You do not need to apologize," Andrei said. "If you had tried to fight her, you would have ended up dead like me. At least now you're alive and still fighting."

"I hate that witch for killing you. Once I find my mother and defeat Chernobog I will kill Baba Yaga too."

"No need to try to gain revenge," Andrei said softly. "After all, it was my stupid idea to go into her hut, remember? She didn't kill you because you didn't steal anything. She was only protecting her possessions."

"You are right, I just feel an emptiness inside every time I try to think of revenge. I'm sorry."

Andrei pointed to the hulking, pale humanoid standing by the sandy beach, less than a hundred yards away. "Who is that monster?"

Ilya turned and looked before facing his best friend again. "Oh, he used to be an American soldier. His name is Patrick Gyle, I think."

"What happened to him? He looks like a cross between a crocodile and a vampire."

"Raven told me that Noah gave him some sort of magical plant and he ate it. He may not look human anymore, but he has the strength of a hundred men and can withstand bullets with that thick skin of his. He moves like a bolt of lightning too."

"He sounds like a superhero. Pity that he is very ugly."

Ilya laughed. "I wouldn't say that to his face, but then again, I doubt he could do anything to you."

"Very funny you little bastard," Andrei said as he shook a fist.

"So what will happen to you now? Will you stay on this island forever?"

Andrei shrugged. "I don't know. I heard from Ozwiena that kids like me might be reborn again, but that would mean we lose all our memories of our previous life."

Ilya smiled. "That is good. I hope you do get reborn again. You deserve another chance at life. I talked to Ozwiena too."

"You did? When?"

"After I escaped from Baba Yaga's hut. I was in the middle of a forest when I chanced upon Radegast, the god of hospitality. He took me to his mead hall and there I met Ozwiena."

"That must have been quite an adventure. I have heard of your deeds when you and another mortal joined forces and defeated an American god. If you keep this up you might be the next Ivan Tsarevich or Ilya Muromets. But of course those two are taller, stronger, and better looking."

"Asshole!"

"What? I was trying to complement you."

Ilya frowned. "Go ahead, make fun of me! Anyway, I was wondering if you know something about that other mortal. Her name is Tara and it seems that she was abducted by a mysterious enemy. Have you heard anything about that in the spirit world?"

"Let me think," Andrei said as he looked down on the ground. "Ah, I have been hearing whispers in the wind about a war between the Dokkalfar and the Sidhe. I am not sure but it may have something to do with your friend."

"The Dokkalfar? Who are they?"

"They are also known as the dark elves. They supposedly live under the ground and their skin is as black as the night. They have accused the faerie nobles of abducting their kin."

"Dark elves? I think I must have seen movies about them before."

"Well the real ones are different than what we saw in those movies. They seem much shorter for one, about half your size."

"They are like dwarves then?"

"I think so. They are known throughout the Spirit World as makers of weapons and experts at crafting metalwork. Be careful about them though, I heard that they can be dangerous when crossed."

"Thank you for the information," Ilya said. "I wish there was something I could do for you in return."

Andrei smiled. "I think our meeting here has been quite beneficial for me too. For a time, I was feeling sad and alone. Now that you have gone out of your way just to meet me again I can feel a sense of peace, Ilya. I think I am ready to move on now."

Ilya was shocked. "Where will you be going to?"

"I don't know," Andrei said softly. "But whatever happens, it was nice to see you again and now you can continue your hero's journey. We will be best friends forever. Thank you and perhaps we shall meet again, hopefully in better times."

Ilya's eyes began to tear up. "Goodbye, Andrei."

"At least you stopped calling me Buratino," Andrei said as he laughed before his form shimmered and then faded away into the nearby mists.

The raven had been perching on Gyle's shoulders as he stood near the sandy beach like a statue. They both saw that Ilya was now walking back towards them. The boy's cheeks were flushed as he stood in front of them a few minutes later.

Gyle's voice was guttural, like a moan coming from a deep, dark well. "Are you okay, kid?"

"Yes," Ilya said before switching his eyes to the bird. "Thank you for bringing me here. It was good to see my friend for one last time."

"Well you did earn it," the raven said.

Ilya kept staring at the bird. "What happened to your dog form? I thought gods couldn't be killed."

"It was damaged. Besides, I felt it might be better to assume a more mobile animal, one that can fly," the raven said.

"So you can change your shape then? Into any kind of animal?"

"That's one way of putting it."

"Why don't you just turn into something more powerful, like a dragon, so you can breathe fire on our enemies, wouldn't that make things easier?"

"I don't believe in fighting."

Ilya pointed at Gyle. "Is that why you brought him along? So he could do the fighting for you?"

The black bird began to adjust its wing feathers with its beak. "That's one way of putting it, I guess."

Ilya placed his hands on his hips. "Can you ever just give me a simple answer?"

"Try asking a simple question next time."

Ilya shook his head. "You are really trying my patience. I wish I had another god as an ally instead of a talking bird."

"You should be more grateful. Especially since I saved you from those commandos."

Ilya pointed at Gyle again. "It was him who saved me, not you."

"If it wasn't for me bringing him, you would be back in the military stockade."

Ilya sighed. "Alright, thank you, bird god, for saving me. When I talked to my friend Andrei, he said something about a war between the faeries and the dark elves and that might have something to do with Tara's kidnapping."

Gyle twisted his head to look at the bird on his shoulder. "These beings, why would they go to war over a human girl?"

"Faeries covet mortals to help populate their realms," the raven said. "Since they live forever, time passes quite differently there, and they get bored quite easily. A human guest in their kingdoms might amuse them for a time."

"I've heard of such stories," Gyle said. "They would substitute a fairy when they would take a human child, the creatures they call changelings."

"But there was no substitution when Tara was abducted. She was in a convoy full of soldiers. One of these soldiers told me the story was that they were attacked by chorts. In Russia we call them devils and demons," Ilya said.

Gyle stretched out one of his long arms and the raven perched on his hand. "Do the faeries have demonic allies?"

"Faeries have been called many names, sometimes as demons," the black bird said. "But they prefer trickery over brute force."

"Then perhaps it isn't the faeries who took her," Ilya said. "What about these dark elves. Are they evil creatures?"

The raven looked up into the sunny sky. "How many times must I tell you, boy. No being is inherently good or totally evil. Each have their sides, like that of a coin. The dark elves almost never involve themselves in human affairs."

"Then perhaps someone made them do it," Gyle said. "Regardless, we need to travel to those places in order to find out."

Ilya pulled out some bits of raskovnik from the folds of his jacket. "I still have some of this magical plant left. They will allow me to tell if the faeries and the elves are telling the truth."

"We ought to go to the faerie realms first," Gyle said. "Raven, can you send us over there?"

"As I've told you before," the raven said. "You merely have to use your mind and start walking. The path to the other worlds will reveal themselves to you."

"Then let us get started," Ilya said as he started to walk along the beach.

As the three of them started moving in one direction, the path ahead soon began to shimmer and change completely. Within a matter of seconds, they were now walking along a path while gigantic trees were all around them. They could not see the night sky, but the forest was illuminated by a strange phosphorescent yellow glow. There were a number of fireflies that flew back and forth, like miniature lanterns. They could smell fragrances both wondrous and strange as the entire realm seemed to be made of flowers. Distant sounds of clanging metal and laughter could be heard but they couldn't pinpoint the direction from where it came.

Ilya felt his winter boots were too heavy, but he made it an effort to keep up with Gyle's long strides. "This seems to be a much better place than Booyan. If I were to go into the afterlife as a ghost, I would prefer to stay here."

The raven was perched on Gyle's shoulder once more. "Beware of the faeries and their tricks."

Ilya snorted. "Well, you're a trickster god too if I remember correctly, shouldn't I be wary of trusting you too?"

"As you wish," the raven said nonchalantly.

Gyle stopped and held up a restraining hand to make sure the boy stopped too. "I sense something up ahead. Be on guard."

Ilya rolled his eyes. "That is pretty obvious."

As the armored man and the boy began to walk down the path again, it soon led into a massive clearing that looked to be the center of the forest. A huge bonfire had been started and its flames seemed to leap up into the heavens. Countless little creatures were darting to and fro, using tongs to take glowing bars of metal from the fire and carry them to over a dozen waiting anvils. A small army of blacksmiths that seemed to be the size of garden gnomes were hammering away, trying to forge weapons for war.

"Halt," a voice that came from their left flank said. "Who dares to venture into the faerie realms without permission?"

As the three of them turned, they saw what seemed to be a horde of creatures in all shapes and sizes that began to surround them. Eight-foot tall ogres with clubs, glowing winged faeries the size of large crickets, pint-sized imps and dwarves- all brandishing jet-black spears. The multitude of snarling, raging supernatural beings began pointing their spears, some of them thrusting their weapon points forward, threatening to skewer both Gyle and the boy as they began to hem them in.

Gyle crouched low as he prepared to charge them. "Raven, get ready and take on the flying creatures as soon as I get started. Boy, when I go, you follow close and then head off into the forest as soon as there's a gap. If I'm still alive, I'll find you," he whispered over his shoulder.

Ilya placed a restraining hand on Gyle's rugged elbow. "I have a better idea," the boy said as he used his free hand to take out the bits of raskovnik and brandished it in front of the faeries.

Almost immediately, the front ranks of the horde began to shriek and fall back. Even the giant ogres squealed like scared pigs as they ran backwards, nearly crushing the smaller dwarves and imps that were behind them. The little winged creatures that had planned an attack from the air, instantly flew away towards the sheltering branches of the nearby trees. As Ilya began to wave the magical herbs back and forth in front of him, the once massive army of faeries began to dissolve into scared packs of critters that were running to and fro, desperate to get away from the herbal scent of the raskovnik.

Even though he could no longer show anymore emotions on his leathery face, Gyle was impressed. "Jesus H. Christ. How did you know they have a weakness for that kind of plant?"

Ilya couldn't help but smile as he put the plant bits back into his coat pocket. "The raskovnik is a very powerful herb, according to the folk tales of Russia. It can do almost anything, and I heard that these faeries can be affected by special plants."

The raven had hardly moved from Gyle's shoulder. "So you made a guess? And the right guess at that?" the trickster said.

"I felt that it was worth a try," the boy said. "Thinking your way past a problem is better than fighting your way through one."

Gyle nodded. "Smart kid."

"If you please, my name is Ilya. I prefer to be called that over boy or kid," Ilya said tersely.

The sound of stomping hooves was soon heard as the center of the horde parted and a troop of supernatural cavalry had arrived. Leading the front was a huge black warhorse and a man-sized being riding on an ornate saddle sitting on top of it. The knight was wearing a greenish brown colored armor that seemed to be made of tree bark. His long green beard protruded from the bottom of his ornate wooden helm. Right behind him were assorted dwarves mounted on billy goats, their spears and lances pointed downwards as if ready for an immediate charge. The faeries on foot immediately began to get emboldened by the arrival of their apparent leader, as they began to howl their war cries once more and started to advance behind the cavalry.

The being on the horse instantly raised a gauntleted hand in the air and the horde stopped and became quiet almost instantly. "I am the Erlking, ruler of this realm! How dare you intrude upon my kingdom without permission!"

Ilya immediately remembered the first time he had ventured into the Spirit World. The boy quickly got down to a single knee and bowed his head. "We apologize for coming into your kingdom unannounced, oh great king. We are on a quest to find our friend and companion who was kidnapped by your enemies, the dark elves. We came to you to seek your wise council and perhaps join as allies."

Gyle was confused for a minute, but then he understood and immediately knelt down as well. *Better to let the boy do all the talking*, he thought to himself.

"Took you long enough," the raven whispered in Gyle's ear hole.

The Erlking was impressed as he took off his helm and bowed slightly in return. "You may rise. I thank you for the proper introduction. It seems more and more mortals have been coming and going into my realm but very few know the ways of the fey people. You seem but a mere child, but your cleverness has impressed me, Ilya Volkhov."

Ilya stood up and stared at the king in surprise. "You know my name?"

The Erlking laughed. "Word travels fast when one converses with the goddess Ozwiena! Your deeds are renowned throughout the infinite worlds," he said before looking at Gyle and the bird on his shoulder. "You are Patrick Gyle, once a warrior and now still a warrior, but of a different kind. And of course, how could I not know about Loki!"

"Pardon me, great Erlking, but I must remind you that Loki died in Ragnarok," the raven said as it ignored the shocked stares coming from Gyle and Ilya.

The Erlking put a palm up. "Ah, you are right! How could I have forgotten? You must be Veles then!"

"Not quite, but you're getting close," the black bird said.

The Erlking finally shook his head. "I give up! All of you trickster gods can change your form, just like the fey. And there are so many of you that I cannot name each and every one for that would take forever. How would you like me to address you?"

"Since I have taken the form of a raven here, then that would be sufficient," the black bird said.

"Very well, Raven it is," the Erlking said. "Now onto the business at hand. I must tell you that we fey folk are normally beings of merriment and glad tidings, but we are now preparing for war!"

With those words, the entire horde of faeries immediately began to bang their weapons on their shields while letting out their war cries in unison. This went on for a full minute before the Erlking raised his hand and the fey instantly fell silent once more.

"We've heard that you are at war with the dark elves," Gyle said. "Is there a reason for this?"

The Erlking leaped from his horse and landed on the ground beside them. "Yes, my beloved daughter, the faerie princess Charissa, was kidnapped by the foul race of dark elves, the Dokkalfar. My kingdom now prepares to invade their accursed lands to bring her safely home."

Ilya looked up at the Erlking. "How do you know that it was the dark elves that took your daughter?"

The Erlking took out a black stone from beneath his armor and held it in front of them. "This dark ore was found in her chambers, the type of rock that is unique and can only be found beneath the mountains of the Dokkalfar kingdom. Her chambers were in disarray, it was clear that she was forcefully abducted by them for they had lusted over her for thousands of years. We shall fight to bring her back and then the fey shall have justice!"

As their king said those words, the horde of faeries began shouting and howling once again before falling silent as Ilya raised his hand, and the Erlking gestured at them to keep quiet.

"We are also looking for one of our companions," Ilya said. "She's a girl named Tara and she was my friend. Someone has also kidnapped her and we are searching for clues as to who might have taken her. Do you know if the dark elves have other prisoners in their kingdom?"

The Erlking thought about it for a minute. "The only other mortal that I have met in the past hundred years was another boy like you, not a girl. He too was searching for a way to rescue his sister from a wizard but he was from another part of your world."

Ilya furrowed his eyebrows. "Another boy was here? And he was going up against a wizard? Was this wizard human or was it some sort of other being?"

"These magicians are human mortals like yourself, boy," the Erlking said. "But they seem to be quite malevolent because they crave power in all its forms. There is a whole group of them that are active in your world, and they are causing a lot of strife there."

"Then it's possible that these wizards might know about Tara too," Ilya said. "Can you tell us everything you know about them? What are they called?"

The Erlking snorted as he crossed his arms. "Alas, I cannot tell you any more, my people are preparing for war and while many of them shall die, this is for a glorious cause. We will make whatever sacrifice is needed for the return of my daughter."

"Wait a minute," Gyle said. "There are so many suspects in your daughter's disappearance that I don't think it's wise for you to make war on another race without full proof. Have you talked to these dark elves about this?"

"Well, no," the Erlking said. "But the black ore found in her chambers is proof enough. There shall be no negotiations until she is returned to us!"

Ilya scratched the top of his head. "Are you sure that perhaps the black stone was planted there by someone who was making it look like it was the dark elves that did it?"

The Erlking growled in frustration. "No, it cannot be! The only ones who could know about her are the dark elves or one of the fey! You mortals are confusing us!"

"Well, there's only one way to find out," the raven said.

Ilya nodded. "King of the faeries, if my friends and I go to the kingdom of the elves and try to find your daughter and bring her back to you, will you promise to tell us everything you know about this group of wizards from my world?"

The Erlking nodded. "That is a fair bargain. Very well, we shall refrain from attacking the dark elves until your return. Find out if they are indeed holding my daughter captive. If you bring her back safely, I shall reward you with knowledge and aid you in whatever else we can manage."

"It's a deal then," Ilya said.

As the three of them moved along the paths of the forest, a few winged faeries flew by and offered words of encouragement before flying off into another part of the woods. After their agreement, the Erlking had offered to feast with them but they politely refused and excused themselves.

The raven had mostly been silent but it shifted uneasily on Gyle's shoulder. "Ilya, you made a bargain with these faeries. They will not take kindly to you if you break this contract."

"Do not worry, little bird," Ilya said confidently. "I am thinking of a plan to find out where this fairy princess is."

"You seem pretty sure of yourself," Gyle said. "Almost as if you know what the answer to this mystery is."

Ilya shrugged as he kept on walking. "I have a few suspicions."

"Is that why you asked to see the princesses bed chamber and had a look around?" Gyle asked.

"Yes," Ilya said. "That is also why I asked to question the personal servants of the princess."

Gyle shook his head in disbelief. "And where did you get all these ideas from?"

"From watching TV, of course," Ilya said. "When the cops look at a crime scene, they always ask questions about what happened, and then look for clues. We may be in another world but it is no different."

"Pity those faeries don't watch TV then," Gyle said.

20. The Schemers

Ashkelon

David Zim used his fingers to partially open the Venetian blinds to look out into the street below. As expected, the roads were deserted and only two cars were parked on the side of the street. If anyone was observing them, the surveillance teams must be from nearby apartments, but other than a couple of kids on their bicycles, the entire block seemed to be asleep on a lazy afternoon.

"Coffee is finally here," Dov Bar-Lev said as he carefully placed a tray on the low table in his apartment's living room. A former rabbi, Bar-Lev was now in his mid-sixties but he always wore his yarmulke the moment he got up from bed, even indoors. He was typical of the people who were now in the cities all across Israel, men and women deemed too old to be called up for reserve duty. All that remained of civilians in the safe zones were now just the elderly, the unwanted, or the children.

David turned around, walked back to where the living room was and sat down on the sofa facing the other three men. Bar-Lev wrapped his stubby hands around the ceramic coffee pot and poured a steaming cup for each of them.

"Thank you," Amel Kasem said as he accepted a cup of coffee from the former rabbi. Kasem was a Druze who was now in his early thirties, very close to David's age. His family had been staunch supporters of Israel for several generations now. Although occasionally mistaken for Muslims, the Druze followed their own teachings which included elements from Gnosticism, Christianity, Judaism, and Hinduism to create a distinct and secretive theology that believed in successive reincarnations until the soul was united with a cosmic mind.

Of the four of them, Aviv Lerner was the youngest. He was in his late twenties and a Haredi Jew. His family was staunchly anti-Zionist and he had refused to serve in the IDF, which was mandatory for every adult citizen of the country. While David and Kasem were clean shaven, Lerner's brown beard and sideburns was kept as long as possible, in keeping with his Haredi traditions. The young man was also wearing a black suit and white dress shirt, unlike the others in the room who wore just casual clothing due to the oppressive heat of the day. He had placed his black fedora beside him and like Bar-Lev, wore his skullcap indoors. Lerner silently accepted his cup of coffee with a nod of thanks.

"I'm sorry I don't have any cakes to offer you," Bar-Lev said as he poured himself a cup. "But all the nearby stores have been closed and that meant I had to wait for the next bus to go to the outskirts of town. If only this meeting wasn't scheduled at the last minute, I could have bought something to go with the coffee."

Kasem smiled. "It's alright, I'm still pretty full from lunch myself. This coffee is perfect to stop me from falling asleep."

David looked at Bar-Lev. "I think we might as well get started. My wife will be looking for me very soon and I have to get back to Beersheba."

Bar-Lev said nothing as he merely nodded.

"Alright then," David said. "We've already made some short introductions to each other so I will just get right to the point. We are all meeting here to state our concerns about what is happening to our country and to discuss ideas on what we can do about it."

"There's no need to be diplomatic, David," Bar-Lev said as he scratched his salt and pepper beard. "We all know what's going on so we might as well be blunt about it. Don't hold back."

"We all know," Lerner said. "But what can we do about it? There's only four of us."

"I have been to the front lines and the IDF general staff knows about me so if I tell them I'm fit for duty, they will not hesitate to bring me back in. I think I can get close to Rabbi Ba'al and end this once and for all," David said softly.

Bar-Lev adjusted his glasses and stared at David. "So you want to kill him? Then what will happen? Do you think all of this will suddenly end?"

Kasem put down his half empty coffee cup on the table. "It sounds drastic but what we've been doing … it's a war crime. I was there when we went into the Palestinian towns in the West Bank because I was a lieutenant in the Sword Battalion. When I protested to my superiors, they threatened to put me in a military jail. The only reason I was thrown out was that I had been a decorated officer and several commanders vouched for me. I hate to say this, but we're turning into the Nazis."

Bar-Lev clasped his fingers together and leaned back on his chair. "We're not getting a lot of news here in the cities as you well know because everybody is out in the front lines. Tell us what happened?"

Kasem's eyes were looking down on the floor. He took a deep breath before he started talking. "We were ordered to round up the Palestinians and bring them to the central processing camp near Jerusalem. All the men, women, even the children. Many of them were scared because we had tanks, gunships, and artillery, so many of them didn't resist. We even had loudspeakers telling them we were moving them to safer areas. That was obviously a lie. Of course, many of the younger men and their police forces did try to resist so we took them down hard. Some of them tried to hide among the civilians while shooting at us so we didn't hesitate. Our superiors made sure none of us had any mobile phones or cameras to record anything. I saw two Palestinian men armed with rifles run into a house with a family still inside of it. We just poured all our firepower into that whole building until there was nothing left but a pile of stone and concrete. In the end, they knew they couldn't resist but some did anyway. It took us three days to take all the people from that town ,and it's been like that throughout the rest of the West Bank. Gaza has been quiet but I know we will go in there and empty it soon. That damned rabbi needs more souls."

"I've heard that the people in Gaza know what's happened in the West Bank, and they will fight with everything they have," David said. "Last thing I heard was that the IDF wanted to nuke the whole place rather than take any more casualties trying to capture the people there. The Gaza front is quiet right now but that could change within hours if the IDF starts placing more troops close by."

"And you're sure that Rabbi Ba'al is behind all of this?" Bar-Lev said.

"I'm certain of it," David said. "You all know my uncle. He's a member of the Knesset and from he told me Elijah Ba'al is practically running the country now. Whatever he wants he gets. The IDF and the Prime Minister have become his lapdogs."

Lerner kept shaking his head from side to side, his long sideburns were flapping like furry ears. "This is not the way of the Jews. We are a righteous people and what that meant was that God entrusted us to be a shining beacon of light, an example for all mankind to follow. We are supposed to love our neighbor as much as we are to love ourselves. What you've told me is horrific beyond imagining. We have abandoned the teachings of God. Justice, truth, and peace are nonexistent now."

"About two weeks ago one of Rabbi Ba'al's political allies gave a speech on live TV," Bar-Lev said. "Yakov Porat, a senior member of the Defense Committee. He said that the Palestinians were nothing more than a tribe of Canaanites and that according to the Tanakh, God had commanded the Israelis to exterminate them without mercy. I cannot support any of these views."

"We're all of the same side here," David said. "The question is what do we do about it?"

Lerner also looked down on the floor and raised a finger. "I support your plan to assassinate Elijah Ba'al. Please do not even call him a rabbi for he is a heretic, and his name shouldn't even be mentioned any longer."

"I'll try to help in whatever way I can," Kasem said. "But even now, I think the IDF command is starting to distrust the Druze and the other minorities in the military, they are purposely placing us in the front lines, as far away from the Palestinian areas as possible. The Sword Battalion took a lot of casualties in the battle of Amman. The only reason why I'm here right now is that they threw me out of the unit before that battle started, and I was sent back here to await a new assignment, if that ever comes. I'm afraid that once they run out of Muslims, they may go after my people next."

"That heretic, he has begun to recruit his own followers," Lerner said. "Already, ten students of my kolel in Jerusalem have quit their studies when they were offered an apprenticeship to train under him. He is poisoning the entire Jewish religious community in this country. Pretty soon he will have a large following of blasphemers to serve him. If we don't do something, he will be unstoppable soon."

"He seems pretty unstoppable now," Bar-Lev said. "Even if David is able to succeed, how can we be assured that the government will not continue his work?"

"Ba'al has some sort of magical book. The Sefer Yetzirah. Yes, I know it's supposed to be a very common book, but he told me personally that he has the original copy, with spells and incantations for creating demonic creatures. Once he's dead, I need to find and destroy that book." David said.

Lerner was shocked. "He has the original Sefer Yetzirah? T-that's astounding! Surely we must preserve that book in order to research the knowledge it contains. It can open up a brand new horizon on the subject of Jewish mysticism."

Bar-Lev shook his head. "Look at what he has wrought by using that damned book. I'm with David, we need to destroy it."

Kasem shrugged. "I don't care either way. As long as we put a stop to this madness."

"But that begs the question," Bar-Lev said. "Assuming we succeed. What then? Do we condemn the state of Israel as slaves of the new Babylon? I don't like what's being done, but I can see why the government and the military went along with him."

"I would suggest that you do not destroy the book right away," Lerner said. "Perhaps we may be able to find a solution against those demons without having to sacrifice people to create golems in that book."

David sighed as he rubbed his hands over his face. "Look, I don't even know if I could pull this off. In the end this could end up as a one-way trip for me. We need to find out more information and we need to recruit others that can help us."

"A lot of people in my community are starting to get concerned, so I 'm sure I could recruit some of my friends and colleagues," Kasem said. "But then again, there are places where we are not allowed to go to."

"The one thing that can get us through IDF checkpoints is mission orders," David said. "If we can find someone who can forge them so that we can pass through sensitive areas to get to the processing camp, then we might have a chance."

"I can talk to the head of my kolel. I know that he has been in contact with that heretic and if I could find out and get some sort of authorization to get into that camp then I will get it for you," Lerner said. "But I have to be careful as to who I ask because if any of them are loyal to that magician, then the game will be up."

"He has to have the book somewhere close by him because he uses it all the time," David said. "If we can pinpoint where he lives in the camp, then we can approximate where the book would be."

Kasem rubbed his elbows after crossing them. "What if that book is secured? What if it's in a safe?"

"I don't think he would secure it that much," David said. "He needs to have that book handy so it must be readily accessible to him."

Bar-Lev emptied his cup of coffee. "Do you know what the book looks like?"

David shook his head. "Well no, but—"

Bar-Lev put his hands halfway up in the air. "Then how will you know if you got it or not? Will you search through his pile of books after you've killed him?"

"Maybe killing him is too risky," Lerner said. "Why not just steal the book instead?"

"He has to die," David said. "If we just take the book from him, he will have plenty of resources to recover it. The whole program centers on him. Ba'al is the head of the snake and our only chance to take back the country is to eliminate him."

Lerner glanced over at Bar-Lev. "We will be branded as criminals after this. They may very well arrest us all or even shoot us."

"There is a special law called the Law of the Pursuer, the din rodef," Bar-Lev said. "If one is pursuing to murder another then a bystander is allowed to kill that man. Elijah Ba'al is a rodef, in my view, and it's perfectly legal to kill him."

Lerner frowned. "That is the same defense that the assassin of one of our previous prime ministers used. The courts didn't believe him."

"That man assassinated a prime minister though," David said. "Ba'al isn't a head of state."

"But he has been recently appointed as one of the Chief Rabbinates. He is now the supreme rabbinic and spiritual authority for the entire country. That would make things very complicated," Lerner said.

Kasem looked at David. "Assuming you are even able to pull off the kill, how do you plan on getting away?"

"I haven't even gotten to that part yet," David said. "This is all just preliminary planning for now."

"Well, whatever it is we're going to do, we will need to decide soon," Bar-Lev said. "The Palestinians and the other Muslim refugees are up against the clock."

The drive from Ashkelon to Beersheba took close to an hour. David rode in Kasem's car. Both men were mostly silent with barely any small talk. The warm air that passed through the open windows whipped through David's hair as Kasem drove them into the outskirts of Beersheba before turning into a residential street, just a few blocks away from the apartment.

David pointed to a sidewalk ahead of them while they waited for the traffic light to change. "You better let me out over there, if a car drops me off near the house, Tzipi might get suspicious."

Kasem drove the car over to the sidewalk before stopping. "You realize that this is a suicide mission if you go through with it. Ba'al is surrounded by IDF troops. There's no way you will get away with it," he said softly.

David turned his head and looked at him while putting his hand on the door handle. "If I fail, can you see that my wife and the child get to safety?"

Kasem looked out at the front of the car. "I will try my best. But where can I take them? There's nowhere on Earth that's safe anymore."

"Whatever you do, just get them out of Israel. If I'm dead and Rabbi Ba'al is still alive, there is no doubt he will try to exact revenge on them. They won't be safe here."

"What about your uncle in the Knesset?"

"They may go after him as well for keeping me out of military jail. We can't depend on him."

"If this plan goes through, they will come after all of us," Kasem said wistfully. "My family will be in danger as well."

"So we do nothing then? Is that it?"

"I don't know what the answer to that is. Only you know it. But if it comes down to it, I think the best chance is to bring our families to Gaza and try to link up with the Palestinians and get away by sea."

"What about through Egypt?"

"Something is happening there as well," Kasem said. "There's a complete blockade at the border and we have several brigades of front line troops nervously waiting for a possible attack. That's as far as I know. You're in the Mossad, surely you know more than I do about it."

"Egypt has gone silent since this whole thing began and nobody knows what's going on over there. The few scouts that we sent over the border never came back. My guess is that one of the ancient gods is on loose down there," David said.

"So you want to take your chances there or across the sea? I've heard strange rumors about the Mediterranean. No one wants to go by boat anymore."

David opened the car door before shaking his friend's hand. "Whatever happens, good luck. Shalom."

"Shalom, my friend," Kasem said. "If we ever meet again, let it be under happier circumstances."

As David opened the front door to the apartment, he saw Tzipi was sitting in the sofa and looking at him intently. He slowly closed the door behind him and went over to the kitchen and took out a drinking glass from the cupboard.

Tzipi stood up and put her hands on her thighs. "Where have you been? I've been looking for you for almost two hours! The baby is sleeping in the room but as soon as I was done with her, you were nowhere to be found."

David filled the glass with water from the refrigerator and took a sip. "I was out."

"Out where?"

"I met up with a few friends," David said as he placed the half empty glass in the sink.

"David, I don't like this," she said softly. "Uncle Ariel did a big favor for us when he got them to allow you to come home. I should be at the front with my unit, but I'm here with you, but then you go off somewhere so I know you are up to something."

David leaned forward as he placed his hands on the kitchen counter. "I'm not up to anything. I just needed some air that's all. Two days being stuck here, in this apartment, and all I could hear is the baby crying so I needed some time to myself."

Tzipi's mouth trembled as she looked away. "I know you're lying. You may be with the Mossad but I can always tell when you lie. Please don't throw away this second chance, David. You have a family that needs you."

David sighed. There was no way of hiding it from her. "If anything happens to me," he said softly. "Make sure you take care of Leyla's baby. She's ours now."

Tzipi's hands were balled into fists as she moved quickly and stood beside him. There were tears in her eyes. "What are you saying? What are you planning to do?"

He stood in front of her and placed his hands on her shoulders. "I have to do something. I cannot, in good conscience, allow what that rabbi is doing to this country. He is condemning us all to spend an eternity in Gehenna."

She started to cry. "David, what's happened to you? I can't believe this. Why would you even be doing this? Why you?"

"Because I'm the one who can get close to him," he said. He loved her and wanted to be with her forever but he knew that his plan needed a sacrifice.

"There's nobody else who is willing to try. Somebody has to do it."

"What are you going to do? Kill him? David, you'll be throwing your life away, and you will destroy this family! Is that what you want?"

"Of course not, but it has to be done. I am doing this for you and for everybody in this country. I love Israel, and I will not see her soul corrupted."

"Why does it have to be done? Don't you know that if you do this, our lives will be over as well? How can we ever live a normal life as a family if you're gone?"

David bit his lip as he looked her in the eyes. "Don't you get it yet? The gods have come back. No one on this planet will ever live a normal life ever again. Now it's all about choices. Do we survive as a nation while turning away from God and everything we have ever believed in? Or do we follow our traditions and do what's right?"

Tzipi looked away as she brushed the tears from her cheeks. "All that's happening. I … I just can't bear it! Why are you putting me in this situation?"

He wrapped his arms around her shoulders and hugged her tightly. He had a feeling he would never see her again. "When we first met, you knew I wasn't that religious. And neither were you. All we cared about was graduating from university, remember? I joined our intelligence organization because I believed in fighting for this country, but I really didn't know what it meant to be a Jew. But after all that's happened, it's opened my eyes. We have survived as a people for thousands of years because we believed in what was right and we never strayed from that belief. It's what kept us as a people no matter what part of the world we were in, no matter how many times they tried to kill us. We have a covenant with God, and we need to preserve that covenant or else everything we worked for, everything we fought and died for, will mean nothing. Elijah Ba'al, that man, he is turning us away from God. As a Jew, as an Israeli, it's my duty to prevent our people from losing that covenant."

She buried her head on his chest and her tears stained his collared shirt. "I … I can't deal with this! I can't accept this, you're going to die and I'll be alone!"

David placed his chin gently beside her cheek. "We've talked about this before, remember? We told each other what would happen if I went on a mission and I never came back, right? It's no different than before."

She pushed herself away from him. "But there is a difference! You were told by your superiors where to go. Now what you're planning to do is something entirely on your own! People will think you're crazy!"

"This will be my most important mission," David said. "I'll have a hand in directly saving my country and our people."

Tzipi's sadness was turning into frustration. "What if I say no to all of this? I can turn you in."

"Then you'll still lose me," David said. "And we'll all be in hell afterwards. So help me."

"Help you? How? I don't even know if this is the right course to take."

"Do you trust me?"

"David..."

"Do you trust me?"

She looked down at the kitchen floor before meeting his eyes once more. "Yes, and I love you."

"Then trust me now that I'm doing the right thing. I wouldn't be doing this if it wasn't important. Our existence as a people depends on it."

Tzipi thought about it for a minute. Then she realized that he was right, even though a part of her still couldn't accept it. "Are you even sure this is going to work?"

"If we can get the right people to help us, then I would say there's a good chance that it will work."

21. Dialectics

Manhattan

Detective Valerie Mendoza and Dr. Paul Dane walked up the stone steps leading to the main entrance of the American Museum of Natural History together. Although the front of the museum looked normal enough, the building had been gutted from the inside when a gigantic larva manifested itself in the basement level, and then grown to gargantuan proportions as it had burst through several floors. It had taken months of clearing the debris using heavy construction equipment and numerous safety checks by city engineers to make sure the remaining parts of the building complex would not collapse in on itself.

"Have you been here since that incident?" Paul said to her as they both passed through the front barricades. There was a squad of heavily-armed Marines guarding the entrance and they went through after they showed their newly-issued DOD identity cards.

"Not really," Valerie said as she put the Glock back in her hip holster after it was examined by the soldiers. "That whole experience gave me nightmares for days so instead I just concentrated on work."

The moment Paul and Valerie walked into the Theodore Roosevelt Memorial Hall, they saw that the adjoining passage in front that was supposed to lead them into the central part of the museum no longer existed, instead there was a gaping hole as whole sections of the floor had collapsed and they could see the basement level down below. A massive tarp was placed over the roof where the gigantic worm had burst through to prevent rainwater from seeping in. The whole scene looked like as if a massive bomb had exploded and demolished the place.

A short black man approached them from the adjacent hall that was still intact. He was bald and wearing a dark blue NYPD windbreaker with his badge dangling on a chain necklace. "Professor Dane? Detective Mendoza? Hi, I'm Detective Lemond Bell, Crime Scene Unit," he said as he shook both their hands. "If you'll follow me, I have a few things to show you."

Valerie smiled as she shook Bell's hand. "How are you, Lemond? It's been a long time."

Lemond returned her smile. "Very, very busy, Val. But it's good to see you again. I heard about your heroics when you were here, and I gotta say we need more of that. But let's start moving because I've got a lot to show you."

"Lead the way," Valerie said as the three of them began walking through the side halls of the building.

"As you can see, this side of the museum didn't collapse, so we set up a command and gathering point over at the Ross Hall of Meteorites at the farthest end of the building compound facing Columbus Avenue," Bell said as they all turned right and began to pass through the Grand Gallery near the side entrance. "It took us months to sift through the rubble but once the Feds got involved, things started to move a little bit faster."

"We sort of just got back on the team," Paul said. "How long has the DOD been here with you guys?"

"We've been working together for three weeks now," Bell said. "The NYPD Forensics Investigation Unit is still leading the operation but we're getting a lot of government support like providing us with generators, so there's electrical power in some parts of the building as well as computers so we can link up to their FBI database. Things really got into high gear just a week ago when we found video recordings of the basement."

Paul's eyebrows arched. "Were you able to find out what really happened?"

Bell just grinned as he pointed towards the entrance to the Hall of Meteorites. "You'll see."

The hall itself was circular, with black painted walls to simulate outer space. A large asteroid had been left in an upraised platform in the center of the room. A number of standing floodlights had been placed strategically around the hall in order to illuminate it. Dozens of folding tables had been placed beside the meteorite displays along the walls; a number of lab-smocked technicians with surgical gloves and forensics tools were busy pouring over the items that were identified as evidence.

As the three of them slowly walked around the examining tables, Bell pointed at the set of computers that had been set up beside the central asteroid display. A half dozen men and women wearing business suits were working furiously through numerous consoles. Both Paul and Valerie noticed that one of the men was Special Agent Lawrence Johnson of the FBI. As soon as the three of them started walking up the elevated platform, Johnson noticed them and he stood up and walked over.

"Welcome, Professor Dane and Detective Mendoza," Johnson said as they quickly shook hands. "As you can see, this is a joint operation and we're working with the police department to make sure that no stone gets left overturned."

Valerie nodded. "I'm impressed. Still DOD, but the whole set up seems different. So far the only military people I've seen are the ones guarding the entrance. Inside is all pretty much FBI and NYPD."

Johnson grinned sheepishly as he rubbed the back of his head. "Secretary Arctor wanted to make sure that the military will be at the disposal of Professor Dane and will not be in command this time. I'll be your official FBI liaison, by the way."

"If y'all would excuse me," Bell said as he started to walk down the platform. "I need to head over to the basement level, we're about to clear the remaining rubble down there so I want to be the first to have a look at it."

Valerie waived as he left. "See you later, Lemond."

"So far so good," Paul said to the FBI agent. "Detective Bell said you might have something for us?"

"Yes," Johnson said as he gestured at one of the FBI technicians manning a computer console before pointing at the monitor of his own workstation.

"If you'll take a look at this. It's a video feed that we were able to salvage from the surveillance cameras in the basement area at the time of the incident. When the team that came in was able to restore emergency power to the museum, the video recording devices were also able to come online. We were able to access the tapes only after we dug through the rubble."

The monitor soon showed a recorded video of the late Dr. Edwin Worlich walking into the basement area of the museum. Within a few minutes, he was setting up a standing camera before opening up the sealed crate that housed the artifact. The video feed flickered for a bit as the next scene showed Dr. Worlich carefully examining the petrified tree trunk that was recovered from Hatteras Island. Captain Laura Niven was seen walking around in the background as she seemed to be making sure that the area was secure.

"That was when I left them to go check upstairs," Valerie said softly.

As Dr. Worlich continued to examine the tree trunk, the edges of the video feed began to get blurry and even flickered to the point where the video was nearly obscured by static.

"Now I can barely see anything," Paul said.

"There was plenty of static interference in the video at this point but we managed to clean it up a little," Johnson said as he used the computer mouse to adjust the controls for the video feed. "It ought to be clearer now."

Although there was still some static lines in the recording, the scene became somewhat clearer as they all could see that the camera on the tripod beside Dr. Worlich had begun to wobble, as if being shaken by some unseen force. Less than a minute later, it looked like something invisible had tipped the tripod over and sent his camera crashing down on the floor.

"That was when we lost video feed from our headquarters in Brooklyn," Paul said.

Valerie gasped and pointed as the video feed soon showed two men entering the field of view. They were both dressed in ill-fitting suits; one was taller and seemed to be physically supporting an emaciated old man with long, silvery hair. Since the recording had no sound it looked like Dr. Worlich had noticed them as he turned around and it looked like they were having an argument of some kind. Less than a few seconds later, Captain Niven entered from the other end of the video, and she pointed her assault rifle at the two men.

What happened next seemed unbelievable as some sort of flickering came up from behind Captain Niven, grabbed her, and then threw her across the basement as if she was nothing more than a crumpled piece of paper.

Valerie was almost in shock. "Oh my god, what was that?"

"I don't know," Paul whispered. "It was like some sort of invisible ghost or spirit."

The next few seconds of the video showed Dr. Worlich grab at his own throat as he fell down on his knees. Both Paul and Valerie let out a gasp as they saw their colleague die before their eyes. As the video continued, the two men had slowly made their way towards the tree trunk on the wheeled platform. The old man then pressed his hands on the trunk and they saw it shudder as if it was alive before it began to open up like a wound. The taller man seemed to hesitate at first as they saw that both he and the older man seemed to be arguing about something. Then the taller man got on his knees as the old man took something white and squirming out of the tree trunk and moved closer to his companion.

Valerie's mouth was open. "What is he doing? Was that the worm that burst through the museum?"

Paul said nothing as he continued to watch, mesmerized.

Valerie could barely hide her disgust and she shrieked when she saw the old man placing the large maggot into his companion's mouth. The taller man looked like he was about to choke, but in the end, he got the larva down his throat. Less than a few seconds later, the tall man had begun to get nauseated as he fell down on the floor, his whole body began to convulse and the look on his face was one of intense pain. Meanwhile, the old man just stood there, staring at his companion. Soon, the taller man's features began to get bloated as his skin began to sag and he seemed to have ballooned in size. Within minutes, all that was left of him was a mound of flesh that seemed to be getting larger by the second. The final scene of the video seemed unreal as a gigantic maggot that was the size of a small car had burst through the sack of skin and began growing. Then the monitor screen flickered out.

Both Valerie and Paul said nothing as they just stood there in shocked silence.

Agent Johnson waited for a few minutes before he started talking. "Those two men in the video, do you know them?"

"No, never seen them before in my life," Paul said. Valerie just shook her head.

"We've been trying to identify that old man the moment we saw the video," Johnson said as he clicked on the mouse on his workstation again. "Here is an enhanced picture of him from the feed."

As a close up of old the man's face was shown on the monitor screen, Johnson continued to observe Paul and Valerie's reactions. So far, their body language had indicated that they were not familiar with who it was.

Valerie turned to look at Johnson. "Have you been able to identify who he is?"

Johnson nodded. "We believe so but we have no confirmation. My entire team has been working nonstop for the past three days in identifying him. With the internet and electrical grids down, we had to deploy as many agents on the field to follow every lead and we ended up with plenty of dead ends. But I think we may have a breakthrough." With those words, he took out a folder from his desk and handed it to the two of them.

Paul started flipping through the pages. It showed a dossier and pictures of an old man who looked quite similar to the one in the video feed. Valerie stood beside Paul as she read along with him.

"We believe that his name is Seth Solomon," Johnson said. "Approximate age at between seventy-five to eighty-five years old; we don't have a copy of his birth certificate so we can't be sure. He is a resident of Manhattan and owned an apartment overlooking Central Park. We raided that place just yesterday and found that it hadn't been lived in for months. We tried looking at his financial records, but all we could find was that he was living off of a trust fund his late father had set up for him."

Valerie looked up at the monitor screen again. "So it looks like we have a suspect that may be responsible for the museum incident? But that doesn't explain what's been going on with the rest of the world."

Paul gasped as he noticed the picture of the black sun wheel that was included in the dossier. "Oh my god, I dreamt of this symbol a few weeks ago."

Johnson turned and looked at him. "What symbol?"

"This one," Paul said as he held up the photograph. "It's an occult symbol called the Schwarze Sonne, which in German means black sun. The symbol is part of a painted floor in a castle somewhere in Germany. It was once used by the Nazis as the headquarters for the pagan religious rites of the SS. The castle itself has some occult significance among arcane societies."

One of the FBI researchers, a woman dressed in a grey office suit and had braided hair, stood up. "I think I may have found corroborating information with that symbol as well as the insignia of the UFO that attacked Berlin."

Paul's mouth dropped open. "What? There was an attack on Berlin?"

Johnson nodded before pointing to the woman. "What follows is classified information that was just recently passed down to us from EUCOM, our European Command based in Germany. Communications have been unreliable so they had to risk sending an aircraft over to us with the details. Go ahead, Sarah."

"Right," the FBI researcher said. "Approximately a week ago, an unidentified airship that was hidden in a massive cloud formation appeared over Berlin. The reports stated that the UFO looked like an all-metal airship that was powered by unknown means. There were massive discharges of lightning that came down onto the city. Hundreds of thousands of people were killed and large areas of the city were destroyed. A helicopter crew was able to take a video of the UFO and that symbol that you just described was on it. After bombarding the city for a few minutes, the vessel disappeared into thin air."

"Jesus," Paul said. Valerie just shook her head in a mixture of shock and disbelief.

"We've tried to gather as much information on that symbol," Sarah said as she looked down on her console and started clicking on her mouse. "And it has been traced to an organization called the Temple of the Black Sun. Its headquarters are in Germany and our suspect was apparently a former member."

Valerie crossed her arms. "Temple of the Black Sun? What kind of an organization is it?"

"It was apparently categorized as a sort of mystical order of magicians," Sarah said. "The German government attempted to classify it as a cult of some sort. But the Temple's lawyers and influence among the politicians were able to get that case quashed."

Paul adjusted his glasses. "Magicians? That proves it."

Johnson pulled out a notepad from his jacket and began to take notes. "What do you mean, Professor Dane?"

"This whole crisis that's happening worldwide," Paul said. "It's supernatural in nature. Now all of a sudden, we have a bunch of magicians who can seemingly do what was once considered impossible. Either they must be causing this whole thing, or they might know how it started."

Valerie took the dossier from Paul's hand and started going through it. "Are there any leads as to the suspect's location?"

Johnson shook his head. "We originally thought that he might have been killed when that worm grew in size and collapsed the floor above the basement, or perhaps he left not long afterwards. We put out an all-points bulletin on him but so far, nothing. He could be in hiding among one of the many abandoned buildings in the city, or maybe even in the subway. Right now, we have no way of knowing where he is or if he's still alive."

Valerie placed a hand on Paul's arm. "Do you think he killed Dr. Worlich and Captain Niven with some sort of … magic spell?"

Paul shrugged. "I don't know, but he apparently became dangerous when this whole thing started. How many members of the Temple are there?"

"We don't know," Johnson said. "It's a guess but there could be dozens, maybe even hundreds."

Valerie frowned before looking at the image on the video monitor again and then pointed at it. "Wait, look at his right hand, it looks like something shiny."

Everyone looked up at the monitor screen.

"Hold on," Sarah said as she started typing on her workstation console. "Let me see if I can enlarge it."

A few seconds later the image on the top screen was centered on Solomon's hand. The resulting enlargement made it blurry but the object was clear.

Johnson squinted his eyes as he kept looking at the image. "It looks like some sort of shiny ring that he's wearing. It's pretty big."

Paul let out a deep breath. "Oh my god. The seal of Solomon. Could that be it? Jesus. It all makes sense now. His name, that ring, and he's a magician too. It's all mind boggling."

Johnson turned and stared at Paul. "Seal of Solomon? What's that?"

"The seal of Solomon is purported to be some sort of magical ring that can control demons," Paul said. "The earliest stories came from Medieval Jewish tradition, and it told that God had given King Solomon a ring engraved with his true name on it. The king then used his power over demons to compel them to help him build numerous temples until one of the demons tricked him and stole the ring from him."

"So let me get this straight," Johnson said. "We have a gang of wizards from Germany. One of them is this Solomon guy, and he has a magic ring that controls demons. Then he kills one of his companions and creates a giant worm? This sounds like a science fiction movie."

"Except that it's all true," Valerie said. "I was here when that worm burst through the ceiling. And I was also here when the nuke that the military had planted was about to go off."

"I'm not arguing with you, Detective," Johnson said. "I'm just having a hard time trying to put all of this together, is all."

"Well we need to pull everything together," Paul said. "And fast. If this guy is out there and he can control demons then we need to find him as quickly as possible. What I would like to know is if this Solomon fellow had this kind of power for years, or did it just start when all the old gods came back."

"If he had all this power before then surely he would have used it way back when," Valerie said. "It feels like it's tied in to everything but it doesn't seem to be the underlying cause."

"So what is the underlying cause?" Johnson said.

"I don't know," Valerie said. "Though it's a start."

"But we're getting somewhere," Paul said. "We know a lot more now than what we knew just a few days ago. We're moving in the right direction. If the gods are real and the demons are real, then our suspect has also proved that his ring might be real. Then other objects must exist as well."

Valerie looked at him. "Other objects? What do you mean?"

"Think about it," Paul said. "If the seal of Solomon is real, then there must be other mythical objects out there. Swords like Excalibur, or Thor's hammer, must exist too. These magical weapons could enable us to fight against these gods and demons."

"So do you want us to scour the globe for religious artifacts?" Valerie said, "Like the Ark of the Covenant or something?"

At that moment, Johnson's walkie-talkie began to squawk. He quickly took it from his belt strap and activated it. "Special Agent Johnson here."

The voice on the other line was from Bell. "It's Lemond Bell. Can you bring Professor Dane and Detective Mendoza down to the basement area? We found something."

"On the way," Johnson said before putting back the walkie-talkie on his belt. Paul and Valerie didn't need to be told to go as they followed the FBI agent back towards the side halls.

The basement area was largely cleaned up, but there were still piles of debris that was lying around. Several teams of forensics investigators from the NYPD and the FBI were slowly going through the room as they checked out each minor detail. Paul, Valerie, and Special Agent Johnson walked down a wooden ramp that was installed a few weeks before.

Detective Bell waited for them at the bottom of the incline. As soon as they met, he turned around and started walking towards an alcove at the far end of the hall. "Follow me," he said. "We've found something out of the ordinary."

The three of them followed until they all stood facing a grey, concrete wall in between two large crates that housed museum artifacts. The wooden containers were damaged from the floor collapse but it didn't look like the forensics investigator was interested in what was in them.

Bell pointed at the recess on the side of the wall. As the three of them looked at the bare concrete, the forensics investigator took out a handheld ultraviolet flashlight and shined it on the base of the wall. Almost instantly, a set of strange symbols and what looked to be writing appeared over the bare concrete as the pale blue light shined on it.

Valerie ran her hand through her hair. "What is that?"

Bell kept pointing his flashlight at it. "We think it's been written on that wall quite recently. Whoever wrote it used blood."

"But you needed a UV light to see it," Valerie said. "That only happens when someone wiped the original stains off, right?"

"Normally yes," Bell said. "But we didn't detect any cleaning agents nor were there any signs that it was cleaned in any way. Also, we're not sure if the blood is human."

Valerie didn't take her eyes off the symbols. "If the blood isn't human, how could you tell?"

"We normally mix the blood with anti-human serum after we collect a sample of it," Bell said. "The serum is made from lab animals that have been injected with blood type O negative. If the blood coagulates then it's human blood. We tested a small amount and it came out negative."

"So it's the blood from an animal then," Johnson said.

"We're not sure about it being from an animal either," Bell said. "The main composition of blood is normally plasma, red and white blood cells, and platelets. When we looked at the sample under the microscope, there were other types of cells that we couldn't identify as well as traces of an unknown fluid that we have never seen before. And that's not even the craziest part."

Valerie twisted her head and looked at Bell. "What do you mean?"

"One of my assistants said something peculiar when she looked at it under the microscope," Bell said softly. "She told me she thinks the blood is still alive somehow."

Johnson's eyes went wide as he backed away. "What?"

"Dead cells have broken down membranes that can be penetrated by a special dye," Bell said. "Live cells have intact membranes that will resist this dye- so if we put the dye on them and shine a light and they don't glow then they must still be alive. We tried that test on the sample, and we're sure they're still live even though there is no metabolic activity. No living being's blood can do this. It's totally nuts."

Paul spoke up.. "It's because that blood is neither animal nor human, it's demon blood."

The three of them turned to face him, their mouths open in disbelief.

"A demon," Johnson said. "Like in hell and damnation kind of demon? Like Satan?"

"Yes," Paul said. "Something like that."

Johnson closed his eyes and looked away. "I-I just can't believe all this. It's like I've been in a nightmare for the past few months and I'm hoping I wake up every morning and think it's all just a dream."

"What makes you think that it's demonic blood? It could be anything else," Valerie said.

Paul leaned closer and pointed at the luminous symbols. "These signs are a form of script. Its writing that's very similar to ancient Latin and some of those symbols are also on the tree trunk from Hatteras. The suspect possessed the ring of Solomon and legend says that it allows the possessor to control demons. The writings that we are looking at are called the demon's mark, or otherwise known as a diabolical signature. The myths explained that they are signed with the name of the demon and they are written in blood."

"But why would a demon leave a telltale sign like this? I would have thought that they preferred to cover up whatever it is that they do," Valerie said.

"Ancient stories state that demonic beings operate on their own set of rules," Paul said. "I don't know why it is so, but they sign a pact with a mortal using their signature."

Johnson frowned. "Signature? Like as in a contract or something?"

"Exactly," Paul said. "The legend of Faust is a prime example of it."

"Never heard of it," Valerie said. "But then again, I grew up listening to my mama and her Aztec stories."

"It's got Germanic origins," Paul said. "Basically, it's about a man who wasn't happy with his life, so he summons a demon by the name of

Mephistopheles. He makes a pact with this being to get unlimited riches and knowledge in exchange for his soul. They sign a diabolical contract for a set amount of time. So for seven years or so, Faust enjoys himself until the end when his body and soul get carried off to hell. It's a morality tale about the dangers of too much ambition and the corruption of one's soul."

"A literal deal with the devil," Johnson said. "And you think that this Seth Solomon has made a sort of pact with this demon?"

"That's my assumption, yes," Paul said.

"That's one hell of a theory," Johnson said.

"I agree that it's just a guess," Paul said. "But it's my best guess based on the evidence that we have."

"Well, we don't have anything else to go on," Valerie said as she looked at Paul. "But based on what we did in this place before, I think it's a valid assumption. So now what?"

Paul looked at Detective Bell. "Have you got a standing UV light so that I could study these writings?"

Bell turned off his UV flashlight and dropped his tired arm to the side of his body. "Sure, I can have it set up for you. I think we might still have pieces of bark from that tree trunk you mentioned as well, shall I have the whole package laid out for you here on some tables?"

"Yes, thank you," Paul said to him before flicking his eyes over to the FBI agent. "My books burned up in my library along with my house in Boston. I need books on demons as well as any old books about magic that you can find. I'll write down a list for you."

"If you want books, hell, I'll have my teams open up the New York Public Library for you," Johnson said. "I heard it's got one of the largest collections of books in the world."

"That would be good," Paul said. "Also, when you went to Solomon's apartment, were there any books in there?"

Johnson nodded. "Yes, a lot. He had a bunch of really old hardbound books in leather and other materials. We packed them off in evidence boxes and we were planning to ship them to FBI headquarters, but I can have them reroute the stuff here."

Paul smiled and shook his hand. "I would appreciate that."

"Let me get cracking on it then," Johnson said as he turned around and started to walk towards the ramp leading to the upper floors.

Valerie placed a hand on Paul's elbow. "What are you planning to do?"

Paul winked at her. "Summon a demon."

22. Stepping Stones

Otherworld

Patrick Gyle looked up at the towering trees above them as the entire forest itself seemed to glow with a faint bluish luminescence. "Are we still in the faerie realms? The trees look different."

Ilya Volkhov was slightly ahead of him as the young boy made his way along the mossy ground. "No, we have left that world and entered into another. This is a place that I had been to before."

Although the thick, pale leathery skin made him seem bulky, Gyle's long, sinewy legs made it seem like he was walking on air as he lengthened his gait and was soon walking alongside Ilya. The raven continued to perch on his left shoulder and said nothing. He could see a star-filled night if he looked high enough, but the trees were gigantic and blotted out the sky, their trunks stretched out hundreds of feet into the air.

"I thought we were supposed to go to the realm of the dark elves," Gyle said. "This doesn't look like a cave to me."

Ilya shook his head as he kept looking at the ground while he walked. "Have you not been listening to that bird god? If the Dokkalfar live in an underground world, then we need some sort of light to see in there."

"Why don't we go back to Earth then? There are plenty of flashlights to be found there," Gyle said.

"I don't want just a flashlight," Ilya said. "I want something that burns so bright that it could be used as a weapon."

"Ah, very clever," the raven said. "You have read up on your folk tales very well, Ilya."

Gyle twisted his neck so he could look at the bird on his shoulder. "What is he looking for?"

"A firebird," Ilya said. "If we are in the forest where they live, then we should have no problem tracking one down."

Gyle looked confused but his features were so thick that it didn't show. "A firebird? What is that?"

"It's a magical glowing bird," the raven said. "It can bring both blessings and doom to its captor."

Gyle nodded. "Like a phoenix then?"

"Yes, except that it doesn't rise up from its own ashes after its death. I guess they may be considered as a related species according to your scientific categories," the raven said.

"Holy cow, look!" Ilya said as he pointed at something on the ground that was near him.

Gyle turned and looked at where the boy had pointed to. There seemed to be a small pile of glowing dirt beside a gargantuan tree root. The radiant color it gave off seemed to be a combination of orange and yellow.

"Firebird droppings," the raven said. "That means it must be close by."

Gyle looked up at the tree branches that towered above them. "Do either of you have any plans to catch it if we find it?"

Ilya smirked as he started to look up as well. "Not me, you. We don't want to catch it- that might bring us bad luck."

Gyle stared at the boy. "If we aren't going to catch it then what do we do then?"

"All we need is a few feathers. It is said that the light from just one of its feathers can light a large room," the boy said.

Gyle sighed. "So you just want me to grab it and pluck a few feathers out of it? Why don't we just wait till it drops some?"

"We don't have the time to wait for that," Ilya said. "We need to get to the Dokkalfar kingdom as quickly as possible."

Gyle snorted. The kid was pretty bossy and annoying, but he seemed to know what was going on. Less than three months ago, he was a CIA field officer in Iraq before all hell broke loose. After the old Babylonian gods retook the region, he encountered the oldest man in the world, a man known to many as Noah, a survivor of the Great Flood, although he preferred to go by the name of Atrahasis, his original Babylonian name. When they escaped the clutches of a renegade Israeli rabbi, Atrahasis brought Gyle into the Otherworld for the first time. It was also Atrahasis who gave him the last petal from a magical flower that was once possessed by Gilgamesh, an ancient Sumerian hero. When Gyle ate the petal, it transformed him into a creature of great strength and speed, but he no longer looked human. He had sacrificed his humanity in order to fight against these old gods and perhaps be reunited with his family. Atrahasis then introduced him to the trickster, a talking raven who could very well be another god. They soon left Atrahasis behind in relative safety in another part of the Otherworld, but the wise old man had tasked him with retrieving two very special children in order to have allies in this final war. And now he was here, looking for a mythical bird in a forest that could not possibly be on Earth or even on another planet.

As he stood there looking up at the trees, a flickering light seemed to reveal itself near the edge of his vision. Gyle immediately pointed in that direction. "There," he said. "Is that one it?"

Ilya turned and squinted his eyes in order to try and focus. At the far end of the trees was another bird. But unlike the black feathered raven that was with them, this bird had a very long neck and resembled a peacock, though it had vulture-like wings. Its tail was long, with paddle shaped fathers at the end. The animal itself was also glowing brightly, like a miniature sun.

"That's it!" the boy exclaimed. "Go get it, both of you!"

The raven launched itself from Gyle's shoulder as it flew on a parallel path towards the firebird. "I'll keep it in sight," the black bird said. "Just follow me, boy."

Gyle tensed his legs and jumped up almost forty feet into the air as he grabbed onto a tree branch the size of a pine trunk, before shifting his body towards the direction of the bird and then making another massive leap.

The firebird instantly noticed them as soon as Gyle had made his first jump. It immediately flapped its wings as it flew off to escape, deeper into the forest. Gyle continued to leapfrog from one tree branch to another, hoping he could get close enough to make a grab at the magical bird. Just as he nearly got his claws on the firebird's wings, the animal quickly banked right as it flew around a giant tree while Gyle had to swing using his arms on a lower branch in order to turn around.

As the firebird flew in between a group of trees away from Gyle and on towards relative safety, the raven had flown ahead and was waiting for it. Without warning, the black bird flew right into the firebird's path, startling it. Gyle seized his chance as he made one last leap while fully stretching out his body and caught the bird's tail with his outstretched hand. The firebird let out an ear-piercing cry as Gyle's weight sent them both tumbling down towards the ground at the last minute, Gyle used his other arm to grab onto a nearby branch and it was able to slow his fall enough, it enabled him to land on his feet onto the forest floor.

Ilya was out of breath when he finally ran over to where Gyle was. The boy had to squint his eyes due to the intense light that the magical bird was giving off from its own body. The raven flew over and perched itself on a nearby tree branch as it watched the proceedings below.

The former soldier was holding onto the shrieking firebird as the animal struggled in his grasp. Gyle's eyes had nictitating membranes that shielded them against the firebird's intense glow. "Come on, Ilya, hurry up and take your feathers! I can't keep holding onto it for long."

The boy immediately got in front of Gyle and grabbed at the firebird's tail. Although he was using all of his strength to pull some of the feathers loose, he was unable to. Ilya gritted his teeth and leaned back but the feathers still wouldn't budge.

Gyle was having a hard time trying to hold onto the shrieking animal. He was afraid that if he used all of his strength, he would end up crushing it in his arms. In desperation, the firebird lashed out with its beak and tried to gouge out his right eye. Gyle instinctively closed his eyes and looked away as the animal's beak was unable to penetrate through his thick eyelids. However, the attack did distract him enough that he inadvertently loosened his grip on the bird.

Ilya cried out as the firebird started to fly upwards and began to drag him along with it.

Gyle quickly opened his eyes and reacted as he saw the boy being dragged aloft by the fleeing bird. He bent his knees and quickly jumped up almost twenty feet in the air as he was able to grab onto Ilya's torso. Gyle had thought that the boy would have just let go of the bird by this time, but he apparently wasn't giving up. As he noticed a nearby tree branch, Gyle twisted his body and made a grab for it. He was able to get his hands around the wooden limb just as the firebird made one last, desperate dive to try and shake them off.

Ilya's eyes were fully closed while he gritted his teeth and kept pulling at the feathers. All of a sudden, he could feel an intense pressure around his waistline as Gyle's arm had wrapped itself around him and it had turned into a tug of war. He could hear the firebird shrieking as its wings flapped so intensely that the vibrations were running down his arms. Suddenly, the pressure had quickly died down as he heard something snap. When the boy reopened his eyes, he was thirty feet off the ground and being supported by Gyle's sinewy arms. In his hands were three brightly glowing feathers.

Gyle was able to get both of them back on the ground in just a few leaps. He noticed that the firebird had flown off and he started feeling his face for any damage. The former CIA field officer had noticed that every time he got hurt, his wounds tended to heal quickly, sometimes in a matter of minutes.

Ilya held the glowing feathers up triumphantly. "We have it! Now we can go to the elves."

The raven flew down from a nearby tree branch and landed on Ilya's shoulder. The boy staggered for a bit before finally compensating for the extra weight on his body. "For a moment there, I thought that the firebird had carried you away for good," the black bird said.

Gyle walked over to them. "I'm surprised you just didn't let go the moment that firebird started hauling you through the air."

Ilya smirked as he placed two of the feathers in his coat pocket. "You both think so little of me."

Gyle nodded. "Atrahasis told me you were special, looks like he was right. You're a pretty clever kid with a lot of guts. I used to think that with all these gods around, we humans wouldn't stand a chance. But if we had more people like you, I think we might just turn this whole mess around."

"Thank you," Ilya said. "But we all did it."

Gyle looked at the raven on Ilya's shoulder. "So what can you tell me about these elves?"

"Ancient tales state that the Dokkalfar dwell in the land of Nidavellir, sometimes known as Myrkheim," the raven said. "Their abode is deep under the earth in dark caves where there is no light. Their skin is deep black, like the color of night. These people are great craftsmen and the items they create are sought by the gods themselves."

"If these elves can create powerful weapons," Gyle said. "Then it's possible that human beings might want them too."

"Yes, like those magicians the Erlking was talking about," Ilya said.

Gyle nodded. "Do you think that these black elves and those magicians might be working together?"

Ilya tried to shrug both his shoulders but only ended up doing one. "There's only one way to find out."

Gyle had been in a state of melancholy ever since the nightmare in Iraq but he couldn't help but grin at the boy. For the first time in months, he felt that he was on the right track. "Lead the way, kid."

Ilya turned away as the transformed man grinned at him with fanged teeth. Although he liked Gyle, the man just looked scary. "Follow me then," he said as he started along a nearby path.

As the both of them started moving forward, the path in front began to get darker while the trees all around them began to fade into a solid black wall of nothingness. Within minutes, it had become so dark that Ilya had to hold a glowing feather in front of him. Gyle's eyes could see in the dark since he could see into the infrared wavelength, but even he had a hard time trying to see what was around him. The grassy ground underneath them soon gave way to smooth stone.

A short time later, all three of them were now walking along a massive rock cavern. The tunnel that they were moving through seemed smooth and circular, as if hewn by hand for thousands of years. The only light source that they had was the glowing feather Ilya held in his hand.

Gyle kept looking over his shoulder as they continued onwards. The air was still but he could sense a thousand eyes hidden in the darkness just staring at them. "Any idea as to where we ought to be going?"

"This tunnel must lead to somewhere," Ilya said before looking at the raven on his shoulder. "Do you know where we're supposed to go?"

"These caves shall have many tunnels and each path will be different," the raven said, "and each tunnel leading to a different fate."

Ilya snorted. "You are speaking in riddles again."

Sure enough, they soon came upon a twenty-foot tall cavern that had a half dozen intersecting tunnels that branched out in multiple directions. Pieces of black ore were all over the cave floor. As Ilya began to explore the cave, he noticed bits of metal strewn about. The boy bent down and picked up something familiar as he held it up in front of his glowing feather. It looked like an iron rivet, a kind of shaft that welded large sheets of metal together. The raven flew from Ilya's shoulder before landing on a boulder.

"Stay here," Gyle said as he pointed to a nearby tunnel at the opposite side of them. "I'll check out where those holes lead to. If there's trouble then start hollering."

"Alright," Ilya said as he kept poking around the cavern floor. "Do you want a feather so you can see?"

"No need," Gyle said as he started walking into a side tunnel. "I can see in the dark pretty well."

As he made his way down one of the tunnels, Gyle's eyes soon adjusted to the darkness. He could see that the walls along the cave itself seemed to give off a phosphorescent glow, like tiny specks of light from a distant Christmas tree. Venturing deeper into the tunnel, he could hear some sort of faint clanking noises in the distance, like the sound of gears grinding together. Could these so-called elves actually create pieces of complex machinery?

Gyle followed the sounds until they got louder. A few minutes later, he had come upon an underground chamber of some sort. The cavern itself was thirty feet across its width, and there was some sort of raised stage made of solid rock at its center. He could still hear the sounds of machinery and they seem to have been coming from underneath the stone platform. The edges of the stage seemed to have been embedded on the cavern floor. On the base of the platform, there seemed to be some sort of strange glowing hieroglyphs chiseled on it. Gyle leapt up on the stage so he could take a closer look.

"Patrick?" a familiar voice behind him said.

Gyle quickly turned around, prepared for action. The moment he saw who it was, his once powerful knees began to buckle. Tears that he never knew he could shed after his transformation, began to form in his eyes. His long, sinewy arms that he had held out in a fighting stance now hung limply beneath his shoulders.

A woman stood before him. He instantly knew that it was his wife, Marie. Her long brown hair was radiant as it flowed down her shoulders. Marie's high cheekbones accentuated her smile as she seemed to welcome him back from the nightmare that had begun all those months ago. He could see that she still wore the tight white blouse and the blue denims that they had purchased the last time they went shopping, just before he was due to return to the Middle East.

Marie held out her arms to him. "Patrick, I've missed you so much."

Gyle had to concentrate in order to keep himself from breaking down. He could hardly move as he just stared back at her, unable to find the words. He had thought the worst may have happened to Marie and the children when the gods came back. Seeing her just standing there smiling made him forget everything. Perhaps, the whole thing about his unit in Iraq being wiped out, of seeing all those people being crushed underfoot by the demons of Babylon, perhaps all of that was nothing more than just a hallucination. Marie would make everything right.

Then a blinding aura of light manifested itself behind him as Marie's body suddenly began to shift and became blurry. The spell was broken as Gyle suddenly became aware that he had been looking at an illusion. His wife was nothing more than a simulacrum, and his mind was thrust back into bitter reality. Gyle whirled and realized that Ilya was standing at the edge of the tunnel, holding a pair of glowing feathers together. It was the boy's presence and the bright light from the magical feathers that returned him back to his senses. A sudden rage washed over him, his feelings of tranquility and satisfaction were replaced by the heat of anger that was partly born of shame.

At that instant, Gyle cursed aloud as he brought down his stubby fists onto the base of the platform. His first blow had somehow cracked the stone foundation as the glowing glyphs were now in disarray. Gyle continued to smash the floor, his multiple blows finally ripped through the stone base as the attack exposed the machinery underneath. When the upper stage finally gave way, he saw a multitude of grinding gears that were interlocked together, like the insides of a clock. Gyle drove his hands through the inside and pulled out large metallic springs as the rivets began to give way. In a matter of seconds, he had reduced the stage into a wreckage of metallic parts and crumbled stone.

The raven had been perching on the boy's shoulder as it surveyed the damage. "Well, it looks like it won't be doing any distractions anymore."

Gyle heaved great gulps of air and exhaled a puff of steam as he walked off the ruined platform and stood in front of a wall. He felt a great humiliation at being swayed by an illusionary trap. Ilya walked over to the side of the stage and took out some bits of raskovnik with his other hand to try to get some sense as to the true purpose of the machinery.

"Remarkable engineers they are," the raven said. "Such complex machinery. I didn't think the Dokkalfar would be capable of this."

Ilya closed his eyes as he used his other senses along with the raskovnik to examine the machine. "It wasn't a trap. It seems this machine was built to experience past memories."

Gyle had finally cooled down as he walked over to them. "I-I couldn't help myself. I was so pissed off that I just lashed out and destroyed it."

The boy put the magical herbs pack into his coat pocket. "The dark elves didn't build this on their own, they were guided by humans from our world."

Gyle looked down and surveyed the wreckage. "What did they build this thing for?"

"I don't know," Ilya said. "Perhaps as a form of entertainment. Anyway, I don't think it's going to work again until it gets repaired."

Gyle started walking towards the tunnel exit. "Let's move on then."

For the next hour, they explored the other branches of the tunnel complex. Gyle kept trying to map the tunnels that they had already explored by leaving a claw mark on each passageway that they went through, but when they doubled back after coming upon a dead end, his marks along the walls seemed to have been removed. Ilya was sure that there were eyes watching them but every time he shined the light of the firebird feathers in a darkened channel, all they could sense were animal-like shrieks and the quick shuffling of feet.

"We're being watched but they haven't come at us yet," Gyle said as they started into another passageway. "I have a feeling we would have been fighting through hordes of monsters if it wasn't for those feathers of yours, Ilya. Good thinking."

"Look," Ilya said, pointing to a branching tunnel up ahead of them. "There's some light coming from there."

"Where there's light in this underworld, there must be creatures that use it," the raven said.

"Stay behind me," Gyle said as he moved forward towards the passageway.

Moments later, they came upon an ever-widening tunnel that led into a gargantuan cavern. Ilya put the firebird feathers in his jacket as there was enough ambient light for him to see dimly. Gyle could see that the cave ceiling was hundreds of feet high; the upper walls of the cavern were studded with great glowing gemstones that shone like stars in a subterranean night. There was heaps of phosphorescent lichen growing on large stalactites that were size of small buildings. As their eyes adjusted to the strange and wondrous sight, they noticed movement along the cave floor and the walls. Within minutes, they had finally seen what the inhabitants of the world looked like.

They were small, dwarfish humanoids with jet black skin and silvery long hair and beards. With thick, stumpy legs attached to barrel like torsos, the dark elves kept scurrying about as they continued to toil and mine the black ore that seemed to sprout like mushrooms everywhere. Elevated metal platforms and ladders that were several stories high were a testament as to how extensive the work that was being done. The upper walls of the great cavern were dotted with numerous grottos that these elves would seemingly come in and out of.

"They seem to be working pretty hard," Ilya said. "But for what?"

Gyle pointed at the far end of the cavern. "Over there."

At the outer edge of the great cave, there seemed to be a raised metallic platform. Numerous ramps from the stone floor were attached to it as a constant stream of elves carrying silvery sacks of ore on their backs were streaming towards it. At the edge of the dais was what looked to be a huge polished mirror that was supported by iron struts in order to keep it upright. As Ilya peered closer, he realized that it wasn't a mirror at all, it looked like a vertical pool of silvery liquid that sloshed about. It seemed to be alive, like a membrane of some sort. A few minutes later, they saw a figure seemingly coming out of the surface of the pool and walk upon the platform. It was a man wearing goggles and dressed in a black robe.

"I thought it was a mirror," Ilya whispered. "But it looks like a doorway of some kind."

"A portal that leads to another world, to be exact," the raven said softly.

"Humans and these creatures are working together," Gyle said. "But whatever it is that they're working on clearly isn't doing the Earth any good."

Without warning, a dozen small hands grabbed Ilya from behind and started to pull him back into the dark tunnel that they had come out of. The raven instantly flew up to avoid an elf that attempted to grab at it as the boy let out a cry for help. Gyle turned and used his arms to swat away over a half dozen Dokkalfar, throwing them thirty feet into the air as he started to make his way to Ilya.

The robed man was standing about fifty feet away when he noticed the commotion at one of the side tunnels. He parted his robes and then pulled out a metallic, cylindrical device with a handgrip attached to its bottom as he shouted out an alarm. Within seconds, another man wearing identical robes emerged from a cave mouth three stories above as he too cradled a similar device.

Gyle had almost fought his way to the boy's side when a man-made lightning bolt struck his back. The former CIA officer screamed as he fell on his knees, his body wracked with pain as he sensed his back was burning. The dark elves were able to overwhelm Ilya as the boy was mobbed by over two dozen of them, they dragged him kicking and screaming through the dark passageway.

But just as the robed man in the caves above them had pulled the trigger on his lightning gun for a second blast, the lightning bolt hit a bare patch of solid stone as Gyle instantly sprang up and landed on the ledge beside him. The robed man quickly turned and brought his weapon to bear but Gyle was much too fast for him. The former CIA officer had been transformed into something that was more than human as Gyle's claws went through the guard's torso and tore out his heart. The robed man on the platform saw what had happened and fired his lightning gun at the ledge where his colleague was, hoping to kill that pale monster before it could get to him. Gyle easily leapt out of the way as the blast from the weapon tore through some of the scaffolding and pieces of metal began cascading down to the cavern floor.

Ilya struggled as a dozen hands were trying to hold him down but he managed to get one of his arms free. He then pulled out the firebird feathers from the pocket of his coat. The tunnel was instantly engulfed in a blinding light as the dark elves shrieked and backed away, covering their eyes. Ilya sat up and then quickly got on his feet as he kept showing the brightly shining feathers between him and his assailants.

The robed man in the platform had fired over half a dozen times, hoping for a hit, but Gyle kept leaping from one scaffolding to the next as he easily dodged the lightning bolts coming his way. As Gyle got closer, he could see the robed man in the platform below was now in a state of panic as he fired one more shot at him that narrowly missed, before turning around to run through the portal. Gyle quickly sprung and landed on the man's back just as he was about to go through the membrane.

A brief surge of energy cascaded through Gyle's body as he transitioned into another world. The next thing he knew, he was lying on top of a squirming man while on a barren rocky landscape. He could see mist-laden mountain ranges stretching out into the distance. The sky was an overcast grey but the daylight was a welcome sight over the lightless, suffocating caverns that he had just come from. It reminded him of the time when he took the family on a vacation in Alaska, the barren tundra was miles in every direction. Only this time, instead of arctic grass, he seemed to be surrounded by crumbling, fossilized rock. Looking around, he saw that there were over two dozen giant piles of black ore nearby.

The robed man continued to struggle feebly underneath him. Gyle had finally had enough as he placed a clawed hand over the back of the man's throat. "Calm down, I'm not gonna kill you."

The robed man whimpered. "P-Please don't eat me!"

Gyle snorted. He could smell a pungent, sulfurous odor. The man had evidently pissed on himself. "I don't eat people," he said. "So just take it easy."

Hearing a vibrating noise behind him, Gyle turned around and saw Ilya step through the portal while still holding his firebird feathers. The raven was perched on the boy's shoulder once again.

"Thanks for the rescue," Ilya said. "If I hadn't gotten one of my hands free, I would have been torn apart by those dark elves."

"Oh they weren't going to harm you," the raven on the boy's shoulder said. "The Dokkalfar were just planning to take you captive, as per their orders."

Ilya rolled his eyes. "Well, that makes me feel better then! To be a prisoner rather than be eaten alive, how could I possibly choose between those two choices?"

"I'm sorry," Gyle said. "I was going to restrain this man and then go back in after you."

The robed man was sobbing. "Please, don't kill me!"

Gyle stood up and grabbed the man by his robes with one arm as he held him aloft like a dangling piece of meat. "I won't kill you as long as you answer our questions."

The man was so terrified of Gyle that he kept looking away from him. "I-I saw you kill Martin with those claws, p-please, I have a family!"

Ilya rolled his eyes. "What a coward."

"I already said I won't kill you," Gyle said. "But if you don't answer my questions, I might just change my mind and then feed what's left of you to my little black bird."

"I prefer moose," the raven said nonchalantly. "The taste of humans is so …vile."

"There were two of you in that cavern," Gyle said to the man. "Are there any more?"

"N-No," the man said haltingly. "We had just relieved the last guard shift for the portal."

"When is the next guard shift?"

The man closed his eyes. "Not for at least s-six hours."

Ilya moved closer but quickly stepped back when he caught the smell of the robes. "Are you from Earth?"

"Y-Yes," the man said. "My name is Heinrich. F-From Germany."

Gyle looked closer at Heinrich. The man looked to be in his thirties. Sharp nose and blond curly hair. "Why are you wearing robes?"

"I-I'm a member of the Temple."

"Temple? What temple?"

"T-The Temple of the Black Sun," Heinrich said nervously. "Our Grand Magus says w-we shall be the new rulers of Europe."

"I've never heard of this Black Sun before," Gyle said to him before looking at the boy. "What about you?"

Ilya just shrugged his shoulders.

"W-We are an order of magicians, our power has somehow increased when all these old gods returned to our world," Heinrich said. "I was only recruited a few months ago, please have pity on me."

Ilya took out some raskovnik and held it out in front of him. "He's telling the truth about his organization, but he's lying about how long he's been a member. He joined up three years ago as a security officer."

Gyle's other hand instantly grabbed Heinrich by the throat. "We can tell when you're lying. Do it again and I'll rip your head off."

"Ahh!" Heinrich cried. "I'm so sorry! I promise, I will say nothing but the truth! Please don't hurt me!"

"Now," Gyle hissed. "Tell us everything, from the top, what are you doing here? What kind of alliance you have with those elves, where's the faerie princess, and where's Tara?"

Heinrich gulped. He knew he needed to tell them everything. All he cared about now was to just try and stay alive. "Princess Charissa is in the tower, a-along with that other girl. The king of the Dokkalfar is in the battleship, he is being held hostage there. As long as the Temple has him, the dark elves are cooperative. If he is freed, the elves will revolt against us and throw us out of their world."

Ilya's eyes widened at the news of Tara. "Where is this tower?"

"Over there," Heinrich said as he pointed to a mist-filled mountain range in the far distance. "It's built on the base of that along with the dry dock for repairs. The elves constructed the whole thing and it's powered by that cauldron. That is what makes it float in the air."

Gyle gently placed Heinrich down on the ground. "Cauldron? What cauldron?"

"I-It's an old metal cauldron that we found a few months ago," Heinrich said. "The Grand Magus said that it's magical, it used to bring the dead back to life during the time of legends, but it was damaged so we used the help of demons and the elves to repair it somewhat. But the repair work wasn't exact and the artifact is flawed somehow, instead of bringing the dead back to life, all we could do is put sacrifices into it and the dead souls would transform into some sort of mystical energy to power the ship."

"So you have a flying battleship powered by the magical cauldron," Gyle said. "What does your Temple hope to do with that?"

"Conquer Europe," Henrich said. "We already bombarded parts of Berlin and it will just be a matter of time till the remaining countries fall under the Temple's domination. The giants and the Fomorians can't touch us because we are in the air. The dragons and the other flying creatures may be a problem, but the lightning cannons mounted on the ship should keep them at bay."

Ilya picked up the lightning gun that was on the ground. It was bulky but surprisingly light. "So this is one of the weapons you are using?"

Gyle quickly took the weapon away from the boy. "Be careful with that, it almost killed me."

Ilya frowned as he crossed his arms. "Why won't you let me have a weapon?"

Gyle snapped the lightning gun in two and let the bits fall to the ground. "You haven't been trained to use it. If you don't know how to use something as powerful as this, it's better to leave it alone."

The boy didn't argue any further as he moved behind Gyle and took a look at his friend's back. "You were burned somewhat, but I can see that your back is healing quite quickly."

Gyle stood upright and stretched his back. "Still hurts though."

Heinrich looked down on the ground. "I am ashamed and would like to help if I could. I just want to get back to my family. I don't want to die."

Gyle turned his attention to Heinrich once more. "That tower, how many guards are in it?"

"Perhaps a few dozen at the most," Heinrich said. "We are training new apprentices there, but most of them are too inexperienced to operate the lightning guns, so they won't be much of a problem for you."

Gyle pointed to the piles of black ore beside them. "Is this some sort of transit point for the ore to bring it to the tower?"

Heinrich nodded. "The Temple needs the ore to repair the battleship with. A group of horse drawn carts will be here soon along with a few men to transport the ore to the tower and then to the dry dock. From there, it will await the battleship's return from earth."

"That's it then," Gyle said. "We make a plan to insert ourselves into the castle using the ore transports."

"And then rescue Tara, and the faerie princess, and the king of the dark elves too," Ilya said.

Gyle nodded. "And kill everyone else."

23. Law of the Pursuer

Israel

David Zim stood outside of the entrance while the camp guards took his mission orders to the command post. The refugee processing center was located a few miles to the southeast of Jerusalem. The inner buildings of the camp were formerly an apartment complex at the edge of the Israeli settlement of Har Homa before its residents were evacuated deeper into Israel, and the rest of the place was allocated back to the government. That was where he needed to go, since the inner camp served as the personal proving grounds of Rabbi Elijah Ba'al and his followers. David could see that the outer ring of the camp was more rudimentary, with several miles of temporary shelters encompassed by a series of chain linked fences and guard towers. Several children could be seen playing beside a number of tents, oblivious to the fate that awaited them. He couldn't help but notice the parallels between this place and the other times in history when helpless innocents were victimized by an inhuman government.

A few minutes passed before the guard finally came back out and walked towards him. David was relieved the guard didn't have his M-16 rifle on the ready. It meant they believed his papers to be authentic. So far so good.

The guard handed him his papers back as he signaled the others to open the chain linked gate. "Here are your mission orders, sir. Please wait in the administration center and one of the staff will escort you to the inner compound."

"Shalom," David said as he placed the papers in the front pocket of his collared shirt and walked inside. With Amel Kasem's help, he had created the mission orders and forged the signature of his Uncle Ariel Weizman along with that of his chief administrator in the Mossad. With all the frantic orders that had been issued by the military and the government due to the ongoing crisis, they had hoped that there would not have to be any sort of security confirmation in order for David to pass through the numerous checkpoints. So far, their paper-thin plan to get into the inner compound was working.

The administration building was once a large house that now served as offices for the numerous departments that ran the camp. David leaned on a nearby wall as a number of guards walked past him. All of the camp sentries were wearing the standard IDF olive-green field uniforms, but with black armbands to denote their status. He tried not to make any eye contact lest someone he knew might recognize him. The Israeli military and intelligence communities were small enough that all of the major players knew one another. The last thing David needed was for an acquaintance to come up to him and start asking questions.

After a wait of almost half an hour, a young bearded man in a black suit and wearing a yarmulka came down the corridor and walked up to him. "Shalom, are you David Zim from the Institute?"

David nodded as he showed the other man a sealed folder marked TOP SECRET. "Shalom, yes, I am David. I'm here to see Rabbi Ba'al with an urgent report for his eyes only."

The young man was obviously one of Ba'al's rabbinic recruits. "It's best you give those papers to me for now. Rabbi Ba'al is rather busy, I'm afraid. He cannot see anybody today."

David shook his head. "I'm sorry, but my orders were to give it to him personally."

For a short while, both men just stood there staring at each other. David had hoped that they would not attempt to call IDF headquarters to confirm that the order was given. If that happened, he would be caught for sure.

But the other man turned and started walking as he beckoned David to follow. "I cannot guarantee that he would see you, but perhaps I can ask him to take a minute or two to take a look at your message."

David smiled as he moved right behind the young rabbi. "Thank you, I really appreciate this. My superiors would not be pleased if I didn't place these reports in his hands personally."

The other man said nothing as he just kept walking while David followed. The two men walked out of the building and moved through a pathway between two sets of chain linked fences. David could see a guard tower manned by IDF soldiers with rifles on the ready above them, while two women emerged from a nearby tent on the other side of the fence. The women were dressed in black from head to toe as their dark veils covered everything but their eyes as they just silently gazed back at him with tired, pleading stares. As they made it to the outskirts of the inner camp, David estimated that the outer camp must have been housing over a hundred thousand Palestinian and Jordanian refugees. He didn't see a single Arab man of fighting age, almost all of the people in the tent areas were the old, the women, and the very young.

"Through here," the young rabbi said as he opened up a door that lead into a building compound.

As they walked inside, David could see that the whole character of the camp had changed dramatically. Gone were the signs that said REFUGEE SANCTUARY and FOR YOUR PROTECTION in Arabic. He could see that the walls and ceiling were fully enclosed and were sound proofed to prevent anyone from the outside to know what was happening in here. The whole building they were in resembled some sort of sterile lab. The passageway that they were moving in was also deserted, there didn't seem to be anyone else around.

They soon turned into another corridor that had two-way mirrors along its walls. As they started walking towards a set of doors at the rear, David saw a crowd of several hundred Arabs in the other side, apparently unaware they were being observed from the hidden corridor. The large room that they were in was fully enclosed, and quite a number of them were just standing or sitting down on the tiled floor. The ceiling above the crowd seemed to have multiple metal panels on the top of it, like vertical swinging doors but they looked so unobtrusive that only someone with a keen eye would have spotted them. David stopped as he tried to figure out what the crowd was doing, but it seemed like they were waiting for something. There didn't seem to be any guards with them either, the Arabs were seemingly left alone to fend for themselves. Children darted in and out amongst the crowd while being chased by their mothers as the older people just kept sitting down from apparent exhaustion. The crowd was subdivided into smaller groups as people seemed to be talking to each other, but David couldn't hear what they were saying.

The rabbi noticed that he had stopped following him, so he turned around with a smile on his face as he walked over to David's side. "Oh, you haven't seen this part, have you? In that case let's stick around for a short while because the next stage is about to begin."

David paid no attention to him as he continued to observe behind the mirrored glass.

Less than a minute later, a terrible thing happened.

As the crowd in the other room continued to mill about, the panels on the ceiling had begun to shift as they slid open, revealing vertical holes above. Some in the crowd looked up and pointed upwards, but it was too late. Strange, misshapen humanoids that were the size of small dwarfs and looking like deformed fetuses, instantly leapt out from the holes of the ceiling and landed on top of the terrified people in the room. David gasped as he realized that the twisted creatures were homunculi, artificial beings created by Rabbi Elijah Ba'al's black magic. But what made the whole scene even worse was that the crowd didn't seem to panic with the exception of the children. People attempted to get away as more and more homunculi emerged from the holes in the top, but they seemed to react in slow motion. The monsters quickly overwhelmed several dozen of the people in the room. David could see the creatures bringing their disfigured, snarling mouths right next to their victim's faces as the other homunculi held them down.

It was then that the nearest homunculus breathed in and began to magically drain the life essences of the sacrifice in front of it. One old woman had her mouth open in shock as a red mist emanated out of it, and the haze was quickly swallowed up by the swarming creatures around her. One girl of about seven tried to climb up to the hole in the ceiling, but another homunculus dragged her down from behind before draining her life essence, leaving a wild-eyed corpse on the floor. An old man tried to push his way past a dozen of the little imps, but they finally brought him down before leeching out his soul.

Within minutes it was finished. All over the floor were bodies that resembled mummified husks surrounded by heaps of clothing. The homunculi quickly darted back up through the holes in the ceiling before the panels closed behind them once more. Seconds later, David saw the steel double doors in the other room had opened as a cleaning team wearing chemical suits came inside and started to pile the withered corpses on wheel barrows before taking them away, leaving trails of ash from where the bodies were.

David closed his eyes as his forehead leaned on the mirrored glass. "Feh! All those people, the children!"

The rabbi shrugged. "Our chief rabbi says it is justified, for the Arabs and the Palestinians are one of the tribes of Canaan. Therefore we are duty-bound to exterminate them without mercy. The Torah said so. At least their sacrifice is going for a good cause."

David turned to look at him. "W-Why didn't they try to resist?"

"They were drugged before they were placed into that room."

"What?"

The rabbi had a blank look on his face. "You should have seen the first batches we sacrificed to the homunculi, they put up such a fight and the creatures were so hard-pressed that it took hours for them to drain all the life essences from all their targets. From then, on we spiked the internee's food and drink. It works pretty well since they don't revolt in the outer camp either. The demand for life essences is growing at an alarming rate too."

David had finally had enough. He whirled and smashed his fist across the bridge of the rabbi's nose. The young man instantly fell on his back as David drove his right heel into the man's chest. Then he knelt down on top of the stunned rabbi and used his thumbs on the man's throat to crush the trachea. The rabbi gargled and died.

Breathing heavily, David stood up and closed his eyes in order to calm himself down. He needed to stash the body away somewhere before it was discovered and the alarm was raised. David quickly moved over to where the door was at the end of the corridor and opened it slightly. As he peered out, he noticed that there was another deserted passageway. He then moved over to where the dead rabbi was and began to drag him until he got to the edge of the door. David then moved out into the second corridor as he tried to open the doors along the passage. The first door led to an unused office, while the second opened up to a supply room.

David then ran back to the corridor he came from and dragged the corpse into the storeroom. He searched the dead man through force of habit before stripping him of his clothes. In less than fifteen minutes, he was not only dressed as one of Ba'al's new rabbinic assistants, he also had keys to the whole complex. As he locked the storeroom behind him, David then went over to the office room next door and began rummaging the desk for anything useful. His thoroughness was rewarded when he saw that there was a pistol in the desk drawer. David took it out from the table and examined it. The gun was a Jerico 941 pistol with a full magazine of 15 rounds. *Good enough*, he thought as he racked the slide to put a round in the chamber and placed the gun behind his jacket before leaving the office.

The third corridor fronted a glass enclosure. David could see a number of other black suited rabbis performing incantations at the squirming homunculi that were captive in closet- sized vivariums. As he watched in horror, the life senses of the victims in the previous room seemed to be exhaled out from the gibbering mouths of the homunculi and through some unknown technique, drifted out from the top of the glass cages, and then settled downwards again until the crimson gas somehow seeped into an earthenware jar with strange symbols written on it. As soon as one of the containers was filled to the brim, another rabbi immediately placed a clay stopper on the top of the jar in order to trap the life mist. The rabbi then picked up the pot and walked out of the room.

There was a voice from behind him. "Are you alright?"

David turned. Standing to his rear was another rabbi. He seemed older than the previous one and had a long brown beard. "Yes, I'm new here so all this has been quite surprising to me," David said.

The second rabbi nodded. "I felt the same way when I started last month. But we must remember that we are doing God's will and that this helps to protect Israel. If you keep that in mind, then all will be well."

David smiled. "I will do that, thank you."

"Shalom," the rabbi said before turning away and he headed out to the second corridor.

David sighed with relief as he kept on walking. The end of the corridor now led into a vast warehouse that looked similar to the factory site in Dimona. There were about three hundred golems in various stages of construction. The farthest part of the vast hall had mounds of red clay that were passed on to hundreds of sculptors and their assistants, who used their hands and various tools to turn the clay pieces into humanoid form. David noticed that the once famous Palestinian artist Khaled Hadawi was still among them, with an armed guard watching his every move. A door across the other side of the massive room seemed to be the only alternative exit so David started walking towards it. As he tried the doorknob, he realized that it was locked so he took out the set of stolen keys from his pocket and began to try them out, one at a time.

By the time he had gotten to the sixth key, David saw that it fit the lock perfectly so he twisted the door open and stepped inside. Almost immediately, the shock of seeing what was in the succeeding room gave David an urge to step back out, but he was able to control it as he composed himself and closed the door behind him.

Like the preceding factory hallway, this room was massive. But instead of having corrugated steel and concrete walls like the previous room, this one had gigantic black drapes painted with esoteric symbols all along its walls, giving it an eerie atmosphere. The only light sources for the entire place were from great metal braziers that burned with unnatural green fire; these were situated along the sides of the walls and as well as surrounding an upraised stage in the center of the room. As he looked up, David also noticed that the ceiling had been painted black with strange constellations illustrated using incandescent gold. Over a dozen rabbis were standing in front of the stage; some of them were carrying Uzi sub-machineguns that were strapped over their shoulders.

As David walked closer, he finally saw his target. Rabbi Elijah Ba'al was standing on the raised platform with his back to the audience. Beside the chief rabbi was an antique wooden bookstand that had an old leathery book lying on top of it. *That must be the true Sefer Yetzirah*, David guessed as he stood just behind the other rabbis.

Rabbi Ba'al had his hands raised as he intoned some sort of incantation while facing a gigantic boulder made of black basalt at the rear portion of the stage. David saw that there was a strange blue glow on the rock that seemed to grow with intensity. Within a minute, everyone in the audience gasped as a giant eye manifested itself as it seemed to float just above the boulder. David's mouth was wide open as he sensed that the eye was looking directly at him so he tried to hide himself behind the others in the group. All of a sudden, there was a loud noise that reverberated across the entire room as if some colossal gong had been sounded. The huge eye quickly disappeared and the basalt boulder's glow had begun to weaken.

"My invocation was a failure!" Rabbi Ba'al bellowed as he turned and faced the group. "The only way this could have happened is if one of you was unfaithful to me!"

It's now or never, David thought as he started moving away from the group while pulling out the pistol from the back of his coat. Two other rabbis in the assembly quickly noticed him and cried out in alarm. As David leveled the pistol at Rabbi Ba'al, another rabbi ran onto the stage and placed himself in front of the target.

David didn't hesitate. His first shots brought down the other rabbi who stood in front of Ba'al as the other man fell back on top of his target and both men were down in a heap. David hissed in frustration as he moved sideways, away from the onrushing group and jumped on top of the stage to get a closer shot. One of the other rabbis in the group pulled out his Uzi and tried to fire but he had forgotten to rack the slide in order to place a round in the bolt, so it just made an audible click.

Rabbi Ba'al tried crawling away from the dying man on top of him but he soon saw David standing over him. "I know you, traitor!" the chief rabbi hissed.

"For the innocents you sacrificed," David said as he pulled the trigger.

The first shot hit Rabbi Ba'al on the shoulder and he cried out in pain. The second shot hit him squarely on the forehead and he instantly stopped squirming as his eyes glazed over. Another rabbi from the crowd was able to get his Uzi working, and he fired a full burst at his master's assailant.

Several rounds hit David on his back and he fell forward onto the floor of the stage, his body wracked with pain. As he started to bleed out, he could hear screams and the klaxon of a general alarm coming from all around him. His final thoughts were of his wife and that floating eye which seemed to manifest itself again and it looked at him just as he died.

Tzipi Zim stood on the pier while watching the waves come into the beach. The afternoon sun reflected off the water like millions of tiny mirrors. The baby girl that she was holding had finally stopped crying and was now fast asleep. Both she and David had agreed that the baby would be named after her mother, Leyla. The wharf was largely deserted with the exception of Amel Kasem's family, who were sitting down on wooden benches just a few feet away. She had known Kasem for a number of years and had been invited to his family compound many times so she wasn't a stranger. She looked at Kasem's little nephews and nieces running around the pier and wished she still had their childlike energy. That was when her thoughts strayed over to the memory of David. She let out a single tear before wiping it off with her sleeve. Tzipi knew he was dead. She got that premonition the moment the emergency sirens started blaring all over the city, and the reports on the radio said that there was an incident at a camp near Jerusalem. When the tone of the news reports changed from cautious optimism to preparations for a general evacuation, that was when she knew her husband had succeeded. Tzipi had already gotten to the port city of Ashkelon with forged identity papers to meet up with Kasem's family. They were set to leave.

Kasem's grandmother walked over to her side. "You had been standing there for a long time. Would you like me to hold the baby for awhile?"

Tzipi smiled as she gave the sleeping baby to her. "Thank you."

"I will go sit with the others," the old woman said as she turned around and headed back towards the stone bench. Along with the five small children, there were a number of middle-aged aunts and uncles who were also there, waiting for the boat that would take them out of the country.

Tzipi tensed up a bit when she saw a car approaching the pier. She still had a pistol in her waist holster but her worry soon turned to relief when she realized that the car belonged to Kasem. The sedan stopped at the front of the pier and several more of Kasem's relatives came out. Two of the smaller children ran over to them as Kasem himself came out from the driver's side of the car and walked over to Tzipi.

Kasem stood beside her and sighed. "I'm sorry but I have some bad news."

Tzipi nodded as she looked away. "He's dead isn't he?"

"Yes," Kasem said softly. "But he was able to neutralize the target. The last reports I got from my friends that are still in the IDF is that the golems went berserk and started rampaging through the camp the moment that rabbi died. It seems there was a massive battle in the camp so I'm sure David succeeded."

There were tears in her eyes now. "We won, but we also lost."

"He knew it was a one-way trip, but he went ahead with it anyway. He didn't hesitate. That's something to be proud of."

Tzipi nodded. Her husband did it for all of them. In her eyes, he was a righteous man who died for what he believed in. In a time of gods and troubles, that was a noble thing. "So now what?"

Kasem exhaled. It seemed like he was holding his breath for the longest time. "We wait for the boat. We all have papers for Cyprus. From there we will be safe. Then we can decide on what to do next."

Tzipi didn't answer. The one man in her life was gone and the authorities would be looking for all of them. But it didn't matter now. Israel would fall within days now that the golems couldn't be controlled. The news on the radio was grim. The Babylonian hordes would soon descend on the country and a new exodus would begin. She estimated that the beaches would be filled with people trying to get on any boat that they could find by this evening. If the ship didn't come for them soon, they would be lost in the crowds as well.

One of Kasem's older uncles stood up and pointed to the sea. Sure enough, a small fishing boat with Greek flags came steaming towards them. As Tzipi walked over to the bench to get her baby daughter, she knew that her journey was just beginning.

24. The Invocation

Mary Arctor gingerly made her way through the corridor in order not to trip on the numerous power cables on the marble floor. Both the Speaker of the House and the Senate President were anxious as to whether any progress had been made with her newly reformed task force, so she felt compelled to find out for herself. Mary had postponed her meetings with the NORTHCOM staff in order to assess the strange requests that Dr. Paul Dane had asked for since she placed him fully in charge of the team. When he had requested that mobile generators be installed in order to provide more power to the museum, she had complied without much protest. Then things began to get even strange. Just a few days after that, Paul made another request, this time for the top cryptography teams in the FBI's Cryptanalysis and Racketeering Records Unit to come and join him in order to work on something. After her reluctant approval, she then received his request that the NSA reactivate its exclusive intranet for his task force. Mary then had to face a barrage of criticism from the Speaker because of the tremendous effort and resources that Paul's team was now using. Even after she had succeeded in getting him all that, Paul still did not divulge what he was doing. Now that she finally ran out of excuses and obfuscation to the government in Virginia, Mary needed to see something, anything, to keep them off her back.

One of her bodyguards nearly tripped over a thick cable that had been snaking along the Memorial Hall. The M-4 rifle that he had been carrying had fallen to the floor with a loud clatter as several nearby FBI agents instinctively had their hands beneath their coat pockets, ready to draw their own weapons before they realized that it was a false alarm.

"Be careful," Mary said to him as she started walking down the ramp that led to the basement area.

Paul was leaning over a folding table in the middle of the massive hall. Beside him were Detective Valerie Mendoza and a group of people that Mary didn't recognize right away. Several teams of cryptographers had workstations along the sides and back of the room and were busy typing away at their keyboards. When the Secretary of Defense had come down from the ramp and walked towards him, Paul glanced her way at first, but then quickly realized who it was as he stood upright and then smiled as he held out his hand.

Mary shook it. "Good afternoon, Professor Dane."

"And a good afternoon to you, Madame Secretary. What brings you here?"

Mary sighed. "Well, I just wanted to see what your team has been up to. It's been almost a week since you made your last request, so I figured you must be getting close to whatever it is that you're doing."

"We've all been working round the clock," Valerie said. "No one on the team has gotten much sleep lately."

"Perhaps it's better that I explain what this whole project is about," Paul said before turning his head and gesturing to one of the women manning a nearby workstation. "Sheila? Could you come over here for a minute?"

A tall woman, dressed in office wear with a pair of large, thick glasses and brown curly hair, came over to them. "Paul, we've uploaded the last algorithms into the system. We can expect the results any minute now," she said.

"That's great," Paul said as he gestured at Mary. "Sheila Giraud, this is Ms. Mary Arctor, the Secretary of Defense. She's here to look at our progress."

Sheila beamed as she shook Mary's hand. "Oh, I'm sorry I didn't notice you, ma'am. I was distracted by what we've been doing."

Mary had a quizzical look on her face. "It's really no problem. I just came over to see what everybody's been doing even though I have no idea what it's about."

"I'll give you the short version," Paul said. "We've gotten proof that a demon of some sort had materialized in this very place and now we're trying to find a way to bring it back here."

Marry nodded slowly. "I see, is this what you want me to tell our government that's been holed up in Raven Rock and facing an outright civil war? That we've spent all our resources on some sort of magic trick?"

"Oh, it's not a trick," Sheila said. "We've made huge breakthroughs in the last few days. We're just now starting to figure out the logic behind magic and so forth."

"Logic behind magic? I thought magic had no logic to it," Mary said to her. "Wait, your name is seems familiar to me. Was your father a certain Professor Giraud?"

"Yes, he taught advanced mathematics at Harvard," Sheila said. "I think he was the reason I got recruited to the NSA after I graduated high school and ended up on one of the teams for the Consolidated Cryptologic Program."

"Okay," Mary said to her before turning to look at Paul. "You are claiming to study magic, yet you've basically drafted the entire cryptanalysis team that the FBI has available and you've got the NSA's intranet, which is a closed network with unlimited access to data, at your complete disposal. You're making it seem like this magic … is some sort of mathematical problem."

Paul smiled. "We believe that magic is in fact, a sort of algorithm."

"What? You've lost me."

"In mathematical terms, an algorithm is a set of step by step instructions," Sheila said. "It's an exact formula that must be performed to either solve a problem, or to come up with a solution. What we've discovered is that there is a sort of science to it. The first step was to upload all the so-called books of magic that the suspect had possessed into our database, and then see if we could weed out anything that truly wasn't magical until we were left with the actual steps to perform true spells."

"But I thought all those occult books were crap," Mary said. "All they could do was to fire up one's imagination. How could you possibly find a real magic spell that works in all that?"

"Because we have an actual working model as our guide," Paul said as he pointed to an alcove. "We discovered an authentic demonic signature that was written on the far side of that wall over there. It was made using demon blood. We're pretty sure that's where the demon materialized along with the museum suspect. We also found esoteric symbols and glyphs from the old tree trunk that housed that worm. So all we had to do was to find similarities between the writing that the demon made on that wall with anything that we have in the occult database. These demons have their own sort of code and that's why I requested the nation's top cryptographers to come here and join me in decoding their hidden language. If we can find out the demon's name and the steps it takes to summon it, we will have made a major breakthrough."

"Assuming that this is all on the level, how close are you?"

Sheila clapped her hands in excitement. "We're almost there! First of all, we think we know the demon's name. Second of all, we think we've finally pieced together most of the incantation spell that will bring it to that area." She then pointed to man-sized glass enclosure towards the rear of the hall.

Mary saw that there was some sort of mystical diagram that was written on the floor of the glass cage. "What is that? Some sort of devil circle?"

"It's a variant of the Sigillum Dei," Paul said. "Also known as the Seal of God. It's a magical diagram composed of a pentagram, an outer circle, and three heptagons. The symbols written all over it is supposed to be the name of God and his angels. Legend says that whoever could construct the true seal would have power over all creatures except the angels. What we've found after comparing the symbols with a cryptanalysis of the demon's mark is that the name in the circle is in fact the names of demons. With the new information we have, we then went ahead and altered the dimensions of the diagram to conform to its proper size. We then removed any non-magical glyphs and replaced them with the true symbols that we deciphered."

"What do you hope to achieve with that?"

"That glass cage should entrap the demon once we've summoned it. Once we have properly detained it then we can try to find out whatever we can in regards to finding a solution to the problems that the whole country is facing," Paul said.

"It will be just like interrogating a suspect," Valerie said. "If we could compel any of these supernatural beings to answer our questions, it will go a long way towards ending this whole crisis."

"That's a big if," Mary said.

Right after she said those words, there was a shout that came from one of the cryptanalysis teams. Agent Lawrence Johnson quickly grabbed a piece of paper from them and then ran over to Paul and his group. "I think you might want to read this," Johnson said before handing the paper over to Paul.

Paul looked at it and smiled before handing it over to Valerie and Sheila. "That's it. We've cracked the last part of the incantation. We can begin."

In less than an hour, the entire basement level was evacuated, save for two people and a multitude of recording devices. Paul and Valerie stood in front of the glass enclosure while the rest of the team were on the floor above. The FBI agents and special forces operators were all on alert with their weapons on the ready as they observed the two below from concealed firing positions. Mary and her bodyguards were closer to the entrance of the museum as they watched the proceedings remotely from the security room.

Valerie glanced at her wristwatch as she stood beside Paul. "It's almost midnight. The start of the witching hour."

"That's pretty ironic," Paul said. "Are you sure you want to stay with me down here? It could get pretty dangerous since I've never done this before."

Valerie did a brass check on her Glock pistol, making sure that there was a round in the chamber, before putting it back on her hip holster. Although she was offered more powerful weapons by the FBI, Valerie declined. She figured that if a gun couldn't stop the thing that they were about to summon, then everything else they had would equally be just as useless. "For better or for worse, I'm sticking with you from now on."

Despite the fact that he was nervous, Paul looked at her closely and smiled. "Are you saying what I think you're saying, Val?"

She winked back at him. "Let's get through this first and then we can talk seriously about us."

"Okey dokey," Paul said as he stepped forward and took out a small bottle of an amber colored fluid from his trouser pocket. The container held Abramelin oil, a ceremonial potion blended from aromatic plants and used in magical rituals. Although Paul followed the traditional recipe of blending myrrh, cinnamon, cassia, and galangal root, he deviated by using distilled demon's blood that they had scrapped off from the glyphs on the wall and combined it with the bark of the old tree trunk from Hatteras. Paul carefully poured the magical oil around the enclosure until it formed a complete circle. Then he walked back over to where Valerie was.

Valerie looked up at Sheila who was in the upper floor behind a pile of sandbags. The NSA agent smiled back at her and gave the thumbs up sign. That indicated that all the remote cameras were working fine.

Paul started an incantation in Latin and then started speaking in what seemed to be gibberish. He held up a clipboard that contained the encrypted words of some mysterious language that no one on Earth had previously understood. As soon as he was finished, Paul placed the clipboard on the folding table to his side and held out his hands. Then he began a number of palm gestures that he had practiced with just two days before. Paul's arms and hands began gyrating back and forth. "By the power vested in me, I call forth the demon that had manifested itself in this place. The past, present, and future are all one. I call upon the demon's true name: Dantalion, the seventy-first spirit!"

Valerie could see that some sort of strange mist started to form in the glass cage in front of them. She instinctively started to rub the jade Aztec charm on her neck, while her other hand clasped a small vial of holy water that was in her pants pocket. Her mother Josefina had given it to her just a few days ago, when Valerie told her what they were going to do. Within seconds, the ring of magical oil around the cage began to glow with a pale amber hue.

"Dantalion!" Paul said. "Show yourself this instant! You cannot resist the summons! Reveal your true form!"

Mary Arctor gripped the chair that she was sitting in and then leaned forward. The security office near the front of the museum had multiple video monitors that were keyed into the basement. Even with different angles they were all showing the same thing. Something had manifested itself within the enclosure. At first she couldn't believe her eyes that it was happening. Everything that Paul claimed was coming true.

"Oh my god, this can't be real," a female FBI agent who stood behind her said.

"Shut up," Mary said tersely as she kept her eyes glued to the monitors.

The mist in the glass box soon became as tall as a man. Paul could see some sort of human-like form that shifted and shimmered as if it was trying to stay invisible. Valerie's hand slid down from her neck and started to wrap itself around the Glock's pistol grip.

"Who dares summon me," a voice coming from all around the room said. The sound carried so much power, it felt like the air was vibrating. Valerie could smell something sweet and sickly, like a combination of blood, honey, and vomit.

Paul felt his knees weaken as if the demon was trying to intimidate him by sneer alone. He kept concentrating as he tried to remember the binding words to keep the creature in check. "You are compelled to do as I command, Dantalion! You are not to break free, for the circle of power hinders you. You are not to leave, for the words of might controls you. You are to obey, for I command you!"

A tremendous roar reverberated across the entire room along with a powerful gust of wind that seemingly came from nowhere. Valerie cried out as she almost fell backwards but she was able to grip the side of the table right next to her. Paul nearly lost his balance as well but he had anticipated something was going to happen by bending his knees and leaning forward. The loose papers on the table had flown upwards to the upper floors as if sucked up by a miniature tornado. The fully armed men and women above them did not break cover as they continued to observe while tightly gripping their weapons. In a nearby corridor, a medical team dressed in hazmat suits, remained hidden as they crouched down near a display wall above.

Paul could see the form clearly now. He wasn't sure if the video feed saw the same thing, but the being looked like a ghostly young man wearing a smart business suit. The demon just seemed to float within a cloud of mist that filled the glass cage.

"You must forgive me, master," Dantalion said. His voice was like lilac and rose, but with a hint of hidden maleficence behind it. "It has been a long time since I have been summoned like this. What is it that you wish of me?"

"First, you are to answer my questions," Paul said. "And you are to state the truth and only the truth."

"But as with all things, master, there are many truths, just as there are many sides to every tale. Nevertheless, I shall answer you faithfully."

Paul nodded. He knew the truth could be twisted. And with a treacherous demon facing him, he knew he had to word his questions carefully. "Why have all the ancient gods and their servants returned to the world?"

Dantalion giggled. "Many gods have many reasons. Some have returned for vengeance, others for power. You of all people should know this, Paul Dane."

Valerie clenched her fists as her eyes opened wide, but she said nothing and stood her ground. Her faith was being tested.

Paul shuddered. He remembered that Dantalion was a great duke of hell and it could read their thoughts. He tried to empty his mind and concentrated on the script that he had memorized. If he didn't stick to the plan, this whole encounter could go very badly for them. "The man who you had brought here to this place, is his name Seth Solomon?"

"Yes."

"Where is he now?"

"That depends. He travels a lot, mostly."

"From one part of the Earth to another?" Paul asked.

"And in other worlds too. Such is the power of one who holds the ring."

"Then he has the seal of Solomon with him?"

"Yes."

"What are his plans?"

"He plans to take his first bath in weeks within the hour. Then he hopes to debauch himself on a few of the younger nuns later this evening."

Paul frowned. "So he is in a church? Where is this church that he is in right now?"

"He is in the world's largest church, and has its most powerful priest in his thrall."

Valerie was tempted to pull out her small notebook and to start taking notes, but she soon realized that it was already being done by the others who were watching. She, along with the rest of the team had been briefed by Paul that the summoned demon would be talking in half truths, and so it was important that they all remember and write down every minute detail that it spoke about.

Paul fought the urge to smile as his questions were starting to bear fruit. The demon had a tremendous ego and if asked the right questions, it might divulge information that it wasn't expected to. "The giant maggot that manifested itself here, why did it disappear?"

"Because its old form was no longer needed," Dantalion said. "It took on a new aspect."

"Was it because of our actions here?"

The demon laughed. "What you did here was meaningless! Let me tell you, Okeus and Ahone were merged not through your silly actions, but rather because of the machinations of two children who traveled to the Otherlands. All those deaths that occurred here were for nothing. Nothing!"

Valerie let out a deep breath that she had been holding for a long time. So many of her fellow cops died that day and now the sad truth came out. Their sacrifice had been pointless. *But at least I prevented a nuclear weapon from obliterating half of Manhattan*, she thought. *That ought to count for something.*

Paul was onto something now and he knew it. "These children, were they from our world here?"

"Yes, of course."

"What are their names?"

"The girl goes by Tara and the boy is named Ilya."

Paul thought about it for a minute. "The boy, is he from Russia?"

"No."

"Ukraine then?"

"No."

"Then where is he from?"

Dantalion was getting impatient. "Siberia."

Paul rolled his eyes. This was taking longer than expected, but his adrenaline kept him going. "The girl, Tara, where is she from?"

"Scottsdale."

Several floors above them, Sheila Giraud was writing furiously on a yellow pad. Even though everything was being recorded using separate video and audio streams, she had a distinct feeling that it could all be erased and so she stuck to the old try and true method of writing by hand.

"This girl, Tara," Paul said. "How was she able to travel to these Otherlands?"

"With the help of the trickster," Dantalion said.

Paul breathed deeply. "The trickster god? Which one of the tricksters is helping her?"

The demon's form shifted slightly as it became mistier. "How do you know that they are not all one god?"

Paul thought about it for a few seconds before answering. "What is the name of the trickster that led her into the Otherlands?"

"Bibsy."

Paul had a confused look on his face. "What? There is no such trickster god that I know of who has that name."

"That is what its master called it."

Paul growled. "I am not asking you what the others called it. I am asking you, what does it call itself?"

Dantalion exhaled deeply. It knew it had lost this round of questioning. "Coyote. Sometimes Raven."

Paul couldn't help but smile this time. He felt he was now gaining the upper hand. "So, Coyote the Trickster has helped her. Why did he do it?"

"Because she gave him some chocolate."

Now it was Valerie's turn to get confused. "What?"

Paul cut her off with a wave of his hand. "So they are still together then, this Coyote and Tara? What are they doing now?"

"They are …separated as of this moment."

"Explain."

"The girl has been taken ... prisoner. The trickster is now with the boy and the warrior to try and find her."

"Taken prisoner? By who?"

"The Temple."

Paul scratched his forehead. The information overload was almost too much but it was starting to make some sense now. "The Temple? You mean the Temple of the Black Sun?"

"Yes."

"So they are in Germany?"

"No."

"Then where are they?"

"The Otherlands," the demon said wistfully.

"So this Temple has somehow relocated to the Otherlands? How many members of this cult are out there?"

"As of this moment, there are about one hundred and two members of the Temple that are still living. Although I have a distinct feeling that number will go down once the boy and the warrior reach their castle."

"This warrior that you're talking about, is he from Earth too?"

"Yes."

So he must be a soldier then, Paul thought. "What is his name?"

"His wife calls him Patrick."

"What is he called by his superiors?"

"Gyle."

Paul had hoped that the people watching them heard all that and that they would be researching his name right away. "How did he get into the Otherlands?"

"He met the oldest man in the world."

Paul paused for bit as he tried to remember the myths of Sumer. "Gilgamesh?"

Dantalion snorted. "You are a poor man of knowledge. Gilgamesh died many, many millennia ago."

Paul tried to think about it again. "Noah?"

"About time," Dantalion said. "I doubt you will recognize the warrior, he has transformed his mortal form …into something else."

Paul nodded. "The girl, what is her surname?"

"That, I do not know," Dantalion said. "She never mentioned it."

"And the boy's surname?"

"Well, he mentioned it to Radegast. It's Volkhov."

"Radegast, he's a Slavic god," Paul said aloud. "Are there any pantheons that have not returned to the world?"

"The Norse gods," Dantalion said. "For obvious reasons."

"Because they were killed in Ragnarok?"

"You catch on quick."

"But there have been reports of giants in Northern Europe. Didn't they all die in Ragnarok too?"

"There are plenty of giants," the demon said. "Not just the northern ones."

Paul nodded. *Now for the ultimate question*, he thought. "Alright, so where is God in all of this?"

"God? I've been telling you the names of many gods that are already present. Have you gone all stupid all of a sudden?"

Paul shook his head. "Not them. You know, the one god- goes by the name of Yahweh, the Lord, and Allah. And Jesus too, where is he in all of this? With all that's happened, why hasn't he showed up yet?"

The demon laughed so hard that even the walls shook slightly.

Paul frowned. "Well? You didn't answer my question."

Dantalion kept giggling. "You already know the answer to that."

So Jesus wasn't real then, Paul thought. *I kind of expected that.*

Valerie was livid. "Are you going to tell us, or not?"

"I am compelled to give you the answer," the demon said. "And I did."

Valerie turned to look at Paul. "He's just spinning us around. Talking half-truths and puzzles."

"It's in his nature," Paul said softly to her before looking at the creature again. "Will the Aztecs invade us?"

"Soon enough," the demon said.

"Why haven't they done it yet? What are they waiting for?"

"They are consolidating," the demon said. Paul could see a hint of a smile coming from its shadowy form. "But they shall be here quite soon."

Valerie narrowed her eyes. "How do we defeat them?"

"The usual way," the demon said. "Blood and sacrifices. Plenty of them."

Valerie grimaced. The monster wasn't telling them anything new. She hoped that the others that were listening would know that the demon wasn't on their side.

Paul remembered something else all of a sudden. "The separatists in Kansas, are they truly the Lord's chosen? Is Jesus really helping them?"

The demon laughed again. "They certainly believe so, don't they? How I admire their convictions."

"You're saying that they're just delusional? That the Christian god really isn't on their side?"

"They have been quite successful so far without any divine help. If they can keep it up then your question becomes rather irrelevant."

Paul turned to Valerie and started whispering in her ear. "I'm going to try a different approach, maybe we can get ahead of this game if we try something daring. Just be ready to get the hell out of here if anything goes wrong."

Valerie's grip on her gun began to tighten. "Are you sure about this?"

Paul winked at her before looking at Dantalion again. "Demon, since you have been commanded to do what I ask, then you must bring someone here to me, now!"

Thirty feet above, Sheila Giraud stuck her head out from beneath the sandbags. *Wait a minute*, she thought. *This wasn't part of the plan!*

Mary Arctor stood up from her chair as she was watching everything from the security room. "What?"

Agent Lawrence Johnson immediately drew a Glock 22 pistol from his shoulder holster and had his hand on the door knob. "Should I go down there, ma'am?"

Mary held her hand up, palm forward. "No! Let's see this play out."

The swirling, misty form that faced them began to coalesce. "What? This wasn't part of the agreement! I have answered your questions and you will release me from the binding ritual now!"

"This ritual will only cease when I wish it," Paul said. "Now I compel you to fulfill one more task for me."

They could see that there were now two glowing eyes from where the head of the creature was supposed to be. A palpable sense of anger began to manifest itself like some invisible force all around them. "And if I refuse?"

"Then I will not release you," Paul said softly. "You shall be bound to that cage. I will have the people here seal this place so that no one from the outside will be able to discharge you, not even Seth Solomon. You will be trapped here for a long, long time."

Dantalion hissed with rage. "CURSE YOU, PAUL DANE. YOU HAVE MY ETERNAL ENMITY. BY ALL THE HELLS, I SHALL STOP AT NOTHING UNTIL I HAVE YOUR SOUL, THIS I PROMISE YOU."

Valerie could feel a chill in her very soul as she looked at Paul., but she could see that he was unmoved by the demon's curse. There was a certain sense of stoicism in him and it gave her some courage as she too stood her ground, just as a mysterious wind began to manifest itself in the entire building. A shrill, grating noise that seemed to be coming from all directions was also heard by everyone. A few FBI agents looked towards the exits as some of them thought the entire museum was about to collapse but so far, nobody panicked and ran.

Paul chose his next words carefully. "As a final task for this ritual, I compel you, Dantalion. I compel you, o Duke of Hell. I compel you to bring forth one mortal to my presence here, in this very place. He is to be of a safe and sound body, completely unharmed. I shall not accept simulacrums, or changelings, or doppelgangers. It is to be this one person, and it must be truly him. Once he is to be brought forth and of these conditions met, then I shall grant you your release. Of this task there is to be no deceit. You must use your utmost power to succeed. There will be no tolerance for failure."

Dantalion's voice had turned into a low rumble. Everyone could still sense the malice in it. "Of this task, it may well be beyond my power to make such a feat without a cost in blood. You know this. All works require payment of equal cost."

Paul bit his lip. The demon was right. He was reaching out too far ahead and playing with powers he did not understand, but he was so close now, he needed results. Paul made a decision and pulled out a small pocket knife from his pants pocket. "I shall give you a little of my life essence, but not my soul."

Valerie grabbed Paul's shoulder. "Paul, what are you doing?"

Paul gently took her hand away. "Trust me," he whispered to her before unfolding the knife.

The demon's form appeared to be shaking its head. "If all you can offer is your partial essence, then all I can do is to give you a glimpse of your desire."

"It's a start," Paul said as he moved forward until he was just a few feet away from the glass enclosure. He then pulled back his shirtsleeve from his left arm and held his wrist near the circle of glowing oil. Paul grimaced as he made a cut on the inside of his left wrist and the droplets of blood began to fall onto the oil. The moment the blood began to conjugate with the glowing ring, the demon's form began to solidify once more.

Dantalion seemed to be enjoying himself. "Aaah, it has been a long time since I have tasted the blood of a righteous mortal who voluntarily satiates my eternal hunger. Name the person that you would like me to provide a glimpse of."

Paul's face was contorted as he continued to bleed but he maintained his focus. "Show me the President of the United States. Reveal his current state."

"As you wish," the demon said. Within seconds, a darker cloud began to form in the same cage at the edge of the glass. The mist began to take shape and an image of the president appeared. He seemed to be tied to a chair and was moaning in agony but no sound could be heard from his lips.

"Oh my god," Valerie said as she quickly moved and stood beside Paul. She could see that he had lost a lot of blood as he strained to hold out his left arm. She quickly held him by the elbows to keep his knees from buckling.

Paul could barely concentrate. It seemed as if his blood was being drained out of him by some unseen force; he could see that there was now a steady line of blood running from the slit on his wrist, and it connected with the oil on the floor like a crimson colored string. "Is that really him? You are commanded not to lie to me!" he yelled at the demon.

"That is indeed him," the demon said. "That is his true self as of this time in the land of Kansas."

Paul groaned from the pain and weakness. "I command you, make his form material so that I can see his true flesh and body!"

Valerie's mouth was open as she looked at her lover. "Paul, are you sure about this? You're getting too weak! You need to break it off! He's drawing the life out of you!"

Paul violently shook his head as he struggled to concentrate. "No! We must keep going! Dantalion, open a conduit to him in Kansas!"

"As you wish," Dantalion said. For a few brief seconds, it looked as if the president was halfway through as his body had now solidified. They could see the beads of sweat on his pale forehead and the wrinkles on his face. The president's eyes were closed and his mouth was in a contorted, painful grimace. There was no mistake that they were looking at the actual person, it was as if he was in two places at once.

Paul realized that it was now or never if his trick was to succeed. Quickly mustering his remaining reserves of willpower, he lunged forward and pushed through one of the side panels of the enclosure. The glass paneling was meant to be only a divider and so the hinges that had held it in place quickly gave way and it fell on top of Dantalion, pinning the solidified demon down to the floor. Paul quickly got his hands onto the president and began to pull him out of the magical circle.

Valerie stood in momentary shock as Paul brushed past her and knocked out part of the cage. But when she realized what he was doing, she quickly ran over and started to help him.

Several special forces operators that were upstairs quickly reacted. Two of them got out of their firing positions and started running down the ramp to see if they could help while four others sighted their scopes until they had the best shots at the demon and waited for the order to fire.

"Go!" Mary Arctor shouted as the FBI agents in the security room ran outside to see what they could do to help.

The NSA technician who ran the video monitors listened to her headset briefly before looking at Mary. "Delta is asking for clearance to fire at the monster."

"Wait until Dr. Dane and Mendoza are clear," Mary said tersely.

Dantalion roared with anger as he realized what had happened. With supernatural strength, it instantly shattered the glass that was on top of it and stood up. Just as the demon turned its attention to its mortal enemies, it quickly saw that Paul had succeeded in getting the president to fully materialize into the area. Dantalion quickly grabbed onto the president's ankles, the only part of him left that was still in the magic circle.

Both Paul and Valerie screamed as they were knocked to the ground. Just as they were about to heave the president out of the glass cage, the demon quickly grabbed onto the old man's legs and immediately began to pull them back. It was a brutal tug of war and the president cried out in pain as the sudden jolt on his spine was unbearable. The two of them didn't want to hurt the head of state and so they began to slacken their grip as the demon pulled the president back into the circle once more.

But just as the tide seemingly turned, one Delta Force operator disobeyed orders and began shooting at the demon with his M-4 rifle. The first two shots hit Dantalion in the lower torso and the demon wailed in pain as it loosened its grip on the president. Paul instantly saw what had happened, and he used all of his strength as he stepped forward to use his own body as a pivot to throw the president out of the circle.

"Damn you!" Dantalion screamed as he saw that the president was now lying outside of the ring. That was when the demon noticed that Paul had accidentally stepped inside, past the protective glyphs. That was all he needed.

Paul saw the two soldiers running towards him, and he had just begun to reach out to them when some terrific force pulled him backwards, and he was suddenly engulfed in a black mist that blinded him. He cried out in terror as he began falling into a cold, lightless abyss.

"No!" Valerie shrieked as she tried to make a grab for him. She was able to grasp his outstretched hand and it was like clutching an iceberg. The cold was so intense it felt like her hand was burning but she quickly got her other hand on Paul and refused to let go no matter how intense the pain had become. Within seconds, the darkness unfolded over her as well.

Mary Arctor had gotten down the ramp and into the basement area in less than five minutes after she told everyone to move. All she could see now was the medical team looking over at the president, who was lying on the floor. The glass cage had collapsed in on itself, and all that remained were some black ashes where the magic circle was. Almost everyone had their guns drawn, but the demon was gone. Paul and Valerie were nowhere to be seen as well.

Sheila Giraud let out sob as she pulled out her handkerchief.

"I shot it twice, but all it did was piss it off," a Delta operator muttered to no one in particular as he just stood there with his rifle pointing downwards.

Mary walked over to Sheila. "Can you tell me what exactly happened here?"

There were tears in Sheila's eyes but she kept her composure. "Professor Dane tricked the demon into bringing the president over to us. But that thing took its revenge by taking him back to whatever hell it came from. Val tried to help him and she ended up being taken with him too."

One of the medical technicians who was crouching on the ground nearby looked up. "He's waking up! The president's alive!"

A loud cheer erupted in the room as Mary made her way to where the president was. *Task Force Omega lost its leader, but Paul had succeeded in taking back the head of the country*, she thought as she looked down at the old man lying on the floor.

The president wore a slightly ripped undershirt and dark trousers. His hair was a mess and he started blinking his eyes. His mouth was slightly open and he had two-day stubble on his chin. He looked somewhat emaciated and tired but was otherwise normal it seemed.

"Mr. President," a medical technician said as he kept shining a penlight on his eyes. "Can you hear me, sir? How are you feeling?"

The president mumbled something softly, then closed his eyes.

Mary leaned over closer. "What did he say?"

The president opened his eyes again. Only this time his irises seemed to have changed color, they went from light brown to blue. Then he opened his mouth. "Omnes aeternis maledicam ... the quick brown fox jumped over the lazy shit! My fellow Americans, we must ...ut omnes manducare prandium forngs! Someone help me ...non proderunt tibi iram dei diabolo! Can you not see the truth? Nisi mortale et caducum, et faciem. Make war upon the blasphemers in Kansas! In nostro mundo est..."

"He's hysterical," a physician on the medical team said.

"I don't think it's circulatory shock," a second medical technician said as he took the president's vital signs. "Blood pressure, heart rate are all normal."

"Must be an acute stress reaction," the physician said.

The president then tried to sit up and started flailing his arms. The medical team had to hold him down as he began talking in gibberish again, saliva and bile streaming down his mouth.

Sheila shook her head. "It's not anxiety."

Mary looked at her. "What else could explain that?"

"Look at his eyes," Sheila said. "They keep changing color every time he blinks. He's been possessed by something."

25. The Raid

Before the crack of dawn, a hand-picked force was on the move as they made their way through the forest. Hours before, the strike teams had already dismounted from their vehicles and made rapid sweeps of the area using their night vision equipment for any signs of movement. So far, they didn't encounter anything at all, not even a small animal. It looked like the entire town was deserted. By the first crack of dawn, the advance teams had already made their way along the nearby streets and were now right beside the castle grounds. They were dressed in black from head to toe and wore heavy body armor, their silenced rifles at the ready as they remained hidden in nearby alleys and houses.

Colonel Anton Wegener of the German Army and Colonel Mike McGrath of EUCOM slowly made their way to the edge of the forest. It was now first light and they could see the triangular facade of Wewelsburg Castle, less than half a mile away to the east. Moving right behind them were two radio operators carrying portable communications units as well as a squad of bodyguards.

"Colonel," one of the radio operators crouching behind them said. "The battery at Paderborn is now in position."

Colonel Wegener nodded. Paderborn Lippstadt Airport was less than two miles away to the west of their location. "Looks like we're now in position," he said to his American counterpart in unaccented English.

"This is your show, Colonel," Colonel McGrath said softly. "My men are just here to lend some support."

Colonel Wegener smiled at him before using his binoculars to scan the castle and the surrounding area. "It seems quite deserted. There is apparently no one in the town and possibly in the castle either. Your grateful support may be all for nothing."

"It's no problem. Better to be over armed than under armed is my motto. How sure are you that this might be the place where that UFO airship came from? If it was based here, we surely would have seen it by now. You can't hide that big of a ship out here without someone noticing."

"Our intel reports say that this castle has the same symbol that coincides with the insignia on the side of that airship. And there was supposedly some sort of a magician's cult that was associated with the purchase of the place for a private company. I think it all fits somehow."

"Magician cult, huh? No shit," Colonel McGrath said. "Well, if they're in there and they are able to communicate with that UFO, then it might just bring 'em over here."

Colonel Wegener nodded as he kept looking through his binoculars. "Yes, that is what I'm expecting. That's why we brought your unit along."

"We're good to go. Ready when you are."

Colonel Wegener put down his binoculars and turned to his radio operator. "Tell the advance teams to move in," he said tersely in German.

The moment they received the go-signal, several teams of German special forces commandos immediately started sprinting towards the castle. Two teams moved quickly from a nearby copse of trees in the south and soon went past the southern garden. A third team came out from behind an abandoned restaurant and ran along the road, up towards the stone bridge that led to the main entrance of the citadel. But as soon as the lead trooper made it to within twenty feet of the castle walls, he was instantly stopped by some unseen force as his momentum threw him back to the ground. Less than a second later, half a dozen commandos had bounced off an invisible wall as they started looking around in confusion. One trooper tried pounding the force field with his battering ram but it seemed to just bounce off the air. Their commanders quickly got on the radio as the teams ran back towards cover.

"Colonel," the radio operator said. "Advance teams report an invisible shield is somehow surrounding the castle. They cannot push through."

Colonel Wegener cursed. "Tell the Leopards to advance. Warn them about the invisible shield."

"Jeesus H. Christ," Colonel McGrath muttered. "Did they know we would be coming?"

"They are not fools. I have no doubt they expected us. If infantry can't get through a shield, let's see if our Panzers can."

In less than a minute, two Leopard 2A6 main battle tanks rumbled along the street. The tanks drove into the southern lawn and parked themselves less than three hundred feet from where the supposed invisible field was. There was a droning noise as their turrets rotated and they leveled their main guns at the southern facade of the castle.

"I would suggest they not try a straight shot," Colonel McGrath said as he looked through his own binoculars. "Just in case the shell ricochets or something."

Colonel Wegener had one hand on the radio receiver while the other was holding up his field glasses. "Leopard team, try an angled shot first. Just shoot one. Use a sabot round."

One of the Leopard tanks turned its main gun slightly to the west and fired. The shell that erupted from the 120 mm smoothbore gun was essentially a finned metal dart that traveled at a speed of 5,700 feet per second. As soon as it was fired, the sabot immediately separated from its cone-like casing as it flew headlong towards the castle wall. A split second later, the dart instantly crumpled as if an unseen hand stopped it in midair. The pieces of the sabot round flew off towards the western tree line surrounding the castle, while a slight shimmering could be seen in the air where it had initially been stopped.

Colonel McGrath was astonished as he kept peering through his binoculars. "What in the hell! Did you see that? Holy shit, that's just unbelievable!"

"Yes," Colonel Wegener said tersely before switching to German again. "Leopard team, try using a HEAT round this time. One shot."

The same Leopard tank fired a second shot at the same angle. The HEAT round that was fired this time was a different sort of warhead. As soon as the impact sensor on the shell tip hit anything solid, the force of impact would drive a shaped charge backwards into the device and would detonate it instantly. Theoretically, the resulting explosion would propel enough energy from the point of contact and into whatever was behind it. The succeeding shot impacted the exact same spot in the air as the force of the blast seemed to cascade in all directions. The shockwave made the two tanks shudder while the reverse torrent of energy made cracks on the castle wall facing it.

Colonel McGrath nearly jumped in the air as he saw what had happened. "Hell yeah! Now we're getting somewhere! It didn't penetrate that damned force field, but the shockwave is damaging the castle, at least."

"Leopard team," Colonel Wegener said on the radio. "How many HEAT rounds do you have, over?"

"We have about a dozen HEAT rounds each, sir," the Leopard team commander said over the radio.

"Okay, fire about six rounds each. Use angled shots and move back a bit so there's less of a force wave hitting your vehicles," Colonel Wegener said.

Right after he said those words, a gigantic shadow suddenly loomed over them. As everyone in the forest looked up to the sky, they saw that a gigantic, metal hulled airship had seemingly materialized out of thin air and was hovering right above them.

Colonel McGrath's eyes were wide open as he stared at the monstrous craft floating overhead. "What in the hell?"

"Alarm! Everybody, take cover!" Colonel Wegener screamed.

Kurt Orlok frowned as his hands gripped the railings on the side of the bridge. He was watching the enemy soldiers below using the gigantic crystal ball that was mounted at the front of the chamber. Even though he had been living in the ship for over a month now, he still wasn't quite sure how it all worked. Was this infernal craft a mechanical creation by the Dokkalfar, or was it powered entirely by magic? His best guess was that it was a combination of both. His bridge crew was now a combination of humans and dark elves. The Dokkalfar couldn't stand the light that shone from the crystals in the ceiling, so they all wore darkened goggles to prevent blindness as they scurried about.

Helmut Krause stood beside his master as he pointed to the northern edge of the image in the mirror. "Grand Magus, there's a pair of tanks just south of the castle."

"Yes, yes, I can see them," Orlok said as he pointed to another Temple crew member. "Helmsman, bring us about so that we can bear our guns against those two tanks."

"At once, Grand Magus," the helmsman said as he started turning a large, golden ship's wheel while standing in front of it.

Within a few seconds, the aerial battleship moved just above the castle. They were now in range. Their test run over Berlin had proved that the closer the lightning guns could bear on a target, the more powerful the damage to it would be. They also needed to get closer since the targets this time were smaller.

"We are at optimum firing position now, Grand Magus," Helmut said.

"Fire," Orlok said.

Colonel Wegener watched helplessly as the two Leopard tanks were instantly incinerated by several bolts of lightning that erupted from the airship. They had all moved back deeper into the forest but they still had a line of sight to the castle. For the first time, he had finally seen the UFO with his naked eyes. He grimaced at the power of it.

"Time for our contingency plan," Colonel McGrath said as he pulled aside his American radio operator. "Tell the battery team to open fire as soon as they get a lock on that thing."

"Yes, Colonel," the operator said as he started to key in his receiver.

A few miles to the west, the Patriot battery unit stationed in Paderborn Lippstadt Airport immediately went on full alert as its crew began to track the unidentified airship. The MIM-104 Patriots were equipped with an AN/MPQ-53/65 Radar set that served as a passive electronically scanned array system. With multiple guidance subsystems, the Patriot's powerful radar suite was able to track the airship in less than a minute. Once the radar systems had calculated the target's speed, heading, and locked into its massive cross-section, the first Patriot anti-aircraft missile was launched. Since the target was so huge and he had received direct orders to use everything he had, the Tactical Control Officer ordered his entire battery to open fire. In less than a minute, twenty-four Patriot missiles were in the air.

The first missiles impacted into the starboard side of the airship. The entire vessel shuddered as the Patriots detonated their proximity warheads just a few feet from the ship's main hull. The multiple explosions from the 200-pound warheads dented and cracked the thick metallic hull in several places.

Orlok turned to another crew member that was manning a console with gauges and levers to his right. "Damage control."

"We have about six batteries on our starboard side inoperative," the crewman said. "I think two of the guns have misaligned lenses because the explosions jarred them out of focus, but they can easily be repaired. The other four would need to be repaired at the dry dock because they took direct hits. Our fuselage is still intact. Though we may take severe damage if they try this again at the same spot."

Orlok looked over to the ship's helmsman. "Huber, use our port side and face the airport. Then hit those fools with everything we can."

"At once, Grand Magus," the ship's helmsman said as he turned the ship's wheel once more.

The Patriot battery in the airport was still in the process of reloading its missiles when the lightning bolts hit them. The sheets of electrified plasma instantly incinerated the mobile launchers and the towed radar array. The cargo trucks that carried additional missiles instantly detonated, causing the entire side of the airport that faced them to collapse. Countless soldiers exploded from the inside out in a fraction of a second as the electrical bolts of death spared no one. Within a matter of minutes, the entire Patriot missile battalion had ceased to exist.

Colonel McGrath pounded the grass with his fists. "Goddamn them!"

"Howitzer team," Colonel Wegener said as he spoke into the radio. "Can you initiate direct fire against the target?"

"Yes, sir," came the reply. "Engaging now."

From the northern edge of the forest, a pair of Panzerhaubitze 2000 self-propelled artillery vehicles lumbered into position. They were essentially large howitzer artillery pieces mounted on a tank chassis. Although designed for ground to ground fire, they were able to traverse their cannons high up into the air as their commanders used a basic line of sight optic to aim at the huge floating airship above them. In less than ten seconds, each gun fired three 155 mm shells at their target.

Since the aerial battleship had turned its port side to face the airport, the massive howitzer shells coming from the other side instantly impacted the already damaged starboard side of the vessel. A number of dark elves and humans were instantly killed as the artillery shells smashed open several sections of the starboard hull. A large groan seemed to emanate from the damage hull as pieces of loose metal began to grind in on itself.

Orlok cursed. "Where did that attack come from?"

"From the eastern edge of the forest over there," Helmut said as he pointed to the right side of the scrying mirror looming above them.

"Helmsman, turn our port side to that forest and begin a full bombardment. I wanted nothing but ash and dead trees in that entire area!"

"At once, Grand Magus."

The airship turned once more as another set of artillery shells impacted its port side. The lightning batteries instantly returned fire at the mobile artillery pieces below. After a few minutes, what was left of the forest had been engulfed with smoke from the multiple fires that raged down below.

"Helmsman," Orlok said. "Activate the engine power and let us return to our sanctuary in the Otherworld. The moment we finish repairs, I shall come back and finish Germany once and for all."

26. Double Down

Kansas

Pastor Erik Burnley immediately stood up as soon as the private elevator opened its doors. The self-styled President of Christian Kansas walked around his office table and stood in front of the three men. One of them he already knew as Lloyd Mallory, former United States Governor of the state and now his vice president. The two men from the south were strangers to him, but he hoped that by the end of the meeting that they would be good friends by then.

After his handshake, Mallory gestured at the shorter man with his open palm. "This here is Clay Sheldon, he is the newly elected Grand Wizard of the new, Southern Klan of America."

Pastor Erik smiled as he shook the man's hand. "Welcome to the Republic of Kansas, Mr. Sheldon. First time in our great state?"

Sheldon smiled back. His teeth were crooked and had major gaps in between them. "First time I've ever been away from the south, Mr. President. I must congratulate you in the founding of your new country. It's been an impressive achievement."

Mallory pointed to the second, taller man wearing a cowboy hat. "This here is Lemuel Winger. He represents the Klans of the Midwest."

Pastor Erik shook the second man's hand as well. "A hearty welcome to you, Mr. Winger. Gentlemen, why don't we sit over by my couch there, I think it will be more comfortable rather than those stuffy office chairs by my desk."

Both men laughed as Pastor Erik led the way. Within minutes, all four men were sitting happily on the leather couches and chairs in the center of the vast office. Lloyd Mallory quickly poured a glass of bourbon for everyone before taking out his cigar and lighting it.

Sheldon raised his tumbler as he smiled at the pastor. "To the great new country of Christian Kansas. May she last a thousand years."

Mallory chuckled as he drank to the toast. "Let's hope Jesus comes back sooner rather than later, we're being deluged by non-stop problems now."

Pastor Erik waived a finger at his vice president. "Now, now, Lloyd. The pressing problems of running a brand new country are minuscule when compared to our security," he said before turning his attention at the other two men. "Now gentlemen, I hear that the Klans are uniting, is that true?"

Sheldon nodded energetically. "That is indeed true, Mr. President. I'm proud to be part of a new organization and we are officially calling ourselves the Southern Imperial White Knights of the Klu Klux Klan. Since these ancient gods came storming back to the world, the various different Klan organizations began to meet and recruit new members. As you well know, the reason why there have been so many independent organizations in modern times is because the Federal Government of the United States was able to infiltrate our ranks with impunity. The only way we could have survived during those years was to stay small and secretive. But now that the Feds have been dealt numerous blows, we feel that it was time that the different groups unite and bring back the Klan into prominence. So far, we have been very successful. Our membership has increased to over thirty thousand active members and we can now openly display our allegiance to the one true race, and the one true god. And I must say, we owe quite a lot of our success to you."

Pastor Erik beamed. "Why I'm flattered, but surely you can't really give me any credit for the rebirth of the Klan, could you? You ought to pat yourselves on the back for doing all the hard work."

"You were and remain a great influence to us, Mr. President," Sheldon said. "You have become a de-facto independent state in the heart of what was once the United States, and you have your own army to protect it. You proved to us that such things are possible. That's why we're here. We want to negotiate an alliance with you."

"Before we go on, I must say this, gentlemen," Pastor Erik said. "My allegiance is to the teachings of Our Lord. The Rock of God Church is the One True Church and our actions have proven it. We are a holy sanctuary against the forces of Satan. I cannot, with good faith, enter into an alliance of any kind with people who are not part of the word of God."

Sheldon put his palms up. "Mr. President, we are fully prepared to be part of your great church. The inner circle of leaders has given me full authority to say this. We all want to join your flock. We know that it is the one true path to salvation in these terrible times."

Pastor Erik raised his eyebrows in both surprise and satisfaction. "Are you fully prepared to accept the church's teachings as well as to proclaim me as the personal prophet of our Lord Jesus Christ?"

"We'll be more than happy to do that," Winger said. "Like Clay here, I too was chosen to represent the various Klans of the Midwest for this meeting, and I can tell you that we are also fully prepared to be under your church. There's a lot of survivalist enclaves that my people can recruit from and spread the word of your church."

Mallory grinned as he adjusted his white leather hat. "I told you this would be a productive meeting, Pastor."

Pastor Erik nodded in assent as he kept looking at his two guests. "Both your offers are very generous and enticing so far. What kind of an alliance do you propose?"

Sheldon drank the last of the whiskey in his glass and set it down on the coffee table before continuing. "Well, for starters I can tell you that my organization has set up a new Klan Bureau of Investigation. In the last few months, we've had many Fed agents from the FBI and other agencies who have secretly joined up with us and pledged their allegiance. This means that we now have a network of spies that can function as an early warning system in case of specific threats against your country. The Klan can function as an ally in that regards."

"That's wonderful," Pastor Erik said. "But can you trust these so-called new recruits to tell the truth? How do you determine whether or not that they might be double agents or something?"

Sheldon laughed. "Oh, we've been testing them for loyalty every now and then to make sure that they stay true to our cause. For example, I ordered a whole batch of FBI agents to murder their own director. As a sign of faithfulness to the Klan, so to speak."

"I think I might have heard it over the news a few days ago. What happened?"

"About six of them got close and shot the director," Sheldon said. "He's in a coma from multiple gunshot wounds from what I last heard. Four other agents balked at the operation and so the Klan inner circle had the rest of the group execute them."

Mallory giggled. "You guys sure don't mess around."

"I admit that our numbers are few right now," Sheldon said. "But we will keep on growing. The South is pretty much a giant swamp thanks to the constant rains and the Fed government can't help. The Klan now has a number of enclaves all over the place and we can increase our territory but we need your help."

Pastor Erik rubbed his chin. "What kind of help do you need?"

"Guns," Sheldon said. "Lots of guns. Preferably military hardware. Maybe even a nuke or two. We're gonna need technical specialists to set up those nukes though."

"I can supply your group with guns, that won't be a problem," Pastor Erik said. "The nukes, we have to be very careful with how we deploy them. If we started to freely give those away, the Feds might come down hard on us. I heard over the radio that one of their generals had to be restrained because he wanted to nuke the whole of Kansas after we set off our nuclear device in Cheyenne Mountain. It's a very tenuous situation right now."

"Oh, but we're not planning to nuke the Feds left and right. We just want a couple for our own protection, just like what you're doing. We figure that once the Feds know that the Klan has nukes, they will leave us alone too."

Pastor Erik sighed. Just days ago, he had talked to a senator from Virginia.

The Feds were secretly trying to negotiate with him to put an end to the conflict. They were willing to cede him de-facto control over Kansas, provided he stayed where he was and not to attempt an expansion. The Feds also demanded the return of the president and Admiral Zimmerman as a sign of good faith. But if he made this new alliance, the war against the Feds might enter into a new and more dangerous phase. "Let me think about it," he said softly. "I can offer you all sorts of assistance but as far as the nuclear issue goes, I can't give you an answer at this time."

"Fair enough, Mr. President," Sheldon said. "We can spread the word of God using our influence, and I feel we can ultimately make America white again. Who knows, if we keep this up, perhaps you may ultimately become president of the entire country."

Pastor Erik smirked. "That really is my one dream right now. If I can just bring the entire country under one church- my church- then we will be an unassailable beacon of light and hope throughout the rest of the world. First, Kansas. Then, the United States. And finally, the rest of the world. I truly believe this. If all of humanity can embrace the teachings of my church, then we can throw these demons back to the hell that spawned them. I think that's the reason why Jesus hasn't come back yet. He is waiting for me to fulfill my destiny."

"We'll be with you every step of the way," Mallory said.

Winger raised his glass. "Amen to that."

The elevator doors opened again. Steve Van Dyke strode into the room, he kept moving until he was directly behind Pastor Erik and began to whisper in his ear. Mallory just shrugged as he poured himself another glass of bourbon.

Pastor Erik's face was flushed as he stood up. "Gentlemen, you must excuse me. I have some matters that need attending. Lloyd, can you continue the meeting? I'll be back as soon as I can."

The other three stood up as he walked with Steve back to the elevator. The moment they got into the lift and the doors closed, Pastor Erik slapped the steel walls with an open palm. The clanging noise reverberated for a few seconds before subsiding. Within a few minutes, they were on their way down, heading for the basement sub level.

Pastor Erik let out a deep breath. "You told me he was tightly guarded by two teams on constant rotation."

"Yes," Steve said softly. "The men were handpicked by me."

"So how in the hell could he have disappeared then?"

Steve just stared at the closed elevator doors. "I don't know."

"Goddamn it! He was our bargaining chip. Now our chances of being attacked by the Feds have increased exponentially."

"I don't believe it was an inside job. Nobody saw the president leave his cell."

"What about the video? Isn't there a constant surveillance on his cell?"

"Yes, there is."

"So what happened then?"

"I think it's best if I show it to you."

The elevator doors opened and they were greeted by an armed escort of five heavily-armed SOL troopers. They walked for several minutes until they came upon a steel door that was labeled Security Room. There was no doorknob so Steve just knocked twice and looked at the video camera above them. Seconds later, the door opened and they walked inside. The soldiers that accompanied them stayed in the corridor.

There was only one technician in the room and he was trying to adjust the quality on a number of video feeds. Dennis Walden, the security chief, was also present. When Steve and Pastor Erik entered the room, they both instantly stood at attention.

"Play the recording again," Steve said.

The technician sat down at his console and pushed a button. The central monitor immediately began a replay of the last few minutes of the president's disappearance. It showed the head of state sitting on a chair in his cell. For a few seconds nothing seemed to happen until a black mist suddenly appeared behind him. Then it seemed that the president looked directly at the camera and began screaming.

Pastor Erik leaned over the console as he tried to look at every minute detail on the video monitor. "Is there any sound to this?"

"No, sir," the technician said. "We only have it available for video."

The president seemed to be in obvious pain though they couldn't determine if it was the mist that was causing it. Within less than a minute, two shadowy hands came out of the black fog and drew him into it. Then the mist rapidly dissipated until there was nothing left but an occupied cell. It was as if he just walked out of there.

Pastor Erik looked away. His face had turned white as snow.

Dennis glanced at Steve. There was a dejected look in his eyes. "I'm sorry, it was under my watch and I thought that everything was secure. I-I thought that God looked over us and that Satan could never enter our sacred ground."

Pastor Erik glared at him. "What are you talking about? How dare you doubt God's will and power!"

Dennis' mouth was trembling. "B-but Pastor, you said that Satan could never arrive at this place! You said that the word of god protects us. I heard you say it!"

Steve grabbed the man by the throat. "Watch what you say, you blasphemous bastard!"

"B-but can't you see? We're damned," Dennis blubbered. "Maybe God isn't truly with us after all."

Pastor Erik quickly thrust his face in front of the terrified security chief. "You just don't get it, do you? God allowed that demon to take the president away because that man is now in hell! Look around you, only the righteous deserve to be in Kansas and we are purging all the deceitful, pagan fools from this land! Do you want to be exiled away from God? Do you want to end up in the fires of damnation like that fool of a president?"

Tears began to roll down Dennis's cheeks as his knees buckled and he got on his knees. He began to sob as Steve had to lean forward to keep holding onto his shirt collar.

Pastor Erik grabbed the security chief by his hair and tilted his face upwards. "Answer me!"

"I-I don't want to be a part of this anymore," Dennis said softly. "I just want to go home. I want to go back to Wyoming with my family."

Steve shook his head. "You're just pathetic. Look at you, no guts at all.

Just because one demon takes a prisoner away, you start pissing in your pants. I should have never promoted you as security chief."

The video technician just remained sitting in his chair as he passively observed the commotion in the room. He was scared too, but he didn't dare say anything.

Dennis closed his eyes and grimaced. Trails of mucous streamed down his nostrils. "Please just let me go. I-I won't say anything. Let me just get to my car and pack up a few things. I can't take the lies anymore. I'm done."

Pastor Erik was incredulous. "Lies? What do you mean lies? Explain yourself. Now."

Dennis opened his eyes once again and looked around. "All this, it was all a lie, wasn't it, Pastor? You kept saying that we're saved as long as we follow you, but you can't even keep a man safely locked up as a prisoner. Admit it, you're not really giving us the word of God are you, you're just a fake!"

Steve's words were slow and deliberate. "You are treading on very dangerous ground, mister."

Pastor Erik said nothing. Instead, he backhanded Dennis across his face. The security chief's head turned slightly sideways from the blow, but he twisted it back to face them as he stood up and wiped away his tears with his shirt sleeve. Pastor Erik could sense a growing sign of defiance coming from his body language.

Dennis smirked at them. "I get it now. You're all just making this up, aren't you? The ancient gods are real, but it's obvious now that Jesus isn't," he said as he pointed an accusing finger at the pastor. "You've been lying to me all this time. You've been lying to everyone."

Steve placed a hand on his side holster but didn't draw.

Pastor Erik laughed. "So I'm the liar now, am I? Look around you, you fool! It was my will that made all of this possible! And you know how I did it? By the grace of God, that's what. You are so pathetic that one little glimpse of the devil has made you renounce your faith. You are excommunicated you asshole. You will die along with the other heathens and you will go to Hell."

Dennis didn't bat an eye. "If you truly are the instrument of Jesus, then prove it."

Pastor Erik's eyebrows were contorted. "What?"

"He doesn't have to prove anything, dipshit," Steve said menacingly.

Dennis glanced at Steve first. "Oh yes he does. Come on, Steve, we're friends! We've been working together for months now, and you've trusted me just as I trusted you. So trust me now," he said before turning his attention to the pastor. "If you are truly the prophet of Jesus, then give me a sign. Come on, do it! I've seen videos of demons, and of the ancient gods on the news, but I have never seen anything about Jesus. Not one little bit! So why is that? Because these other gods exist, and he doesn't. So come on, I dare you! Show me something that proves Jesus is real!"

Pastor Erik's face was a mask of stone. He didn't betray any emotion as he slowly turned his head and looked at Steve. "Show him, Steve. Show him a sign that our Lord is with us."

"With pleasure," Steve said as he drew his Wilson Combat 1911 pistol and fired. Dennis caught the bullet in the center of his forehead and fell backwards into the linoleum floor. His mouth and eyes remained open as a pool of blood began to form at the back of his head.

The technician instantly shrieked and stood up as he held his hands up in the air, both as a sign of mercy and supplication. Steve pointed his pistol at him and the man screamed for leniency. A split second later, the technician took two shots in the chest and went down. Steve stood over his convulsing body and fired a third shot to his head.

Pastor Erik walked over to the video controls and pressed the erase button. He deleted the camera footage in the cell where the President of the United States was taken away, and he also deleted the recording for the security room. His ears were still ringing from the multiple gunshots.

By force of habit, Steve reloaded a fresh magazine into his pistol before thumbing the safety and holstering it. "There were four other men who watched the video and opened up the cell when they found out he was gone," he said.

"Have a talk with each and every one of them thoroughly," Pastor Erik said as he rubbed his still painful ears. "If any of them has any doubts, then execute them. We need to purge our nation from unbelievers and traitors. The taking of our prized prisoner is just another test from God. We will still prevail."

27. Assault on the Tower

Otherworld

As he watched the final approach towards the tower on the airship's bridge, Kurt Orlok suddenly felt some tightness in his left arm. As he pulled back the long sleeves of his black robe, he noticed that his left hand had begun to wither again; the skin on the back of his hand had suddenly shriveled and it looked like a flaky spider web had formed on top of it. That meant that his body had begun to deteriorate once more. *Looks like I will need to use the rejuvenation pool again*, he thought.

"Preparing to dock with the tower," the ship's helmsman said as he carefully maneuvered the ship's wheel.

The tower was in fact, a gigantic cone of rock that jutted out from the base of the mountain range. Made of smooth black stone that stretched upwards for two miles, the top of the cone had a mooring mast so that the airship could attach its bow to it. Along the side of the tower was a gigantic iron platform that could then be pivoted to the side of the airship in order to facilitate the transfer of personnel and for repairs.

Orlok turned to his aide who was standing beside him. "Once we dock, I want you to supervise all the repairs and recharge the gun batteries. We will teach the German government a lesson they won't forget."

"Yes, Grand Magus," Helmut Krause said.

Ilya Volkhov held a tight clench around Patrick Gyle's thick, leathery neck. The boy had been holding on as he rode on Gyle's back for almost half an hour now and he didn't dare look down. His legs were wrapped around Gyle's torso for an extra grip just in case his arms felt too tired. The wind whipped at his blond hair, sometimes getting into his eyes, but he dared not pull one of his hands free to part it. If he lost his grip, the fall would be a long way down.

Gyle had been steadily climbing the smooth face of the tower for some time now. The boy clung onto his back and he hoped that Ilya had the strength to keep up with this. Gyle was using his claws to wedge his way up since the rock was too smooth for any kind of grip. Just before they started the climb, they had tied up and gagged Heinrich and then left him at the base of the tower. When a small team of men and horses had met them at the portal, they were instantly overpowered and bound. Using the horses, Ilya and Gyle made the journey to the base of the tower a few hours later. But since there was no visible entrance at the bottom, they figured it would be best to climb up.

Ilya looked up. "I think I can see a window or a ledge above us."

"That's good," Gyle said as he continued to use his claws. With one arm at a time, he would dig in and then pulled the other arm free and up before clawing into the stone face again. Gyle then used his clawed feet to push himself up using the holes he had already made.

Just as the two of them made steady progress, a gigantic shadow suddenly loomed over them. Looking up, they both saw a gigantic metal airship several hundred feet above as it slowly maneuvered until its nose had moored at the tip of the cone. Gyle noticed cracks and multiple holes along the side of the airship.

"There," Ilya said as he used one hand to point at a ledge just above. "It looks like an open window."

"Okay, hang on," Gyle said as he slowly made his way upwards until his head was now level with the ledge. The window looked more like a porthole as it led into a deserted stone corridor. Perched on the side of the opening was the raven.

"Took you long enough," the black bird said as it ruffled its feathers.

"Shut up," Gyle said before turning his head to stare at the boy. "Okay, Ilya, can you climb over my shoulders and go on in?"

"I will try," Ilya said as he used the remaining strength in his arms to pull himself up and through the window. But just as he got his knees on top of Gyle's shoulders, his hand slipped and he nearly fell backwards. Gyle reacted as he instantly used his left hand to hold the boy aloft to gently placed Ilya on the window ledge.

"That was close," the raven said.

Ilya took a deep breath as he saw that the wagons below were but tiny specks in the ground. "Thank you, Patrick."

"You're welcome," Gyle said as he looked up again. "You go ahead and find Tara. I'm going to climb up higher and see if I can sabotage that airship that's floating above us. The dry dock is just another few hundred feet above so I should reach it in about ten minutes."

Ilya looked confused. "Ten minutes? It took longer than that just to climb up to this first window."

Gyle grinned as he showed his fangs. "Now that you're not holding onto me I can start jumping around. I should be able to leapfrog my way much faster now."

"Okay then," Ilya said. "Pity you didn't allow me to carry one of those lightning rifles. I don't have any weapons so what do I do if I encounter one of the bad guys?"

"It's better if you sneak around rather than fight your way past them," Gyle said. "You're not a killer so leave the killing to me. Do your best to hide out of sight and not be seen."

"But what if they see me anyway?"

"Then run."

Ilya frowned. "I am not joking. You can fight because of your claws and all that but I have nothing. They will probably take me prisoner if they see me."

"There's no other humans on this level," the raven said. "They're mostly at the top of the tower now that the airship has returned."

"And they will stay up there because I'll be bringing hell with me," Gyle said just before he started climbing up again.

Ilya watched him go up until he couldn't strain his neck anymore. Then the boy slid off the window ledge and into the corridor. There were glowing lamps that were embedded along the walls to provide illumination, giving off a faint, orange light.

The raven flew up and landed on Ilya's shoulder. "I think I know where Tara is being held."

"Let's go then," the boy said.

Orlok and Helmut stepped off the airship ramp and walked onto the dry dock. Standing on the platform were half a dozen robed occultists from the Temple. As their subordinates bowed, a dwarf that was the size of a small dog darted in from behind and stood in front of them. The little creature was wearing a red cap and had a long, silvery bread that extended all the way to its little, stick-like knees. Tock the dwarf had been an invaluable ally, and Orlok acknowledged him with a slight bow of his own.

"Welcome back, Grand Magus," Tock said. "I can see that the ship hath borne signs of a great battle."

"I am tired, Tock," Orlok said. "Can you prepare the rejuvenation pool for me again?"

"At once, Grand Magus," Tock said. "Once ye return to thy chambers, ye shall hast been regenerated." With those words, the dwarf instantly took off towards the doors leading back to the tower.

"Helmut, you're in charge of the repairs," Orlok said nonchalantly as he slowly made his way to the exit.

Ilya and the raven had already made it to the next level above. The twisting corridors still looked identical to the previous one as they passed through massive rooms that contained vacant workshops and forges. A number of empty rooms also contained unused bunk beds. In one set of rooms, Ilya had noticed a small group of women dressed in black robes preparing food in what was obviously a kitchen; he had narrowly avoided detection by temporarily hiding underneath one of the dining tables as they were setting up a meal. Once the servants had temporarily left the hall, the boy quickly ran the other way and ended up in a stone stairwell so he started going up. Now that they were on another level, Ilya noticed that there was now some sort of plush carpeting on the floor. This part of the tower was obviously reserved for the Temple leaders.

As he kept moving along the corridor, Ilya ended up facing set of double doors at the end of the passageway. There was an ornate metal lock with strange symbols that kept it sealed.

"This is evidently the master's chambers," the raven said.

Ilya placed his ear on the door to see if he could listen in but he didn't hear anything. "Do you think he's in there?"

"Only one way to find out."

Ilya snorted as he pulled out a small wad of raskovnik from underneath his jacket and rubbed them against the lock. Almost instantly, both doors opened inwards and he walked inside while putting the magical herbs back in his pocket.

The large room had a high, arched ceiling and was gaudily furnished. Rich tapestries hung along the walls and there was a four poster bed at the far side, near a large, open window. Ornate Persian carpets covered the stone floor and there were large cabinets made with lacquered wood on one side of the room. In the opposite side of the place was a sunken pool that faced a raised stone slab. On top of the slab was a lozenge-shaped object that looked like a giant lemon drop.

The raven flew off of the boy's shoulder and landed on the tawny-colored lozenge. "She's here."

The boy quickly ran over and stood beside the capsule. As Ilya looked down, he could see Tara's face. It looked like she was embedded within the object, like an insect trapped in amber.

Ilya gasped. The boy noticed that there were holes along the side of the capsule and he could see a glowing pink liquid seeping out from them and into the pool. "What have they done to her?"

The raven smoothed its feathers before it started talking. "It looks like they are using her essence to extend their leader's life."

The boy took a step back. He was both disgusted and shocked. "Is she dead?"

"No, but she will eventually die if this keeps up. I have a feeling the Magus will need more than just a bath in his pool now."

Ilya's mask of shock quickly turned to anger. "No! They cannot do this to her! How do we get her out?"

"Well, this pod that she's encased in is really a cage, and all cages have locks."

Ilya quickly took out all of the raskovnik he had in his pockets and started spreading them on top of the lozenge. For the next few minutes, nothing seemed to happen.

"Why hasn't it opened yet?" he asked aloud.

"Because ye hast not said the command word," said a shrill voice that came from the entrance of the room.

Ilya turned. Standing in front of the door was Tock the dwarf.

The little creature grinned at him as Tock held up a glowing golden medallion that was on his neck. "Ye are a clever boy, just like that other who had me exiled from the faerie realms. But thy magical herb cannot unlock that coffin until the spell that surrounds it is broken!"

"You are not a Dokkalfar," Ilya said. "You seem to be from the land I just visited, a magical forest ruled by the Erlking."

Tock hissed. "Beshrew that name! Ti's that foul king that had me exiled. But I had my revenge! For I stole his daughter, the faerie princess Charissa, and plotted to have the Myrking as a hostage. Along with mine human allies, I shall soon overthrow the accursed king of faeries and taketh my rightful place among the fey once more."

Ilya frowned. "So you are the one behind all of this, you are the cause of the war between the dark elves and the faeries!"

Tock grinned once again as he pulled out a dagger from beneath his tunic. "Aye, and I shall also be thy death."

Helmut thought he had seen everything. He was there when the Grand Magus came out of his room in Wewelsburg Castle one day and proclaimed that the ancient gods had returned. The others in the inner circle were skeptical at first but then came the news reports. And then the world stopped turning as everything ground to a halt. That was when he started to believe. Then the next few days became a non-stop whirlwind of activity as the entire Temple began their rituals; those were strange times, filled with wonder as they all saw the beings of myth and legend come alive before their eyes. Everyone was on a learning curve then, it was a race to find out which spells and enchantments would work and which of those that were fake. Weeks had passed, but by then Orlok had mastered enough magic to cast protective wards around the castle and that had protected them from the creatures lurking out in the lands. And that was when people from all over the area had come, seeking sanctuary against the giants, dragons, and demons that were out there. Days later, more and more refugees came pouring through but there was always plenty of room since each and every one of them were sacrificed. By then, the Grand Magus was able to master the necessary rituals to open up the gates to the Otherworld, the place beyond Earth where all the supernatural beings dwelled.

Weeks later, the Temple began to transfer most of their members and new recruits to the tower, a fortress in some previously unknown planar world. A renegade dwarf named Tock soon approached them, promising an alliance that would benefit them all. With Tock's help, the men of the Temple were able to enslave the dark elves after they had kidnapped their king. This was where they repaired the Pair Dadeni, the legendary magical cauldron from Ireland that could raise the dead. But the repair work done by the Dokkalfar was flawed, and all the cauldron could do now was to convert the souls that were sacrificed into it and transform them into energy. That was when the Grand Magus instructed the Temple and the dark elves to build a powerful ship that could float in the air. As Orlok had retired to his personal quarters in the tower, Helmut had ordered the work crews to begin the repairs. Suddenly, a creature leapt up out from underneath the platform and landed in front of everybody. It was a tall, gangly thing with thick, bloodless skin. Completely hairless and naked, it stood before them like a ghostly albino with claws and fangs. Everyone just stared at it, speechless. They had never seen anything like it before.

That was when one of the repairmen, a young man from Berlin named Josef, pointed his finger at it and said one word, "Nosferatu."

And then all hell broke loose.

The creature flew up into the air as everyone panicked. Workmen tried to defend themselves using their tools while the guards tried to aim their lightning guns, but it was of no use. The pale monster moved so fast, it was like seeing a blur. It raked its claws and sunk its fangs into the guards first, then it started on the repair crew. Anytime somebody tried to take a shot at it, the creature would just leap away and then come right back down as it crushed its foes like pieces of paper. For some strange reason, it seemed to ignore the dark elves as it concentrated on killing all the humans.

That was when Helmut truly saw everything now as he ran screaming back into the inside of the ship, trying desperately to close the outer doors before the thing could get in.

Gyle stood on the bloody platform as the last human lying on it gurgled, then died. His estimated body count was a little over fifty and he had done it all in less than five minutes. He saw the remaining men run into the ship and seal its doors but he knew there were other ways to get inside. His hands and mouth were dripping with blood.

There were about a dozen dark elves just standing nearby. They all just stared at him with tinted goggles over their eyes. None bothered to react or run away when the fighting started. As Gyle just stood there, contemplating on how to next to proceed, one of them moved forward and walked right up to him.

"Please," the dark elf said as it pointed its black stubby finger at the airship. "Our king, is in the belly of that machine."

Gyle nodded before turning around and then leaping up into the air. Less than a second later, he landed on top of the ship's fuselage with a loud thump. From there, he could see a small observation tower made of glass near the bow. He quickly balled up his fists and shattered it with one blow. Now he had a way in.

As Tock chased Ilya around the master's chambers, it resembled a deadly serious game of tag. The boy was about a foot taller, but the dwarf moved with uncanny speed and there were times that Tock's dagger thrusts had almost landed, but Ilya was able to get away at the last minute as the dwarf ended up knifing some furniture instead.

"I will get thou, lad," Tock said as he sliced the dagger in the air, narrowly missing the boy's back by mere inches.

Ilya was sweating now and he was getting tired of running around. The boy knew he couldn't keep this up as he jumped on top of the four poster bed, and then tried to leap off towards the other side. But Ilya's foot caught a crease in the silk sheets and he fell face down on top of the bed. He was able to turn and lie on his back just as the dwarf had jumped on top of him and tried to bring his dagger down onto Ilya's throat.

The boy shrieked, just able to get both his hands on Tock's wrist as the dagger point was a mere inch away from his throat. Tock used his other hand to hold Ilya's face down as he focused on pushing the knife into the kid. The dwarf had tremendous strength as the edge of the blade was almost touching the boy's throat.

It was at that moment that the raven landed on top of the dwarf, curled one of its claws around the medallion on Tock's neck, and then flew up, ripping it away from him. The dwarf screamed with rage as he pulled away from Ilya and tried to run after the bird. But the raven had already flown over the lozenge that held Tara and dropped the medallion on it. As soon as the golden pendant touched the capsule, it glowed and melded with the lozenge.

Tock screamed as if he had been the one who was stabbed. His entire body began to wither and burn as he dropped his dagger and leapt out of the open window. Ilya got up and ran over to where the lozenge was.

The capsule soon began to glow brightly and then there was a loud noise of something breaking. It was right at that moment that a great crack appeared along the side of the lozenge. A few more seconds passed and there were multiple fractures all along the capsule.

"Take cover," the raven said as it flew down behind the wooden table. Ilya ran back to where the bed was and dove underneath it.

A split second later, the capsule exploded in a multitude of crystal shards that tore through the room. After the sound of breaking glass had subsided, Ilya crawled out from under the bed and looked around.

Lying on top of the stone slab where the capsule had once been was Tara Weiss. The fifteen year old girl was naked and covered in pieces of amber crystal. She began to stir and soon sat up. Then she brought her hands up to her face and screamed.

Ilya grabbed one of the smaller bed sheets and ran over to where she was. The boy quickly wrapped her body around the sheet and tried to comfort her. "Tara, it's me. It's Ilya. Can you understand me?"

Tara looked at the boy. She was wild-eyed but quickly regained her composure. "Oh my god, Ilya!" she cried as she hugged him and started sobbing.

Ilya smiled as he hugged her back. They had been separated a long time, it felt like years to him. "How are you feeling?"

"Oh god," Tara said softly. "I felt like I was in a nightmare and I just couldn't wake up. The last thing I remember was lying in some sort of armored car as those Russian soldiers said they were taking me to Moscow."

Ilya drew back so he could see her face but he kept holding her arms. "Yes, you were apparently kidnapped by an evil wizard but I got some new friends to come and rescue you."

Tara stood up and looked around as she kept the bed sheet wrapped around her body. "Where are we? How long have I been here?"

Ilya got on his feet as well as he scratched the back of his head. "I was held prisoner by my country for a few months too. I was only able to escape a few days ago. We are in the Spirit World now."

That was when Tara remembered about her talking dog. "What about Bibsy?"

"I'm right here," the raven said as it perched by the window. "But I'm not a dog anymore."

Tara walked over to where the bird was. "So you've got some sort of a new body now?"

Ilya's eyes opened wide. "Be careful, the dwarf is near that window!"

"He's gone," the raven said as it walked up along Tara's arm. "The medallion held his power on this world. He is weak without it."

Ilya rolled his eyes. "For a god, you sure didn't help me very much. I nearly died."

"What is going on here?" a voice coming from the door demanded.

All three of them turned. Standing by the doorway was Kurt Orlok. The old man was visibly angry as he relied on his staff for balance. The Grand Magus stared at the wreckage around his room and let out a gasp.

Tara stared back at him. "Who are you?"

Ilya slowly moved to the center of the room as he noticed Tock's dagger lying on the side of the bed.

"A very powerful magician," the raven said. "He kept you prisoner in that capsule so he could use your life essence to keep him from growing too old."

Orlok was amazed. There was a talking bird along with the two children. He felt that it must be either a god or one of Odin's ravens. But what shocked him the most was that his captive was now free. He needed her powerful essence, or he would die soon.

"So you're the one who kept me prisoner all this time," Tara said softly. "I feel so weak too. It's like I've been drained of blood or something."

Orlok held his staff in front of him. "I was not the one who kidnapped you. That was my former protégé, Seth Solomon. He did give you over to me as a sort of gift. That talking bird of yours is right, however. I am afraid that I will need your life force in order for me to continue living."

"No!" Ilya shouted as he threw the dagger at him. Orlok was able to activate his defenses just in time as an invisible shield deflected the thrown knife away. The Grand Magus reacted swiftly as a bolt of lightning erupted from the point of his staff and struck the boy in the chest. Ilya flew backwards and landed in a heap on the carpeted floor.

"Ilya!" Tara cried as she ran over to where the boy was. Ilya's clothes were in tatters and there was smoke coming from the burned fabrics. There was a massive red blotch on his chest and the boy's eyes were closed. His breathing was faint. The raven landed beside Ilya and just stared at him.

Tara looked back at the old wizard with fury in her eyes. "What have you done to him?"

"The same thing I shall do to you if you do not submit," Orlok said tersely. "Now you must surrender so that I can begin the binding ritual. Don't worry, it won't be painful. You will just be in a deep sleep like before. It's better than dying."

Tara stood up. "You won't be doing anything."

Orlok laughed. "Oh? Why shouldn't I be? I plan to live forever. This is a great time to be a wizard now that I know that magic is real. I consumed part of your life essence, and I'll keep doing it until I have it all."

"No you won't," Tara said as she held her hand up and pointed all of her fingers at him. "I've been taught by a brujo to control my spirit. This means that I can feel every aspect of my being. And you know what?"

Orlok frowned. He had a feeling he wouldn't like the answer. "What?"

Tara looked at him with pity in her eyes. "You never digested my life essence, it's still in your body. You only borrowed it."

Orlok's eyes opened wide. "Impossible!"

"Let me show you," Tara said as she started to take a deep breath.

The next thing he knew, Orlok couldn't move his hands. He made a slight step backwards, but then he couldn't move his extremities anymore. A slight shriek came out of his mouth before he realized that his entire body was now paralyzed. That was when he saw a strange, silvery white mist emanating from his own skin. The staff fell from his frozen hands and clattered on the floor.

Tara closed her eyes as the life force began to drain from the old wizard and started to seep back into her body. As the seconds passed, she began to feel more alive. After less than a minute, she felt reenergized. It was as if she had been made whole again.

When she opened her eyes a moment later, all that was left of Kurt Orlok was a mound of grey dust on the floor along with a black robe and a metal staff that lay nearby.

Gyle stood in front of the doors that lead to the engine room. He tried pounding it with his fists but the thick metal only incurred a few dents. He could use his claws but it would probably take hours to get through. As he looked around the metallic corridor, he could note where the rivets were bolted on and the grated floor underneath him. *This whole place is like an old steamship*, he thought as he remembered taking Marie and the kids to a steamboat museum in Texas once. That was when he realized that there was a massive golden tube underneath the grating.

Using all his strength, Gyle tore through the flooring and then pulled against a patch that seemed to have been riveted on the massive piping. A squeaking sound of twisted metal followed as he ripped off the sheet of iron and exposed the exhaust as the hot mist exploded around him. Gyle's skin had become less sensitive to pretty much anything so he ignored the slightly warmer feeling as he crawled inside and began to make his way past where the doors above him were.

When he burst through underneath the flooring, there were still about half a dozen occultists in the engine room. They were expecting him to get through the door first so their backs were behind him as he tore his way out of the floor and stood upright. Two of the guards had set up a more powerful lightning weapon that was mounted on a tripod, but it was useless since the gun was facing the door. Gyle made short work of them and then he smashed the weapon by stomping on it with his feet. Three more had knives and lead pipes and they charged at him. Less than a minute later, there were just pieces of them on the floor as the blood and entrails began to seep down the grating.

Gyle looked around. The massive chamber was dominated by a vertical glass tube that was surrounded by pistons, snake-like tubing, and revolving gears. Wisps of steam would periodically emanate from numerous vents and ducts, as the humming sound of the engines reverberated all around him. He noticed some sort of movement within the giant cylinder. There was something alive inside of it.

"Please … don't kill me. I give up," a voice from a nearby alcove said.

Pivoting quickly, Gyle crouched, ready to strike. The man that was hiding was Helmut Krause. He had wedged himself in between two consoles, but it was clear he would be found sooner or later, so he did the most logical thing and decided to give up. Helmut squeezed his way out from his hiding place and fell on his knees.

Gyle stood over him as he wiped the blood from his lips. "You in charge here?"

Helmut had wet his pants. "No. The Grand M-Magus runs everything. I-I'm just his assistant. Please don't kill me!"

"I'll probably let you live if you answer my questions," Gyle said as he looked at the vertical pipe. "Is there somebody in that glass tube?"

"Yes. The Myrking is in there. We, I mean, the Magus t-trapped him inside the engine so his form could channel the energy needed to run the airship."

"Myrking? Is he with the dark elves?"

"Y-Yes, he is their king. As long as we kept him alive as our hostage, they would not revolt."

"Good, get him out of there."

"What?"

Gyle grabbed Helmut by the hood of his robes and held him aloft using one hand. "I said let him go!"

"B-But if we release him then the energies keeping the ship in the air will cease to function! We will crash to the ground below us!"

Gyle threw him down on the floor. "Do it, or I'll rip your guts out!"

Helmut whimpered slightly as he crawled over to a control panel and then began to push levers and buttons. Within moments, a loud siren emanated from every corridor. He hesitated a little but when he saw Gyle's bloodshot eyes looking straight at him, Helmut bit his lip and pulled the final bar.

A loud clanging noise erupted in the engine room as the glass cylinder began to break. Cracks formed along its opaque surface. Gyle noticed a dark hand press itself against the glass. Moments later, the glass finally caved in and the Myrking pushed his way out. The leader of the dark elves was a tall man wearing strips of black rags. His skin was jet black and his long hair and beard were of the whitest silver. But the most otherworldly thing about him were his eyes, the all-white pupils glowed with a pale hue.

The moment that Myrking saw Helmut, he instantly ran over to him and grabbed him by the throat. "By all the hells, you and your accursed kind has kept me trapped in that infernal machine for the longest time! By all that is mine, you shall die!"

Helmut screamed a final time as the Myrking held him, locking eyes with him. A pale, grayish mist emanated from Helmut as his life essence was torn from him and the Myrking drank his soul greedily. When the king of the dark elves finally let go, all that was left of Helmut was a dried out husk and bones.

Gyle just stood there as he watched it happen. When the Myrking was finished, he started to speak. "He told me that you were keeping this ship afloat in the air. I think we better get out of here."

The Myrking stared back at him for a long time without saying anything. But then the ship began to shudder and they could feel a bit of weightlessness before the whole chamber began to tip sideways. "I thank you, changed one. Lead the way."

Gyle nodded before taking off like a lightning bolt. As he looked over his shoulder, he noticed that the Myrking was keeping up with him almost step for step. They both moved quickly across corridors that began to twist and sway as the ship started to break apart. Since they were near the underbelly of the airship, Gyle took another route as they made their way towards the gun ports. Sure enough, he noticed that there were gaps in the armor where the last attack on earth had damaged the airship. They both quickly tore through a weakened part of the hull and made a leaping jump before landing on top of the dry dock. Moments later, the airship collapsed in on itself as it fell backwards and tore off the mooring at the top of the tower. They watched as a once powerful weapon of war crumpled and dropped down into the valley below.

The Myrking pointed towards the hole that was at the top of the cone. "That is where the cauldron of evil lies. The Sidhe princess is trapped inside, I felt her cries of help as the soul energies coursed through us."

"Wait here," Gyle said as he jumped up, jackknifed in the air and dived into the hole that was left when the mooring gave way. The vertical drop was almost two thousand feet. *It's like falling into a volcano*, Gyle thought as he plunged down head first. The great cauldron was at the bottom and was surrounded by a mountain of bones. The Pair Dadeni was once used to revive the ancient heroes of Ireland, but it had been turned into a reactor that fed on the souls of people that were sacrificed to it. Princess Charissa was chained along its side as she screamed while her powerful life essence was used to channel the mystical energies upwards. Gyle's velocity had increased in a matter of seconds as he twisted his body and rammed feet first into the bottom of the cauldron. The resulting collision shattered the Pair Dadeni into a thousand pieces.

There was a small crowd that stood at the edge of the portal that led back to the world of the dark elves. Tara had managed to steal some clothes from the tower and she was now wearing a pair of jeans underneath her black robes. She was crouching on top of the platform beside the makeshift stretcher that had Ilya lying on it. The boy's breathing was erratic and Tara had a distinct thought that he might die.

A pale, silvery hand placed itself on her shoulder. It was Charissa. "Do not worry, Tara. My people, the fey, we will nurse him back to health. He may be but a boy, but he is strong and clever."

Tara's mouth trembled as she stood up and hugged the princess. "Please, make him well again. He's my one true friend."

Charissa nodded as she signaled the four Sidhe knights that came from the faerie realms to take up the stretcher and carry it through the portal. "We shall send a messenger to you as soon as the boy is well again," she said before waving goodbye and stepped through to the other world along with Ilya.

The Myrking bowed before Gyle as he was being surrounded by the dark elves. "I thank you, warrior. I return now to my own realm. If you ever wish to visit us again, you and your companions will always be welcomed as honored guests."

Gyle nodded. "Just stay safe and keep the peace."

"That we shall," the Myrking said before disappearing through the portal along with his entourage.

The raven just sat there as it watched the numerous farewells before turning to look at Tara. "It's going to take some time for the boy to heal. It's because time flows much slower in the faerie lands compared to Earth."

Tara wiped her eyes with the sleeves of her robe as she was tearing up again. "Ilya went out of his way just to rescue me. I can't wait till he comes back. I made a promise to him that we would find his mother."

Gyle turned away in shame. "It was my fault. I should have been with him first before taking out the ship. I thought they were all at the top of the tower."

"It doesn't matter," Tara said softly. "At least he's alive and will be back in once piece soon."

The raven looked at both of them. "So now what?"

Tara sighed. "Has the world gotten any better while I was a prisoner?"

Gyle shook his head. "Nope. It just seems to be getting worse."

Tara pulled the robes closer to her. There was a chill wind coming across the mountain pass. "Then let's go. There is so much to do."

"To do what?"

"What else? Save the world."

28. Coda

Oregon

There was a small stream less than a hundred yards from the shelter, so she always volunteered to gather some plants just so she could visit it. Although one of the more enterprising people of the group had set up a deep well with a water pump within the compound, she preferred to go out into the forest as much as she could. The shelter was basically a single passageway dug into the side of the hill that led to numerous chambers. Even though she had a room for herself and the kids, it was still quite stuffy and claustrophobic inside. The weather was getting colder by the day so she wanted to spend as much time out in the wilderness as she could, despite the possible dangers that lurked around.

The group had been living for months now deep in the heart of the Umatilla National Forest, near the center of the state. When the Glooming began, she had her heart set on staying with the kids in Dallas but when the continuous streams of bad news kept coming, her brother Tim had driven all the way down from Oregon to pick them all up. She hadn't wanted to go at first, thinking she ought to wait for her husband, but then the news about the debacle in the Middle East stunned her as well as everybody else. Deep in her heart, she had believed that the news her spouse had died would one day reach her and she would have to live with it. But what made it even worse was she hadn't received any news at all. The reality was that all the overseas troops were largely cut off. Even if he was alive, there was probably no chance he would make it back to America until the crisis was over.

It had been a good thing that she decided to lock up the house and head to the Pacific Northwest with Tim. Just days later, the entire southern half of Texas had been lost to the hordes of demons coming in from the southern border. The journey to Oregon had taken a long time, and they had seen things that she thought could have only been possible in the movies. Her two daughters had cried and been scared for the first few weeks but when they had finally made it to the compound, they had adapted to a new life very quickly. She had been fortunate her brother was a hardcore survivalist; he and his friends, along with their families, had been preparing for that very day when all hell broke loose. And it had.

Now the days were spent planting and gathering food. Hunting was reserved for special occasions. They had all learned the hard way to kill the animals of the forest only when it was necessary. One time, when Tim and his friend Richard had killed over a dozen wild turkeys in a single hunt, something came out from the darkness the next evening and took her brother's friend. They had found Richard's remains a few days later. That was when a shaman from the Tillamook tribe visited them and told them that they had angered the Great Spirit. From then on, they would only kill no more than two animals at a time, and they would pay their respects to it, using silent prayers and rituals. Tim had lived in fear for days when he killed a doe that still had an unborn baby in its womb. He had sat at the edge of the compound and fasted for nearly a week in order to placate the Great Spirit. After that, they all had to make sure that they would kill only the animals that were old enough to die from something else.

She had left her daughters with the other families as she came out with Tim and headed towards the stream that day. By this time, she had taken a crash course in finding edible plants, so she picked up a few and put it into her cloth sack as she moved towards the creek. There was plenty of pickle weed near the banks of the stream and her youngest had taken a liking to them. Her boots were wearing out, but they were still serviceable.

Tim waved at her as he stood on a nearby ridge. His Remington 700 was slung over his back. "I think I saw a grouse about a few yards that way," he said, pointing at a nearby tree line. "I'll be away from visual range but if you need anything, just holler."

"No problem," she said. Her Mossberg 500 tactical shotgun was slung over her shoulder as well. Her husband had seen to it that she take lessons and knew how to handle herself. "Just be careful. You don't want to have to fast for another week if you screw up again."

Tim shook his head before walking away. "Very funny."

When he walked out of sight, she bent down and looked at her reflection in the water. She was nearly forty now, but she still had her youthful looks. Wrinkles had begun to form near her eyes but she guessed it was more from stress than anything else. Just as her thoughts began to stray, she suddenly saw what looked like someone else's reflection in the water. It had pale skin and red eyes and seemed to be standing behind her.

She quickly turned around as she dropped her sack and readied the shotgun. She saw what looked like a blur from the corner of her eye but didn't see anything. "Tim?"

For what seemed like a long time, all she did was look around. The forest was strangely calm and all she could hear was the slight howl of the wind. Suddenly, cawing sounds coming from the trees above her made her jump and her index finger almost pulled the trigger on the shotgun.

As she looked up, she saw a black raven perched up high in the pine branches above. She was tempted to shoot at it for scaring the heck out of her, but then she realized that the Indians considered those black birds to be sacred animals, and the last thing she wanted to do now was to piss off the Great Spirit. She didn't want to waste precious ammo either so she pointed the shotgun away.

"Marie," a guttural but familiar voice beside her said.

She stood completely still. Her heart was pounding with terror and her breathing was shallow. She was tempted to turn and bring the shotgun to bear, but something was telling her not to.

"It's alright, Marie. I'm not gonna hurt you."

She turned around slowly, the shotgun cradled in her arms pointing downward.

That was when she saw him. He was completely naked. His thick leathery skin was as pale as milk. All of his body hair was gone and it didn't even look like he had genitals anymore. His pale red eyes were too ashamed to look at her directly.

She let out a deep breath before the words came out. "Patrick?"

Patrick Gyle said nothing as he just looked away and nodded.

"Oh my God, I thought you were dead. What happened to you?"

"I made a choice," he said softly. "I needed to be something …more than human if I was going to fight them."

"Fight who?"

"The ones who threaten this country. The ones who threaten my family. The ones who threaten you. I'm a soldier, it's all I know."

Marie fought back tears. She wanted to put her arms around him, but he just looked so different. "Are you coming back to us now?"

"Not yet. The Aztecs will be coming soon, and I have to get ready for them."

"What about us? What about the kids?"

Gyle held his arm out for her to see. His stubby hand ended in black, razor sharp claws. "Just tell them that I'm alive. Please don't tell them I look like this. I can't face them looking like this."

Marie couldn't hold it back anymore. She let out a sob. "Oh, Patrick."

His voice was almost a whisper. "I have to go. I'll try to see you again. If I don't come back, just don't forget about me."

"Patrick wait—"

And then he was gone. He moved so fast, it was like a distortion in the air. One minute he was there and the next it was as if never existed. All she could see were the trees and the flowing waters of the creek.

By the time Tim got back to the area, he found his sister Marie just sitting by the side of the stream, crying her eyes out.

Otherworld

The old wizard gingerly stepped over the crushed glass amidst the wreckage of the former master's chambers. That was when he noticed the pile of ash near the center of the room. Seth Solomon was tempted to pick up the lightning staff that was lying on the ground, but it just wasn't his style. He preferred to let others do his fighting for him.

Tock the dwarf had boils all over his body. When he was stripped of his golden medallion the aftereffect somehow cursed him and he was in constant pain. Perhaps the trickster god may even had placed a hex on him. Either way, he wanted revenge. Tock walked over to the side table beside the four poster bed and grabbed an old, leather bound book from the drawer. The renegade dwarf then made his way towards his new master.

Solomon took the book from the dwarf's tiny hands and flipped through the thick pages. It was essentially a collection of old papyrus scrolls that were bound together in human skin. He could see the complex hieroglyphs and arcane symbols in its pages. "Ah, so this is the Book of Toth. How wonderful indeed."

Tock scratched at his beard and became annoyed when a whole tuft of hair underneath his chin came loose. The curse was worse than he ever imagined. "Aye, and what shall thou be doing now?"

Solomon laughed. His greatest rival was dead and the remaining followers of the Temple were now slaves of the dark elves. But Orlok had done enough damage to Germany that the rest of Europe would no longer be a threat to his empire in Rome. He was pretty much left to his own devices now. The next phase of his master plan was about to begin.

The story continues in:

A World Darkly
Wrath of the Old Gods
Book III

Coming Soon

Join John Triptych's mailing list for the latest news,
exclusive discounts, and FREE books!

It's FREE to join in and you can unsubscribe at any time!
http://eepurl.com/bK-xGn

J Triptych Publishing
Spellbinding literary entertainment at an affordable price!

Crime Thrillers:

The Opener: John Triptych's gritty debut novel of South East Asia's expatriate underworld. A sordid society in which one man is determined to succeed at all cost. Recommended for mature readers.

Science Fiction and Mythology:

Wrath of the Old Gods Series: The entire world is thrown into turmoil as the ancient gods of myth and legend return. An epic, post-apocalyptic series with multiple characters, mythical beings, and world spanning adventures.

The Glooming (Book 1)
Canticum Tenebris (Book 2)
A World Darkly (Book 3)
And more to come!

Wrath of the Old Gods Young Adult Series: A complete and standalone series for young adults that ties in with the main Wrath of the Old Gods series. This trilogy centers on a young British boy and of his quest to save his country from supernatural forces.

Pagan Apocalypse (Book 1.5)
The Fomorians (Book 2.5)
Eye of Balor (Book 3.5)
And more on the way!

Look for these books in e-book and paperback formats via the internet or by request at your local bookstore!